# *A Candle For Lucifer*
## *An evil priest beyond redemption?*

– ANDREW DE BERRY –

FASTPRINT PUBLISHING
PETERBOROUGH, ENGLAND

*Andrew de Berry*

# A CANDLE FOR LUCIFER
## AN EVIL PRIEST BEYOND REDEMPTION?
Copyright © Andrew de Berry 2009

All rights reserved.

No part of this book may be reproduced in any form by photocopying or any electronic or mechanical means, including information storage or retrieval systems, without permission in writing from both the copyright owner and the publisher of the book.

ISBN 978-184426-657-9

First published 2009 by
FASTPRINT PUBLISHING
Peterborough, England.

First published Bloomington, Indiana, U.S.A., 11/08/2005
ISBN 1-4208-7138-2 (sc)

Printed by
www.printondemand-worldwide.com

*Andrew de Berry*

# *Acknowledgements*

To the many people who gave me encouragement along the way. To an assortment of proofreaders, JPs, police officers, prison officers and indeed to a memory bank of many in prison, including those sad psychopaths – not all of whom are locked up!

Also to Andrew Dobell for the cover design at andrewdobell@hotmail.com, as well as to New Writers UK. at w.w.w.newwritersuk/co.uk

## To Nicholas S

A Candle for Lucifer is not entirely a work of fiction. Andrew de Berry knew Nicholas S, with both of them attending the same theological college. Both went on to become vicars only for N to be de-frocked and sent to Wormwood Scrubs prison, during the writer's time as a chaplain there. Doing a life sentence for the serial abduction of young teenage girls, N ended his life whilst in prison.

'The truly just is he who feels half-guilty of your misdeeds'
                                                    Kahlil Gibran
'I lie better than most people tell the truth'
A psychopath's rare admission.

# PART ONE

*Andrew de Berry*

# Chapter 1

Leaving the body in church was obscene. Nor was death dignified on that Friday evening in mid summer when, as sometimes happens, a coffin might be kept overnight ready for burial next day.

More to the point, Saturday's thoughts were focused on *LIFE* and young love. Not on *DEATH*. For in that sweet-scented atmosphere of lilies, freesias and pink carnations where tomorrow's bells would ring in celebration of a wedding, the corpse was abhorrent.

Crudely hidden and not yet cold, it belonged to that of a bright, pretty teenager called Stacey Witcombe.

In the mediaeval church of All Saints, evil mocked innocence.

As was his custom on a Friday evening the Reverend Christopher Wilkes had called in towards the end of choir practice and, with other members of the choir starting to leave, she had hung back to speak with him.

'Christopher,' she had asked (he liked the intimacy of Christian names). 'Can I speak with you for a few moments?'

'Why, of course you can,' he had replied. With the church

now empty he nudged the outside vestry door shut and turned towards her with an encouraging smile,

'How can I help you, my dear?'

The evening was warm as it had been all week. She was dressed in jeans and a white T-shirt, a small locket on a delicate chain being her only adornment. Invariably her footwear consisted of trainers. Slight but lithe in physique with long corn-blonde hair, she carried an imitation suede jacket over her arm. Her face glowed, not from make-up – she wore none – but from many hours spent playing tennis.

She exuded health and happiness.

'I need to ask you a personal question,' she responded with her own sweet smile, 'and I thought you'd be the best person to talk to, even though I'm a bit embarrassed to ask.'

'Well I'm here for that purpose. Don't be embarrassed, Stacey. You know me well enough by now, don't you?' His fatherly tone masked the inner frisson, which she aroused in him.

Few teenagers would have even bothered to ask the question, still less of their vicar. But Stacey had been brought up on traditional values and she sought his reassurance. Yet even as she spoke, she shattered the hidden feelings he'd harbored for her and which he liked to think she harbored for him.

The question cost her her life.

Despite his contempt for the opposite sex, he'd always taken delight in charming the women, doing so as a matter of course through his use of flattery and guile. More often than not, they – at least the women members of his church fell for it.

But Stacey and a few young ladies like her were different. Behind their youthful charm was a tantalizing innocence that even he could not deny. Supposing it to be love, when clearly she had no such thoughts for him, contempt collided into another dangerous emotion – the longing to control. Even so might his loss of control that in one way had felt so effortless – almost tender in its brevity – be called murder?

It was just that the sensual smile in the sultry silence of the vestry, followed by the disastrous question had left him no choice. For he preferred to suppose that her surrender had still been voluntary in some way; a sacrificial love that she could never own upto in this life - beckoning yet out of reach.

For as the question left her lips, his response had been so swift that she neither cried out nor offered any resistance. In an instant the sweet open adolescent expression, hazel eyes in a Botticelli face framed by sun-bleached tresses, had distorted more into a look of surprise than terror. Between her wide-eyed look of innocence, and his having snatched the cord from his alb to twist it round her neck so violently that she had passed out before dying, the deed had been done with lightning speed.

Two minutes was all it took, and so sudden was her encounter with death that her eyes remained open. Nor did he think to slip his fingers across her eyelids to close them.

Lying at his feet - a slight figure of waxed ivory, her expression bore him no malice.

It was as though both of them somehow understood.

In his prime Christopher Duncan Wilkes had been a tall man of six foot three, who blessed with good looks might have seemed like an unlikely figure to enter the church. His was a muscular frame with strong hands and where, despite late middle age, he remained slim although his bearing, as can be the way with taller men, stooped as though in condescension to those of shorter mien.

His large head once crowned with a full crop of curly

brown hair had peppered itself gray, while his face with its smooth skin and well-spaced eyes retained a certain youthful charm. Perhaps an over-fleshed mouth and cheekbones too high marred any direct comparison to film star good looks. Yet the charisma was undeniable to his many women admirers. A further distinguishing feature to endear him to them was that his eyes, although brown, were of a slightly different shade to each other.

Favoring tweed jackets or light-knit cardigans and chino style trousers he always dressed with an easy elegance. And if there was a quirk in his dress code it was rare to see him without a 'dog' collar. Regardless of the weather or time of day his collar, of the slip-in variety, would invariably be lodged into a black or gray hand-tailored clerical shirt.

Traditionally the width of a vicar's collar defined his or her churchmanship, narrow if you were 'high church' and wide for the evangelical. That preferred by the Reverend Wilkes – medium-sized – reflected a churchmanship somewhere 'middle of the road', which in his case meant that he held no strong views. More to the point although he didn't *believe* in God as such, the Establishment thought well of him given that charm and flair were commonly thought to equate to holiness.

Rare also for a man of the cloth was that he had no money worries. Not only had he married well, he had acquired a very substantial inheritance from his father's coffee plantation in Kenya, leaving few to guess that his wealth ran to the tune of several million pounds. An understated Rolex on his wrist, along with clerical shirts designed to take opal cufflinks set in gold were but discreet hints at his wealth. And as a connoisseur of good shoes purchased from an exclusive Chelsea retailer, others who notice such things might have recognized him as being 'well heeled' all round.

First impressions of Christopher Wilkes were that he cut

a persuasive image as a priest, and the fine figure of a man in his prime.

But now with the body of the girl resting foetus-like at his feet, measured rage and an icy calm were followed by panic.

*'Christ Almighty!'* whispered the minister, whose blasphemy now came as readily as any entreaty of that name in a thousand prayers before. In the immediate aftermath of murder he knew what he had done, as did the One 'from whom no secrets are hid.'

Yet even in his moment of admission and even if *'He'* saw, the vicar's instinct raced towards a plan to ensure that Stacey's death remained a secret – at least to everybody else. For by reacting swiftly nobody need ever know. The girl would simply and tragically have disappeared.

Naturally it was risky to return to the vicarage some fifty yards away from the church, while leaving the body in the vestry where it lay. But by securing the church's outer door it felt imperative to clear his head and plan a course of action, this being best done at home.

With a busy weekend ahead a shortage of time presented the main challenge; not helped when upon unlocking the back door to the vicarage the kitchen phone rang.

'Ketborough 413610,' he answered.

The last thing he wanted was a baptism inquiry or some other pastoral request.

'Is that Kevin?' inquired a male voice.

'No, I think you must have the wrong number.'

'Is that 412610?'

'No, 413610.'

The line went dead. He hated those callers, who after dialing a wrong number would hang up without a word of apology.

Replacing the phone his upper torso suddenly became

numb, requiring that he extend his arms downwards so as to lean against the pine kitchen table. For a moment he couldn't move, even as his throat constricted to turn him breathless. The cold beads of sweat that began flowing from his forehead down his neck and staining the collar band of his shirt, these were entirely new sensations.

It was the rattle of the cat-flap that jolted him back into action. To loud purrs the black cat, which his wife had adopted as a stray, bumped against him with its old familiarity. Nudging it away with the toe of his shoe, he sought composure by pulling up a favourite chair. The yew and elm Windsor had always been a steadying place of repose for collecting his thoughts, and by pushing back into the seat and grasping the arms tightly, he managed to check a sudden bout of violent shaking. The shaking reminded him of an epileptic parishioner he'd once tried to help, who'd had a seizure during one of his services.

Was he ill? Perhaps he'd caught the summer virus doing the rounds, and which was said to induce strange mental side effects. For a moment everything went cloudy. Surely he couldn't have killed the girl. Maybe it hadn't happened at all? But even as denial sought to offer its reprieve from what had occurred no more than twenty minutes earlier, his reason reminded him of how he'd half-premeditated the deed in earlier fantasies.

Stacey's innocence had aroused feelings of anger months ago.

It was a quarter to ten. There'd be nobody else at home, at least not for another three hours. Then quite suddenly, despite the shock and subsequent shaking, he felt strangely elated - a part of him beginning to feel no regret at all. For although he hadn't planned to kill the girl – at least not that night – the pleasure that washed over him was *orgasmic*; a climactic thrill superseding anything experienced before.

So of course the girl was dead, with immediate action being called for.

Time had to become his ally, its rule being dictated in the kitchen not by the flicker of the turquoise digits from the cooker, but through the ponderous tick-tock of a large 'station' clock hanging on the wall. With its Roman numerals etched on to a white face, the clock's presence lent urgency to his task.

*'Damn!'* The phone rang again.

'Ketborough 413610,' he said as the cat nudged up against him once more, its miaows signaling its demand for milk.

'Sorry to trouble you, Christopher, it's Jonathan here.'

Jonathan Sharpe was his organist and a good one for sure, but like other inquirers who can invade a vicar's life at all hours the last thing he needed was Jonathan on the line – too conscientious for one thing. Yet even when phone calls might infuriate, they always necessitated a civil and Christian response:

'Yes, Jonathan, what can I do for you?' He marveled at the reasonableness of his tone.

'I forgot to check whether we have enough copies of *Jerusalem* for tomorrow's wedding,' replied the other.

The great patriotic hymn was not an entirely unusual request for a couple getting married.

'It's not in our standard Hymns of Faith,' he continued, 'and I'm not sure how many copies of Ancient & Modern Revised we've got hidden away.'

Having practiced the hymn earlier that evening the choir had their own copies. So it was more a case of the congregation being provided for. 'Shall I come over and check out how many books we've got available? We're going to need at least a hundred and fifty.'

'*No*, don't trouble yourself, *I can do it!*' urged Christopher. 'And if there aren't enough copies, I'll get back to you.'

'I can easily come over myself,' offered Jonathan. He only lived five minutes away by car.

'*Don't* worry!' said Christopher tetchily. '*I'll* see to it.'

'Right. By the way,' asked Jonathan, 'forgive me for asking but was everything okay with Stacey this evening? She seemed a bit flustered during choir practice.'

'Yes, she's fine,' answered the vicar, now fearing the limits of his composure. 'She just wanted to clear up a minor problem, and only stayed for a few moments before catching up with her friends.'

'Great! Then, I'll leave the matter of the hymn books with you.'

'*Yes*, Jonathan!' As he hung up he knew he'd been close to losing it. The organist's job wasn't to worry about the congregation, and whether they had enough hymnbooks. Why too in God's name had he asked about Stacey?

Of course All Saints was lucky to have acquired the services of so gifted a musician. He was an organ scholar from Leeds University and good organists were hard to come by. But Jonathan was an unpredictable sort, sometimes turning up in church when least expected.

At least the organist's concern for Stacey helped to focus the vicar's thoughts. Yet despite the urgency of what to do next, the rhythmic ticking of the clock still allowed him to remain calm.

'First, feed the cat!' he spoke out loud. Going to the refrigerator, he was forced to use two hands to steady the flow of the near-full plastic container into a saucer, almost dowsing the creature as he did so.

'At least that'll stop the infuriating cupboard love.' Again he voiced his thoughts.

He then had a bizarre wish to go and look at himself, Might there be some telltale sign? Would he *look* like a murderer? He wondered. What was that saying about the eyes being the window of the soul?

Yet beyond the bloodless, unblinking expression, the mirror reassured him. As usual an air of charm and look of innocence would come to his rescue, it taking no effort to conjure up his dependable smile.

Narcissus smirked. 'Butter wouldn't melt in your mouth, would it?' he said to himself. 'Who me, Christopher Wilkes – Guilty? *Unthinkable!*'

A further look in the mirror assured him that he was the gentlest and most caring of souls.

Slowly his confidence returned. Of course, once news of Stacey's disappearance got out he would be as shocked as everyone else, his ashen expression conveying suitable sorrow. But then he'd have to be strong for others. So come Sunday, he would ensure that his rich baritone would stay constant with the choir and, although serious in tone, his sermon would urge people to have faith that Stacey would surely return home shortly. Keeping his composure was crucial for everyone's sake. Nor must he be distracted for tomorrow's wedding, having no wish to let down the couple on their special day.

But he was now one of the damned. Any innocence had become lethal camouflage - the chameleon on the rock slipping like an alligator into its swamp. More dire than the mild ravages of late middle age, Wilkes would come to look haunted; *hunted* even – suspicious that he was being watched, even when no one was watching. But then he wasn't to know that those with second sight, so to speak, might catch another expression. For behind its ever-benign smile his face – Janus-like, could leave in its shadow an expression of sheer menace; a mask straight from hell.

Not that he believed in *hell* or any of that stuff! Any beliefs he had about the devil were as vague as those he held about God. Of course there was that verse about 'no man serving two masters, for he will end up hating the one while serving the other,' and although the devil went by a variety of names – Satan, Beelzebub, Lucifer, as far as Christopher Wilkes knew he served no-one but himself.

But to have committed murder and then to feign innocence ensured that whatever allegiances he once had, however vague, consigned him to a darker domain.

The deal was being done and, with thoughts only of evasion, the last thing he now contemplated was to call the police and say, 'I've committed a murder. For God's sake arrest me and put me away!' Or to contact some trusted priest with the plea, 'I have to make my confession. Please can I see you immediately.'

'*Like hell!*' The phrase erupted from his lips, even as he thought it.

For even if Wilkes didn't see it that way, the pact between the devil and his valuable new recruit was already signed and sealed. For contracts to be exchanged, Lucifer required no signature

For had he felt a bat squeak of remorse at the moment when the soft cotton of the ligature claimed her, now it was only the elation that rode high. Deep down he'd always known that his life as a vicar was a sham. Notwithstanding his obsession with the institution, he'd never had any divine experience; never 'seen the light' as they say or been called. Nor, unlike a few of the clergy he knew, did he feel anything for God – let alone Christ.

So upping the stakes felt good. What with a large inheritance, public school education plus fine athletic record, along with a good degree from Oxford – he was made for life; one of the 'old school' as they say, plausibility being his birthright. For even when he had no belief in God, he'd grown confident about bluffing others into believing so that most of his admirers considered him to be a devout, if not holy, man.

If charm was to be confused with holiness so be it!

For the shepherd who was no shepherd but a wolf in sheep's clothing, the exhilaration now felt at having killed the girl was perhaps the nearest he'd ever come to being *himself*. Murder had invited his true persona onto center-stage. It was up to others to discover the wolf in their midst, and to chase it from the fold.

Too much in love with his status and of his future prospects, a betrayal of this other self was unthinkable. As vicar of the prestigious Midlands town parish church of All Saints, Ketborough, no vestige of conscience could be summoned to make amends for the pretty teenager, now dead and who, from his point of view, had been leading him on anyway.

If he were to ponder these considerations at all, he would do so in the future. What mattered now as he prepared to leave the kitchen was to keep his cool and act decisively.

'Come on, man!' he urged. '*Get with it!*'

He had already decided what to do with the body.

# Chapter 2

'Good evening, Nick, what'll it be?'

'Good evening, Nick, same as usual.'

Such was the gentle repartee between Nick Cochran, landlord of The Magpie and retired detective inspector Nick Hagan, one of The Magpie's regular but modest drinkers over the past seven years.

Of the three pubs near the center of Ketborough, The Magpie was but a stone's throw from the parish church off the High Street. Unlike the Hetherington Arms just opposite, the 'Pie' was a case 'of what you see you get'. Nor did it seek to compete with the trendy Staff of Life, a renovated pub half a mile away and the new watering hole for the local youth.

Stubbornly unpretentious, the pub's interior offered neither a pastiche of polystyrene beams, nor a profusion of brass knick-knacks to give it some fake ye olde look. A couple of gaming machines were the only concession to a rowdier clientele, with the bar-billiard table and dartboard being largely monopolized by the regulars. Where traditional pubs were fast disappearing all over the country, it was through serving decent beer and keeping the place relaxed, while not wasting excessive amounts of money on the place, that landlord Nick Cocheron managed to stay in business.

Like its no-nonsense decor, Cocheron and most of his drinkers were down-to-earth folk, tending to know everybody's business, whilst arriving through conjecture and idle chit chat at what they *didn't* know.

Stocky and with a large open ruddy complexion, black 'tache and thinning hair slicked back – the landlord observed the world with that bitter/sweet humour that seeks to make life more bearable. Having several customers by the name of 'Nick,' he'd secured a tradition by which the only one to keep his first name after the mutual greetings would be himself. The other Nick-locals would have to answer to derivatives, 'nick' names in fact.

Nick the retired detective inspector, was addressed as 'DI' as in the fist syllable of Diana. Then there was Nick the builder who, having served a short term of imprisonment twelve years ago for shoplifting and who might have secured a ready pun on his name, had been left to settle with the label of 'Crooks.'

The third of the local Nicks was a traveling salesman, who known as a bit of a ladies' man got dubbed – quite unjustly in his view – with the title of 'Lech.' It was the sort of pub where people couldn't forget their past, but where former lifestyles were only referred to good-naturedly.

Setting down a pint of stout for the most reputable of the Magpie's three Nicks, the landlord observed, 'Grand evening again Di although this weather's playing havoc with my carrots and broccoli. This hosepipe ban's doing my head in, not to mention my back – lugging around all those watering cans. Good weather for drinking; lousy for beetroots!'

The landlord's obsession for his allotment at the back of the pub held no interest for the retired detective. Besides Di chose to have his summers hot and dry any day.

'Suppose so, Nick,' replied Di. 'For myself I prefer to

grow my fruit and veg out of the supermarket trolley. Trimming the privet and mowing the lawn are quite enough to be going on with as it is. I can't understand how you chaps spend hours slogging it out in the garden, and sometimes with nothing to show for it. What with droughts, slugs, flies, not to mention blackbirds and pigeons and two-legged thieves running off with what's left, why waste your time and effort instead of leaving it to the professionals?'

With his record-breaking marrows and tomatoes, Nick Cocheron tended to regard himself *as* a professional, enjoying an allotment safely walled in at least from human intrusion. But wishing to take the conversation in another direction, he had no wish to argue the point.

'Run out of time now that you're retired, eh Di? What with that and your church, don't forget,' observed the landlord. 'You weren't like that at one time, remember?'

'Ah well, that's as may be,' replied the other guardedly. Examining the contents of his glass with a special interest, he pretty much guessed what was coming.

An awkward silence followed.

The garden talk – as everybody knew – was but a pretext for what was the talk of the town, the disappearance three nights ago of the choirgirl Stacey Witcombe. Reference to the church, by which he meant All Saints, was the landlord's way of getting on to the subject of Stacey. After all, if anyone had an opinion about what had happened it ought to be Di Hagan.

But Hagan was naturally cautious and never one to voice off-the-cuff opinions, more so given that the landlord's query had caught the attention of the other two Nicks.

These days he could only take out his pipe while keeping it unlit. But it remained a helpful distraction. Clamping his teeth around his meerschaum, he could at least bite his tongue, so to speak. Let others do the talking, if they so wished.

That wasn't to say he didn't feel tempted to say something. Up until his wife's death seven years ago, the sixty-one year old former detective hadn't given much thought to religion. Only thanks to the outstanding support shown him by the then vicar, Rev Jack Bishop during his bereavement, had Di's faith in God or in the Church been restored. Sadly eighteen months ago Di suffered a further loss, when his good friend Jack – who wasn't averse to a glass or two in the Magpie – died without warning from a massive coronary.

Having been the vicar of All Saints for almost eight years, Jack had persuaded Di not only to attend church and join the Parochial Church Council, but had then got him elected as churchwarden. A few years earlier, agreeing to such an appointment would have been a complete joke to a sceptical copper who, if not an atheist, had always been a confirmed doubter. So truth being stranger than fiction was nowhere more apt than when Di Hagan got religion, it being a source of endless amusement to both men,

'I reckon that new vicar's a right weirdo . . .' Nick Crooks' blunt comment interrupted the widower's lonely introspection. 'Not so long ago, he looked right through me, when I said Good morning. It felt like he didn't want to know me.'

'Well maybe he's got good taste!' said Lech, giving Crooks a friendly prod. 'But joking aside, I've got to admit it, this Wilkes bloke just don't match up to good old Reverend Jack.'

Nick Cocheron ventured an opinion through a question, 'Do you think you'll be staying on, then, as churchwarden, Di? You don't seem like half as happy now that Wilkes has arrived. I agree with Lech and Crooks, he's not a patch on dear old Jack. What's more, with all the hoo-hah over young Stacey, it's been three days now that she'd gone missing, I'd want to keep away from that church - all the associations as much as anything. God's-truth, Di what do you reckon happened to her?'

'Well, you can be sure that the police have, by now, turned their investigations into a major missing persons' inquiry,' replied Di. He refrained from adding that when someone went missing for more than seventy-two hours, along with the phrase about 'growing fears for her safety,' the police tended to fear the worst. Nor did he wish to comment that even with computer printouts of possible abductors and their whereabouts, the likelihood was that they would have turned up next to nothing.

'Yeah but what about the *vicar?*' urged Crooks. 'After all, he was supposed to have been the last person to have seen her.'

'Oh come on, so what does that prove?' Lech's interruption was timely. 'You could be the last person to see your best friend before he died in an accident. It doesn't mean you *killed* them!'

Di also knew that although the vicar had been the last person to see the girl before her disappearance, this proved nothing. In fact if anything he'd shown exemplary concern by going to visit the Witcombes that same very night. Had he 'done a runner' or lost his cool in some way, then the spotlight would have fallen fair and square upon him. But he'd reacted just as you'd expect of 'a man of the cloth' by doing everything he could to help.

Yet Di knew how this Wilkes fellow left him feeling uneasy, in a way that Jack Bishop never did. Jack had a knack for putting all and sundry at their ease, except for those 'pious' souls who perversely preferred their vicars to be 'holier than thou.' Nor was old Jack averse to cracking a joke about sex, or to expressing his views about a pretty girl. The previous vicar was, in Di's opinion, as in the eyes of his drinking associates, a bit of a *Jack the lad* but in the nicest sense and in the best possible taste. For with his open cynicism about the Church and ready rapport with ordinary folk, the nearest that the late vicar would have got to promotion was when people referred to him affectionately as 'Reverend Bishop.'

This new fellow was just so different. Charming but cold, such humour as he had was of a joyless kind – short clipped witticisms that weren't remotely funny, at least in any relaxed sense. If anything Wilkes was horribly normal, too normal even. Nor would he have ever risked a dodgy joke had he deigned to enter the plain-speaking atmosphere of The Magpie, which he never did.

'I read somewhere about this bloke – some sort of serial killer in Scotland in the seventeenth century . . .' It was the landlord's turn to imply an air of suspicion about the new vicar. 'This guy lived his life like nothing had happened, even when he'd killed six or seven women. In fact he behaved so normally that he was the *last* person anyone suspected.'

At this point another local chimed in, 'they say that about serial killers. I'm old enough to remember Peter Sutcliffe, the Yorkshire Ripper – nobody suspected him of being anything other than a loving husband. Everyone said at his place of work how "You could always count on good old Pete in a crisis".'

'Who was that civil servant who killed all those young lads and slept next to them after having sex?' asked Lech.

'Dennis Nielsen,' responded Di, remembering the case clearly, more so on account of how Nielsen looked so completely harmless.

'Yeah, but they're as nothing compared to Dr Harold Shipman,' countered the landlord. 'There was your caring Manchester GP giving all those trusting old dears shots of morphine like there was no tomorrow.'

'And there was no tomorrow for – was it nearly three hundred of them?' added Di.

'*Fuck him!*' said Lech and Crooks in unison. 'The trouble was' added Lech, 'he topped himself before he even got tried. That Shipman was some evil bastard.'

Di recalled how Shipman looked every inch your typical family doctor, where with his conscientious pose nothing seemed to be too much trouble. In fact it was his very air of *professionalism* that stopped anyone from ever expressing an opinion against him for years.

Why are these psychopaths such bloody good actors? He nearly voiced his thought out loud.

'So when do you reckon they'll find out?' asked Crooks. 'Find out what happened?'

'Don't hold your breath,' said Di. 'These things can sometimes drag on for an eternity.' God, how he wished he could light up his meerschaum; hide behind the smoke for one thing.

He felt sick thinking about Stacey or, for that matter, on the peculiarities of his vicar. The seventeen-year-old was a girl of startling good looks, with a lovely sunny outlook on life, making him identify with her loss almost as though he'd been her father.

Downing his stout with unusual abruptness, the retired detective declared, 'I must be off!' explaining how upset he was by the whole crisis. To mutual murmurs of sympathy, he left them to their conjectures while returning to the solace of home where he could think alone.

Di knew he'd escaped lightly from the inquisition at The Magpie, more so given the absence of the pub's most vocal customer – a Pole called Zbierski.

For, as he rightly guessed, Zbierski would up the ante

big-time about what had happened to the girl.

Hagan's home life wasn't one of complete solitude. Having had no children, he and his wife had consoled themselves over the years with a number of cats and dogs. Now in bereavement, Di's two companions were in the form of a large, ten-year-old ginger tabby called Sleuth and an eighteen-month-old border-collie bitch called Snap.

Snap, a sweet but demanding creature, had been acquired when Di was in mourning for Jack Bishop's passing, while the bonding between Sleuth and his master had consolidated over the past ten years. He and his wife had chosen Sleuth as a kitten, and it was now in widowhood that Di found him half believing that the tomcat could understand him, was even able to read his thoughts in some way. For when it came to mulling over problems, Hagan would unashamedly consult his feline friend. There was the time when he'd quizzed Sleuth over a prospective new lady friend, only for a reproachful glare to leave him in full agreement that the lady in question wasn't somehow suitable! Too soon for someone moving in to join him, or should he say *them?*

For a man, bereaved and pensioned off, which in police terms meant surplus to requirements, his pets had become inseparable confidantes.

Returning from the pub, the retired detective settled down to talk with Sleuth.

# Chapter 3

Hiding the body had worked like a charm, the task having taken no more than ten minutes.

For upon hurrying back to the vestry that Friday evening he'd scooped up the corpse along with her suede jacket, while picking up the delicate chain and locket which had broken off in the near non-existent struggle. As he took the body down the aisle towards the large antique chest he was surprised at his coolness. Secured up against the west wall, the chest was an ideal place for leaving her overnight. Besides he had the only key to it. After opening it he casually wrapped her in a discarded calico altar cover, securing it with some residue sash cord also found there. Then locking the chest and remembering to replace a brass baptism jug on its lid, he returned to the vestry. It was like he'd done no more than change some altar linen.

No sooner had he returned to the vestry than the outside door opened to reveal, like an apparition, Jonathan Sharpe.

Momentarily shaken, Christopher then recalled his organist's request about the anthem *Jerusalem*.

'Oh, hallo!' he said to the younger man. 'I thought I told you not to worry about the hymn. In fact I was just going to see to that now.'

If the organist registered surprise that Christopher appeared to be on his way out, having clearly overlooked his assurance that he would check out the hymnbooks, he passed no comment.

'No, I wasn't worrying about that,' Jonathan responded. 'I thought I should have one last practice at Widor's *Toccata* for the recessional after the wedding, since I won't have time to do so tomorrow morning. So if you don't mind, I'll just have a quick run through now.'

*Good God!* Thought Christopher. Why doesn't the man ever let up?

'I'm sure that you'll play it perfectly,' said Christopher. 'But by all means go ahead but please do so *not* at full volume!'

After checking that they had enough copies of the 'Jerusalem' hymn, Christopher bid Jonathan goodnight, asking him to be sure to lock the church with his own key when he left.

Returning to the vicarage, he broke into a further spasm of shaking and an outpouring of sweat.

*'Jesus, that was close!'* he whispered. 'If he'd have come ten minutes earlier, he'd have tripped right over her!'

People like Jonathan unnerved him, their unpredictability for one thing, making him question whether his excuse for returning was only to rehearse a piece of music. Flushing Stacey's broken locket down the lavatory, and returning to the kitchen he sat down once more in his Windsor chair. He could think through his strategy while waiting for the inevitable phone call.

It was shortly after ten when the phone rang with Stacey's parents in near panic, 'Vicar have you seen our Stacey after she left choir practice?' Mrs. Witcombe's voice trembled, 'She's not come home!'

Measured concern, left Christopher replying, *'Goodness!*

No, I fear I haven't. She left church just after nine after we'd had a brief chat. She said she wanted to share a problem with me. But she didn't stay long and I asked her if she would like a lift home but, thanking me, she said no and that she'd catch up with her friends.' Had Stacey perhaps called to see Martin her boyfriend, he inquired, given that Martin's house lay directly en-route between the church and her home on the council estate about a mile away. But that possibility had already been checked out. She'd neither called to see Martin, nor had she been seen walking along the High street. 'Besides, she's always so good about time,' continued her mother. 'I've never known her late before. She always tells us where she's going and if she's running late. I tell you vicar, we ain't half worried!'

Seeking to console Mrs. Witcombe with phrases like, 'You know what young teenagers are like!' and 'It's been such a lovely evening that maybe she's just lost track of time,' Christopher then said that he would have a drive around to see if he could see any sign of her daughter.

After murder, lies seemed to come so easily. Trussed up dead in a seventeenth century coffer at the back of a mediaeval church, it felt like simplicity itself to fob off the girl's parents with a few decoy suggestions. An icy calm had begun to take over.

It was fortunate that his wife Frances and their elder son had gone to Dorset for the weekend, visiting her elderly uncle and aunt. Dominic had willingly accompanied his mother, getting in some driving practice before his test in a fortnight's time. Only his teenage daughter Katy would be around and she'd gone out to some disco, having promised to return home by one am at the latest.

'Keep up the good work. Don't panic!' Christopher counseled himself. 'Do the obvious thing and visit the parents.'

*A Candle For Lucifer*

Stepping out into the warm summer night to go to the garage, the magnificent strains of Widor's *Toccata in F* became clearly audible from the church; the great swell alternating with the intricate higher notes. Even with muted stops the young organist was excelling himself. But tonight of all nights to be playing such a piece! For a few moments the vicar found himself transfixed by the music. For such was the composition and the organist's rendition of it that here was a fanfare both to love and joy; music even to raise the dead back to life. Listening to the toccata, the last thing he intended was to inform his organist of Stacey's disappearance.

'For God's sake, go home Jonathan and *give it a rest!*' he found himself pleading, under his breath.

Jumping into his car, he went through the pretence of looking for his victim before calling in on the Witcombes. With the night's warmth clinging in the air along with a hint of mauves and reds on the horizon, tomorrow promised to be every bit as warm.

Theirs was a typical but neat semi-detached house on the apex of a crescent, which housed Ketborough's only small council estate. With most of the house lights on and the curtains left open, the brightness spilled on to a garden better tended than most and on to the luminous markings of the white Ford Focus parked on the kerb.

The Witcombes had two daughters and it was Stacey's elder sister, Philippa, who answered the door, framed in the background by her father. He was startled to see how similar the two girls looked, more like identical twins than sisters.

'I had to come and see you!' explained Christopher, standing on the doorstep. 'You were obviously very upset and understandably so. But surely there has to be a simple explanation. Have you heard any news yet?'

'No, no sign of her at all!' Mr. Witcombe gasped. 'Come

in, vicar. In fact the police have just arrived.'

Clearly distressed Philippa excused herself by saying she needed to make some phone calls, leaving him to be ushered into the front living room where two youthful officers were seated with one taking down a few notes. With both their radios kept on at low volume it was as though they were going through the motions of an inquiry, rather than giving the matter their full attention.

'Good evening reverend, we understand you were the last person to see Stacey. How did she seem?'

He couldn't get over how young they both looked; officers hardly out of their teens or so it seemed.

'She seemed to be all right although perhaps she was a bit more excited than usual. But that's only guesswork and when she left me she appeared to be happy enough. I thought she was going to catch up with her friends,' replied Christopher before adding 'It's been such a lovely evening. Maybe she got waylaid, perhaps deciding to go to the Staff of Life or somewhere.'

'She didn't hang out with any of them who went to the Staff,' said Mrs. Witcombe, her tone catching but indignant enough to suggest that the pub would have been off-limits for their daughter.

No great distance from the church, the 'Staff' recently under new management had become the new venue for the youth of the town. Not that he the vicar entirely approved of the place or, for that matter, that his own daughter Katy had begun some part-time work serving drinks there.

'Besides, there's no way she'd be late, like this,' added Mr. Witcombe, his anxiety making him angry. Not only did the vicar appear unreasonably calm, the unhurried attitude shown by the officers was, if anything, following similar lines namely that when Stacey returned she'd be full of apologies, explaining how she'd lost track of time.

'What's more,' added Mr. Witcombe, 'I've been out all over. She always lets us know where she is. If she went anywhere out of the ordinary she'd take her mobile. As it is her phone is still upstairs. *So in God's name, what's happened to her?*'

The vicar stayed for around half an hour, during which time the officers asked him a few further questions about what he and Stacey had talked about, and where else might she have gone after leaving the church. Declining to make mention of the 'question,' he invented a story about the girl wishing to clarify something about the Trinity for the mock RE 'A' level which she'd just taken. After that she'd left the church presumably to catch up with her friends. Then for added effect while lowering his voice he repeated, 'she did seem a bit excitable, however, as though maybe she could have been planning something else before going home. Young love and all that!' he half-smiled as he looked at the two officers.

The questioning remained informal with the policemen nodding at the vicar's suggestion – that 'for all that she's a good girl,' Stacey had simply lost track of time and been diverted by friends. Upon her return, the two constables would be more than willing to have a word with her about being more considerate in the future.

'For want of a single phone call, teenagers can give their families endless grief, more so when they leave their mobiles at home' suggested the marginally older of the two policemen.

Hopes surged only then to be dashed by a phone call from Stacey's boyfriend Martin, asking if she had returned home yet. By repeating that he'd still heard and seen nothing, Mrs. Witcombe became hysterical, giving Christopher his cue for leaving with the parting request of 'please let me know as soon as you hear *anything*!' His better judgment stopped him from repeating the mantra about Stacey losing track of time and so forth.

For even as he was expressing his pastoral concern, even as he sat in the Witcombe's living room being solicitous, his brain had been busy working. Calling to mind the proverb about Fortune favoring the brave, he'd decided what to do with the body, but that he must be prompt and unswerving in his actions.

Upon leaving their house it was distracting to catch a further glimpse of Philippa.

'*My God,* she's the spitting image of her sister!' he thought. Being so near to a physical resurrection of Stacey spooked him.

First thing in the morning he'd drive up to the Lake District and dispose of the girl on some steep roadside slope overgrown with bracken. From his many visits to the Lake District, he knew that under bracken the carcasses of sheep could lie rotting and undetected for years.

Returning to the vicarage, he was relieved that with the church lights out the phantom of the opera had taken his leave. Even then, he half-expected Jonathan to jump out of the shadows, to tap him on the shoulder perhaps with some further request. Upon double-checking that both doors to the church were locked, and attending to one or two church matters he retired to bed just before midnight, more with the purpose of avoiding his daughter Katy than for sleep. Rest would also give him time to relax, before making what would be a six-hour return journey.

Around an hour later, he identified his daughter's return by the distinctive tones of her boyfriend's Lotus Elise. Reassured that Katy was now indoors and that her companion had driven off, Christopher relaxed in the knowledge that when he slipped out of the house in the early hours, Katy would still be fast asleep.

Dawn shrouded itself in a lace of mist; nature's signal that the heat wave that they'd been enjoying all week stood to last over the weekend. He'd not slept badly as it happened, and tiptoeing downstairs just before five a.m. he ate a hurried breakfast of cereal and toast. Then switching off and depositing his mobile in his desk while switching on his answering machine, he left a note for Katy to say he'd not be back until later. In virtual silence he then let himself out through the back door.

The likelihood was that his daughter would sleep soundly until at least ten, and stay blearily indifferent either to her own or to her father's whereabouts for a good hour after that.

The trickiest part of what was to follow was transferring the body into the rear of his estate car. The short distance between the vicarage and the church was dissected by the garage, which lay mid-way between the two on its own apron of tarmac. Seeing no signs of life either on the main road or in the adjacent houses, Christopher set his plan in motion.

Unlocking the vestry door, he strode down the central aisle to the west wall. With the first rays of sunlight penetrating the east window, the light stirred colour from the flowers and ribbons for the wedding later that afternoon. The pew ends had been exquisitely decorated with small displays of lilies of the valley and pink myrtle – myrtle, the symbol of young love consummated in marriage. It was rare these days to have a traditional wedding, and one for which Stacey and the choir had made careful preparations.

Removing the brass baptism jug, he unlocked the chest and lifted the lid. Her clothes were soiled and a slight smear of mucous and blood was visible around her discoloured lips. Mild nausea hit him as he removed her body, noting how its slightness seemed accentuated by death and whose extremities had started to stiffen and putrefy. A further bloodstain had seeped on to the altar cover, while several wisps of corn-blonde hair had shaken loose onto her T-shirt. Wrapping the jacket and altar cloth around her hunched form, as well as gathering up some further sections of sash cord, he held the bundle in one arm while relocking the chest and placing the jug back on its lid.

It unnerved him holding her so close, the coldness for one thing. Yet she seemed to nestle into him like a sleeping child; an involuntary pose of trust had it been in real life. Even in death it was as though she kept her innocence.

Sounds were amplified. The winding mechanism of the church clock gave him a sudden start as it struck five fifteen; the chimes resonating like a call to prayer. Pigeons cooed menacingly as they scuttled along the apex of the roof. Outside on the road a number of vehicles suddenly came to life, including a council lorry whose swishing sounds relayed that it had been commissioned to spray the dusty streets. And if birds could speak, the whole dawn-chorus seemed to be rousing itself in a cacophony of accusation.

*'Stay cool!'* a voice within commanded as he stood momentarily at the vestry door.

Like a child briefed on the first rules of the Highway Code, he waited to 'Look and listen!' He checked his daughter's bedroom window, which overlooked the church. Although the curtained stillness reassured him that Katy was fast asleep, this was his most dangerous moment. *No mistakes!* At all costs avoid some chance witness who might observe what was going on.

The short distance to the up-and-over door of the garage that he'd already opened took seconds. Gently he lowered Stacey's body, still wrapped in its altar cloth and jacket, into the back of his midnight blue Volvo Estate. He'd make the bundle more secure later, covering it for the time being with a piece of loose carpet and a large car-rug. He returned to lock the vestry door, doing so in virtual silence.

Having prepared a flask of coffee and some sandwiches, he had no wish to delay further. He started the car, affronting the Almighty by praying that its motor would neither awaken Katy, nor cause some curious neighbour to twitch back a curtain. Fortunately Saturdays were for lying in and, standing in its own acre of ground, the vicarage was largely obscured from other properties by a perimeter of silver birches and leylandii.

Nobody appeared to see the Volvo pulling out onto the main road. From there he'd soon joined the motorway, making rapid progress up the M6, before turning west on the road to Lake Windermere.

The drive made him jittery. Had he left his answering machine on? Might the police call on the off chance? What if there was some major traffic hold-up or his car broke down? Needless worries he told himself at least concerning the car. Having had his vehicle from new, he spared no expense on its regular servicing, and where after three years it had just passed its first MOT examination without a hitch. Knowing that a Volvo in mint condition was an improbable vehicle in which to break down, he relaxed. The car's only problem was an air-conditioning malfunction, due to be fixed under warranty in a few days time.

Near to Windermere he had the presence of mind to find a phone-box and call the Witcombes, inquiring if there had been any further developments. The heart-rending sobs of Mrs. Witcombe allowed Christopher a suitable pause, before informing her, 'I am still upholding you all in my prayers. Whatever we do *we mustn't lose hope!* Please try to hang on!' Inconsolable cries required him to replace the handset, as he muttered 'Goodbye.'

*'You're a bastard!'* said an inner voice approvingly as he

resumed his journey. Weariness from his short night's sleep, and the encroaching heat of another scorching day made him irritable. It was vexing that despite the car's otherwise impeccable order, the air-conditioning remained un-repaired. For although it wasn't yet eight thirty in the morning the sweet fishy smell exuding from the rear of the car persisted, even with his front windows wound fully down. So he was relieved when he came to a wooded section on the road running west of Coniston Water.

He stopped at a lay-by, free of any other vehicles apart from a yellow Volkswagen Caravanette, which just at that moment was pulling away. This was exactly the sort of place Christopher had in mind – wooded and with dense undergrowth, falling away steeply to the lake below.

Having made an earlier halt to ensure that the bundle was tied securely, the disposal of Stacey's body was as straightforward as her death. Given that it all felt so easy it was like someone was looking after him. One heave over the dry-stone wall and the bundle had rolled into a dense oblivion of ferns and rhododendron bushes; a location so inaccessible that it would deter even the most intrepid fell walker or inquisitive dog.

With the finality of Stacey's disappearance it felt like a burden, not unlike the one just discarded, had lifted. Suddenly he felt so much better. Congratulating himself on having been so coolly efficient, he drank two cups of strong coffee and ate a couple of sandwiches before making a swift and uneventful journey home.

With only the oppressive heat to contend with, he arrived back at the vicarage in less than three hours, pulling up at ten minutes to twelve. A message from his daughter told him that she'd gone shopping, and that did he want anything for lunch? If so, she would be back around twelve thirty. His answer-phone flashed two inconsequential messages and, reassured that Katy had gone about her normal routine, he resumed his role as vicar.

The gamble had paid off. Deciding to make a further call to the Witcombes, he learned from a neighbour minding the phone that Mr. and Mrs. Witcombe were down at the police station. He asked the neighbour to let the Witcombes know that he had rung, before having a bite of lunch.

After eating he then took a shower so as to be in church refreshed and in good time for the wedding.

# Chapter 4

'Yoo-hoo, we're home, darling!'

'Is that you darling?' called Christopher, knowing as soon as he saw the Renault Clio pull up the drive that his wife and son had come home. It was early on Monday evening following their weekend visit with her aunt and uncle.

Pretty in a neat airbrushed way, his wife Frances was of medium height, having a preference for jacket and skirt outfits either in pink or beige. Wearing her dark hair in a bob and notwithstanding the overall pleasing effect, a keen observer would have detected the strain behind the pretty blue eyes – her clear complexion having long been marred by the pallor of insomnia. If she wore earrings, they were usually small gold-framed studs with onyx or pearl insets. For the drive home, the onyx earrings were in place, although she had discarded the suit in favour of a white ribbed cotton cardigan and maroon slacks.

'How was everything?' inquired Christopher. 'How are Uncle Josh and Aunt Maude? Did you have a good journey?'

'In answer to that,' replied Frances, 'yes, and nearly yes! They're in good spirits considering his diabetes and her lameness. And yes, we had a good journey apart from a near miss on the way home when *kiddo here* misunderstood an oncoming driver's signal to turn right, when *we* had to make a right.' With a whimsical smile, she added, 'Nearly wrote the car off . . .'

'It wasn't as bad as *that* Mum!' complained Dominic, his young manhood bruised that he hadn't completed a flawless journey to mid Dorset and back. 'Anyone could have made the same mistake.'

'Well, you're probably right. The other driver certainly didn't make his intentions plain. Anyway, how are you are darling? How's Katy? I tried phoning early on Saturday evening but neither of you can have been at home.'

Offering her cheek for the cursory kiss, this was the only intimacy indulged in for years. For despite the sprinkling of 'darlings' theirs was the proverbial marriage of convenience - functional and polite, yet one sustained by the forces of inertia for twenty-five years.

Responding to her question, he said, 'I'm fine. All the services went well. I got pretty tired on Saturday after taking the wedding and then having to go on to the reception. The more receptions I attend, the more I feel out of place and hate going as a sort of token presence. I don't think I shall go to any more, unless we happen to know the couple really well. Katy's fine and should be back any time.' He paused. '. . . Of course you won't have heard what happened last Friday, will you?'

Frances and Dominic stopped in the hall, their arms laden with paraphernalia from the car.

'Stacey . . . Stacey Witcombe in the choir.' By blurting it out he hoped to emphasize his alarm. *'She's gone missing!'*

*'Good God!'* gasped Frances uncharacteristically.

'How? When?' asked their son.

'Well, she stopped after choir practice to talk to me briefly and then left, as I supposed, to catch up with her friends. She can't have been much more than five minutes behind them, when somewhere between the church and her home she simply disappeared. It's terrible, more so now that the weekend has passed with no further news. Stacey's parents are going out of their minds with worry.'

Visibly stunned, mother and son stood silent for a few moments before going upstairs. Some eighteen months older than the seventeen-year-old Stacey, he had certainly fancied her. But she was more outgoing than the tall, somewhat donnish chess-playing Dominic and so, despite being friends, they hadn't actually gone out together.

Christopher helped carry his son's laptop and two of his carrier bags upstairs. Hoping to strike a balance between showing too much concern and callous indifference, he didn't wish to dwell on the Stacey incident overlong.

'Of course, I've been to visit the Witcombes and called a couple of times, but feel pretty hopeless about knowing what to say or do. Naturally the police had to interview me, because I was the last person to see her alive. I can only conclude that she's chosen to run away.'

'Who with? *Martin?*' Frances looked incredulous. Stacey's boyfriend was an undergraduate, known to the Wilkes because he did holiday work at the local newsagent.

'No, he claims not to have seen her at all last Friday.'

'So why on earth should she want to run away?'

'I don't know, it's just a hunch I've got.'

'Well, from what I know of Stacey,' said Frances, 'she's just not that sort of girl. She's not only sensible but comes from a very close family.'

Reasoning that too much guesswork might appear odd, he had to agree.

'I bet Katy's very upset. How is she?' asked Frances. 'She was very fond of Stacey.' Use of the past tense made Dominic wonder, if not his father, whether his mother had felt a sudden instinct that Stacey's disappearance was final.

'It's shaken her badly, of course,' replied Christopher. 'After all, she was out until after midnight on the same night that Stacey went missing.' He managed to add, 'She's not the only one shaken.'

Almost upon the mention of her name, Katy appeared at the front door. Wearing a black beret, Monica Lewinsky style, her shoulder-length brunette hair framed her mother's bone structure. She wore a corduroy maroon snug-jacket, a loose fitting floral dress and brown slip-on boots.

'Hi, Mum! Welcome home! I can tell Dad's told you the news? I didn't want to phone you or worry you while you were away but isn't it *dreadful*? I'm surprised you didn't see it or read about it.' As an afterthought, Katy muttered, 'and Stacey of all people!'

'We didn't really bother with the news,' replied her mother. 'Dominic spent hours playing chess with Uncle Josh. Maude and I spent most of the time nattering.'

'I'm really *frightened* for her,' continued Katy. 'Stacey's mum and dad must be going out of their minds. ...Hi Dom!' she called in a quiet voice as she saw her brother's head appear over the banisters.

Dominic came downstairs. Despite being very different, brother and sister got on well together. He was gangly and non-athletic, with a professorial air borne out by a high forehead and tortoiseshell-rimmed glasses. With hair of a tousled mouse-brown already hinting at a receding hairline, he had his father's colouring with soft-brown eyes. Less academic but athletic like her father Katy had a firm frame, which allowed her to excel at tennis, swimming and netball. A girl well on the way to becoming exceedingly pretty, whose good height was dispensing with a slight chubbiness, her eye contact with the cornflower blue eyes of her mother was arresting.

Both had been to private boarding school but Katy had

come unstuck through an episode best forgotten – at least by her parents – which had made it necessary to re-route her education through the local Girls' High School. She had just re-taken and passed some GCSEs, before going on to do her 'A' levels. Six months older than Stacey, Katy was a year younger than her brother who, having just passed his 'A' Levels with top grades, was going to Cambridge that autumn.

Mortified by the news of Stacey, the vicarage conversation having taken place between the downstairs landing and the staircase petered out. With Frances going to the kitchen to prepare a meal, Christopher retired to his study to reflect on events that weren't yet seventy-two hours old.

God, he'd had a heavy weekend! Murder; concealment; a drive to and from the Lake District; Saturday's wedding that included consoling a distraught choir and then going on to the reception. Then there'd been the two CID officers calling later that evening, fortunately after Katy had gone out. Sunday followed with an increasingly agitated choir, and where at all three services there'd been the call for prayers to be offered up for the girl's safety.

And what had the two police officers asked him? He could only remember their numbers, not their names. More mature than the two young upstarts he'd met at the Witcombes, the pair may have introduced themselves but he recalled them only as officers 442 and 331. Following questions about his family and background, the interrogation had been a bit too close for his liking.

With officer 442 asking most of the questions, it had been 331 who was the more unpleasant.

'We need to know exactly how long Stacey stayed to talk with you, sir.'

Answer: 'About five to ten minutes at the outside.'

'Why did she want her friends to go on?'

'Because she said she wouldn't be long and would then catch them up' – a response indeed corroborated by her young female companions in the choir.

'What did she want to speak to you about, sir?'

'It was a personal question concerning her boyfriend.'

'We need to know what it was, reverend.'

Christopher paused. Much as he disliked having to say it, there was no reason for not telling them the truth. 'She asked me whether it was right or not for her to have sex with her boyfriend.'

'That's seems a bit of an odd question to put to a vicar,' interjected Officer 331.

'Stacey felt she could trust me with such a question.'

'Why? Was she giving you the come-on in some way? It wouldn't be the first time that a choirgirl has given her vicar a bit of a tease. Maybe she fancied you?'

'That's quite absurd! I'm a happily married man.'

'That doesn't mean anything, *sir!*' 331 seemed inclined to use the titles 'sir' and 'reverend' as terms of abuse.

'Well, how did you answer her?' probed officer Nice Guy.

'I told her that I strongly advised against it. Having premarital sex is wrong in the eyes of the church. And as the father of a teenage daughter I give the same advice to Katy, not just on religious grounds but in my capacity as a parent.'

'What were your feelings about Stacey, Vicar?' asked 442.

'What do you mean?' replied Christopher sensing the *double entendre* of the question.

*'Give them a pious answer!'* ordered a voice of stone from within.

'Well what did you *think* about her? What *do* you think about her?'

'She was a very nice girl. Very co-operative, very willing.'

*'Was!'* Who says anything about *was?*' Officer 331 seemed hell-bent on rattling him, before adding 'And what do you

mean by *willing?'* – a further 'sir' then being tacked on for good measure.

Christopher recalled reading somewhere how investigating officers working in pairs, would often operate on the principle of one being considerate and polite, while leaving the other to act the bully.

'I meant *was* in the sense of how much she had given to the life of our church in the past. She has been a member of the church following her confirmation three years ago and I've got to know the family since I arrived here twelve months ago. She was very *willing* to assist in the life of the church!'

'So what do you think happened to Stacey?' asked 442, maintaining his sweet reasonableness.

'I think that tragically there must have been something playing on her mind; something that she'd kept hidden from her parents as well as from me. Although I sought to guide her in her personal life, my hunch is that either she had some close-guarded secret to which none of us was privy and chose to run away, or that she was abducted.'

'Pretty unlikely that she'd be abducted in what was still broad daylight,' said 331, 'just after nine on a hot summer's evening with people walking up and down the High Street. Presumably she went home along the High Street?'

'She left by the porch door,' replied Christopher. 'I offered her a lift to catch up with her friends, which she declined. So I presumed that she would head back in the direction of her house by the most direct route, or that she'd visit her boyfriend whose house is also close by.' Pausing, he added, 'perhaps if there was something on her mind she didn't go straight home. Or maybe she met someone she knew who then abducted her.'

'So you think that someone who knew her may have picked her up and that she went *willingly?'* asked 442.

'It's just a hunch. After all, we're all left guessing.'

'Someone may know more than the rest of us, reverend,' added 331 slyly.

The interview continued for some time longer, with Christopher requesting that if they had further questions, then please to reserve them for another day. He had Sunday's services still to finalize, and it had been a busy and distressing day for all concerned. Before leaving, Officer 331 put one further question to Christopher. 'Can you tell me how you spent your time this morning, sir?'

With no mention of his six-hour journey to the Lake District, he told them about driving to a beauty spot to do some sermon preparation.

And then as the two officers were leaving, what was that about 442 slipping back to apologise? 'You'll have to forgive my colleague, vicar. If he seems a bit rude it's just on account of his having a daughter nearly Stacey's age. I'm sure you understand given that you say you have a teenage daughter as well.'

Trying to recall every nuance of that interview, had he slipped up in some way? Did somebody somewhere know something that he did not?

His thoughts were interrupted with his wife calling her darling husband to supper.

# Chapter 5

He'd been born in Mombasa Kenya during the second war, the younger brother to an elder sister of parents who'd felt the call to live in Africa as missionararies. Mr. and Mrs. Wilkes senior belonged to the Plymouth Brethren church.

Despite the interruption of war encouraging some ex-pats either to return to Britain or move north to Ethiopia to fight the Italians, Harold Wilkes chose to do neither. For in tiring of his calling and the pittance that went with it, he took the family from Mombasa to the Nyeri district near Mount Kenya so as to venture into coffee planting. Having purchased the freehold of his rented property along with some additional land, his newfound venture became highly lucrative with coffee providing, to his mind, his contribution to the war effort.

Despite the Nyeri area being in the heart of Kikuyu land – with the Kikuyu tribe later instigating the Mau Mau uprising of the 1950s – the region was a popular enclave of British colonialism. Alongside the dozen or so British coffee growers, there was an assortment of retired military men and their wives living there adjacent to a migrant aristocracy, which included the ageing Lord Baden-Powell and founder of the Scout Movement. It was a gerontocracy choosing to end their days in the Garden of Eden.

From the turn of the twentieth century, European settlers and the British in particular considered Kenya to be 'the seat of paradise,' and where despite the threats faced by crop pests and malaria there was no place to compare. Who wouldn't put down roots in a country of magical beauty, whose climate was largely temperate and where, by exploiting the native labour, fortunes were almost impossible *not* to make? Compared to the stark alternatives back in war-torn Britain, an investment of one's life and resources in the playground of Kenya was, for those in the know, irresistible.

Yet by showing contempt for the country's tribal people as well as a callous disregard for the land itself – unlike the wandering Masai, who only borrowed the land for their cattle without ever laying a claim to it – the rapacious colonials came to uproot the fragile lifestyle of centuries.

'Are you married or do you live in Kenya?' typified what the blueblood 'Happy Valley Set' stood for; their notoriety widely affirmed for being a group of shady people having their place in the sun.

To the indigenous Kenyans, the 'valley set' were despised for their intrusion. True they provided work for countless servants, but with their English squires and other hangers-on their arrogance knew no bounds. Often they'd 'forget' to pay their staff, taking perverse delight to inconvenience them at every opportunity. Servants kicked around at will, were sometimes there only to perform solitary tasks like pouring out the pink gins or claret. That said, with alcohol being imbibed into the small hours, often to be resumed after breakfast, a drinks servant could easily be run off his feet.

Others of them doubled up as drug couriers. Being readily available via Port Said, cocaine was the drug of choice, with morphine running it a close second. Even living extravagantly, it took no more than an annual income of around £2,000 for the Happy Set to live like royalty. Waited on hand and foot, along with their morbid dread of taking too much sun the 'veranda farmers' offset their boredom in pursuit of ever-new forms of depravity.

By distancing themselves from that race-going, drug-besotted set for whom idleness was a way of life, Harold Wilkes and his wife, Ivy, set high store on their own personal probity. He remained aloof from those philandering 'Rogers' who would make a point of sleeping with any woman just so long as it wasn't their wife, as did she in steering clear of the sad wives of those 'Rogers' who, with their 'champers' and fading looks, ended up doing nothing.

Arguably in terms of their personal morality and zest for hard work, the former missionary and his wife were not 'shady' at all. Yet when it came to sharing in the white man's trespass – to pillage the land at will – Mr. and Mrs. Wilkes felt under no such constraints. For were not the spoils of pagan Africa theirs for the taking - spoils to be claimed as a God-given right?

During the 1930s, Harold Wilkes had joined the movement known as the MR.A, or Moral Re-armament Crusade, which as its title suggests sought to improve the morals not just of the western hemisphere but of the world. Having swept across the United States, the 'moral re-armers' sought to convert Britain before advancing to many parts of the British Empire including East Africa and her colonies.

Unfortunately Harold Wilkes' moral zeal that went way beyond the ideals of that movement included Ivy found, herself a fellow conspirator. For both parents were rigorous disciplinarians where, for good measure, the four 'absolutes' of honesty, purity, unselfishness and love, and on which the MR.A modeled itself, came to be ruled within the Wilkes' household by a fifth 'ideal' – that of absolute discipline.

Harold ruled servants and family alike with a rod of iron

or, more precisely, with an assortment of flogging implements that included several canes and a rhino whip, the latter being wielded almost on a daily basis. It was not uncommon for him to flog his Kikuyu and squatter servants not just until the blood ran, but until either he or his victim dropped from exhaustion.

In the event of a family failing, little other than the mild entreaties of his wife would restrain him from punishing his children with equal severity. As often as not the father took it out on his son, who was no more than six years old when the assaults first begun. If dread inspired affection, Christopher remembered his father more by phrases addressed as though to make him an equal, but which were invariably used in the demeaning of others.

'Treat him so that he knows who's the boss!' he had ordered Christopher when forcing him to ride a stallion far too big for him. This was said with father lashing at the animal with a pointed stick.

And, 'Get back up and be a man!' was the command given when the small boy had fallen, severely bruising his shoulder.

Such was the urge to make a man out of his son that Harold would sometimes victimize his wife as though her humiliation along with that of all women was part of the son's initiation into adulthood. 'Don't forget, you're here to do my bidding!' was one of his pet phrases addressed to Ivy and their daughter.

Wilkes Senior's loathing for women, even when they came from his own family, was akin to the servants whom he tyrannized. When discovered at play with some of the Kenyan children on the plantation, Christopher remembered his father laying into him with a strap, emphasizing each word with a blow. 'Treat the natives for the pagans that they are. Do you hear?'

No defense could be made for Harold Wilkes' behaviour. For, despite living at a time when his British counterparts assumed an almost despotic power, he exceeded their standards by far.

After school on one occasion Christopher overheard a reference to his father spoken by one of the parents: 'the man's totally insane. We may have our faults but he's a so-called *Christian*, yet he'll cheerfully flog a servant until he drops.'

This observation came after two of Wilkes' servants having undergone a flogging of such severity, had dragged themselves some twenty-five mile journey to Nyeri in search of help.

In today's lexicon of psychological types, Harold Wilkes was a psychopath whose erratic mood swings would alternate in an instant between relative kindness and abject cruelty. But even his kindness was twisted, Christopher recalling perverse displays of paternal fun, which included hiding him and his sister in the cellar, or putting them down in public, especially at the dinner table. But that was preferable to those times when even at mealtime he might take them out to beat them for some supposed misdemeanor.

Even to his ex-pat contemporaries Wilkes was regarded as insane; a twisted bastard whose pretensions to Christianity only made matters worse.

Barring the tyranny of his father, there was another side to Christopher's childhood that was joyful. He displayed an exceptional athleticism at a young age and could hold his own running barefoot with other young Kenyan runners, in what became his later specialty of middle distance. Yet his greatest love was reserved for climbing. He could shin up any tree, especially the fragile acacias and flame trees that surrounded the family lodge. The more sinuous the tree the greater the challenge! How intoxicating was the scent of those sweet-smelling acacias as they drew him upwards, until their feathery branches creaked a warning to go no higher.

The dread with which the plantations' servants regarded his father was not, with typical generosity of spirit transferred by any mistrust towards their employer's son, given that his childhood friendships enduring for as long as he stayed in Africa. How could he ever forget Namdi and Samja or Okutu? It was to Okutu, with his darting movements and hissing laugh, that Christopher awarded the nickname of 'little snake.' They in turn called him 'Chrees' or 'Bambo' – their English pronunciation for Baboon, in recognition of his primate-like agility for swinging through the acacias with rarely a mishap.

During the weeks he boarded at the Christian primary school in Nyeri, leaving the weekends or school holidays to hold him in thrall. Arising at dawn in the crystal air, he would secretly summon his friends. 'Samja, Namdi, Okutu, quick, get up. Let's go fishing'! Or 'Let's go hunting'! Or 'How about some climbing'?

Often their day would begin by creeping up to the nearest wadi to cause mayhem among the gathering flamingoes, wildebeest and zebra. They tried to imitate the hunting skills of the lion by stalking these gracious creatures of prey as they lifted and lowered their necks to drink. Creeping as near as possible, the group would suddenly erupt skywards, scattering God's creation in all directions. With whoops of excitement they would then plunge into the vacated wadi and, with improvised fishing tackle, attempt to catch a few small roach or carp. The hippopotami, they too, were another favourite. Maori legend told how the hippo would stay under water during the heat of the day to tell each other jokes, only emerging around sunset to laugh. Their grunts and wheezes certainly sounded like laughter, causing Christopher and his friends to fall about laughing themselves.

Climbing the blind-side of the family's water-tower presented an alternative excitement to tree climbing where, using the services of his friends as look-outs, Christopher would complete a daring abseil. Cameos such as these all served to enrich memories of the Kenya that he loved. Beyond the malevolence of his father there'd always been a kaleidoscope of shimmering colour and laughter.

'Chrees like Africa!' said Namdi more than once in his broken English. Along with the rippling giggles of his friends, these were memories that Christopher would never forget.

Aged thirteen, his ties with Kenya were rudely severed when his parents sent him to school in England. Escape from the cruelty of his father to a prestigious public school presented a new torment, with a sadistic housemaster and a group of prefects groomed in the ways of their adult mentor.

Public school reinforced the tyrannical experiences learned from his father. Seeking out miscreants during the day only to beat them after lights-out, the prefects hunted in pairs or sometimes in packs. Upon his own elevation to prefect, Christopher shared readily in this covert torture. Morning cold baths and cross-country runs in all weathers all added to a regime of unremitting harshness.

Five years at public school gave him far more than what was supposed to be a good education. He would grow up with men who, a few years later, would reach the upper stratas of society. Fellow pupils would emerge to become doctors, lawyers, High Court judges, City underwriters, even a sprinkling of private under-secretaries destined for the Cabinet; men who like himself were schooled within a system where the vices of cruelty, greed and guile were extolled as virtue.

*A Candle For Lucifer*

In his sixteenth year Christopher was allowed to return to Kenya for the summer holidays.

He had long promised himself an ascent of Kenya's highest mountain, the volcanic crater of Mount Kilimanjaro, in anticipation of climbing the far tougher peak of Mount Kenya which he achieved two years later. He made the ascent of Kilimanjaro with the aid of a neighbouring tea planter called Jake and his son. He never forgot the short one-liners, which Jake taught him. 'Let your mind do the talking, even when your lungs scream out that they've had enough!' Or, as he inched his way over the last few thousand feet of ancient scree, 'Make the scree work for you, fella! Take little steps rather than big ones! Balance as though you're on tiptoe!'

Jake taught him the vital lesson of avoiding the European disease of 'overdo,' which produced splitting headaches, cramped thighs and delusions brought on by dehydration. 'Don't be afraid to climb but don't acclimatize too quickly. And *drink* like you've never seen water before!'

In preparation for his ascent of Mount Kenya, Jake and the old volcano had taught him well.

Upon completing his 'A' levels with the guarantee of a place at Oxford University later that autumn, the summer allowed him one further opportunity to visit Kenya. Having been stricken with a bout of malaria Harold Wilkes was near to death, signaling that the son was close to inheriting his father's fortune.

What the old man lost in terms of posing a physical threat tended to turn inwards through his growing paranoia. The Mau Mau had been operating within the area for eight years now, and with glimpses of them peering murderously through their heavily fortified homestead, Harold Wilkes guessed correctly that he was no more than a spear's throw away from death.

So serious had the threat become that only Ivy remained alongside her husband, their daughter having left Africa to get married back in England.

# Chapter 6

'I have to admit it, old chap, I don't just dislike the man, I *detest* him! He gives me the creeps! How he got the job as vicar beats me. But then again, he can switch on the charm and so many people in the church seem to love that sort of thing, *a smoothie*, who appears to excel at his job!'

Di Hagan was talking to Sleuth; adding for the cat's benefit as he ruffled his neck, 'I bet you'd like to charm the birds out of the trees the way he does!'

Having left The Magpie earlier that Monday night, the landlord's questions had along with the knowing glances from the other locals, disturbed him even more than he was disturbed already.

His three-bedroom bungalow was a place of sad memories, but it was home and he'd settled himself into his favourite armchair. Chosen more for sentiment than comfort, the winged reproduction Chippendale with its floral patterns was the place of repose used by his late wife. The cat had jumped on to his lap as he wriggled to reach for his tobacco pouch to take further respite in the filling and lighting of his pipe. The pipe, tobacco pouch and armchair, were along with Sleuth essential items for the ex-detective to get his head into gear.

Purring loudly, Sleuth pirouetted on his master's lap and then curled into a ball. Used to lending an ear to his master he would, despite all appearances of being asleep, remain his ever-attentive confidant.

Biting on his meerschaum, Di muttered, 'I must be honest about what I really think and feel. After all, there's all the difference between being churchwarden and happening to dislike him, let alone suspecting him of *murder!*'

He knew well enough that his merits as a detective, retired admittedly and one unashamedly belonging to the old school, had been widely respected in his prime. For Di had been known to rely heavily on shrewd observation and informed hunches. Nor had he made any apology about his resistance to all the fancy technology of modern investigative work. Of course, DNA along with the other newfangled detection toys were light years away from the crude methods of detection used when he first became a copper. But he hated how modern forensics had become the new deities, often making redundant those carefully honed tools of intuition and sixth sense. Nothing could dissuade him from his belief that on the seesaw of modern-day detective work while forensics rode high, reliance upon steady graft and the careful pursuit of hunches was at an all-time low. Besides it wasn't unknown for a clash of egos between forces to sabotage all the good done by forensics and where, notwithstanding all the new gadgetry, a suspect's chances of staying at large could be greatly enhanced through idiotic rivalries.

'Speaking of which,' said Hagan, raising his voice, 'what about those two railway rapists around Hampstead, John Duffy and David Mulcahy? School friends, who turned into *demons from hell!* Between them they killed at least three young women, terrorizing many more. At the age of eleven, they made a pact never to betray each other and although

Duffy got arrested and convicted twelve years earlier, it was thanks to a series of police cock-ups that Mulcahy remained free for so long. Four forces – as I recall it – failed to co-ordinate all the evidence. Time and time again *pride and stupidity* can undo the best forensics going.'

Getting worked up more than was good for his angina, Sleuth's hackles appeared to rise as though in sympathy even as Di went on speaking:

'That David Mulcahy was an evil piece of work although, no question, he'd got class. He still evaded capture, long after he and Duffy posed in front of police stations mocking their photo-fits. *God Almighty!* With all our technology and they still managed to operate like a pair of Wild West desperadoes,' said Hagan catching his breath. 'Mind you, Mulcahy was another of your Oscar winning actors, where by all accounts even his childhood sweetheart and mother to their six kids claimed to know absolutely nothing of her husband's other little sideline. And come to think of it, from the family snaps of him in the paper, there's no denying that he wasn't just good-looking he'd got form all right. All I can say is 'Never ever underestimate a psychopath!'

Yet just because he disliked the vicar, Di had to be careful not to let his hunches run away with him. His feelings should be reserved only as a yardstick for the sort of person Wilkes *might* be, nothing more!

With the long-suffering Sleuth staying in attendance, Di went on, 'They always say that the longer a crime goes undetected, the more likely it is to go cold. Of course Wilkes comes under suspicion with the regional and national crimes' squads. He has to. He was the last person to have seen Stacey. But he's so cool, so smooth in his role as the caring priest that he could have us all fooled. The question that needs to be asked is that if he killed Stacey, not "why did he do it?" but "What did he do with the body"? The body's everything. Without that we've got zilch!'

Acting on the assumption that statistically it was a near-impossibility for no one *not* to have seen Stacey on a summer's evening just after nine, whether outside church or along the High Street – one conclusion seemed inescapable.

'What of her friends in the choir who must have been keeping an eye out for her to see if she was following them? Stacey was a good-looking girl, pretty enough to turn heads and earn a second glance. I'm an old man and I know that she caught my eye! If she had left the church, chances are that someone would have seen her. But nobody's come forward to say they either saw Stacey, or witnessed her getting into some stranger's car, or whatever. Besides her friends would have hung back had they seen her hurrying towards them, if as Wilkes claimed they'd have been separated only by minutes? So it would seem that the girl never got out of the church alive. In which case, the vicar did something with the body while coolly going to visit Mr. and Mrs. Witcombe. . . . *Bastard!*' The expletive came involuntarily, prompting Sleuth to extend a not entirely benign set of claws across his knees as though to concur with his thoughts. The cat then reverted to its endless purr.

Hoping that his hunches weren't running away with him, he resumed, 'Even though Wilkes implied that he was around on Saturday morning, maybe he made a daring getaway with the body, dumping it somewhere before returning home. Naturally, disposing of the body in a short space of time would mean dumping it in a lake somewhere, or in some other secluded place. He certainly wouldn't have had time to bury the body, unless he'd premeditated the murder and dug a hole somewhere beforehand. . . .The graveyard possibly?'

For a moment the horrifying thought of Wilkes actually using All Saints' graveyard flitted across his mind. But with

Sleuth extending his claws, giving a yawn and ceasing to purr, Hagan recognized the cat's dissent. 'Not possible of course,' he told himself, given that as churchwarden and custodian of the graveyard, no grave could be dug without his say-so.

'I favour the undergrowth idea.' For a moment Sleuth looked up with wonderment. 'So what one really needs to know is whether Wilkes did some unaccounted-for mileage on Saturday morning, perhaps driving away as far as possible. *I must try and look into that!*' he promised himself.

'But how did he murder her and where did he put the body?' Shutting his eyes, Hagan could visualize Stacey clearly with her regular features, flawless skin and beautiful full hazel eyes. She had the sweetest smile, perhaps coquettish but that went with the territory of any pretty teenage girl. Despite her athleticism her physique was slim almost to the point of delicacy, leaving him to recall how the first choir robe she'd worn some eighteen months previously had nearly dwarfed her.

'Certainly Wilkes would have had no problem strangling her if he so chose. You've only got to look at the man's hands to see his strength. Easy enough to have stifled her screams and left her body in a cupboard or in the belfry,' he thought. 'Come to think of it, he could have dumped her in somewhere like the chest at the back of the church – an ideal place for concealing a body at least for a short time.' And then he remembered, 'My God, he's got the only key too!'

His master's sudden brainstorm caused Sleuth to stand up, arch his back and bump his muzzle against the stubble of Di's chin.

But had it even been there briefly, Wilkes would have had no choice but to move the body before Saturday's wedding. No *body*; no case to answer for! That was how Hagan viewed it, as would the crime squad. By now the squad would have gone off in hot pursuit of a list of suspect abductors and other weirdoes, living within a hundred-mile radius or more of the town. It would take time before they even considered looking nearer to home - their scattergun approach invariably being how they did things these days.

For the time being the heat would be off Wilkes. After all to the police authorities such a well-placed cleric, of supposedly unblemished character, wouldn't begin to figure on their radar. But as Hagan knew, always consider the unexpected, act quickly and *never cease to be surprised!* Delay meant a trail petering out. Keep the pressure on! And if need be – vicar or no vicar – *keep him sweating!* Let him know that you know or let him *think* that you know.

*'Action Stations!'* declared the man for whom the inaction of having been retired for too long had nearly driven him insane.

Plan a strategy! Tomorrow would be Tuesday. Sleuth hopped to the floor as Hagan sprang to his feet. Snap too chose to look attentive.

With the cat wrapping himself around his ankles as he paced the floor, he urged himself: 'Try and get a check on Wilkes' mileage. Even if I can't find out what his mileage was last week, at least I can find out when his car was last serviced, and perhaps arrive at some conclusions. Without official backup there's no way I can do a formal check on his car.

'Anyway, the first thing is to go to the church and do a search. It won't have been cleaned since Friday, prior to the wedding. Between now and then they may have picked up a few loose petals, swept up some stray confetti, but they'll have been no serious vacuuming done. The cleaning rota's not due until this coming Saturday.' The following Saturday was one of the few weekends when there was to be no wedding, allowing the church cleaners ample time to prepare for Sunday's services.

'So check out the vestry tomorrow morning,' he muttered aloud as he thought through his tactics. 'Wilkes may look in, but you can easily offer an excuse. As churchwarden you've *every right* to be there. Besides he knows I'm conscientious. Either he won't suspect anything or, if he does, it will have the desired effect of *unsettling* him!'

After giving Sleuth a dish of milk and walking Snap for his constitutional around the block, he retired to bed; his head spinning with the possibilities of what he might turn up next morning.

Following their weekend away, Frances and Dominic were also in deep thought that evening. While daughter Katy was the independent one, the home-loving Dom and his mother were close – more like brother and big sister. Now with the disappearance of Stacey still uppermost in their thoughts, they were in the kitchen.

'Mum, what the hell do you think happened?' he asked. 'She used to come here quite a lot to see Dad over bits and pieces for the choir and I got to know her quite well. She's just not the sort of person to go waltzing off without telling her parents where she was going.'

'I agree, Dom. I phoned through to Caroline's mum to ask what Stacey said to her when she hung back to speak with Dad.'

Caroline had been Stacey's closest friend, both at school and in the choir. Hitherto inseparable, it was only by having first time boyfriends that they saw less of each other.

'What did she say?'

'Well, she made out that Stacey said that she'd catch them up after she'd spoken with your father.'

'*God!* Caroline must be in a state.'

'She is. She's on medication and can't go to school right

now. Poor kid. What on earth can you say?'

'Martin can't be much better,' said Dom thinking of Stacey's boyfriend.

'Yes, he's in a bad way as well. I've phoned his mum as well and she says he's gone completely into his shell. What a way to begin your summer holiday. Apparently he won't come out of his room or talk to anybody. Normally Stacey pops in to see him after choir practice, but she'd told him that she wanted an early night because she was playing a tennis match first thing in the morning. Apart from church, she'd planned to spend most of Sunday with him.'

A cloud of sadness hung between them as absent-mindedly he started to clear some dishes and cooking utensils, while she completed their supper. Beyond their agreement that Stacey's disappearance was inexplicable and bizarre, they dared develop their thoughts no further. For what both knew was that the family's breadwinner had, as was so typical, shut himself away; sharing the same roof while living perpetually in his own world.

That other world consisted of the inner sanctum of his study - a no-go area for the rest of them unless granted access after knocking. Hours seem to get spent on his computer, often on the pretext that it was to do with church business. Yet notwithstanding the crisis over Stacey, nothing had caused him to break from this routine whether just to talk or commiserate further over the girl. Closeted in his study, his weird and secretive lifestyle continued as normal.

As it was on that occasion he'd retreated to his study, not so much to work online as to escape the troubling presence of his wife and son. For it was as though both were reacting strangely to him of late.

So let him forget all his current disruptions, so as to call up some earlier and more agreeable memories. When life became stressful he could always escape into the labyrinth of happier times. He loved it how memories of Africa could always do that; transport him out of himself, especially when he recalled the time of his near miraculous ascent of Mount Kenya. For notwithstanding the growing threat posed by Kikuyu terrorists at the time, his return to Africa that summer had been specifically to climb the mountain.

His inspiration to do so had come after reading the true story of three Italian climbers who, during the war, having escaped from their POW camp at the base of the mountain had all but made it to the summit. If three undernourished and ill-clad climbers could accomplish such a feat then he with the best available equipment and with three companions, could do the same. One of his companions was his trusted childhood friend Okutu who'd brought his friend Benjamin, along with an experienced guide called Nguyu from the Mbulu tribe.

Although not as high as Kiliminjaro, Mount Kenya is every mountaineer's dream. Rising from the fertile savannahs encircling it, the initial climb begins with a testing slog through bamboo jungle and thick forests, until an area of moors and glaciers is reached at around 11,000 feet. Even here the landscape resembles – what it is – an elevated national park for rhino, elephant and other big game.

Ascending beyond the plateau, the night frost had strengthened markedly as they moved higher through fig trees, lobelias and giant groundsel cacti. The groundsel provided excellent fuel for night fires with which to repel wild dogs and leopards as well as the cold. That night they'd slept in a circle around the fire.

Up first thing in the morning, they trekked through the tussock grass rimed with frost and, even as they ascended to 15,000 feet buffalo and other wildlife were still plentiful. Venturing higher they entered prolific vegetation of leopard orchids and exotic flora, before meeting the ice zone.

With vast sheets of ice draping themselves over huge outcrops of rock their climb was reduced to a near crawl. He knew how his three companions believed the mountain to be inhabited by the Kikuyu god of creation Ngai, while waited upon by a hideous dwarf called Gumbi. By producing snow on the equator, Mount Kenya was revered as Ngai's sanctuary where for thousands of years only the very bold or profane would dare to venture, and it was as the three natives began to hallucinate in the thin air that Okutu supposed that Ngai now wished to strangle them.

Spurred on only by their wages, his guides grew increasingly fearful that yet more terrifying punishments might be unleashed by Ngai, enraged at their intrusion onto Meru, the second of Kenya's twin-peaks.

For when angered the god had been known to shake the heavens and unleash huge rocks. Some climbers on the way down had been known to self-asphyxiate. Others could be broken at will, whether on the ice crags or later even when they returned to the mountain's base. While holy men might stay for weeks close to the peaks of both Meru and Kenya to return radiant and in their right mind, proud men might simply disappear or who having escaped with their lives might do so only with their minds in disarray.

On approaching Kenya's summit, they faced a blizzard that lasted three days. Sheltering in an ice cave the three guides huddled in terror convinced that Ngai was about to kill them. But instead of reassuring them, Christopher had relished the opportunity for a moment of revenge. Several thousand feet below, his guides had laughed at him for shrinking in fear at the sounds of the tree hyraxes, such shrieks being well able to chill the marrow of anyone unfamiliar with such sounds. Now, it was he who could laugh as they cowered from the crashing thunder and wind.

*A Candle For Lucifer*

As though drunk on champagne in that rarefied atmosphere a strange ecstasy had overcome him, and one where even in the teeth of the storm he'd carried on to complete the final 1,500 feet by himself. Assisted only with crampons and his ice axe, he'd forged upto the summit like a man possessed. Several hours later he returned still manically ecstatic while showing scant regard for his companions who, exhausted through terror and cold, were in a pitiful condition.

As they made their descent surprisingly none had ended up suffering from altitude sickness, although his three guides had peripheral frostbite to their hands and feet. As for Christopher, he carried his elation right back to his parents' homestead, where only upon seeing the police and military jeeps did he appreciate that something was wrong.

As though it were yesterday he could still see the senior white police officer, dressed in his immaculate khaki, who approached him,

'Excuse me, sir, might you be Mr. Wilkes junior?'

'Yes, what's happening? Why all the soldiers?'

'Someone told me that you have been up the mountain. Is that correct, sir?'

'Yes, we've just returned, as you can see.'

'Well in one sense, sir, you've been extremely fortunate. Can you brace yourself for some very bad news?' He paused. '... I'm afraid to have to tell you that both your parents have been murdered. There's no doubt that you would have been killed yourself had you been here.'

Even when asked to view the bodies, the police officer had observed no flicker of emotion; no revulsion shown for parents who had been all but decapitated in a panga attack. Despite the Mau Mau's penchant for always killing white folk in the most brutal fashion the son, neither then nor later, shed a tear over the demise of Harold and Ivy Wilkes.

He became the sole legatee of his parents' fortune, with nothing being passed on to his older sister.

Rubbing his eyes as he sat in his study, it was not memories of his parents' murder that brought him back with a jolt. Nor was it the Kenyan police officer in his impeccable uniform that had given him the news.

It was of a murder much nearer to home, and of the two police officers who had so recently cross-examined him.

# Chapter 7

First thing on that Tuesday morning he unlocked the church using the side door. Sadly, and regardless of the fact that Ketborough was a 'respectable' town, All Saints like many churches had to be kept under permanent lock and key. These days vandals, arsonists and other undesirables could spring up anywhere.

Absurdly by entering a holy place with dark suspicions on his mind, the churchwarden now back in detective mode felt like an intruder himself. Tentatively, he went into the room adjacent to the organ console, which doubled up as both the vicar's and the choir vestry. Since Stacey's disappearance, there had been a wedding and three Sunday services.

Of course no corpse would obligingly drop out from Christopher's robe cupboard. Nor did the carpeted floor of durable maroon cord offer a trace of any evidence. With magnolia walls pristine in not showing so much as a fleck of blood anywhere Hagan started to feel stupid, even to ask if he'd gone completely over the top with his paranoia for the vicar.

Still he planned to carry on as he started. Perhaps a signature in the service book might betray an unnaturally shaky hand. Yet the confident swagger of the vicar's name penned four times for each of the services over the weekend appeared self-assured as ever. Any scene of foul play was conspicuous by its absence, for if murder had been committed there, it was the very ordinariness of the vestry that made it extraordinary.

As he was reflecting on what else to look for, the key rattled in the door.

*'Good God!'* he thought, 'Look *calm.*'

After a few further rattles of the key it was pushed open, encouraged by the churchwarden calling to say that the door was already open. Relief surged over him when he saw that it was the vicar's wife. He quite liked her in fact. For there had been other occasions when having met he felt that Frances Wilkes possessed none of the spooky vibes of her husband.

'Hallo, Nicholas!' she said (she was unaware of how The Magpie referred to him). 'How are you? I'm just coming to check the flowers to see if we can make them last until next Sunday.'

'Oh right!' replied Di, then feeling obliged to explain why *he* was there: 'I thought that I'd clear out some of these old choir robes, so that we can increase the space for the newer outfits. I understand that our choir numbers are due to expand with some of the new confirmation class expressing an interest in joining.'

He could hear the deadpan intonation to his voice.

'Yes, let's hope that we won't have to fill Stacey's place,' replied Frances, 'and that she'll soon return. Isn't it *terrible?* I only heard about it yesterday. Christopher told Dominic and me after we'd come back from being away at the weekend. I gather the news has been full of it, but we watched little or no TV while we were away.'

'It's very worrying indeed!' replied Hagan. As he spoke he was reminded of the fact that Wilkes had, apart from having his daughter Katy at home, been on his own over the weekend; a detail that would have made Stacey's disappearance that much more straightforward: 'I dread to think what Stacey's parents must be going through. Your husband did his best to reassure everyone at the weekend. We not only had the wedding at which the choir had to sing a special anthem, we had all of Sunday's services to contend with. Her absence hung over everyone like a cloud.'

'What do *you* think happened, Nick?' asked Frances out of the blue. 'After all you're the detective!'

No sooner had she spoken than she judged her question ill considered. For its directness seemed to disconcert him.

'Well, we can all start guessing,' he said defensively. 'That's the trouble. There are so many possibilities. Have you heard any more from the police?'

'Not as yet! Having asked Christopher a number of questions last Saturday night they may want to interview me.'

'I would imagine that they've cast a hypothetical net of suspects far wider than just around here,' said Di. 'Although Stacey is officially registered as a missing person, I fear it will have been registered as a national murder inquiry by now.'

'That's *scary!*' whispered Frances giving an involuntary shiver.

'Well, we just have to hope and pray.' After a pause Di said, 'Changing the subject, would you mind popping back home to ask your husband for the key to the large chest by the west door. Some of these robes are clearly past it and are not in a fit state to use, so I might as well dump them in there for the time being. There are other things that need sorting out in here but, given the day's going to get hotter, I'm not going to do too much right now.'

'Of course,' replied Frances, in answer to the request for the key: 'I need to go back and get some more oases, so I'll be back very shortly.'

On his own once more, he made a further quick examination of the vestry before walking down the aisle to the chest, which stood at the far end near the great west door. Despite the hot weather, the church remained cool with the wedding flowers having spilled only a few petals onto the blue carpet.

Upon asking her husband for the key to the coffer and as requested by their churchwarden, Frances had noticed Christopher start ever so slightly. But this husband of hers from whom she'd been estranged for more years than she could remember, was well known to her for his nervous mannerisms. To those familiar with the code of body language such jerky reflexes might have told their own story but she couldn't, or chose not to, read anything more into them.

Typically she'd caught him at his computer. While he seemed to derive so much comfort from the endless clicking of a mouse and keyboard, she wanted as little to do with technology as possible. Dom had shown her some of the ingenuities of his laptop, which he used largely for his chess games. But for someone wrestling with her own loneliness, the realm of cyberspace and emails only added to her sense of isolation. Staring into a screen and typing out endless messages seemed so unreal and impersonal. It was a relief to return to the church and to the homespun churchwarden.

'Here it is!' she said presenting him with the key.

Thanking her but wishing to scrutinize the chest at leisure and on his own, Di diverted himself by visiting the belfry, leaving her to water and sort out the flowers. Despite his intense dislike of the vicar, Di had no such problems with his wife; found her endearing even. For Frances had the careless habit of speaking before she'd always thought through a remark, which despite its lack of finesse suggested openness. He could see too how the lines around her face and jaw line disturbed an attractive bone structure, lines which to Di spoke of a love unfulfilled. It was as though any residue loyalty to her husband came from a forlorn sense of duty.

Upon hearing the vestry door being pulled to, he descended from the belfry to collect some of the more threadbare robes from the vestry, before striding back to the coffer. He reminded himself of a golden rule once taught him by an old police sergeant, 'Never forget your five senses, especially your sense of smell; the first whiff at the scene of a crime can be crucial and it may be the only one you get!'

With his nostrils flaring in anticipation they wouldn't teach that nowadays. He'd also brought with him a large magnifying glass. But it was by smelling that might tell him more than anything he might actually see with the naked eye.

He stood by the coffer for a moment before opening it. Of no great value it was one of those seventeenth century pieces, a common enough item of oak furniture found in many churches and used at various times to store robes and other vestments. Being paneled on top with matching panels on an uncarved front, it stood well clear of the floor on its original stiles. Security ensured that it had been bolted to the wall. As far as anyone knew, the chest had always been at All Saints and was pretty much in its unaltered condition, with its original key-plate, lock and staple hinges. Apart from a brazing repair along its stem, the key too looked original. From the day of manufacture the chest's ebonises effect acquired its own rich dark patina.

Over the years he'd developed a psychic 'nose'. Even as he removed the baptism jug on its top and lifted the lid he couldn't be sure what he smelt. The smell of polish was more pungent than anything else. Yet upon opening the chest did he pick up the faintest musky odour of flesh; a fleeting malodorous hint that a corpse had been kept there for a short few hours?

What his eyes did tell him was that some sash cord along with a discarded altar cloth had disappeared. Before Wilkes had laid claim to the key, he clearly remembered depositing various lengths of the cord removed from the fanlights just over a year ago. An old altar cloth and less frayed sections of cord might always come in useful for some purpose later on.

Of course he wasn't to know whether Christopher might have opened the chest at other times. The interior of the box, which was five feet long by two and a half feet deep, was remarkably clean, free of any cobwebs or noticeable debris. It looked completely empty, bereft of further clues. Unlike its exterior, the interior displayed the mellow gold look of old oak revealing no obvious stains whether of excreta, saliva, semen, blood or fibers.

Yet had it not been for Frances making a surprise return visit, use of his magnifying glass would have revealed the most damning evidence of all.

'I thought you might like to sample a glass of my iced tea,' she said smiling. 'I find it's one of the most refreshing drinks in hot weather.'

An assortment of distractions now led him to make what in detection terms was an elementary mistake. Not wishing to appear overly suspicious like some sort of Sherlock Holmes from the past, he slipped his magnifying glass into his pocket and then out of common courtesy and genuine thirst, gratefully accepted the drink. As he did so, he bundled the robes into the coffer before closing the lid. She stayed long enough for Di to down the iced tea and then said she'd let him get on with what he had to do.

But of course he'd blown it! A schoolboy cock-up in fact! For by disturbing the robes and then returning them to the chest, he'd cross-contaminated any further evidence had it been there. 'You daft bugger!' he cursed himself, his only option now being to take a more general view of things. Nothing suggested any movement of the chest from its set indentations in the carpet, nor could he see any suggestion of scratch marks or broken fingernails on its interior. If the girl had been placed in her overnight sarcophagus, she'd have been dead beforehand.

Leaving the church, he remained furious at himself for having made such a basic mistake. At least before returning the key, he could follow up the rest of his plan by checking the mileage of the vicar's car. This might prove useful in that Wilkes happened to mention his car going for its MOT test that previous week. Observing that the blue Volvo Estate had been left on the drive and was out of view from the study window, he hoped to get a reading of the mileometer unobserved.

Nonchalantly he made a slight detour onto the garage drive approaching the driver's side of the car. Memory allowed him to recall the mileage without a second glance. It stood at 41,002. Looking as relaxed as he could, he then sauntered across to the vicarage, only to realize that Frances had been watching him from the open kitchen window. Returning the key to her through the window, he said, 'I've always liked those new Volvo estates and wouldn't mind owning one myself.'

'I didn't think you liked cars' she responded half confused.

'Well I've been thinking about getting back into driving.'

But given that medical advice had warned against it, Di's other problem was that

he was a hopeless liar.

Even as he replied, he could hear the false timbre to his voice.

An hour or so after Di's visit to the church, Frances felt an urge to go out. 'I'm just going to the cleaners, darling,' she called through to her husband in his study.

'Righto, darling,' came the response. 'I may be out when you return. Could you post the letters in the hall?'

'Will do!' And with that Frances left the vicarage.

Having met at Cambridge University, when he was studying for ordination and she was an undergraduate, they had married some four years later. Despite first favourable impressions their union, based more on shyness and mutual need than on any mating of souls, quickly declined into an arrangement of respectability. Indeed given that they'd hardly ever had meaningful sex or, more to the point, *couldn't* have sex it was a misnomer to speak of any 'union' - their early abstinence in marriage having given them an excuse to sleep in separate bedrooms for as long as she could remember.

Even with the visible offspring of Dominic and Katy, the arrival of their children into the world had come by way of a closely guarded secret.

In compensation for her lack of love, and not a little perversely, Frances aspired to become that increasingly rare commodity – the perfect vicar's wife. Imbued with a strong moral sense from childhood, flight from her marital situation felt unthinkable; still less any prospect that she might have embarked on having an affair. Furthermore, unlike many clergy spouses who take outside work to bolster the modest income of their partner, hers and Christopher's private means had made that unnecessary. It was as though given her circumstances Frances threw herself, almost fanatically, into her husband's work and where martyred in marriage she completed the sacrifice by throwing herself onto the altar of mother church.

Having elected to go on the flower and cleaning rosters,

she further enlisted as a member of the Mothers' Union with the possibility soon of becoming its leader or Enrolling Member. She led a Women's group and, had she not been somewhat tone-deaf, would have offered her services in the choir. Vicarage life also left her playing out the role of hostess, running errands, taking phone messages and responding to the copious amounts of clerical circulars, which in her more rebellious moments she saw as no better than 'junk mail'. Only through her express refusal to have anything to do with technology or her husband's computer did she give vent to her own needs.

That afternoon after her meeting in church with the churchwarden, she paid a quick visit to the dry-cleaners. Along with two pleated skirts and a trouser suit, she'd gathered up her husband's cassock from church; his underarm body odour tending to become embarrassingly pungent in the hot weather. Besides by taking it on Tuesday Mrs. Myers, the proprietor, would ensure its return in good time for the weekend.

Having posted the letters she called in at the cleaners just a short distance along the High Street from the vicarage. Marjorie Myers was as it happened a keen member of All Saints, as well as being a leading soprano in the choir. Upon entering the shop, Frances sensed an abrupt halt to what appeared to be an animated conversation between the proprietor and one of her customers.

' ...Oh, I know, this weather, it's all very well, but I could start a dyeing business quite apart from a dry-cleaning one. So many people have told me how the sunlight plays havoc with their curtains and carpets. Mine are no different. Do you know we've only just put down a new carpet in our back living room – indigo blue and it's already faded to almost sky-blue under the French windows? And then when you pull the curtains to keep out the sun, it bleaches the colour out of *them!*'

'We had the same,' replied the customer, picking up on Mrs. Myers' deft new turn of conversation. 'In fact we had a new golden yellow carpet some years ago and during the hot spell *all* the colour went out of it. Turned it virtually white, for heaven's sake. We tried getting a claim on our insurance but they weren't having it. It made me mad and we've only just got round to changing it!'

'Oh, Good morning, Mrs. Wilkes!' said Mrs. Myers, acting as though she'd only just seen the vicar's wife now inside her shop.

'Bye-bye, Mrs. Levett, see you soon!' was said to the outgoing customer who left the premises, doubtless consumed by thoughts that ran deeper than worrying about soft furnishings bleached by the sun.

Mrs. Myers was one of those to prefer the use of surnames, more so when it came to addressing the vicar's wife.

'Hallo, Marjorie!' replied Frances, whose preference for first names made her feel more accepted. For she resisted strenuously those strategies where as the vicar's wife, she could feel more isolated than she already was.

'What can I do for you?' asked the more formal proprietor.

'These items need dry-cleaning please, with the cassock coming back for Friday, if that's all right?'

'That'll be no problem Mrs. Wilkes! How are you keeping?' On this occasion the pleasantry by way of a question was incidental to what had become the collective anxiety of the town. 'Terrible about Stacey, isn't it? We've still heard no news.'

'Oh, it's terrible, quite *dreadful!*' Frances replied, her voice trembling. 'You must have known her especially well in the choir.'

'I did. We were all very fond of her. Mr. and Mrs. Witcombe are simply devastated. Nobody knows what to do and we all feel so *helpless!'*

'I wasn't at home last Friday,' said Frances, 'Dominic and I went to Dorset for the weekend. It somehow makes me feel more negligent by what's happened.'

'In fact *I* wasn't there for choir practice as I had a summer cold,' replied Mrs. Myers, 'so I never saw Stacey to pick up if she was acting differently at all. But by all accounts, from what the other choir members say, she seemed perfectly all right. If anything she was in high spirits.' She paused before adding, 'The vicar was the last person to see her, I understand.' Although her tone suggested no obvious insinuation, it was an observation bearing its own significance.

'Yes, Christopher is dreadfully upset and blaming himself for not having taken her home. But Stacey had said she'd be fine just walking back on her own.'

Their discussion about Stacey was becoming too painful to bear.

'I'll just hang the skirts up.' The proprietor's voice faltered, before asking, 'Have you checked the cassock pockets?' Upon turning, Mrs. Myers then blew into a handkerchief before tagging the skirts and placing them on a rail.

Frances hadn't thought to examine the cassock pockets. There were a couple of soiled tissues and some old prayer requests in one pocket. Just as well Mrs. Myers had reminded her. But what was this shiny piece of card in the other pocket?

As she was returning Mrs. Myers was diverted when the phone rang.

Frances pulled out a photograph. *What on earth?* She nearly spoke out of shock.

Not an unseemly photograph in itself, it would have graced any family album and been passed round with innocent delight in the living room of those who knew the subject. But the picture made Frances want to throw up, almost choking her with fear.

It was a recent colour photograph. Lying on the beach propped up on her elbows and smiling broadly with her blond hair falling backwards, while dressed in a bikini was Stacey Witcombe.

Presumably a mutual sense of grief felt by both women would have helped explain why Frances' expression had become so ashen, as she stumbled out of the shop.

Feeling exposed like a lizard on a sheet of glass, she had to do something.

# Chapter 8

Stumbling out of the dry-cleaners on that hot summer morning made her realize that he was the only person she could talk to - the short walk to his house giving her time to gather her wits.

Her sense that Hagan was a shrewd man, quite apart from being a retired policeman didn't falter as she opened the garden gate. His white pebble-dashed bungalow stood in almost half an acre of garden to the front and rear. Clearly the garden was in need of attention, as was the painted rendering showing itself chipped in places. The front door and window frames also looked neglected. The general effect was testimony to how after his wife's death the owner had lost all interest in the place. Plans for spending a happy retirement together had been shattered when, having undergone a routine operation for varicose veins, his beloved Alice had died from an embolism to the brain. Devastating at the time and seven years on memories, sad as well as happy, had put on hold any enthusiasm whether for his garden or their property; even as he remained adamant that no way was he going to sell up.

Use of the small brass fox doorknocker wasn't necessary as his dog was already barking loudly, visible through the frosted glass with the silhouette of Nicholas coming into view behind. With the door opened, the collie was already greeting her.

'Oh, hallo' said Frances, breathless. 'Do you mind if I come and talk to you? I have to see *somebody,* and after speaking with you this morning I knew that you were the obvious person.'

'Of course Frances come on in! Don't mind Snap by the way.' responded Hagan. Nor did he appear entirely surprised to see her. Ordering the dog back inside, he motioned her to follow him along the narrow corridor that led to the living room at the back of the house. In the brief moment that they'd stood facing each other, she observed that they were of equal height. In his open-necked shirt and summer slacks he was despite his age still an attractive man. Even if the gray hair could have done with a bit of a trim she felt drawn to his overall appearance. With the aroma of pipe smoke wafting about him, a reminder of her father, the effect felt further enhanced.

'Sit down. You look pretty shaken up. Let's have some tea or would you prefer something cold? I enjoy limejuice in this weather,' adding with a smile, 'I'm sorry I haven't got any of your delicious iced tea!' The iced tea she'd offered him earlier that morning, resulting in his contamination of the coffer's evidence was all but forgotten.

Clearly agitated and stating her preference for the limejuice she sat down in his second armchair. As he went into the kitchen, with Snap demanding her attention, she too observed that he too looked tired and withdrawn, his movements being slow for one thing. Probably the weather, she thought.

Into its sixth week, the scorching conditions made talk about the English weather more topical still as she called through to him, 'It's absolutely baking out there!'

'They say it will hit 32 degrees this afternoon.' Bringing in the refreshments, he added, 'I don't mind the weather like this. In fact I'm one of those people who can take any amount of heat. I think I acclimatized when I spent some years in Gibraltar.' Passing her a drink and pretty much guessing at what was troubling her, he asked, 'So what's on your mind Frances?'

He was one of the few parishioners open enough to address her by her first name, for which she'd long been grateful.

'Nicholas, I've been worried sick since coming back from our weekend away and learning about Stacey. I feel terrible because I've not been to see the Witcombes, who must be going out of their minds with worry.' Distractedly stroking Snap's head for comfort, the dog was pushing his muzzle up to her extended hand, willing her not to stop.

'We're all tremendously worried,' replied Hagan. 'Of course the lass could just have gone missing but it seems increasingly unlikely. Thousands of youngsters do simply up and leave every year – as many girls as boys. But Stacey wasn't that sort of girl! Take it from me I've seen enough cases of girls running off, and most that do so bear no resemblance to Stacey. Usually they're tearaways with parents who've either disowned them or abused them. From what I know of them the Witcombes are a very close family, which leaves me to conclude that Stacey has been abducted or even . . .'

'*Murdered!*' said Frances, confessing the awful possibility.

'Yes, it has to be said,' he acknowledged.

Even as she hesitated she was resolute, 'Nicholas . . . I've got something else I must tell you. There's no-one else I feel I can share this with.'

'Go on!' he encouraged her gently while trying to keep his voice level. 'And by the way, why don't you call me Di.

It's the nickname they've given me at The Magpie and I'm sort of used to it. Short for DI or Detective Inspector, I believe.'

Nicholas was the name that his wife always used and it unsettled him to hear it spoken by another attractive and more youthful woman.

'All right, Di,' His visitor mustered a faint smile. 'But would you take a look at this?'

Delving into her shoulder bag she presented him with the photograph of the missing girl. Being a good quality photograph, recently taken, it made recognition of its subject instantaneous.

'Where on *earth* did you get this?' he asked.

Swallowing hard and fearing she was about to cross some point of no return, she replied, 'I found it in Christopher's cassock only a few minutes ago. I've just been to Myers Cleaners taking in a few bits and pieces and took the cassock as well. It was only by chance that I discovered the photograph in his pocket.'

In thirty-five years of detective work, even he was stunned. He'd been pondering what he'd found or rather *not* found that morning - sash cord and an altar cloth that had gone missing from the chest, and a mileage check on the vicar's car that might yet tell a story. And now there was this *photograph*!

'Does he *know?*' was all that Di could think of asking.

'Not yet! In fact I've come straight from the cleaners to you. Mrs. Myers could easily have discovered the picture for herself, since I only went through the pockets after she asked me to.'

'Did *she* see the picture?'

'Mercifully not, since she got distracted by the phone just at the moment I discovered it.'

Di Hagan was brought up with a start for another reason.

Had the cassock been in the vestry when he'd been there earlier? To have not examined an article of clothing that might have been incriminating was a clear oversight. Was he losing his grip? Maybe others had been right to treat him as they tended to treat most retired coppers, as a bit over the hill - even 'a dinosaur' as one superintendent had ribbed him. Why hadn't he thought to examine Wilkes' robes?

He consoled himself with the thought that Frances had appeared in the vestry unexpectedly. Furthermore, who would have imagined a photo of the missing girl in, of all places, the vicar's cassock? It was bizarre all right but, as he had to remind himself, good crime detection thrives on being open to the bizarre. And now the bizarre was getting worse with none other than the vicar's wife herself yielding what, by all accounts, was a pretty damning disclosure. Only slowly did he put the photograph down on the coffee table between them.

Going through to the kitchen for their refreshments he felt hugely unsettled. As he did so Sleuth appeared through the cat-flap to begin his usual ritual of bumping against him, only to follow him into the living room. With Snap moving away to lie exhausted by the sofa, the cat jumped on to Frances' lap and where with a couple of pirouettes, subsided into a ball for his own siesta.

His normally steady hand shook as he gave her her drink, making it necessary for him to say something. 'Sleuth's taken to you, that's for sure. Not everyone gets such royal treatment!'

The impact of the photograph of the smiling teenager lying face upwards on the table was almost too much to bear, obliging him to make further small talk. 'I've always considered that animals are a good judge of character,' he went on. 'You should see the way these two are towards anyone they don't like.' Nor did he add how Snap's hackles had risen on the one occasion when Wilkes had called in to see him. Now in the soothing atmosphere of Snap's gentle snores and of Sleuth's uninterrupted purring, the animals helped Frances regain some composure.

'Well, what should we do, Di?' she queried. The use of 'we' indicated how keen she was to take him into her confidence.

'I'm trying to think what's best, Frances.' He knew it was better to ask her outright: 'Tell me truthfully Frances, do you think your husband is involved in some way?'

If she hedged, she did so because of the implication: 'I can't possibly think why he should be. He's a remote man or can be, but he's never been criminal in any way. He's always been a good father, and . . .' here she paused, 'a good husband, at least when it comes down to looking after us . . .' her reply tailed off.

Di's suspicions were confirmed. She neither knew her husband, nor loved him.

In a distant voice, she went on: 'Dear Lord, I wish *I'd* been around when Stacey disappeared!'

'Don't we all!' replied Di bleakly.

Sipping their drinks in silence, each was lost in the enormity of the problem now facing them. Nothing she said could allay his growing suspicions about the vicar. Dislike and mistrust were for him two sides of the same coin, not entirely a charitable response for a churchwarden perhaps, but pretty much consistent for a straight copper, retired or otherwise. For there was no doubt that Revd Jack Bishop and his successor were as chalk and cheese; the one you could take an instant liking to, while the other seemed at least to Hagan to be repellant.

The silence between them was not uncomfortable. Di thought further about this. Of course Revd Jack had been transparently *good*. His easy outgoing manner made him an excellent PR man for the Christian faith. For while Christopher Wilkes was clearly a polished performer, Di instinctively felt that he was a 'baddun' in some way - *phony as hell* in fact. Not to put too fine a point on it, Wilkes made Di's skin crawl.

As she sat there stroking Sleuth it felt for Frances like she was coming out of a deep sleep. It was both a wretched and disturbing sensation - one, which she hardly dare express in her next thought: Here I am sitting with a complete stranger, or at least with someone I've only passed pleasantries with before, and I feel more comfortable with him in twenty-five minutes than in over twenty-five years of marriage to Christopher!

She wanted to slam shut the door on this stark awakening. But the photograph of Stacey still there on the table – semi-naked but radiating innocence – changed all that. It served as a reminder too of how her 'darling' husband had seemed so clinical over the girl's disappearance. He may have said some of the right things, but there was no emotion attached; no identifying with the rising panic felt by others. This man for whom she'd feigned affection nearly half her life, might now be involved in something unimaginable. The realization felt like the tripping a switch in some dark cellar.

In the quiet of his living room, with their unspoken thoughts running parallel, Di had mentally convicted the vicar already.

Seeing that it was well into the afternoon, she broke their silence to say that she must be getting on.

'To do what?' came Di's blunt response.

'Good question! I'm going to challenge him over the photograph.' She put Sleuth down on the carpet.

'Perhaps you should let me hold on to it for safe-keeping.' His proposal was a directive more than a suggestion.

'Of course!' she said. Giving the picture a further heart-rending glance, she left it where it lay. They agreed not to tell Christopher that Di had any knowledge of the photograph, or that it was now in his safekeeping.

'I think you're right. You need to confront him about the picture,' said Di. 'Watch carefully how he reacts – any little give-away expression. Please promise to call me at the earliest opportunity to tell me *what* he says and *how* he says it.'

Despite the risk it might entail, to leave the question unanswered would have put an intolerable strain on the vicar's wife. Too much hinged on how Wilkes would reply for her *not* to confront him. Picking up her bag, she reassured him that she would phone him by early that evening at the latest.

Returning home she caught him just as he was about to go back into his study.

She was point-blank with her question. *'Christopher!'* – the appellation as well as her tone warned him of her gravity – 'When I took your cassock to the cleaners this morning, I removed a photograph of Stacey Witcombe dressed in a bikini. How on earth do you come to possess such a picture?'

'I never asked you to take my cassock to be cleaned.' Despite his reflex answer, the facial twitch and blanching behind his wife's discovery could not be hidden.

'Well you've never complained on other occasions when I've done so' came her equally quick riposte.

Realizing in the circumstances that he could not deflect her, he then chose to sound almost casual: 'She gave me that photograph sometime ago because she wanted me to have a picture of her.'

'That seems pretty odd,' replied Frances. Knowing how he could have a ready answer for most things she continued, 'I can imagine letting her boyfriend Martin have such a picture. But why *you*?'

'Well, I didn't tell you this before darling. In fact I didn't consider it necessary. The fact of the matter was that Stacey had a crush on me. I'm surprised you hadn't seen it for yourself. It was a bit embarrassing really but, supposing that it would pass, I thought that if she really wanted me to have a photograph of herself, there was no harm done. As much as anything I didn't want to hurt her feelings.'

Frances was aware that Stacey had made several trips to the vicarage, perhaps on some pretext for seeing Christopher. But being an outgoing girl, she seemed pleased to see anyone who happened to answer the door whether it had been Dominic or Katy or even herself. Perhaps some adolescent fancy may have surfaced for the charms of her husband, it being far from uncommon for clergy to become 'father-figures' to impressionable teenage girls, or indeed sometimes to certain unhappy women. But having a steady boyfriend who she'd been dating for at least six months, how possibly could Stacey have had a crush on her husband?

Observing her confused expression, Christopher sought to press home his case, 'Honestly, darling, I didn't really want her photograph but I looked upon it as a kindness to keep it. Nor had I thought to get rid of it now that she's disappeared.'

'Well, shouldn't the police have it, or better still Mr. and Mrs. Witcombe?' Cunning lurked behind her question.

'Maybe so,' replied Christopher, knowing for certain that they, whoever *they* might be, would *never* lay hands on such a picture.

'By the way, have you got the photo?' he asked casually.

'Eh, yes, I put it down somewhere,' she replied. 'Now what on earth did I do with it?'

Displaying an uncharacteristic loss of memory, she left him on the pretext of going to retrieve Stacey's photograph from the kitchen.

Having bluffed his way out of trouble before, he presumed she'd go back to being her usual gullible self. With his fleet-footed answers, he felt like a boxer where, not with gloves but with a word-game, he could jinx and talk his way out of a corner; even go on the offensive with his back to the ropes.

For her part, and with the photograph left at Di's house she had never consciously lied to her husband before. But it was as though the photograph had taken her into a new arena. Their marriage having been a sham for so long, her newfound mendacity meant that from thereon they danced no longer even as partners within a marriage of convenience. For if she had moved to accomodate the rhythm of his deceits before, she now counter-bluffed with her own little jig of deception.

Back in his study, he pondered the true explanation for the photograph, and which she'd given him shortly before her death. The girl had called to see him with some question about her mock 'A' level in RE, asking about details for the various names for God in the Old Testament and to discover which of the two Creation stories came first.

It was then that he went on to say, 'Stacey, I don't know if you are aware of it but I'm especially fond of you. I'm sure you're a credit to your parents but to me you seem more like a daughter than a parishioner. Does that make you feel all right by my saying that?'

Despite the slight embarrassment she'd felt at the time, it felt flattering to have such close attention more so from the vicar of an important parish. So responding with a quiet 'Thank you!' she then had the presence of mind to ask, 'But Katy's your daughter – surely you must feel close to *her?*'

'Well, yes naturally I do,' replied Christopher

momentarily jolted by the reminder that his own daughter was almost identical in age to Stacey. But then with typical adroitness he added, 'sometimes fathers don't always get as close to their own children as they do to others.'

'I know what you mean. I don't always see eye to eye with my dad.'

Insofar as Stacey got on very well with both her parents, hers was the reply of an adolescent bartering times and places for when to go out and return home. Not seeing 'eye to eye' for Stacey meant no more than the haggling done between a teenage daughter and a dutifully protective father, and one where despite the grumbles a strong undercurrent of appreciation always existed. Knowing that her parents cared as much as they did meant a lot.

'Ah, you understand then! I'm so pleased. So if every now and again I give you a little hug, you won't mind? You can be my little girl and I can be your pretend daddy. Nothing very serious, just a little secret between us, you understand?' He paused . . . 'Actually vicars quite often get lonely. Not even their wives always understand, so it's lovely to think that someone cares for them in a special way. Is that all right?'

Stacey nodded with a smile which he liked to consider as beguiling, but which she delivered only with typical innocence. 'But we should keep it a secret, yes?' he asked. Again she nodded, her look of maternal protectiveness assuring him of her discretion.

Before he showed her to the door, he placed both his hands on her shoulders and said, 'Do you know what I would really treasure?'

Wide-eyed, the girl shook her head.

'I'd love a photograph of you, perhaps one of you on the beach or playing tennis or something. Have you got one which you can let me have without anyone knowing?'

'Yes, I've got one or two which Martin took of me on

May bank holiday, when his family took us to King's Lynn for the day,' she replied. 'You can have one of those if you'd like.'

'I'd like that very much indeed. Thank you!' came his instant reply.

In teaching their family to be trustworthy, Stacey Witcombe's parents had inadvertently taught her the ill-conceived lesson of sometimes being *too* trusting. Both she and her elder sister Philippa were unusual in that they both remained trusting to the point of naivety.

Having presented him with the photograph a few days later before choir practice, it was only two weeks later that Stacey died.

As husband and wife pondered their separate thoughts over the Stacey photograph, Frances had to admit that his explanation sounded at least half plausible.

Perhaps the girl *had* been infatuated with her husband, and that he'd done no more than accept the photograph so as not to hurt her feelings. Later when he left the vicarage to make a parish visit, Frances immediately got on the phone to Di. She told him of Christopher's explanation.

Instinctively Di knew that the reason given was patently absurd. Yet considering it a safer and wiser course to let Frances go on half-believing her husband at that stage, he said no more than:

'Remember Frances if you ever you need me, I'm here for you.'

# Chapter 9

At least with the Christmas vacation now underway, she had the consolation of having Dom living at home.

Later that week, mother and son came to share a quite separate concern. Having resolved to tackle a mountain of ironing that had been ignored for too long, they were in the kitchen once more when he expressed his concern: 'Mum, I know she's in shock like the rest of us, but Katy seems to have gone completely into her shell of late. In fact I'm seriously worried.'

A prolonged hiss on the steam iron signaled that her son's disclosure had, like other awakenings, touched her on the raw. Bad enough having unresolved suspicions about one's husband without having to worry about one's beloved daughter. But then she thought to herself, 'Better to start facing problems, rather than to go on denying them like I've done for the past, God knows how many years.'

'She's not her normal self *at all!*' insisted Dom.

'Well I can see that she's become very withdrawn,' Frances agreed. 'But she still looks her pretty self, even if she's gone into her shell. Let's hope to goodness that when we get some good news about Stacey, Kate will get back to normal.'

But come Christmas and Kate would show just how much *not* 'her normal, pretty self' she really was.

With the festive season beckoning it was now six months since Stacey's disappearance. There'd been no sign of her or more to the point, *no sign of her body*. Whatever the authorities might say to the contrary, her memory would slowly immerse itself into that much larger pool of missing persons who, despite the denials, were presumed lost without trace.

'Missing presumed dead' wasn't said as such, but after an interval of six months that was how those in the know tended to think.

As for the Wilkes' household, it was beginning to show all the sings of falling apart. Quite bizarrely her husband had just been promoted to becoming a canon of Fordham cathedral, and where in the build-up to Christmas the new vicar-come-canon would choose to go out visiting, or simply steer clear of his wife and son. Whatever other peoples' perceptions about them Frances knew that their marriage was sustained on nothing more than the next event in the church's calendar. And now with Katy's increasing detachment from them as a family had heightened her brother's concern. Upon completing his first term at Cambridge and being 'the only sane one among us,' as his mother sometimes thought of him, even Dom was beginning to suffer.

With Frances seeking solace once more at the ironing board, Dom returned to the problem of his sister: 'Mum, Katy's getting worse. I can hardly get a smile out of her. She's smoking and drinking and, if not back on the hash, then she could be into something worse!'

'O God! Not *drugs!*' The very reminder stopped Frances in mid-flight from ironing one of Dom's shirts. 'That's impossible – after all, she promised.'

'Mum, for God's sake, please get *real!* Kate's a big girl and you know drugs are everywhere – nowhere more so than at that flashy dump where she works. Besides The Staff's got a reputation. And don't forget we know nothing about that iffy character who's meant to be her boyfriend.'

Having rarely spoken so forcefully to her, he went on: 'Anyway if she's not on drugs, she soon could be. The problem's got to be *Dad*. He's become weirder than I've ever known him. Maybe Kate, who always wanted to please him, can't get her head around the way he seems to be over Stacey, like he doesn't really care at all. Maybe she sees that as a reflection of how he feels towards *her!*'

Such perceptions both stung and devastated Frances. There was no way she could nullify what Dom had just said. Katy a drug addict or prospective one, traumatized by a father whose clinical calm over the whole Stacey episode surely spoke volumes as to what he thought, or didn't think, about his own *daughter!'*

Dear God, it was like she'd been asleep all of her life, or for all of her married life! Aroused first by their churchwarden Di Hagan and now by a son who just spoke as he saw, she berated herself. Not only in denial about her daughter's problems, she had no idea as to just *who* played at being the caring vicar while forever toying away at his computer.

Then of late there had been two further distractions in the vicar's life. The first revolved around drawing up and finalizing plans for a parish pilgrimage to the Holy Land. Having been to Israel on two previous occasions as a curate Christopher now saw himself as a bit of an expert. This new pilgrimage planned for early in January had entailed much work, more so as it was to include another group from the nearby parish of St Hilda's.

But on top of that, he had been giving an excessive

amount of time to Mr. and Mrs. Witcombe of late. While the Witcombes clearly needed support, Frances couldn't understand it - given Christopher's complete disregard for his own family. Besides the other family had received counseling from various groups and organizations. 'So how could *he* be of any further use?'

In the circumstances it was probably as well that she wasn't privy to his main motives for visiting the Witcombes.

Philippa had gone through a traumatic two years. There'd been a marriage ending in divorce to leave her with the custody of a one-year-old daughter, and little else. And then there'd been the disappearance of her sister. Always wishing to do 'right by their family,' as they put it, Mr. and Mrs. Witcombe had readily offered their remaining daughter such home comforts as they could provide. Also having Philippa at home did in a tiny way compensate for the void left by Stacey.

It had been Philippa who'd answered the door when Christopher called on the first night of her sister's disappearance. She had done no more than invite him in – he then going in to console her parents and to give a few details to the police. But in his subsequent visits to the Witcombes, the vicar found himself motivated to call on them, more for the purpose of wanting to assist Philippa.

The likeness between the two girls was indeed uncanny. Both were slim and of equal height with straight ash-blonde hair where although Philippa wore hers shorter, it still fell to her shoulders. More intriguingly the elder sibling bore the same air of naive innocence. For despite all her troubles, it was as though Philippa was cocooned in her own world. Whilst other girls might fake innocence, he marveled that like Stacey, Philippa seemed to wear an air of genuine innocence. Furthermore she didn't seem averse to drawing close to Christopher on the sofa when he called at the Witcombe's home, or maybe that was just her rather unusual way.

It was just that with the two young women having mannerisms so akin to each other, he wished to help Philippa in some way.

It was on his third visit that she elaborated on her predicament: 'I don't know if you know it, but I got married in All Saints. It must have been a short time before you arrived. Anyway it was that lovely vicar the Reverend Bishop who took our service, the one who died so suddenly.'

'Yes, I'm sure I've seen your name in the wedding register,' replied Christopher, without wishing to digress on the merits of his predecessor.

'Well, I'm afraid it didn't work out' said Philippa. 'I've learned a lot about life since our bust-up two years ago. Both Ewan and I were far too young and when we had Rosamund, he just took off. Ewan was a self-employed HGV driver and once the baby was born he lost all interest in either of us. It made me angry at the time, only now I simply feel like a failure.'

If Christopher needed a cue to do his fatherly, pastoral bit, it now presented itself: 'Oh, I shouldn't say that. Anyone can make a mistake over marriage, while we in the church should never judge. It must be very difficult for you and Rosamund.'

'I feel full of regrets.' For such a pretty woman she seemed to have a seriously poor opinion about herself, as she resumed: 'For one thing I wanted our baby to have a happy home and to know her father. Now with this happening to Stacey, I feel mum and dad have had all they can cope with. Stacey was one of my bridesmaids. Sometimes I wonder if she could see what was happening to Ewan and me.'

Ever paternal, he responded with unintended honesty:

'well you can't blame yourself over Stacey's disappearance. Nor can you blame yourself if your husband suddenly got cold feet and left. Blaming yourself is the worst thing you can do!'

Observing his brown eyes of a slightly different colour, she returned his gaze with appreciation. 'You're very considerate' she replied smiling. 'It was something Stacey always said about you.'

And when you smile you look just like your sister, he thought before replying:

'Thankyou. Are you able to make any plans, or is it still early days?'

'Well, I ought really to get a job; *any* job. Mum says she'll look after Rosamund. But I'm not too happy about that either. Dad's job looks under threat, because orders are down at his place of work and I don't know how they'll cope if dad's made redundant. What with *Stacey* and then *myself* and then maybe *him!*

'What sort of work might *you* do?' inquired Christopher.

'Well, I've got six GCSEs but I'm not sure what I might do. Before meeting Ewan and getting pregnant, I'd been thinking about dental nursing or something like that.'

It was clear that Philippa was a vulnerable young woman in need of his help.

# Chapter 10

'That was a lovely service, vicar!' said several of the godparents from the assortment of five babies whom he'd just baptized.

'Oh, you do have your way with them, don't you Christopher?' cooed a devoted middle-aged female parishioner.

'Successful yet again, vicar!' chimed in another.

For those Family Service baptisms which he conducted four times a year, the bouquets were thrown as though to royalty. Not only did he have a powerful effect upon his congregation, Revd Wilkes seemed to have the Midas touch - managing to baptize children who, one moment, all out of sorts and grisly could a short time later be restored to their mothers as good as gold.

Half a year on from Stacey's disappearance and, on this Advent Sunday, the church looked pristine and cared for. All Saints was untypical of other churches in the diocese, many of which suffered from mould and neglect. With its sparkling brasses, meter-tall candles and freshly laundered white altar frontal, light radiated from every corner. After a summer spring-clean with the walls of the nave and chancel whitewashed throughout, everything about the place shone squeaky-clean.

In his freshly laundered alb and brightly embroidered white stole the vicar too looked the embodiment of well-scrubbed piety.

'Would you like to take some photographs of me holding little Samantha?' he would coax. Or, 'Where would you like a picture of Emily? Around the font, perhaps?' Or, 'How about a photo with mum holding her under the porch?'

'Aren't we lucky with the weather!' might be followed by, 'Thank you, I would like very much to join you for tea later on.'

And to the inevitable jibe about Sunday being his only busy day, he would reply, 'I'm sure that I could manage to pop over for just half an hour.' Nor would he rarely let an opportunity slip, to coax: 'By the way, if any of you would like to make a further contribution to church funds, do feel perfectly free!' Or, he might wisecrack, 'if you didn't remember the collection plate, then there's always the box at the church door!' With such inoffensive pleasantries, he typified the ever-obliging vicar.

Barring the Stacey incident and the curious detail of having been the last person to see her, life was returning to some sort of normality. With time being a great healer, folk were starting to appreciate once more what a good, if not outstanding, vicar they were blessed with.

Married to a wife who was clearly devoted and more than willing to pull her weight, Revd Wilkes ticked all the boxes. Their two children also as far as they were known outside seemed to be, if not avid churchgoers, then always pleasant and polite. For some time the Wilkes household had been lauded as a role model for other clergy and their families, and where as a 'middle-of-the-road' Anglican, the new vicar played his part admirably. Ready and willing to visit the sick and elderly, if called upon, he was an easily-heard preacher

*A Candle For Lucifer*

whose sermons rarely erred on account of being too long or, for that matter, too challenging. Not only that, his tenor voice was an asset to any choir, unlike his predecessor Jack Bishop who'd been tone-deaf.

Some recognized Revd Wilkes as having the potential for high office. Ex-public school and university educated he still stood to go places. Furthermore as a man of private means in difficult economic times, he was less of a liability and thus less of an embarrassment to the diocese. Compared to those other clergy who wore their poverty like a flag 'C.W.', as his bishop affectionately referred to him, was both charming, witty and yes it could not be denied – *affluent!*

With two-thirds of his regular congregation being made up of women he found it effortless to charm most of them. Furthermore by not rocking the boat, his were a 'safe pair of hands', as the bishop liked to put it; and now with the Stacey episode receding, his future prospects looked good. Who knows an archdeacon's ticket could well be in the offing. Things had already been said or hinted at to suggest as much.

Proof of being in good odour with the bishop came two weeks after that Advent Sunday. Sensing that the vicar, and indeed his wife, had suffered quite enough over the lost choirgirl, and during which time Christopher had shown great fortitude, the bishop decided to confer upon him the new status of 'canon'. This meant that in future an honorary chair, or 'stall' would be made available to him in the cathedral and which, as one of the canons, he would occupy on special occasions.

So with Christmas upon them, the new Revd Canon Wilkes felt confident that the good folk of Ketborough were, at last, coming to terms with the loss of Stacey. Until then prayers had been said continuously for the girl and her family, and if there were any lingering doubts over

Christopher, the girl's abduction – for that was surely what it was – now attached itself to some opportunist rapist said to have been in the neighborhood at the time. The papers had been full of reports about a traveling salesman recently caught for a series of murderous attacks on young women, assaulted between Cornwall and Coventry. Clearly Stacey was but one of his hapless victims, with her abductor having made his getaway via the nearby motorway.

As far as he could tell all suspicions had now lifted. So despite two long and tricky interviews with the police some time back, things were at last returning to normal. Also having twice explained to his wife how he'd come by a photograph of Stacey in a swimsuit, he supposed that Frances like everyone else was now firmly behind him.

It was only one of his two churchwardens, Nicholas Hagan, who remained a bit of an unknown quantity. But having becoming increasingly withdrawn of late, Christopher saw it more as a matter of Hagan still grieving over his wife's death. Besides having enjoyed unusually good rapport with the previous vicar, Jack Bishop, Hagan was bound to be biased somewhat. With vicars invariably being compared, favorably or otherwise, to their predecessors, you couldn't win them all. Thus whilst always remaining civil towards Mr. Hagan, Canon Wilkes contented himself knowing that his other churchwarden, a Miss Gateshead, gave him her unswerving support.

From thereon his task would be to help heal his flock of their memories. To do this he had, quite properly, to bury all knowledge of what may or may not have taken place. Faith must take them forward and he would lead by example.

Unfortunately, even in those parishes where people are inclined to think well of each other and more so of their vicar, few clergy can claim total immunity from those troublesome exceptions who, sooner or later, love to pop up to present problems. Most clergy can call to mind the occasional thorn in his or her side.

By themselves, such individuals stand out more as an irritant; perhaps no more than a goad used by the Almighty for keeping a negligent cleric in line! Of course if they're known to be universal troublemakers, they give less cause for alarm. Yet whatever their purpose, it is important to remain alert to such thorns.

Granville Zbierski was a case in point. Yet despite being an irritant whether towards head teachers over his demands for proper playground facilities, or to local authorities insisting on traffic calming measures, he wasn't beyond winning begrudging respect. An ex-miner, he'd moved himself and half his Polish family down from Yorkshire on to Ketborough's small council estate. Largely on account of his new boss being Polish, he'd been fortunate to secure work as an electrician in a factory nearby.

Zbierski, or Mr. Z, or even Z as he was often known, was not, by any stretch of the imagination, a nice man; at least not in the sense that Ketborites understood niceness. Quite apart from swearing like a trooper - he had indeed done his national service, he drank heavily and more worryingly by getting to know everybody's business became a relentless gossip.

Whether inebriated or not, he chose to tell people as readily to their face as behind their back many a home truth, even if it was patently *untrue*! Nor was he easily heard on account of his thick and often slurred accent – a blend of Polish/Yorkshire, shaken and stirred with the residue of his favourite tipple. So for those whose path he crossed or who judged people by their appearance and social graces, Granville Z was altogether unpleasant – a rabble-rouser whether for district councilors, school governors, the new vicar or whoever.

Although acquainted with the vicar of All Saints, he remained avowedly anti-church, his lapsed Catholicism showing no wish to reform itself 'given what half dem priests get up to'. It was only on account of his two nieces attending the church youth club, and because of his daughter Carol's wish to have her son Frederick baptized, that he found himself tangling with Canon Wilkes. Since her mother's death and her own abandoned common-law marriage, Carol had all but taken over the running of the Zbierski household, nieces included.

Requesting that her son be baptized some time near Christmas, Carol had made an appointment to see the vicar during that first week in Advent. But being an unmarried mother he had shown some reluctance about proceeding with the ceremony.

Putting it as tactfully as possible, he'd said, 'We try to maintain a policy here at All Saints to baptize only those children who are in a secure family unit.'

Explaining further he added, 'we like to hold baptisms only at our family services so that everybody can be present. Not only that we do prefer it if parents and godparents are themselves baptized and confirmed. This encourages people to regularly attend family service so that we can maintain a spirit of participation for everyone involved.'

Despite this explanation, Carol knew that it meant automatic exclusion for her and her son. As a lapsed Catholic she'd been baptized but not confirmed. Nor was there any boyfriend left on the scene to make them look like a family. So, bearing in mind what had been said, of course she had no wish to be paraded like some scarlet woman in a church where, according to the vicar, everyone else seemed to live unblemished lives.

Yet seeking to avoid any possible backlash, Wilkes had

even gone so far to suggest: 'If you like I *could* do a private ceremony for yourself and your son one Sunday afternoon, with just you and the family present so as to avoid any unnecessary embarrassment.'

This concession having been offered for other 'awkward' occasions, it seemed that Carol would agree to the proposal. But all this did was to bring to the boil the fury of her father.

The next day, Mr. Z was on the phone to the vicar. 'I want to come and see yer!'

'Can you tell me your name, please?'

*'Zbierski!'* was said with a snarl.

'Can you tell me what it's about, sir?' asked Christopher, already wincing at the tone of voice on the line.

'Too bloddy right, I can. It's about your friggin so-called baptism policy. Our Carol tells me you won't do her Frederick by way of there not being no father. What the fock's going on? Who do yer bleeding think you are – friggin God Almighty?'

'I'm sorry I haven't quite got your name,' requested an agitated Christopher. Then having checked the details he'd written down during Carol's visit, he assumed that his trusty charm would win him over, 'Ah, yes, Mr. Zbierski. May I call you Granville?'

There was a derisory snort down the line, before a further demand was made to come and talk. Arranging an appointment for the following evening, Christopher was then left addressing a dialing tone.

Arriving the following evening Mr. Z was a small, wizened man scarcely five feet six compared to Christopher, whose additional nine inches loomed over him. Whisky fumes wafted around the front door as with the belligerence of a Jack Russell facing upto a Great Dane, he confronted the vicar.

'I want to know *why the fock* you won't baptize my

grandson!' he declared before he'd even crossed the vicarage threshold.

'Do come in, won't you. Do take a seat,' coaxed his host ushering him into his book-lined study and pointing towards a well-stuffed chair. Ignoring the chair, Mr. Z demanded to know: 'what's going off, then, why won't you do it? Carol's got a perfect right to have her lad Fred christened, and you bain't able to stop her.'

The Jack Russell knew his rights. The law clearly stated how any member of one's family living within the parish boundary could not be refused a baptism, as and when requested. Nor did other circumstances like being born out of wedlock have anything to do with that entitlement, anymore than did the family's lapsed Catholicism, or for that matter having to abide by certain dictates as set out by the vicar and his council. Knowing what was what, the Pole knew that the vicar would have to yield. This being the case there was no call for Zbierski to then follow up his demands with barely concealed blackmail. But that wasn't his way:

'You tell me what's focking moral and right. You're all bloddy hypocrites anyway. Thou's full of chicken-shit. Thou mayest think you act holier than thou, but thou's ten times worse than my Carol - thee and thy pals!'

Had it not been for his liberal use of expletives, the sprinkling of 'thee's and thou's' might have been lifted from the old authorized version of the Bible.

*Zbierski the Prophet!*

Until then, Christopher had looked down on him like the apparition of some Dickens character – Scrooge came to mind, someone to patronize if not speak down to because he was so universally disliked. But what Mr. Z said next changed that notion in a flash: 'Sides her sisters (by which he meant Carol's nieces) have been telling her that thou's been touching their bums in that youth club. What are you, a dirty ol' man or summat? Them lassies swear gospel's truth that thou's touched 'em up. Thou had best be keeping yer hands to yerself, or there's going to be rumours flying about thyself and that Stacey lass – the one that got screwed and murdered!'

Whether it showed or not, he couldn't tell. But seated in his red-leather captain's chair, the vicar inwardly trembled. It was as though out of the blue some deadly intruder had stormed the bridge-house of his cherished vessel, All Saints; a marauding pirate appearing only to hold one of those ancient flintlocks to his head. Despite Zbierski's infamy as a known troublemaker throughout Ketborough and beyond, it was what he came out with and said to others that which made him so dangerous.

Only through will power did the vicar control the knotting in his stomach, hoping that his inner panic or the blood draining from his face wasn't too apparent.

'Granville, eh Mr. Zbierski, that is a very slanderous remark and I shall pretend I never heard it, only because you are visibly upset.' And before the other had time to respond that he knew what he knew, Wilkes hurriedly put it to him, 'I've told your daughter that we can easily arrange a separate baptism for your grandson and we can find a time that suits all of us. Although we could still have Frederick's baptism at our family service, Carol might find it embarrassing to be in church on her own. That was the only reason for making the other suggestion.'

Without a flicker of satisfaction, this concession put an end to any further discussion.

*'Just get on with it! I can't stand you hypocrites. Fock you all!'* retorted the drink-enraged Pole as he stormed out of the study. He then passed a stunned vicar's wife standing in the hall before slamming the front door with a crash.

'What on earth was all that about?' asked an incredulous

Frances. 'I could hear him yelling from the kitchen'

'Nothing, darling, just a very drunk father complaining about our baptism policy for his grandson.'

But as Mr. Zbierski strode out into the night, Christopher felt that he'd not seen the last of his most unwelcome guest.

The man's intrusion was all the more disturbing because nothing of great consequence had prompted it. Having done no more than uphold the guidelines of their baptism policy, even going so far as to suggest a compromise Christopher had had a bucket of slander and invective thrown in his face. As it was the Zbierski clan subscribed to the compromise baptism arrangement made a few weeks later.

He had no wish to be reminded of the recent past; of the unease he'd felt when being hassled by Officer 331, shortly after Stacey's disappearance. But the ferocity of this new verbal onslaught, as well as being so unexpected was all the more unsettling, coming at a time when he was busy reasserting his role as the respectable and caring canon. Getting behind the vicar's defenses in that way, the Pole was a blackguard all right. And besides, how possibly could his allegations about the two young girls possibly be substantiated? True, the girls with their mischievous eyes were precocious ten and eleven year olds, but as far as he knew he'd never laid a hand on them. Possibly once in a while he might have given them a fatherly cuddle. As for the man's remarks about Stacey, those were just typical of his foul mouth – par for the course for those sorts of people who delight in being hell-raisers.

As one, who having worked hard during the day and who upon retiring to bed had – as he saw it – paid his daily dues to society, Christopher had for most of his life slept soundly. But of late his sleep had grown fitful and disturbed. Years ago Frances' insomnia justified their use of separate bedrooms. But, since moving to Ketborough, his own insomnia had grown worse.

Some insomnia is said to arise from the fear of what we might come to dream. Normally most dreams are relegated to a corner of our mind, like the rubbish we throw into our bins and think no more of. Sweeping up the detritus of our daily lives, these nocturnal caretakers can leave our minds feeling tidy and refreshed for the new day. But that is to ignore those other rare occasional dreams, which like some Leviathan can occasionally emerge from the depths never to be forgotten. Such sea-monster type dreams can upon wakening be easily recalled, leaving even the most skeptical amongst us to observe: 'Last night I had this *incredible* dream!'

Even before Stacey's death one such strange and disturbing dream that came to him involved a beloved axe, given to him by his father before his tenth birthday. He'd loved and caressed the implement, learning to hone its edge razor-sharp so as to split logs for fuel during the cold Kenyan nights. From an old chainsaw that ran off a motorized belt used for cutting sections of logs, he then used his axe to split the logs before stacking them into piles. It was always a task he'd found exhilarating even during the heat of the day.

Of late that axe had come into his dreams, beginning with the innocent splitting of the logs in his childhood. But then the tool in his hand would distort into a bloodthirsty and disgusting instrument of death; a sort of double-edged mediaeval hatchet. From there he visualized himself donning a black mask and mounting some ancient scaffold – not in readiness for his own death, but rather to dispatch some unseen victim! Fascinated and bewildered by the dream, he recognized a sensual link between the axe of his dreams and the one he'd wielded in real life. Upon awakening from this dream, usually in a cold sweat, he was relieved to know that he was no more than the innocent woodcutting son of his father. Exploring the dream's symbolism no further, he failed to detect his hidden fascination in knowing how it might feel to kill somebody.

But after Stacey's murder his recent insomnia feared the repeat of what had become a new nightmare. At first he reveled in the opening imagery of what came to him shortly after retiring to bed. For whether he was half-awake or fully asleep, she would always visit him. First the gentle eyes and then the contours of her face came into full view. With her lips half-opened, she presented him with her soft purity, a purity to enchant him with its constancy. For in the dream she seemed more like a child than how he remembered her in real life; her steady gaze offering no hint of recrimination.

For there was his reassuring arm around her slim shoulders, and there she was smiling at him. All seemed well until something frightened her. And it was her startled movement, which he felt sure prompted the white girdle from his cassock alb to come into his hand, and only then to stifle a silent scream did the girdle encircle her neck. But surely even the softness of the cord was no more than some love knot caressingly secured as though by mutual consent, victim and assailant colluding as though in the shared wrapping of a present?

Such now was his necrophilic fantasy and the love he believed that she bore him, would not one party readily surrender if not die for the other? The world might bay for retribution against the innocent victim, but not the enchanted martyr who, in the name of love returns nightly to her lover-devourer; and doing so of her own freewill.

At first the dream always left him feeling calm, even virtuous in some way. For there was no death mask wearing the flowing blonde hair that had so beguiled him. No nocturnal specter rose up to point a skeletal finger, or rasp retribution. No succubus with a myriad other defiled women cried out for justice beyond the grave. For it was as though in death, Stacey seemed *better able to understand*, bringing him comfort and, even if it were being called for - *forgiveness*. From that other world of spirit free both of spite and recrimination, it was as though she approached him with the submission of an enchanted slave. Drawing close enough for him to hold her, theirs it seemed was a love pact beyond the grave, somehow kept sacred on account of her corpse still hidden.

On the night when she died, Stacey had done no more than seek his advice concerning a question about whether or not to sleep with her boyfriend. She'd regarded the vicar as a fatherly figure, more amenable to such a discussion than her parents. Nor could she have ever guessed that Christopher's gentle interest in her welfare was sparked by a raging aberration; an attraction for the opposite sex being directed neither towards mature women of his own age nor indeed to his wife, but towards young innocents like Stacey.

From his perspective over the twelve months that he'd known her, Stacey had of course *flirted* with him. For no sooner had he arrived at All Saints than she'd drawn attention to herself whether through her attendance at confirmation class, or just by making regular visits to the vicarage so as verify hymn and anthem requests for the choir. Then by wishing to speak with him on that Friday night in the solitude of his vestry she'd scarcely disguised her seduction. For had not the question itself been provocative, challenging a response from him to her?

It was from the insanity of such twisted logic and to which he could never own up, that from the nightmare of a real event he sought only to edit a dream of shared innocence. But now the dream of her visitation came with hateful intrusions.

For it was into the intimacy of that recurrent dream that other unwelcome presences now appeared. Behind the smiling eyes of Stacey and the slumping of her form before his feet, new hostile spirits manifested themselves. For behind the immaculate khaki uniform of that Kenyan policeman, and who'd imparted the news of his parents' deaths could be seen the dark blue uniform of what he took to be Officer 331. And then beyond him in the shadows there appeared the outline of former Detective Inspector Nicholas Hagan.

But the clearest image, and whose voice with its jarring obscenities was instantly recognized was that of the drunken Pole – Granville Zbierski.

## Chapter 11

*'Thank God, it won't be long now!'* said Sister Angelique under her breath.

Discarding her nightdress, she clambered into her linen undergarments, followed by tunic, cap, hood and collar over which went the heavy serge habit and white wimple. Pushing reluctant feet into black flat shoes concluded the process. There was no time of the year when the procedure didn't chill her to the bone.

Wanting to stay in bed instead of going to school bore but a faint comparison to getting up every morning before sunrise. They would have all felt it. But such was the discipline over their body, mind and soul that Angelique assumed she alone actually *suffered*. Winter was especially bad and deep down she'd never got over the ordeal of dressing in such ungainly garments, or of rousing herself to face the dawn summons to prayer. Perhaps in the past it had only been her flesh that was weak. Now her spirit was breathing defiance as well.

Six o'clock mass beckoned and her mutterings, although muted, suggested that her shifting tone towards the Almighty was already underway; a detail that, had she confessed it, would have carried severe reprisals. Not only was *'Thank God!'* said in such a way as to be blasphemous, it was said in the knowledge that this her ninth year in the Convent of St Juliana was to be her last. Whether by God's grace or through honest temptation she cared not. Her mind was made up.

She came from a good Catholic family - mass every Sunday, fish on Friday with confession once a fortnight. Encouraged by her mother to enter convent life at the age of eighteen had felt like an inspired choice at the time. For despite a self-conscious prettiness, she sensed that a betrothal to God offered a nobler, if not a more romantic alternative, to that of dating boys only to get married. Along with the repeated encouragement of 'You'll make a fine sister to our Lord, Angela' - as how the Provincial Superior of her convent school kept repeating it, and she'd made her choice. So as a postulant who then went on to complete her novitiate, Angela duly 'took the veil' three years later thereby acquiring the name of Sister Angelique.

St Juliana's, just outside the town of Ketborough, wasn't an order of nuns in the strictest sense of the term. Indeed, she was less shut off from the world than during her postulancy, hers being an Order modeled on their fourteenth century founder to try and assist the needy. Yet despite such charitable ventures as were made into the world, the sisters were still constrained to live within a house of Victorian-style discipline; the last 'victims', so to speak, of convent life to show scant regard for the widespread reforms of Pope John XXIII.

It was through her involvement with two ecumenical charities within Fordham diocese, one for the homeless and another for single mums that things began to change. After some years, as though through her re-acquaintance with life beyond the walls of St Juliana's, a startling reversal of her emotions had begun to take place. Not that there was anything romantic about helping the homeless or giving support to single mothers, but it had brought home to her that reality from which, in her adolescent naivety, she'd taken such hasty flight.

Most of her adult life then had been spent in a world controlled by prayer, the hushed utterances of worship, and the repetition of endless chores. Needlework and hours spent in silent reading were supposedly the nearest she came to doing anything recreational. Noise too was strictly controlled from the clicking of needles to the solitary tolling of bells, or the singing of plainsong. Above the crashing sounds of silence, it was the white noise of starched linen and the rustle of habits that began to torment her most. Nor were domestic tasks such as the scrubbing of floors, or the washing of pots and pans allowed any respite through the therapy of idle chatter or humour. Only during the half hour after supper could the oppressive silence be interspersed with whispers, or the licensed trill of her sisters' laughter. Yet all giggling was muted from the fear of offending Reverend Mother.

With hers being a world of psychotic cowardice where any frivolity was akin to mutiny, Angelique now understood how she had served a term of unremitting torment - eight years of *hell* in fact! Eight years in which the only channel of affection permissible came to be showered upon the two convent cats, obscenely cosseted with names such as 'darling' and 'pusskins,' - terms of endearment which, if transferred from one nun to another, would have suggested instant scandal. As for embraces, these were reduced to the farcical bumping of wimples, knowing that to proffer a cheek for a kiss or to provide an encircling arm for comfort were forbidden. For to touch was to sin!

She must have been *mad,* out of her mind, gullible beyond words to have inflicted upon herself such a fate at the age of nineteen! Eight years of carbolic soap, serge and silence, eight years of groveling and a penance, which went so far as to recommend self-flagellation with a small cord called 'the chastiser'. And what was the penance for? She still didn't know. What Angelique did know was that she'd had enough. Nor could it be denied any longer. It had been eight years without a *man!*

Deluded they may have been, but it wasn't that her sisters were bad people. In many ways they were heroic – seeking, according to their lights, a true devotion to God. But it was a heroism, which for her originated from impossible dreams of piety, ones that imposed cruel and unnatural demands upon her life. In the blindness of adolescence the vows of poverty, chastity and obedience had sounded ennobling. Now in her twenty-eighth year, she was in no doubt that she was being called to become *herself,* to become a woman and display a glorious disobedience by fulfilling a higher vocation of falling *in love!*

As an ecumenical member of the Anglican diocese of Fordham, Sister Angelique was always welcome to join the Clergy Chapter of Ketborough, which met once a month. The point of contact had initially come through the Area Dean who, being Chairman of the Trustees of the charity for the homeless where she worked, had put the suggestion to her. As the formal structure within a diocese, the Deanery Chapter arranges for its clergy and any other invited members to plan and meet for fellowship.

Ketborough Chapter consisted of fourteen members which included two women priests, a majority of male clergy of whom Christopher Wilkes was one and three of whom were parish vicars, several self-supporting ministers (SSMs), one female hospital chaplain and now Sister Angelique from the Order of St Juliana's. And then there was Fr Benjamin

Carter, the man appointed by the bishop to be Area Dean.

It was Benjamin Carter's parish church of St Hilda's just outside Ketborough, which along with All Saints had recently shared in a pilgrimage to Israel, and one led by the newly elected Canon Christopher Wilkes. Not only was this necessary so as to bring some fifty pilgrims together, it helped forge a bond between the two parishes.

Having also been permitted to share in that pilgrimage Angela, as she preferred to be known during that time, had got to know and befriend both Christopher and Benjamin. In planning for the pilgrimage Benjamin or Ben, as he was generally known, considered that he'd done well out of the deal. For while Christopher planned the itinerary plus researching all the information for the sites, Ben had been required to do no more than secure the hotel bookings, see to the welfare of the pilgrims, pay tips and take care of minor matters of administration. It was an arrangement to suit both men – the area dean wanting more time to relax while the canon, viewing himself as a seasoned visitor to Israel, liked to hold center-stage.

Into their seventh month since the disappearance of Stacey Witcombe, it had been important for the folk from All Saints to follow through with the event. Not only did the trip allow the two parishes to 'cluster', as it was called, it provided all of them with an opportunity to focus less on the past and more on the future.

Having returned from that pilgrimage some three months ago, Sister Angelique had had ample time back in St Juliana's to reflect on some of her memories. And now as she attended the Deanery Chapter, in close proximity to the Area Dean, she found it difficult to concentrate. Chapter meetings invariably went on for too long, worse still when in a stuffy room. Usually the programme began with an act of worship, with the host saying prayers or conducting Holy

Communion. Quite often a guest speaker would be invited this being followed by a general discussion, concluding with matters of business and a closing prayer.

On this occasion, the guest speaker was a somewhat dreary industrial chaplain, whose discourse caused Angela's mind to wander off in pursuit of memories of Israel.

'You'd better hold on to me here!' advised Benjamin to Angela as they prepared to explore the tunnel to Jerusalem's pool of Shiloh. She remembered the first thrill of being touched by a man, at no more innocent point of contact than her elbow. Nor was her arm even exposed, since the authorities insisted that women were to keep their arms and heads covered while visiting any religious site.

Flushed and adolescent in response, Angela felt obliged to reply, 'What will the other pilgrims think?'

'Who gives a damn!' was Benjamin's healthy rejoinder. 'If they've got any sense, everyone should end up clinging on to everybody else for most of the time we're here. As you've seen already you can't go anywhere without climbing steps, or grabbing on to handrails and many of the stones are so well worn they're like glass!'

Not only were there the steps to worry about, the three of them – Christopher, Benjamin and Angela – had chosen to wear light cassocks which made negotiating steps still more hazardous. Despite Christopher managing quite well on his own, the cassocks offered various occasions for Benjamin to lay claim to the Sister's arm.

Built on seven hills, parts of Jerusalem resemble one long roller coaster of inclines and troughs. With its camel-coloured buildings and narrow alleyways, most of the Old City obliges people to move only by mule or on foot. More hazardous still were those sites reached through tunnels, whose surfaces were invariably slippery and uneven. It would have been stupid of the fifty or so other pilgrims, most of whom were middle-aged, *not* to have linked arms at the very least. Nonetheless, Angela suspected that no other hand would have conveyed the same intimacy, as the one now encircling her forearm. It felt *divine*.

There were several occasions when the ever-solicitous Benjamin would take her arm, whether to guide her down the Via Dolorosa, up the Mount of Olives to the Church of Mary Magdalene, down to the tomb of Absalom or into the caves of Solomon's mines. But, surely here in the gloom of the Holy Sepulchre, where the stone floor was flat and smooth, did she really need his guiding hand? It was then in the Holy Sepulchre, of all places, that he felt his arm brush her *waist!*

But it was some of the things he said which made Angela's heart beat faster.

'I bet you're pleased to be out of that convent, aren't you, Sister?' he had asked with a mischievous grin. 'What with all the prayers, the constant masses, the lack of conversation, the lack of decent food and drink and especially the lack of proper companionship?'

Nor could she help her reply. 'Well, yes it does get a bit difficult at times. But then that's what I was called to do, and I knew it would never be easy.'

At one point where with the other pilgrims attentive to Christopher's patter about Jerusalem having six gates, only three of which remained standing, and of how some celebrity had survived a bomb attack at the exact spot where they now stood, Ben brushed close to her ear and whispered, 'I admire your constancy, Angela, but speaking personally I couldn't hack all that enclosure. I have to have space and, more importantly, I have to have real flesh and blood people around me. Maybe it's because I'm a man, and women can cope better. But my religion has to take me close alongside people, *ordinary* people!'

He realized that by her commitment to work with the charity for the homeless, he wasn't being entirely fair. But in the heady atmosphere of the Holy City, he had *felt* provocative sensing too how his companion seemed to almost encourage him.

On one occasion their conversation had been abruptly halted, she recalled, with Benjamin striding across an expanse of pavement to where some of their group were being accosted by three Arabs. Postcards, along with an assortment of geegaws and other artifacts carved from olive wood, were being thrust in their faces. She had to smile, as she thought about that particular episode - of how Fr Ben had waded in among the hawkers like an avenging angel, totally at odds with what her convent would have taught as the correct 'Christian' approach! And yet the way he'd sent those pesky Arabs packing, she pondered ruefully, wouldn't have been so untypical of the One who'd upset the moneychangers in the Temple two millennia before.

The interruption of the hawkers had been timely for it spared Angela having to respond to his earlier question. For her remark of wanting to be close to people - *ordinary* people, was to challenge her deeply, and where by addressing the needs of the homeless and single mums she had flagged up her *own* need for human contact.

Standing at some three thousand feet, Jerusalem's atmosphere is a heady one. It can do strange things to people, even making Angela feel light-headed as to what was or was not the correct protocol. It reminded her of a childhood sin when she'd downed a whole glass of sherry without anybody knowing. Stolen waters are sweet, more so the stolen sherry. For it had been a case both of giddy and delectable guilt!

In large numbers pilgrims tend to strike a pose, absorbed by the significance or otherwise of countless shrines and other holy places. But she now found herself distracted, noticing for one thing the virile strength of Christopher who despite his age was in excellent condition. She'd glimpsed the outline of muscular thighs pumping under the light cassock, and the strong hands with which he made light work of pulling himself up to a higher vantage point.

But it was the man who chose to be her escort who distracted her more, and who in her eyes was the finer and more alluring specimen of manhood. More bulk admittedly, but someone solid, warm and genuine, whose passion for life and people was further complemented by a robust, even wicked, sense of humour.

Like her, Ben had taken a vow of celibacy.

Not obese but of ample build, not least on account of his love of good food and drink and into his fortieth year Ben appeared to her to be in his prime. His wholeness as a man and priest was what got to her. Mischievous in the nicest possible way, his mischief had been known to offend some of his parishioners, if not one or two of the pilgrims who saw the whole enterprise of their pilgrimage as something sombre.

Perhaps the strangest side to his ebullience was that although he was a passionate man and strong in his beliefs, Ben appeared not to take his religion too *seriously!* Least of all would he assume any mock air of piety over many of the religious sites, whose claims to originality he hotly disputed, 'No way can Jesus have risen from the dead in three different places!' He didn't care who heard him. Or, 'There's only one mount of the Transfiguration, not two! Someone's pulling a fast one, given that no-one knows anything for sure!'

With his wide open face, the expansiveness of which could no more be concealed by the sunglasses he wore, than could the domed forehead with its retreating hairline under a sun-hat, Fr Ben looked the picture of health and well being. As for his laugh that was enough to get everyone else laughing.

'Surely our Lord would have loved his company, just for its own sake. He'd have enlivened any party and would almost certainly have cheered up the disciples when they were down,' Angela thought to herself.

It was whilst approaching the Mount of Olives that she alighted on a word to describe Ben, and one wholly alien to her lexicon of sisterly language. For the fact that he didn't take his religion too seriously meant something else too. Having taken a vow of celibacy, about which surely he must have been serious in the past, he gave an air of being far from enslaved to such a vow. For it was as they entered the Pater Noster church, of all places, Angela realized that it was these qualities that made Ben *sexy!*

Emancipation from this vow would prove itself for both of them before the year was out.

A rare ripple of laughter woke her up to remind Angela where she was.

The Chapter's guest speaker had cracked a joke. She pretended to have heard it before resuming a pose that looked prayerful, but which was more akin to the dozing state she'd been enjoying as she reflected on her memories in Israel.

She had had feelings for Christopher Wilkes as well. But as the pilgrimage progressed they were markedly different emotions. She knew he was married, had children and presumed that to all intents and purposes he was contented enough. But eight years of denying her own womanhood had not lessened her sense of intuition. For she perceived Christopher to be someone deeply troubled - a man, who for all his formal charm and extensive knowledge over the sacred sites, was clearly someone far from being inwardly *at ease*.

What attracted her to Christopher was not the natural attraction felt for Ben, more perhaps the curiosity of a concerned mother for a troubled son. She knew all about the Stacey affair, and that had she Angela met Christopher in adolescence she too might have been infatuated as, rumour had it, Stacey had been. For there was no question that he had *magnetism* but it was of a kind that, in her more mature self, she felt repelled by. However with the security of Benjamin close to hand, she had wanted get to know the other man better.

'. . . And what do you think about it, Sister Angela?'

'Er, excuse me... I'm sorry, what?' responded Angela, trying to come to, 'I'm very sorry, I seemed to have nodded off.'

An unhelpful if not deliberate pause . . . 'I was asking what you felt about our having a procession on Good Friday, walking around the streets of Ketborough.' The questioner was an evangelical, ever ready to promote worthy causes.

'Oh yes, that sounds like an excellent idea. I'm sure we could do with a more high-profile witness in the community,' answered Angela, still flustered at such a conspicuous display of ill discipline.

*'Sleeping in public, shame on you!'* the voice from within sprang to life, encouraged by the critical look shown by some of the other clergy present, including two of the women. The inner voice that had tried damning her soul for the last eight years had the rasp of Mother Superior. The glint of disapproval in the eye of the evangelical opposite that too replicated Reverend Mother's permanent expression.

Catching a sideways glance from the area dean, Angela knew that Fr Ben couldn't abide this particular fellow. After some further brief discussion, Ben then brought the meeting to a close and she blessed him for his closing remarks: 'We're grateful to our guest speaker, but I'm sorry that we've gone on for longer than usual. As Chairman I should really try and keep the business end of our meetings shorter. If Sister Angela nodded off then who can blame her? If we had to get up before six every morning, then we'd have probably dropped off even before we got here. Let's say the Grace.'

With a small downward smile, she gestured her appreciation. Only then as they bowed to say the dismissive prayer did she notice the hands of Christopher – hands which previously she'd admired for their size and strength, but which in that moment of praying she sensed were cruel.

With over three months having elapsed since Sister Angelique's return from her pilgrimage. Easter was late that year and the convent was approaching its most sombre time in the Church's calendar – the seven-day period of Holy Week. Having observed the austerities of Lent, which included getting up an hour earlier with fasting and longer periods of silence, it was now the eve of Palm Sunday and the sisters were filing into the Oratory for night prayers.

There was Reverend Mother, bird-like, and the other nuns shrouded in the gloom with only the spotlight on the great crucifix above the altar relieving the darkness. Bats rustled in the eaves overhead. As the hushed tones of Psalm 90 wafted antiphonally across the sanctuary pews, Sister Angelique might well have included in her letter of departure some of the verses, which in sacred whispers she and the other sisters floated across to each other. 'O, satisfy us early with thy mercy, that we may rejoice and be glad all our days,' to which those on her side replied, 'Make us glad according to the days wherein Thou hast afflicted us and the years wherein we have seen evil.'

The days of Angelique's affliction were about to end.

*Dear Reverend Mother,* she had written,

*I have seen fit to renounce my vocation within the Order of St Juliana, and will have left forever the convent when this letter comes into your hands. That this will come as a great shock and sorrow to you, I do not doubt. I also feel sorry that I must absent myself by way of this letter, rather than through taking any more formal process of leave-taking. But I choose to keep grief to a minimum.*

*The road to sainthood need not be, as I once understood it, by way of the inscription over this House, of having to 'make of thyself dust, for by so doing I accomplish God's will.' From hereon I seek to do God's will neither through self-abasement, nor through any willful reneging on my vows. But nor do I see holiness enshrined in perpetuity through a keeping of those vows.*

*There is a distinct probability that upon leaving the Order I shall bear children to the man I now love. Nor has such love ever made me feel so completely at peace, or assured that I remain in God's will.*

*If possible, I ask for your blessing, not on account of vows breached but upon my choice to walk in the liberty and love of Christ as I have come to comprehend it.*

*Your former obedient servant, Angelique.*

With a greater solemnity falling upon St Juliana's, her departure coinciding within Holy Week, she would leave that night. As the office of Compline droned to its conclusion, she saw for the last time the floodlit crucifix above the altar – Christ with the blood streaming from his hands and side. From his timeless Calvary the same inscrutable gaze looked downwards, even upon this his wayward daughter.

She'd grown to detest that effigy.

With the sisters self-inflicting their own incarceration, escape was easy. For this was no Alcatraz. One key separated her from the outside world and, at half past ten sharp on a spring evening crystal with stars, she took her leave. Slipping out of her cell, she carried her shoes to walk barefoot by the backstairs down to the laundry and on past the refectory. From there she passed through the chapel into the sacristy out along the corridor to the far side leading to the parlour, which in turn led to the hall and front door. The key to the door, locked at all times, hung incongruously on a hook by the one pay phone. She put on her shoes.

Removing the key and turning it while sliding back two heavy bolts, Sister Angelique unlocked the door and passed into the cool night. It was that simple! Relocking the door behind her, she then deftly cast the key through the letterbox, posting with it her letter of resignation. As she walked along the grass border of the circular graveled drive the scent of jonquils and wallflowers came to her nostrils. There was also enough moonlight to see small violets nestling under the sleeping daffodils. With her sisters locked back inside her heart surged. Yet her freedom came not so much with the drawing back of two bolts and the quick turn of a key. More it came knowing that she was no longer the prisoner of a misplaced conscience.

No turning back! No *reason* for turning back, when she saw the small white Renault of the man she loved. Upon seeing her he too ran towards her, each embracing the other while sobbing and laughing as one. From the grotesque contours of the convent outlined behind her and the deranged twitter of endless chants, the night-sky seemed luminous and alive, as though vibrant with the singing of a heavenly host. On this night in Holy Week with her nun's outfit now disheveled and hair tumbling around her shoulders, how could God disapprove? And if so, on whose side were the angels that now sang?

One last response needed to be made to the grim edifice behind her. In the cool of the night and in the privacy of some rhododendron bushes she shed the indestructible serge of her nun's regalia, replacing it with a set of lingerie, a pair of jeans, blouse and warm pullover all provided by Ben. Even in the chill air she reveled in the comfort of her new clothes, appreciating their softness. Again a pair of flat heeled shoes fitted her perfectly, the leather so much more supple than the unyielding ones of the convent. Then skipping towards the convent's front door she deposited the bundle of her old habit on the top step.

Running back across the gravel she cared neither as to who saw or heard. With theirs now being two separate worlds what matter if Mother Superior, from her tortured and loveless bed, heard a shriek of euphoric laughter? As Benjamin and Angela embraced hard and long in the car, he then drove her to the hostel for the homeless where he worked and where, as a homeless person, she was booked into her own room.

Soon they would be sharing their own home.

# Chapter 12

'Hard to think what her family must be thinking right now!' said Lech. 'When I was a kid, I had a favourite aunt who died near Christmas and that was bad enough. Couldn't get her out of my mind for years.'

The cheerful festive lights in The Magpie belied the subdued mood within. Six months had elapsed since the disappearance of the girl and as Di Hagan feared, the trail had all but petered out. There were rumors, of course, that she'd been sighted. One spoke of some traveling salesman having abducted her, but Di knew from experience how rumors inevitably arose the more that people actually knew nothing. As usual seated in his favourite corner with a pint of stout, he was keeping his teeth clenched to his unlit pipe. On this occasion he'd brought Snap who lay at his feet.

'Shit!' Nicks Crooks and Lech were playing an indifferent game of darts, and one of Lech's darts had hit the wire and fallen to the floor.

'It beats me that somebody must know something and can still keep it secret. *Christ,* if I'd have done something like that I couldn't live with myself!' replied Crooks taking his turn at the dartboard. There was no doubting that the light-fingered thief of a dozen years ago meant what he said, when he added, 'I mean how can anyone sleep at night who does such a thing? . . .Bugger it.' This time one of Crooks' darts had missed the board completely.

Secretly they all hoped that Di might know more than they did, or at least come up with some sort of answer. But the former detective remained his usual unforthcoming self, which as before they put down to grief, yet unresolved, over the loss of his wife.

The subdued atmosphere was broken by the arrival of Granville Zbierski. Noise followed the man like a football crowd, for when he wasn't speaking there would usually be someone who'd find themselves getting wound up by something the hard-drinking Pole had just said. It was like with his weasel eyes he appeared never to miss a trick, and where whatever he saw he would then pass comment on, a dirty innuendo often attached.

'Watcha Z, how you doing?' called Crooks, just as he was about to let fly with another of his wayward arrows.

'Not bad, except I pisses up with the 3.30 at Wolverhampton! Lost twenty five quid, when my so-called buddy told me I'd got an outsider who was a cert.'

'That'll teach you not to gamble!' riled Crooks, momentarily in denial about his own penchant for dog racing.

'Was that the outside favourite - Rough Justice or something?' interjected Lech, 'the one that lost a shoe and came in next to last?'

'Yeaaah!' sneered Z: 'Bloddy thing, I should get a refund. Or they should run the race again. No fockin justice with a name like that! Them bookies just takes your money and that's it. Big farts. I'd like to make *them* run without their friggin shoes!'

'Well it had got bloody guts to finish the race at all. Maybe it'll be a good each-way bet next time round!' said Crooks, winking at the landlord. He enjoyed any opportunity for getting under Z's skin.

The fuse was primed! As it was Nick Cocheron was cultivating the patronage of a new drinker sitting at the bar who just happened to be a bookmaker. Immediately the bookie felt his hackles rise but remained quiet, more out of amazement at the contentious intruder and the landlord's parrying rejoinder. 'Here he is, making everyone else's life a misery, just because *he's* miserable!' And then to keep in with him he offered, 'OK you grouchy old sod, I'll pay. What'll it be?'

With Z laying claim to a pint of best and the bookie keeping his distance, a brief moment of quiet ensued.

Di Hagan saw horse racing for the rip-off that it was, a mug's game and so he had no sympathy. He was glancing through a tabloid reading about some serial killer in America, who'd kept all his bodies under his house only to pour quicklime into the crawlspace so as to keep down the stench. He could do with some edifying conversation. But tonight, like the hapless punter, the odds seemed against him.

'Ee up, Di!' said Z from his barstool, choosing to make Di the target for his opening salvo: 'Seen any more of that Mrs. Wilkes, then?' Being in a foul mood Z always did his best to drag others into his orbit, a skill in which he invariably succeeded.

Di had no idea that the vicar's wife been observed making visits to his house. But as people knew to their cost, Z rarely missed a trick.

His reply was guarded. 'Up to your old tricks again then, Granville! Minding everyone's business but your own, eh?'

Di's answer seemed to deflect Z momentarily from pursuing him further. Yet by making it common knowledge that, for whatever reasons, the former detective had been seeing the vicar's wife there was fuel enough for any fire.

Never a man for small talk, Z's aptitude for gossip reminded him of those rare racing drivers who enter Lap One as though it were their last. No warm up or preliminary gauging of oneself against the opposition. Just straight to the point and away! Or put another way, Di suspected that if and when Z made love to his wife, he would have been adolescent in his demands, fitting into what Hagan described as the 'wham, bam, thank you mam' brigade. For where Z was concerned there'd be no feeling his way onto the track, either as a racing driver or as amorous husband – no foreplay. Whether in sexual or social intercourse, more so when it came to the latest gossip, Mr. Zbierski drove straight for the finishing flag.

'That bloddy vicar,' said Z taking the first chicane at full throttle, 'I told him a thing or two the other day. He wouldn't baptize my Carol's baby. Said he couldn't do it 'cos she weren't married. Anyway he's going to now 'cos I scared the shit out of him when I told him what my Carol had said about him, touching her nieces up on the bum.'

'What you saying now Z?' piped up another regular, Bob Myers, the husband of choir member Mrs. Myers who also owned the Dry-Cleaning business in the High Street.

'I told him he'd best not pussy-fock with me,' said Z 'He ain't going to tell me how to live, not if he was touching up young girls. I told him that we all 'spected him and that Stacey, and how the word'll get around if he starts smart-assing good girls like my Carol.'

*'For Christ's sake!'* said the landlord despairingly. 'You can't start libeling people like that. If the vicar had got anything to do with the Stacey business, they'd have taken him away by now. You'd best give the chap a chance, Granville.' The 'Granville' was said to try and placate him - nobody feeling entirely safe with Z on the loose. 'Anyway, they say he's been very helpful to Stacey's parents. You should know that, since

you live only a couple of doors away from them, don't you?'

'Aye, and there's another reason for that too!' Here Z looked straight at Di, although he stayed canny enough not to mention the missing girl's sister by name. The weasel's eyes gleamed bright as mercury.

This was Di's second jolt of the evening. For what on earth might Z be implying? Certainly the churchwarden had noticed how Philippa had started coming to church of late, and of how absurdly solicitous the vicar had been whenever she appeared. Why did Wilkes treat Philippa any differently from the other parishioners who arrived for worship? Besides, it was the churchwardens' job to make people feel welcome, not for the vicar to come striding down from the vestry just to greet one favoured parishioner.

'You never give up, do you Z?' said Myers. 'You're always on the lookout for trouble somewhere. You never give anyone a fair crack, do you?'

'I speak as I zee', replied the Pole. 'Trouble is most folks around 'ere walk about with 'der eyes shut.'

Although Z made him cringe – 'This Zbierski is *the pits!*' – Di had told himself often enough, 'He really doesn't seem to miss a trick.' But knowing that the last thing Hagan intended at that moment was to be drawn in by Z, he stayed quiet.

'What does *thou* reckon then Di?' came the question that he had no wish to answer.

'I reckon it's getting near to Christmas,' answered Di, 'and that we should give everyone a break. I come here for a quiet drink not to hold an inquisition. You should be careful, Zbierski, if you go muckraking the way you do, you'll get done for libel one day. You can't foul-mouth people without evidence.'

Di's strength of feeling may have given the impression that as the vicar's churchwarden he was displaying a show of loyalty. As it happened, to show feigned loyalty might be no bad thing. In fact Di was reacting not just to the possibility that Z could have been right about Philippa, but because he'd been stung by the Pole's earlier insinuation about him and Frances Wilkes.

Nor wishing to show how shaken he was, Di drained his glass and got up to leave followed by Snap. Sometimes he wondered how much more he could take by being a local at The Magpie. Yet as he said goodnight, he had to admit that Zbierski was a hell of an observant fellow. Uncouth for sure, but one hell of a natural amateur detective nonetheless!

'What's more,' he thought as he pulled up the collar of his coat, 'thanks to Z and the rest of them, the pub was an excellent place for keeping the memory of Stacey Witcombe alive, and for maybe learning more about the vicar!'

Nor, after he left, was he to hear the words of Zbierski who, tapping his nose, said in a hoarse whisper, 'zat Di, he knows more than he's letting on. You'll zee!' he said, then jabbing his finger at the landlord.

# Chapter 13

Not ten minutes' walk from The Magpie, Katy Wilkes had been working at the Staff of Life for nearly a year now and to where, being the best excitement that Ketborough could offer, the local youth flocked in droves. Originally a building of dark Midland brick, the place had been completely refurbished by a national Lottery winner and his wife, whose further ambitions were to convert the pub into a nightclub.

With its Christmas lights, and live music thumping out most nights the place was jammed solid. Strobes whisked back and forth inside and, with this being that time of year, many extra lights had been added to the outside. Little or none of this goodwill spirit of course rubbed off on the surrounding middle-class neighbourhood.

Originally she'd patronized The Staff for getting a slice of whatever action might be on offer. After her earlier work as a part-time dishwasher but now turned eighteen, she'd been offered the better job working behind the bar. More to the point her good looks and intelligent manner were wasted behind the scenes.

Smoking a few joints of hash whilst at boarding school had led to her immediate expulsion and transfer to the local Independent Girls' High School. What at the time had induced mild apoplexy for her parents had in the eyes of her more recent associates been seen as pretty much *normal*. Besides consigned as she was to living in the boredom of her parents' vicarage, the rebel felt if anything further provoked than reformed. So like other disaffected youth, The Staff drew Katy as a moth to flame, with the taking of a spliff or two being perfectly normal.

Along with everything else Katy had been badly affected by the abduction and, what was now commonly assumed to be, the murder of Stacey Witcombe. More especially she hated the response of her parents to the tragedy. Her mother seemed at sixes and sevens of late, while her vicar father just seemed to be switched off. For given that what had happened to Stacey might have happened to *her* - both were around the same age, living in the same town and out and about at the same time, he seemed anaesthetized from it all!

Small wonder, then, that Kate needed the rowdiness of The Staff to help her forget.

'What'll it be?' she asked, grinning at Pete, the boyfriend whom she'd been out with for a few months, as though as yet it hadn't become serious.

'Fussy navel, darlin'!' he replied, testing her knowledge of the drinkers' slang which had become a special feature of the Staff.

'Coming up!' she said, presenting the peach schnapps in a trice.

'Nice one!' he grinned.

Pete's mate Joey asked for a 'Bountiful', which momentarily threw Katy but Sandra, the other barmaid, whispered in her ear that it was a Malibu and Cointreau. This too was presented promptly. The Staff specialized in an assortment of drinks patented as much by trial and error, as by any specific drinking knowledge. There was the 'Tequila Slammer,' tequila and ginger ale to be 'slammed and swallowed'; 'Singapore Sling' consisting of gin and soda water; an Irish whisky and limejuice came to be known as a 'Cement Mixer,' and inevitably there was the 'Orgasm' consisting of vodka, Tia Maria and milk.

*'You'll go far!'* said Joey with the condescending repartee allowed in pub banter. 'Do you reckon you'll stick this job then, Kate?'

'I don't know, the money's reasonable – when you guys tip, that is. But I doubt if I'll stick it for that long. There's got to be better things in life if you go looking for them.'

'You could become a vicar now, with all those women doing the business,' coaxed Pete, knowing how the remark would get an instant reaction.

*'Piss off, creep!'* Talk of church was one of the few subjects to bring out the worst in Katy.

But Katy did want to go places. Canny enough not to divulge a reason why she might only be staying at the Staff for a short time, she and Dominic had recently received a windfall from the estate of their great aunt Maude, whom Dominic and his mother had been to see over the weekend of Stacey's disappearance. In her eighties Aunt Maude had died suddenly, leaving Uncle Josh to fend on his own, while bequeathing a sum of £10,000 each to her great nephew and niece.

Despite sparing no expense in providing for their education, Christopher and Frances had always been careful not to spoil their children, even though they could have given them substantial sums from their own respective inheritances. Money already invested in trusts for them could not be redeemed before they were thirty. So with this unexpected windfall arriving and without strings, Kate and her brother felt flush. Dominic, having passed his driving test wanted to buy a good second-hand car with the proceeds, as well as setting aside some cash to off-set his 'uni' debts.

Katy didn't want to blow her money on a car. For one thing her new boyfriend had a gorgeous dark blue Lotus Elise, a little gem with awesome acceleration that had attracted her to him in the first place. 'Much better looking if the truth were told,' she once giggled to some of her friends. However wishing to have ready access to her great aunt's bequest, she deposited the cash in her local building society.

'Yep, a girl like you could do a lot better than working here,' added Pete. 'You could get into fashion or marketing. Or even a priestess in drag! In fact, nothing to stop you becoming a high-class hooker!' he said winking at Joey.

There was no denying that despite the two-edged compliment, Katy was beginning to become a real 'looker.' She'd started to take pride in her appearance without undue vanity. Tall and well proportioned, she had also shed a few kilos – due as much as anything to all her other worries. With her blue eyes and dark hair and auburn tints, along with a dress sense that was invariably simple but attractive, she was an asset in any pub.

'Hey, *do you mind?*' said Katy affronted. 'I'm not sure what I'll be doing but it won't be *that!* I may even want to get ahead in my education, although these days you can never be sure of what lies out there even after getting a degree.'

'My very point,' said Pete. 'Education's a waste of time. There's loads of them poofters doing it just because they can't think of nowt better. My brother's got some fancy degree in surveying, and as of yet he'd only got a load of credit card debts. I heard of someone else with a PhD or some such crap, and he's out of work as well.'

But Kate knew that his reasoning short-circuited in some way. For living in an age where young people without *any* qualifications could end up bigger losers still, didn't seem to surface on his radar.

'Anyway, I still haven't worked out what you actually *do,*' she said. 'You pose around in that flash car and make out you've got business interests like marketing sportswear, but you're pretty vague about it.'

Something about Pete McCoy didn't stack up. If he wasn't actually well off he certainly appeared to be, which by today's standards amounted to much the same thing. Drive a fancy car, wear snazzy threads and people look up to you because you're flash. A smooth operator could always find ways and means to wheel and deal in telephone number sums of credit.

Theirs was an arrangement replicated the world over, only liking each other in the way that ambitious people, young or old, do so - trading off only what the other has to offer. Short in stature with irregular features, and skin damaged by scars either from childhood chickenpox or acne, she didn't find him physically attractive. But it was his image that made her feel better about herself, while she with her long dark hair and tall good looks became an extension of his ego.

'So what *do* you do exactly?' pressed Katy.

Pretending to have been distracted, his reply as always stayed evasive: 'You'll find out if you stick around with me.' Downing his drink and sandwiching a £20 note between his and Joey's glasses for a refill, he said. 'You and Sandra take one out of there.'

'*Ta, ever so!*' replied Kate mockingly.

'Well, he's not nicking mobiles, you can be sure of that,' sniggered Sandra into Katy's ear.

With time for further chatter being interrupted by a flood of new drinkers arriving, Katy and Sandra went into a mad spin taking orders.

'Catch you later, Kate!' called Pete, grabbing his drink.

'Sure thing!' she shouted back over her shoulder.

*A Candle For Lucifer*

Pete did indeed catch Katy later, suggesting to her after the pub closed that they go to a friend's party. At this stage she was still casually responsible about returning home around midnight. But for some reason with Christmas coming and the way it was at home, she was in her light-headed mood – what she sometimes called her *'Sod it'* syndrome.

Perhaps by staying out late she could wind her parents up for once, get a real 'rise' out of them so as to make them 'mad' – find out whether they cared or not. Of course she knew her mother would be upset, although her father was *something else!* Nothing seemed to change him. Anyway if she stayed out seriously late, she might goad one or both of them into a semblance of anger for once. Test out whether her old man cared in the slightest.

They left for the party around midnight, Joey traveling separately and Katy going with Pete. They drove to the neighbouring town of Kidcharington, about twenty-five miles away. Pete seemed to know the route well, and about as many minutes later they pulled up at an insignificant Victorian terraced house in a quiet street

Slightly drunk from too many peach schnapps plied upon her by patrons in the Christmas spirit, Katy followed Pete upstairs where she was surprised to see a group of a dozen or so men and women, about half black and half white. The air was thick with the sweet smell of marijuana, the party clearly well lubricated by a couple of whisky bottles and carafes of wine also doing the rounds.

'Hi, *man!* Join the fun!' said a large friendly West Indian, who like the others was sitting cross-legged in a circle. He shifted across to allow Katy to join them. Emblazoned on his black T-shirt was a huge fluorescent message 'Increase the Peace!'

'Hi, *woman*, don't mind if I do!' she replied imitating his deep accent and prompting a whoop of merriment from the other.

'Man, I'm going to like you,' he chortled. 'I'm Clive and these here are my mates.' But before he could introduce them, Clive seemed to return to the comatose state from which she'd momentarily stirred him. Nor were others in the group too much bothered with any exchange of formalities.

'We're just here having a little pre-Christmas celebration,' said a male voice beyond the group deep in shadow. His accent was distinctively plummy and upper class.

'Excellent, if Pete brought you here, then you're in good company.'

'Only the best come here,' sounded a female accent that might have come from the same private school from which Katy had been expelled. 'We're all one big happy family!' Her fruity voice was slightly slurred.

It would have reassured her to hear a snigger but the reference to Pete and his family seemed primed and joyless. Katy sensed that her boyfriend wasn't far away but that he too was out of her field of vision.

'Light up for Christmas!' said another disembodied voice.

She felt comfortable enough with the joints of hash doing the rounds. Cannabis posed less of a threat to her than her recent daily intake of some twenty cigarettes, and which had started to impair her abilities in the swimming pool. Wary too of that lethal derivative of hashish known as 'skunk,' she was consoled that the reefer doing the rounds was of the good old-fashioned Afghan variety, washed down harmlessly it seemed with red wine. Yet although this wasn't one of those psychedelic 'jungle' sessions she'd heard about, the group – to the accompaniment of some old Joan Armatrading tracks – seemed focused on getting seriously stoned.

Despite the creeping stupor now overcoming her, she saw

that Pete's pal Joey had joined the circle opposite her, and where in the dull greenish light she noticed a facial disfigurement, which she'd not seen before. Somehow the ghoulish glow drew attention to a series of quilt-mark stitches, removed after what must have been plastic surgery around his nose. She knew that ulcerated nostrils or a split septum meant something. But now she was partying with the rest and swaying to the music, while getting high with slugs of wine and a regular supply of good quality weed.

Pete then appeared somewhere from out of the darkness. 'Hi, how you doing Kate?' he asked.

'I don't know. I'm freaking out. I suppose I'd better get back. What time is it?'

'Hey, stay cool. The night's young.' If by sometime after one a.m. he meant 'young' then he spoke the truth.

'Anyway Kate, mustn't let our standards drop, *must we?* Don't you remember me?' Although the same female fruity voice she'd heard earlier remained in shadow it sounded familiar. With no name given, Kate guessed it was one of the two other spliff taking schoolgirls, who'd also been expelled at the same time as she had been.

'Musshant let our standards slip!' got repeated as the plum accent mulched from quince conserve to mushy jam.

As the apparent host of this old girls' reunion, Pete approached her once more: 'Hey Kate try this, why don't you?' He handed her what was no more than a ballpoint pen stuck into a plastic water bottle secured at the top with tinfoil and an elastic band. An unseen hand held the pipe, with another hand flicking a lighter at the base of the bottle. She had almost taken a deep suck on the pipe before asking, 'what is it?'

'Just try it. You'll love it.'

'Hey, man, what are you trying to force on me?'

'I'm not trying to force anything, babe. *Just try it!* You said yourself that smoking a drug is a whole lot better than injecting it. Treat it just like the hash. Lie back and take a long deep drag, this is what the party's for. The other stuff's just to loosen up with.'

The sod-it stupor was now well in control. Partly from weariness and partly because she didn't want to be seen as a moral bitch, holding out against what the others were doing – spacing out and taking flight on a quiet, friendly trip – Katy took the pipe. She breathed deeply just as you're supposed to do with the hash. Instantly the bitter gunmetal taste made her want to retch, and where only through a supreme effort did she not do so.

Yet no sooner had the nausea passed, an altogether different sensation kicked in. Suddenly a craving for the vile taste made her snatch the bottle back for another hit. The obliging lighter flickered once more. If this was lift-off, then man, all the other stuff was shit. This was 'something else.' 'Whoo-hoo,' she found herself shrieking and tripping as though in some weird and wonderful land of UFOs. Lights popped in her head and she was riding as though at immense speed through the stars. This was *'magic'* to use an out-moded schoolgirl expression. Suddenly she loved everyone about her in that dark, mysterious group of weird and wonderful revelers. Cackling without knowing it, there was nothing she wouldn't do for them. *Boy*, she'd never felt so alive or, for that matter, so happy!

As though on cue the music, which had included Celine Dion singing *'All by myself'*, kicked in with a harsh reggae beat so as to transport Katy into a high-flying diva. For a few sublime moments she was in heaven, ruling from space while wielding a fiery sceptre over all those whom she despised on earth, her teachers; so many of her peers; all those pathetic devotees who attended church. More than ever now she despised that bastard father of hers, who treated everyone else as though *he* was *their* superior. Well, she was in charge now - untouchable, ruling from on high in her raging chariot.

Yet from her celestial heights and perhaps no more than two minutes later, clouds billowed behind her eyelids and sickly vapors started to choke her. As her heavenly craft crashed back to earth to return her into the fetid atmosphere of that upstairs den, Katy went from euphoria to dysphoria.

'*God, what's happening?*' she whimpered. 'Somebody, please help me.' '*Quick!*' said a voice behind her identifiable as Pete's. 'Give her another blast.' The first pipe sucked dry was replaced with another, placed in the fist of her right hand. The flame appeared once more.

'Breathe deep on it, Kate. Feel good again. Forget all your worries.'

The need to do so was overwhelming. The crash from heaven had been straight into a swamp of slime-green monsters. She craved lift-off once more to restore her to her celestial domain.

Again she sucked deeply. Rushing oblivion returned within seconds.

'Oh, G-*o-o-o-o-o-o-o-o-d!*' she yelled as though reaching a climax. With the second rush feeling sweeter than the first, it was like some orgasmic catharsis now engulfed her. As though lifted up on a whole sea of dopamines her entire body longed to surrender itself from the virginity of which she felt so ashamed.

Transported into their charmed circle and with the drug offering its own libation, it felt like her new friends understood. Unasked the drug was violating her and if that's what the drug demanded, so be it. She'd give anything to stay in the temporary ecstasy of where she now found herself.

But no sooner was she lifted up than she was flung back into a vortex of vile creatures and terrifying depression. Only by gulping on the pipe, if not gagging on it, could she find renewed euphoria. For to return to earth was not just to re-enter a place of dark images, but where now the terrifying sounds of mechanized thunder rolled over her or more precisely *across* her. Inches from her brain like some giant theme park ride out of control, the hideous cacophony roared to and fro. Crashing into her and crushing her self-esteem, the one time cool-headed girl felt mangled into a rag doll drenched in sweat. The drug wasn't so much toying with her, as playing with her very life.

This time the bottle of wine was passed to her. 'Take a long deep drink sweetheart,' encouraged the beguiling voice of her boyfriend.

*Sweetheart* be damned! God, what sort of friend was he?' She questioned herself amidst the swirl and the haze. *'Take me home!'* she gasped.

'OK, honey, right away,' said Pete.

He and Joey had more or less to carry her downstairs. The dark-haired beauty who had been there to grace Pete's Lotus now lay sprawled, a drugged and human derelict. The journey back to the vicarage was mercifully quick. During it, Kate heard herself thinking, 'I want my mummy!'

When she did let herself indoors, Frances was indeed standing on the landing demanding to know where in God's name had she been, and what in heaven's name had she been up to? Although her father hadn't so much as ventured onto the landing to see what all the fuss was about, Dominic was standing there as well silently echoing his mother's questions. Too oblivious to register anything more, Katy crashed out on the stairs.

With it being after three in the morning and having castigated her daughter for being so wholly inconsiderate, mother and son managed to get her into bed. Fast asleep even as they pulled the covers over her, Frances still chose to interpret Katy's legless arrival as due to some misplaced binge; one of those pre-Christmas parties where she'd clearly drunk way too much. Although Dominic was in no doubt about his sister, she his mother still couldn't see it or chose not to see it. Not to comprehend that having been seduced with pipes of marijuana and red wine, her daughter had been raped by 'crack' cocaine adulterated with some other substance.

Katy deteriorated badly over the next few days. With the Michaelmas term all but completed, Frances decided to keep her off from school. 'Having caught some virus or other' was said as a cover-up for a 'Class A' drug addict, ready to sell her soul.

Over Christmas the Wilkes household became an ensuing nightmare. While Dominic remained supportive of his mother, Christopher retreated increasingly into his own world, busying himself with final preparations for their parish pilgrimage. Despite their daughter being so unwell, her father's indifference tormented Frances with the remorseless persistence of water torture. In another way his detachment was just as terrifying as what was happening to the girl. The so-called charming prince whom she thought she'd married and who, perhaps better than anyone, could restore their daughter to life, was himself a man imprisoned in ice.

Katy began staying in bed at all hours, occasionally soundly asleep, sometimes sweating profusely, then hallucinating and weeping inconsolably. Throughout Christmas she suffered from a permanent head cold, coughing and with eyes streaming, although this had nothing to do with the winter virus doing the rounds. Her hair had become lifeless, while her skin had taken on the sallow and goose-pimply complexion of a chicken. Worse still was the rash of ugly sores that had broken out on her face and neck. The girl with the once English rose complexion, rendering make-up superfluous, appeared to be decomposing before the eyes of her mortified mother and brother.

Whilst occasional glimpses of her old self might surface briefly, typically her mood descended into one of irritability and withdrawal. Getting up in the late afternoon either to eat nothing for supper or to eat ravenously, she would leave home on the pretext of going to work although sometimes not returning until the small hours.

The New Year was ushered in with Kate not coming home at all, leaving Frances paralyzed with fear and suspicion. By Christmas, Dominic knew that his sister was a complete druggie, leaving him to explain to his mother what he knew about the behavior of addicts - of how they could lie brazenly while stealing from their nearest and dearest.

'Just so long as they can get their fix, they don't care who they hurt,' he'd told her.

Despite her daughter's protestations that she was only going to the pub either to work or socialize, Frances had checked with the landlord of The Staff of Life to discover that Katy had packed in her job some weeks earlier. Upon making this discovery and with Dominic having returned to Cambridge, his mother's loneliness was compounded.

Knowing that Di Hagan was in poor health due to his angina, she didn't wish to trouble him further. Yet the reality was that he alone was her one trustworthy friend.

Of course he was willing, even desperate, to help in any way he could. After all, Frances was married not just to a murder suspect but also to one who, through his total indifference towards Katy, was every bit the 'weirdo' that Nick Crooks and other patrons at The Magpie adjudged him to be.

What had failed to raise alarm bells in Frances' mind sooner was the fact that Katy appeared to be in no need of money, a point raised by Di.

'Theft is the giveaway warning to a family that one of their number is doing drugs,' he told her. 'Have you noticed sums of money going from your purse? Or has your husband suggested that he may be losing money?'

'As far as I know nothing's gone missing and *he's* made no mention of any theft. Mind you, most of the time he keeps his study locked, so she'd have had a problem getting cash from him, even if she wanted to.'

'Do your children receive any allowances?' asked Di.

'We help Dom with his university, of course, and give Katy £5 a week,' said Frances. Suddenly her hand went to her mouth. *'Oh God!* I've just remembered. An aunt of mine died recently and she left both Kate and Dom a sum of £10,000 each.'

'She won't have had to steal with a sum like that, at least not to start with,' answered Di. 'I have a nasty feeling that you'll find that fund sadly depleted. Frances, you'd do well to check out her account immediately.'

With Kate having gone out that evening on one of his typical pretexts, Frances hated having to rummage through her daughter's clothing and personal effects. But she was desperate to check out her Building Society account, which lying carelessly among some clothes in a drawer of her chest of drawers, wasn't hard to find. One glance told her all she needed to know: From the balance of £10,000 deposited five weeks ago, a sum of over £3,000 had already been withdrawn.

After her first introduction to the drug, Katy was quick to discover that 'crack' cocaine was far from cheap. Of course the introductory offer had come free of charge, courtesy of a boyfriend whose line of work was now self-evident. The two 'freebies' she'd been given were but a trifling down payment made for her future enslavement to him as her supplier.

In her more level moments she totted up what her new habit was costing, and although she'd give anything to sustain the half-marathons that she had embarked upon earlier - of getting stoned on six-hourly trips - she knew this was unsustainable. Marathons were of course best since that way you could stay pitched on a 'high' for when eventually the crack did run out, withdrawal was made bearable by the use of barbiturates and the mind-numbing dysfunction that followed.

Sustaining her habit in the fast track necessitated Katy finding other ways and means to supplement her dwindling resources. She raised this question with Pete's companion Joey.

'Fixers and hookers need bread,' he responded, stating the obvious. On account of his being blitzed most of the time, Joey tended to speak in drug-illiterate aphorisms, as though replaying a tape. 'There's no such thing as a free buzz,' was another of his junkie one-liners, along with stupid phrases like, 'Trade for aid' and 'No dope, no hope!'

By then Katy realized that the crude surgery done to Joey's nose resulted from his being a 'snorter' By inhaling a line of coke through a straw or a tightly rolled banknote inserted into one or both nostrils, the addict could fast-track the hit. Yet it was also a sure way for destroying the nasal blood vessels thereby causing the septum to split. She also discovered that snorting the drug as opposed to smoking or 'freebasing' it was done as a cost-saving exercise; only the more well off being able to smoke the drug as a vapor.

As Pete's assistant, it was clear that Joey had been able to fund his habit, at least as a snorter. Nor had she realized earlier that as Pete's pimp, so to speak, he'd been recruited to test out venues like the Staff of Life. For it had been courtesy of Joey that she'd been brought to Pete's attention several months earlier.

'So how can you get the dope?' she asked him in one of his more lucid moments.

'Ask the man!' was his guarded reply.

With both of them hooked into 'the Man', Pete had no reason not to offer helpful suggestions, as to how his customers could more easily stomp up the 'readies.'

'So you want to know how to make enough dough to keep tripping?' he asked her.

'I *have* to!' she replied.

'I told you before. You could go on the game. In the right place you could trade and score and still make a decent profit. I could get you introductions.'

She felt repelled by the matter-of-fact indifference shown her by Pete and his sidekick. Having introduced her to one of the most lethal narcotics on the drugs' circuit, they didn't do remorse. Why should they? For by now despite being aware of her complete revulsion for him, she also recognized her enslavement to a creep who held the key to keep her in golden lights and paradise.

The options were becoming stark. For despite the balance from her building society keeping her going for a while, some residual respect for her late great aunt made her hate having to hemorrhage her legacy in such a way. Only crime or prostitution looked feasible for sustaining a habit that could run up a bill of between £800 and £1,000 a week. Although Kate was now willing to surrender all the moral niceties of her Christian upbringing, the prospect of selling herself professionally was truly to jump in at the deep end, with unknown consequences.

'If you don't fancy going on the game,' said the ever-accommodating Pete, 'then you could go into crime. I know an area of soft crime that's a cinch, where you can make good money and not get caught.'

'Such as?' she asked.

'I'll tell you when you need to know.' Nothing was given away before time, advice being transacted with the same precision to how the grains of dope got weighed out.

Nor could she get over the way this *character* spoke of her welfare with the detachment of someone leading a lamb to the slaughter. Having no feelings for her he was impervious as to how she might feel about herself. She who threatened to self-destruct was being aided and abetted by a nonentity of a human being, who gave not a damn how she or his other clients committed suicide. All that mattered was how long she'd take to do it, even as she kept pressing the readies into his hand and massaging his ego. It was like having the attentions of a euthanasia specialist, to whom one remained of value up until the last post-dated cheque.

Obligingly he later made a further offer, 'There is another way,' he said, slyly peering at her through his cigarette smoke. 'At least it would pay for your habit for a while.'

Without having to ask, Katy knew the deal from the leer in his proposal. 'Better the devil you know . . .' was perhaps the only consoling logic for the arrangement now struck. Nor from the sideways glance could she negotiate, having had no practice at knowing her 'worth'. In her desperation, the promise to keep her fixed up for the first week may have seemed generous but, of course, for the first week she was virgin property and worth more.

New negotiations would shortly become necessary.

## Chapter 14

'I'm sorry to trouble you, but can I speak to Christopher?' asked the extremely attractive young woman with shoulder-length blonde hair. 'He did say that I could call anytime if I felt it might be necessary'.

It was a rare frosty morning in late January when Frances went to answer the doorbell. Still struggling in her role as the dutiful vicar's wife, Christopher had just returned from what, by all accounts, had been a very successful pilgrimage. He certainly looked in good rude health, even as he resumed life back in his study.

For a moment her spirits surged, making her want to burst into tears and throw her arms around her new visitor, to say something like: 'oh, thank God. You're *alive*! You've returned home at last'!

Dressed in a fawn overcoat with a brown headscarf, her breath floated mist-like in the crisp air. For had not the frost flushed her cheeks to heighten her good looks, she could so easily have been *her*. There was the same slightly classic Botticelli face, the same smiling eyes – hazel, if she remembered correctly – and the same trusting expression. Only the cut of her ash blonde hair from seven months ago had altered slightly from when she'd last seen Stacey.

But then it all came flooding back; of how she'd seen the visitor a number of times in church, with Christopher showering his attention upon her. The young woman was Stacey's older sister.

'Er, yes . . . excuse me. Of course! Do come in. He's at home and you say that you don't need an appointment to see him?' He'd tutored her well when it came to stalling tactics to deter unexpected and sometimes unwanted visitors at the vicarage.

'He did say to call anytime, but I'm sorry if it's inconvenient. I know he's only just returned from the parish pilgrimage.'

Frances presumed rightly that *this* particular visitor would be more than welcome day or night.

'Just hang on for a moment will you,' Frances replied. 'I'll see how he's fixed up.'

'Christopher!' - she had decided to drop the 'darling' bit once and for all, 'Philippa Witcombe has called to ask if she can see you.'

Immersed in one of his software programmes where he was hurrying to finalize bits and pieces for February's magazine, he might well in other circumstances have claimed to be too busy. But at the mention of his caller's name, he spun round and jumped up with enthusiasm. 'Yes, that's fine darling, please show her in.'

'Please come through,' she called across to Philippa who was standing in the hall. With so much else on her mind, Frances couldn't disguise the brittle edge to her tone.

'*Philippa!*' cried Christopher, greeting her with the rare enthusiasm he reserved for special guests. Extending his arms, he directed her to an upholstered chair. 'Good to see you! How are you?' he beamed. 'You look cold. Are you warm enough? How about a cup of tea or coffee?'

'No, I'm fine thank you,' replied Philippa, allowing him

to take her coat.

Declining any need for a drink at least excused Frances from playing out any further charade as the vicarage skivvy. For no sooner had she shut the study door than she closed her eyes, leaning against the wall close to breaking point. I can't believe how the man who's a total recluse towards his own family is transformed in the presence of a good-looking female! She reflected with the after-thought: More so, one who appears to be in need of his help.

In this place supposedly called home, she'd just admitted a delectable female into the company of her husband to engage in what clearly was to be an intimate conversation, the like of which she'd never shared for as long as she could remember. Nor had he shown either woman the courtesy of formally introducing them.

*'This is madness!'* she hissed under her breath. 'Here we have Christopher glowing with health and vitality after his pilgrimage while we, the children and I, are hitting the skids. Then an unknown woman, at least unknown to me apart from having seen her in church, gets welcomed into our house like a long lost friend while we, his family, are abandoned like derelicts.'

Moving away from the study door she continued her lament, a lament now erupting into cold fury: 'Fair enough this woman has only recently lost her sister. But *who* in God's name is this man I've been married to for the past twenty-five years? While we're all falling apart, he's the picture of health after gadding around the Holy Land.'

Moving back into the kitchen she sat down. 'Why can't others see that he's an out and out Jekyll and Hyde?' She spoke her convictions in an audible whisper: 'He gets no pleasure being at home whatsoever, yet uses us for posturing as the happily married vicar and family man. Just *what* is going on?'

She'd long come to terms with her husband's love/hate behaviour towards the opposite sex, where he'd use his charm even when she knew how he detested certain women. 'But now, this seeing Philippa is something else,' she muttered darkly. 'For despite all the unresolved questions that linger about him having been the last person to have seen Stacey alive, it's her *sister* who of all people, for God's sake, now rolls up to ask for his advice.'

Philippa's wish to meet Christopher might have been interpreted as a reassuring sign. Instead it left his wife with a yet greater sense of foreboding.

From the manicured and self-possessed woman that Frances had always tried to be, further worries especially over Katy now left the mother facing her own disfigurements: Of skin taking on an ashen-gray look, a jaw that had started to knot visibly while the bags under her eyes betrayed how her insomnia had turned chronic. Everything hung like a fog around her, even the absurd hope that Stacey might yet materialize by coming to the vicarage door. Just like that! Perhaps it had been through clinging to this hope that she'd been shelving the unthinkable!

Meanwhile back in the study, Philippa was pouring out her heart. 'I'm really worried. It looks like dad's going to lose his job. He's fifty-eight and stands no chance of finding any new job, at least not in the semi-skilled work he's doing. It looks like he's going to be laid off around Easter.'

'So, what would you like to do Pippa?' Having heard her parents call her by the more intimate name he presumed to do the same. It was a small test to see whether such familiarity drew them closer together.

Appearing not to mind, she continued: 'Well, I can't or shouldn't go on living at home. Rosamund's nearly ten months now and soon she'll be all over the place. Mum's in a dreadful way, still not knowing about Stacey and that. I've got to get some independence. It's only fair for all of us.'

'By the same token,' said Christopher, 'maybe your family still needs you living at home. It must help take their minds off Stacey, don't you feel?'

'You're *unbelievable!*' It was his inner voice that was chortling. 'How do you manage to do it? . . .to look and sound so sincere?'

'Well, in a way, yes. But we all need some space and have to try and pick up the pieces. What's more, because I look so much like Stacey, I know there are times when I'm just a painful reminder.'

'Well, I'm prepared to honour my promise,' Christopher smiled and looked altogether composed as he extended his hands towards her. 'I'm sure I can help you find a flat, and am more than willing to help you pay your way.'

'You're incredibly kind, Christopher!' said the woman whose eyes, brimming gratitude, reminded him so painfully of her deceased sister.

*'You are indeed!'* mocked the voice.

'How can I thank you enough?'

'I want to help, that's all,' he replied, sensing that same expression of self-effacement that he'd seen in the mirror so soon after losing Stacey.

True to his word, a fortnight later he'd found Philippa a one-bedroom private flat, agreeing to pay the rent for the first six months, while reviewing their arrangement at some later stage. As well as being in near proximity to her parents, the flat was ideal for herself and the baby. For the time being she would receive a job seekers' allowance, with a view to finding other work. It was only through lack of confidence that Philippa couldn't find a job with better remuneration.

Mr. and Mrs. Witcombe were especially grateful to the vicar for being of such practical help in their hour of need.

For his part the vicar was content to know that he'd always be welcome at Philippa's house, should he ever choose to call in for a cup of tea . . .

'Is it convenient to come and see you?' Frances had phoned her friend.

'Of course! Come on right over. The kettle's going on *now*. You know you're welcome anytime.'

Despite Di's poor health, with so much happening it was as though he'd been given a new lease of life. Nor 'despite that blasted Zbierski already knowing more than was good for him' could he deny a growing affection for Frances. In fact there was a part of him that no longer cared what Z may or may not have seen.

She too had grown indifferent to any rumour mills churning out gossip. If anything a new bravado of 'Let them talk!' was by way of a reaction to having lived for so long in her husband's shadow.

With a wordless understanding being forged between them, the common thread of their thoughts was that Christopher Wilkes was their main problem. Obviously he was clinically sick, whilst on the surface remaining well enough to stay in work. But knowing that it was his unpredictable hidden side that could pose a threat, Di sought to do nothing to imperil her safety. For his part of late, he'd done his best to placate Christopher, even hinting at a thawing of relations between them. 'Let him suppose that if he has any accusers left, then I'm no longer one of them,' he told himself.

Arriving at his front door, she was greeted by Snap effusive as ever. On this occasion the collie was relegated to the kitchen without ceremony and Sleuth, perhaps the feline soul of discretion was nowhere to be seen.

'Timed to perfection!' said Di. 'The tea's just made. I've

calculated that it takes you eleven minutes to walk here from the vicarage. You're fitter than me by nearly four minutes. It takes me just under fifteen to cover the same distance.'

For one who'd always prided himself on his general fitness, the calculation was disturbing. Having angina was like never being able to get out of third gear.

'It's got to the stage where I can't stand being at home with him around,' said Frances. 'The tension's getting unbearable, if not for him then most definitely for me.'

Her face flushed from the exertion of walking on an unusually wintry day, made her appear healthier than she was. Truth to tell she was close to burnout. Cradling her hands around her mug of tea, she continued, 'Di, I've got to speak to you about Katy. You may have guessed already, since I've been denying what must be obvious to others.' She paused imperceptibly and then blurted out. 'Katy's a *junkie*, she's on crack cocaine!'

Di's expression and the slight nodding of his head told her that he suspected as much. She choked as she then told him, 'I've been over to The Staff of Life and spoken to several people who've told me that her boyfriend, somebody called Pete McCoy is a drug dealer.'

The disclosure made her break down completely. Going across to the sofa and putting her mug to one side, he held her tightly. The crumpled figure affected him with alternating waves of anger and compassion. Even as he did so, he shuddered at this new disclosure. He was ninety eight percent certain of Wilkes guilt; he knew of the drugs scene at The Staff; he even knew of the dealer called Pete McCoy who'd been a criminal delinquent when he had still been in the Force. But now having his suspicions confirmed about the beautiful Katy, and who'd shown such a zest for life was almost too hard to bear. *God*, how he'd love to deal personally with the 'Petes' of this world! Such parasites on society were worse than vermin, who in his more despairing moments Di would have willingly exterminated.

'Frances, I didn't know how to tell you myself,' said Di, struggling with his emotions. 'I had my fears over Katy. Before she started at that pub, she was such an outward going person, very positive and in a word *healthy*. But it was obvious from what you were telling me that after her eighteenth birthday, she'd started – pardon the phrase – 'of going to pot.'

'But it's *crack cocaine* – not the harmless stuff!' she moaned into the proffered handkerchief. 'It's wrecking everything - her last year at school, her career prospects, of getting married and having children. She could *die!*'

If she'd been naïve before, he could see she was under no illusions now as to the effects of what a Class 'A' drug might lead to. Notwithstanding the Stacey tragedy, here was a family crisis on the edge of a full-blown apocalypse. A vicar who in all probability had committed murder, then turning on his wife who was losing control of a daughter through drugs, and whose other son was being sent crazy by everybody else.

'Frances!' said Di, taking her face in his hands and forcing her to look at him. 'You're going to have to take control, and you need to do so pretty damn quick. You don't need any convincing by me that life at the vicarage of All Saints, Ketborough is, unless you're careful, going into meltdown. I think that by now,' he continued, 'you and I now know each other well enough to trust each other implicitly. Am I right?'

She nodded, trying to hold his gaze through red-rimmed eyes.

'Put simply, you need a game plan in terms of sorting your priorities. Priority one is *Katy!* Are we agreed?'

Another nod.

'Priority two is your sanity and I'm sorry to have to say it, but your *safety* as well. Agreed?'

There was a less emphatic nod this time.

'I say *your* safety, because we both know our thoughts about Christopher. I'm not saying that he *is* to blame over Stacey's disappearance and, in one respect, it's very important that you go on treating him as innocent! But we have to admit that the conditions under which she disappeared are inexplicable and frightening, more so given that he had a photograph of her. Whatever he said about the photo, there must have been *something* going on between the girl and your husband. It may have been a harmless infatuation and nothing more, so you don't have to suspect him outright.'

He had no wish to elaborate further over his suspicions. The church chest certainly raised questions, more so given those missing items once stored there like the altar cloth and sash cord. But nothing was proved. Nor was it right to tell her about the mileage on her husband's Volvo. For on the Wednesday before Stacey's disappearance Christopher had happened to tell Di that his car was being serviced and MOT'd.

This detail of the car's MOT had allowed him to make his own check. Knowing the garage proprietor where Wilkes had taken his car – Di and the proprietor had been at school together – Di had, in the strictest confidence, been given a sneak glimpse of the mileage on the copy-certificate. Between the test-date less than a week before, and when he'd made his later reading outside the church, it transpired that nearly five hundred miles had been added. There had been no clear reason for the vicar to have traveled any significant distance between the Thursday (indeed the churchwarden and vicar had spent the morning together meeting with the diocesan architect) and the following Tuesday. This meant that on a conservative estimate, some four hundred unaccounted-for miles had been driven over a period that included a busy bank holiday weekend of church services.

'Returning to the game plan then, what about Katy?'

'Well, the school knows,' Frances replied. 'Having had her off sick for the best part of a month, I've had to come clean with the Head.'

'And the police?' asked Hagan.

'I haven't spoken to them.' Visibly cringing at the prospect of the vicarage coming under siege from an army of DEA storm troopers tearing the place apart, she expressed her fears accordingly.

'It won't be like that at all,' he reassured her. 'But it's crucial that you contact them and straightaway. Forget all your moral inhibitions. Crack cocaine is lethal and the fellows who are peddling the stuff around Ketborough need sorting immediately.' And taking her hands once more, he urged: 'Frances, I'm deadly serious. We can call the police before you go home, if you'd prefer. If nothing else they need to be given the full picture about what's going on at the Staff of Life.'

'But what about Katy?' she whispered.

'She's the priority, remember!' His craggy features tried to smile. 'You told me that you took Katy to see the doctor. Clearly your GP didn't get it right, although to be fair you took her probably in the early stages of addiction. From thereon you've been trying to treat her on your own. Believe me, what you did was far from untypical! You're not the first mother whose gut reaction is to downplay the problem. But you've said yourself that Kate's a junkie' – he used the word for effect. 'She's got to be assessed and given therapy. And even if she relapses, which sadly can happen all too easily, the drug's counseling services will at least be monitoring her.'

'*Right!*' Desperation was making her resolute.

'Do you want to look at Priority Number 2 at the

*A Candle For Lucifer*

moment, or can that wait? It's to do with *your* recovery but that hinges to no small extent, you'll agree, on Katy getting back to normal?'

'Katy first and last!' Her new resolved allowed them to put their game plan into action by contacting the police.

But with so much else going on, Frances completely forgot to tell Di of the visit made by Philippa to see Christopher.

*Andrew de Berry*

# PART TWO

*Andrew de Berry*

# Chapter 15

It was at short notice that Canon Wilkes had been asked to give an Easter address at the cathedral. The reason for this was on account of the cathedral's dean having been taken suddenly ill. Normally Christopher would have ensured his presence at All Saints, but the invite was both a privilege and an opportunity to oblige the bishop.

This change of plan required leaving All Saints in the hands of his own guest preacher Fr Ben Carter. It being Easter the church would be full, more so, with a number from Ben's church of St Hilda's, having been invited. The idea was to celebrate an Easter communion, given that the two parishes had enjoyed a shared pilgrimage earlier that year.

So in the absence of Christopher, Area Dean Fr Ben Carter was left in sole charge. Various older members of All Saints, including Di Hagan, were pleased with this development given that Ben Carter reminded them of Christopher's predecessor, the thoroughly likeable and easy going Revd Jack Bishop.

Although he was due to retire as churchwarden, Di had been on hand to welcome Ben. His formal retirement date wasn't until May when his replacement would be sworn in at the Archdeacon's Visitation; she being an elderly spinster and near-idolatrous devotee of Christopher.

He was retiring for two reasons. The one expressed publicly was on the grounds of his angina. The second reason he kept to himself. For how could he tell the PCC that, if he had his way, he'd like to arrest the vicar and throw him into the nearest prison? More alarming perhaps was that had he expressed his main reason for leaving, not a few would have been very angry. For despite the unresolved mystery of Stacey, the vicar's enhanced reputation was now looking unassailable.

'He's such a wonderful man, so hard working and conscientious.' 'He'll go out of his way to help you.' 'Nothing seems to be too much trouble for him.' These were typical of some of plaudits that so sickened Di Hagan.

For most of them the Stacey affair, although very sad, was now history. Not only had Wilkes been recently promoted to Canon, he'd been allowed the further privilege of preaching at the Cathedral. So God help anyone, even a retired detective who might imply Canon Wilkes to be someone other than who he was, namely a conscientious and holy man of God!

So it was in that context that Ben Carter arrived at All Saints, ready both to celebrate Easter communion as well as preach. With the big west door swung open for the occasion, a choir made up from the two churches each bedecked in their respective robes of red and blue was led up the aisle. A crucifer who preceded them was carrying an Easter cross, pierced with clusters of primroses, while behind the choir there followed two acolytes and three Readers, with Ben all resplendent in a richly embroidered chasuble completing the procession. Decorated with daffodils and lilies the church offered an impressive setting for the festal hymn of 'Jesus lives!' As the choirs filled the sanctuary stalls, so Ben was ushered to his by one of the acolytes.

A Reader started the service off, followed by the Epistle and Gospel, each being read by a member of the congregation and between which the choir sang the 'gradual' anthem 'Rejoice!' After that Fr Ben ascended the pulpit to give what the congregation assumed would be a short, none-too-challenging sermon, typical of the ones preached by Canon Wilkes.

Only as he was standing in the pulpit did Ben elect to discard the sermon he'd prepared for the occasion, even though he began conventionally enough:

*'It is true! The Lord is risen!'* He was quoting the traditional verse to which the refrain goes: 'He is risen indeed, Hallelujah!' He then cited familiar words from St Mark Chapter 16, where the angel at the empty tomb declares: 'Fear nothing, he has been raised; he is not here. Look, there is the place where they laid him . . .'

Pausing, Ben then asked: 'Friends, tell me what do you *honestly* believe? . . . about Easter, I mean? What does it mean to you personally?' Resting his elbows on the pulpit top, he put his question assuming a pose of sweet reason, even sweeping a disconcertingly open smile across the faces in the crowded church. Turning to the red and blue robed choirs behind him, he asked. 'That was a marvelous anthem you have just sung. *But do you believe it?* Do you believe that Jesus rose from the dead as a resurrected body or, as many now believe, that Jesus rose only in a spiritual way? What's your understanding of this?'

Nor could *he* quite believe it himself. Believe, that is, that he'd discarded his sermon notes entirely only to ad-lib:

'The trouble with the Christian church,' he went on, 'is that we try and maintain a set of beliefs that science and a skeptical world no longer find credible. I mean, there isn't one person present in church today surely, who believes that the world is flat. Yet we might claim to believe things in the Bible that might seem just as contradictory, as though we belonged to some flat-earth brigade!

'Now don't get me wrong, I'm not saying that we shouldn't believe in a way that we find personally helpful or even reassuring. But if we don't dare to *test out* our beliefs, or ask awkward questions and express doubts then we lose credibility, do we not? The danger is that we become a laughing stock, or worse still our faith inspires neither us nor anybody else!

'Let me take you a few steps on. I wonder how many of you really believe in Jesus being the Son of God. You may be adamant that you do. After all, it's easy to recite what we're obliged to say in the Creed. But what do *you* mean when you repeat that Jesus is *"the only begotten Son of God . . . who rose again and ascended into heaven"*?

'To speak of Jesus being the Son of God, because he was born of a virgin and raised from the dead in bodily form surely has to strain credibility. Credibility is stretched further, surely, if we lay aside what physical logic seems to tell us in favour of mystical hearsay. So can we, hand on heart, say, "Yes, we believe Jesus was born of a virgin, and yes, He is God in human form"!

'And here's another thing! Was Jesus actually divine? For around three hundred years or so it didn't seem to much matter whether he was or he wasn't. And although St Paul tried to make the word 'Christ' mean something that it did not, the truth is that a 'Christ' or a 'messiah' as originally understood meant no more than 'an anointed leader'. It had nothing to do with being divine! Indeed not until 325 AD when the emperor Constantine decided to convert to Christianity, did the issue of Jesus' divinity even come up for discussion!

'And guess what! How did they come to a decision? Wait

for it, *by private ballot.* They formed a council at Nicea to vote on it! Just imagine it! You hold a PCC meeting or a deanery synod, and by a show of hands you vote on whether or not Jesus was the Son of God! "Hands up, all those in favour of Jesus being God" sort of idea! Talk about man playing God, and not the other way about!'

It seemed now that Ben had lost all fear: 'Or when we speak of Jesus going down to hell, as we do when we recite the Apostles' creed and where "on the third day he rose again," what on earth are you and I saying? Nowhere in the gospels does it say anything about Him going down to hell. So whose idea was the "harrowing of hell," as it's sometimes called, for it to get adopted by the Church and then inserted into our creeds?

'Or when we declare that Jesus "was incarnate of the Virgin Mary by the Holy Ghost," how many of us, hand on heart, *believe* what you're saying? Jesus made no mention of his mother being a virgin! Nor does St Paul, as it happens. For it wasn't until centuries later that such a belief got inserted into our creed! And going back to the Bible, there is no evidence to suggest that the term "virgin", as *we* understand it, is what was originally written.

'Forgive me if I'm starting to bore you here' said Ben who by this stage felt it was no bad thing to try and humour his congregation. In fact a number of them weren't so much bored as outraged, even as they were forced to listen on:

'Did you know that when the gospel writers Matthew and Luke speak of the virgin birth, they mistranslated a verse from Isaiah 7,14? Not only do scholars agree that Isaiah chapter seven had nothing to do with the birth of Jesus, the Hebrew word used there for virgin referred only to a young married woman, *not* to someone who'd never had sex! And the explanation for Matthew and Luke's mistake is perfectly simple. They only spoke Greek! Not knowing a word of

Hebrew, the language of the Old Testament, they just plain mistranslated the word to mean what we understand virgin to mean today! More tellingly, in St Mark's gospel and because the writer was a Hebrew-speaking Jew *he* makes no mention of Mary being the virgin mother, and the reason's obvious. He knew his Hebrew!'

'*Stone the crows!*' muttered Di under his breath. Rumour had it that Ben Carter could be outspoken, but he'd never imagined anything like *this!* Surely Fr Ben had said quite enough already for the ecclesiastical powers-that-be to burn him at the stake! The media would love to get hold of this. Even as he preached maybe a correspondent from the local press was already preparing an article. No question, Fr Ben's address was inflammatory. Di Hagan could see it now:

"AREA DEAN DOESN'T BELIEVE ANY OF IT!" How's that for an opening paragraph? *"A packed congregation at All Saints, Ketborough and place of worship for missing schoolgirl Stacey Witcombe, heard on Easter Sunday how much of the Easter story is an invention! The guest preacher, Area Dean Revd Ben Carter told how none of the Easter story is properly credible. Jesus was not born of a virgin! He never rose in physical form from the tomb, and He never went down into hell,"* etc, etc!"

How might it go on? Di felt gripped to hear more.

With Ben in full flight, he knew that it was his love for Angela that had liberated him, given him a new love for God as well!

'How much can we actually believe any of this?' he asked. 'Do we really want to go through the motions of saying something, simply repeating our creeds while neither believing nor understanding them? If we have a faith it has to be *credible*, intelligible not only to *us* but to those on the *outside looking in!* Take the story of Jesus' resurrection. Nobody seems to know *who* saw *what!* According to the Bible He seems to have left earth from *two completely different locations* and at *two completely different times!*

'Just for a few further moments allow me to press you further.' And here Ben made a joke as though to curry favour with his captive audience, suggesting to them that he might get away with saying things at All Saints which he couldn't say back in St Hilda's!

'How many of you believe in a devil or hell, or for that matter in heaven? After all, surely, the whole purpose of Easter is to reassure us that Jesus overcame death so as to send the devil packing. It's what as believers we commonly refer to as being *saved!* But if you don't believe in some sort of sulphurous pit presided over by little men with pitchforks, then what's the *point* of Easter? What are we being saved from? And if we don't take any of this seriously, why worry about it at all?

'So what *do* you or I believe? When my time and yours comes, are we going to say to St Peter or whoever's in charge of the keys on that day, "Excuse me, but I have a right to be here! My credentials are such that I'm a paid-up member of the Church of England. This is what I've always said in church so I've secured my place in heaven! *Stand to one side my man and let me in!*"'

An embarrassed titter in the church was rudely interrupted by a helpless guffaw from Di Hagan, choking into his handkerchief while trying to disguise it as a sneeze. *Dear Lord,* thought Di, the man's telling it how I've always thought it!

Ben didn't appear to be distracted by the choked laugh coming from the congregation: 'Somehow I don't think so,' he continued. 'Or perhaps more to the point, I cannot presume to claim any copper-bottom guarantee that because I believe in the Easter story, I have some God-given right to enter Paradise, a first-class ticket so to speak entitling me to live there for eternity. Not only do those ideas fail to make much sense, they segregate me into a group I don't necessarily feel at home with. How many of us have heard it said that if Heaven is made up only of Christians, then please send me to the other place?'

The pin-dropping silence suggested a congregation more stunned than uplifted.

*'Dear God, this is magnificent!'* Half-sobbing with mirth into a now saturated handkerchief, Di was close to shaking uncontrollably. He was almost of a mind to jump up and cast his own caution to the wind, by shouting something like: You tell 'em, Ben. Sock it to the lot of them! But then his more serious ex-police officer's voice chose to caution: The man's crazy; he's got to be out to commit professional suicide. Just why is he being so outspoken?

It was an eye-opener for Di to observe the expressions of others in the congregation. A few of the infrequent attendees seemed to be riveted and agog at what they were hearing, while the old regulars, chins on chests, gave every impression of wishing to vanish under their pews. In fact even those visiting from St Hilda's seemed to be shuffling uneasily to suggest that on this occasion their vicar was, even for him, overdoing things somewhat.

With a further coughing attack of smothered laughter, Di then pulled himself together. He did this by returning to his observations, while noticing one or two people in particular. First he saw Frances, who had clearly decided to stay at All Saints, rather than go through the pretence of supporting Christopher at the cathedral. Alongside her was her son Dominic home for the Easter vacation, and doubtless there to give his mother some support. She looked marginally less drawn, perhaps in the knowledge that Katy was now getting some suitable treatment.

Di sensed that the sermon was bound to appeal to the non-churchgoing Dom but nor was his mother, he felt, rejecting what was being said. Indeed with Ben preaching with such passion, she looked absorbed. Such a change surely from her husband whose sermons dealt only in platitudes.

Scanning the congregation further, he recognized someone else whom he couldn't place straightaway. Although he'd seen the face somewhere before, something about it had changed. The woman in question was clearly hanging on the preacher's every word. Years of investigative work had given him a good memory for faces, and soon it came back to him. The difference was that there was no black serge or wimple, and where there had been hair, once hidden, it now shimmered in shoulder-length gold curls. Surely it was Sister Angelique, whom he'd once met at a deanery supper. Wearing a terracotta blouse with blue cheesecloth skirt, she looked the picture of unrestrained joy.

Although Ben longed to say more, he'd said quite enough! He longed to rail against the whole decadent system of the church; to sound off over the sheer mind-boggling indifference of certain bishops he'd known; to lampoon the pathetic dishonesty of those clergy who played endless word-games; to denounce the Church for its odious chauvinism against women priests, or whatever.

*Love* wanted to propel Ben up and away – to reach a yet higher stratosphere of outspokenness. But the psychic energy now pulling him back to earth felt palpable, warning him that he'd said way too much already. For in that highly charged atmosphere it seemed that even the lilies on the altar, erect with static, were expressing their outrage.

'And so in conclusion, how can Easter be truly real within the Christian Church? How can we speak of Christ's power over death?' And here Ben's expression still impassioned became one also of great tenderness: 'the answer, dear friends, is I believe simple. It's not how we live now but how we *choose* to live now! Anyone can *say,* "Christ is risen!" but if we look as solemn as crows at a funeral then we betray not only ourselves, but our Lord as well. I believe that we've got the whole thing the wrong way round. We in the churches don't ask enough questions, preferring only to say things by rote. But if we ask no questions, we become either bigots or robots. It has been said that the bigot may think he's dead right, but that's just it - he's just as dead as though he were wrong.

'Easter is about being true to ourselves! It's about trusting God more than being shackled to creeds and dogmas. *Easter's all about Life!* It begins when we shake off the fears and taboos of the past. Those fears and taboos may have given us some guidance in former years. But the Christian journey is a journey forward and up. It is a journey of *risk* and *faith* – those two words meaning the same thing. For those who dare not advance, who dare ask no questions or who daren't make any mistakes, Easter becomes an irrelevance! For the heart of Easter is to flip all creeds and dogmas on their backs. It's way too *big* for crusty old dogmas and formulas. Easter can only be lived! Words alone don't do it!'

Di noticed how as the preacher drew to a close he did so with a look towards Angela of such gentle love.

'The message of Easter is primarily for the man or woman who dares to be him or herself, who sees only *LOVE* – the supreme expression of God in us – as the only standard by which to live! For me, Easter only becomes meaningful when we learn the true meaning of love!'

It was then that he paused to say, 'Thanks be to God,' before descending the pulpit to announce the hymn, 'Thine be the Glory.'

'*Wow!*' said Dominic, blowing a gust of air up at his thinning hair and looking at his mum. '*That was something else!*'

'Sure was!' whispered Frances, smiling her assent. She was now persuaded that in Ben she had another much-needed friend; and one, would you believe, who was actually a vicar within the church!

In another corner of the church, Angela rejoiced that she'd found in her most exalted dreams a friend and lover – more than she could ever have prayed for. For from her tomb of St Juliana's, she too knew what Easter was all about!

Along with a small group of parishioners Di thanked Fr Ben for officiating at their service and for his inspiring sermon. A few others did the same passing such comments as, 'Really made me think, vicar!' and 'What you said has needed to be said for years!'

But most said their goodbyes stiffly and if they wished him a Happy Easter at all, did so with that funereal sombreness he'd just lampooned. Clearly for most of them 'Happy Easters!' would be shelved until next year, when the whole rigmarole would be re-enacted once more, preferably listening to the unchallenging tones so cherished by the likes of Canon Wilkes.

Ben's controversial sermon was best forgotten even before people had reached the door, although from the warmth of her greeting Frances told him that she'd been one who had been challenged.

Outside the church, Angela met up with Ben and they walked towards his car. Slipping her arm into his and helping him to carry his robes, a gesture not unnoticed by those who make it their habit to notice such things, she told him: 'Darling, you were *awesome*!'

'Well I suddenly got past caring, sweetheart,' he replied. 'I had no intention of saying all that stuff, and maybe I didn't get it all right. But something reared up inside me as soon as I got to All Saints, forcing me to abandon what I'd planned on preaching. Because although the church looked beautiful and bright, it struck me as being like a sepulcher! For whilst everything's so immaculate at All Saints, it's *cold as ice!* In fact I actually physically shivered as I went into the vestry, even though the heating was on. For me, the atmosphere just felt weird throughout the church. And today, *Easter of all days!* But it wasn't until I climbed into the pulpit that I decided to let rip!'

He stopped to face her, 'I've got to answer to *Him*, so that if He ever says, "Benjamin, Why did you go on speaking all that gibberish whenever you came to preach, boring me and everyone else to tears and in fact making me mad with your half-truths?" I can at least refer Him to today, when I spoke from the heart!

'Besides,' he went on, fumbling for his car keys, 'I really don't care any more. The Church of England has reached its Rubicon. Whether pandering to the evangelicals and their precious dogmas on the one hand or trying not to offend anyone on the other, it ends up standing for nothing!'

Angela chuckled, 'You know something?'

'What's that?' he said, sliding into the driver's seat alongside her.

'Our love has taken us on to a new shore. It's as though we're no longer landlocked within the old Establishment; no longer at sea like so many who seem to use religion like it's a boat without paddles. I just want to burst our laughing,' declared Angela. 'I'm not trying to suggest that we've arrived. But isn't this what Christianity should be all about? Dispensing with the system and all its archaic practices, and not having to say and do things to please some remote hierarchy! We can speak from the heart!'

'We're free to be ourselves,' Ben agreed.

'By the way', said Angela laughing. 'Did you know that the original meaning of the word hierarchy means being *ruled by bishops?'*

Marveling at where she came up with these little gems, he drove the short distance from All Saints to her flat.

'Yep, we've both been sent a signal about as loud as you can get, that we're no longer out to please Reverend Mother or His Holiness the Lord Bishop,' she continued. 'Our God-substitutes can go to hell! We used to be more anxious about pleasing *them,* than ever we were about finding out what *God* wanted. It's so subtle when you're *in* the system, yet so obvious when you step back *out* of it and break the fetters!'

It thrilled him to hear the former nun getting so animated. 'I love it when you talk *dirty* about the church!' he teased. It was as though her infidelity to mother Church made their affair all the more delectable. She too loved to be turned on by a daredevil area dean, who detested the system as much as she did.

'Anyway,' said Angela, 'I reckon that you gave God a real lift this morning. That churchwarden, the older fellow, did you notice him? He erupted at one point, trying to smother his delight with a coughing fit. He was lapping up your every word! If you ask me the angels and all the rest of them up there were creasing themselves as well. I bet they've not had an Easter like that for a long time. It was almost as though I could hear them cheering you on!'

'So it was *okay,* then?' he queried, as they reached their destination and he opened the car door.

'Don't be daft, sweetheart. Remember it's Easter . . . it was out of this world!'

'Race you to the bedroom!' he laughed.

Still dressed in his cassock, his last remark was clearly audible to an elderly couple passing by.

Running from the car, they collapsed in laughter as they climbed the stairs to their flat. Each had discovered their child's heart and both were hopelessly, hilariously in love.

## Chapter 16

Discreet enough not to make the vicarage their love nest, they stayed together most nights in the self-contained bed-sit that he'd secured for her from the Housing Trust. Living there rent-free, the arrangement was that she'd be on call two days a week while keeping a general eye on the place.

Over her final weeks in the convent, she'd given a lot of thought as to what she'd do on the outside. Even as a nun working with the homeless, she'd been amazed to discover how many people tried to make sense of their lives through other channels, or through what the Church would always disparagingly refer to as the 'occult.' It was this that in time would lead to Angela's interest in astrology. For the time being, however, just getting used to life on the outside was what pre-occupied her.

He loved the anticipation of returning to her flat for those clandestine meetings where, for two people hitherto sworn to a code of celibacy, every kiss, every embrace became pure elixir. He marveled too that someone who'd spent eight years in a convent could kiss like that, while she made him laugh by saying how on earth could a man of forty plus and 'of the cloth, what's more be such a raunchy lover!

Having as good as fled naked into the night, her

possessions were minimal. Apart from a few undergarments secreted from the convent, the only other object was that of an alarm clock, which as her most unwelcome companion she and Ben had laughingly disposed of with a hammer. Few, if any, knew where she was; not even her mother who, in sad surrender to God of an only daughter who would bear her no grandchildren, would have been more mortified still to know that Angela had now foresworn her vows. Although in time her father might be more amenable to her decision, she'd made no immediate plans for contacting her family.

On a vicar's stipend, Ben's generosity to others along with his penchant for good food and wine meant that they were both pretty strapped for cash.

Even so, they tried making the flat as comfortable as possible. Nonetheless with its hardwearing cord carpet, a pair of well-worn armchairs, blue Formica table, plus two upright chairs and a bed-settee, the general effect remained spartan. The kitchen too was supplied only with basic cooking utensils, cutlery and crockery. She'd managed to decorate the walls with some posters from Israel, with Ben providing a few other Israeli artifacts that included a Bedouin fleece rug and some dark blue Hebron glass. A vase with its golden string of decorative glass coiled up its stem held a display of daffodils that stood on the wooden mantel housing the electric fire. On the opposite wall, again thanks to Ben, she'd hung a framed print of Van Gogh's 'Sunflowers.'

Normally when he joined her he'd light up the room, so to speak. But upon his arrival later that Easter evening Ben's brow was furrowed, and he was uncharacteristically deep in thought. Setting down a coveted bottle of 1986 Chateau du Basque, he remarked: 'you know, sweetheart, that All Saints set-up really disturbs me! Since this morning, I've not been able to get it out of my mind.'

'Why's that, love?' she asked, basting the small beef joint

and potatoes of what would be a traditional 'roast and four veg', a meal she'd been accomplished at cooking during her teens. Despite Ben's own repertoire of dishes, she had insisted on reclaiming her culinary skills.

'Well, most of the people in that church struck me as being in a deep sleep. They reminded me of Orwell's *1984* – stupefied victims of the 'Thought Police' with everything going precisely to plan, as though they'd been conditioned in some way or were being watched on CCTV. I'm not criticizing them because they don't put on a good show or do things decently. Nor is it that they don't pay their parish quota or anything like that. Quite the opposite! With Canon Christopher in charge, they're *exemplary* in every department! But truth to tell they're *too* bloody exemplary; too perfect in fact!

'I watched the eyes of the people there,' he continued. 'The best way to describe it was like folk swimming under water with fish-dead eyes. Many of them had a vacant expression, and there was absolutely no *feeling* there! Acolytes or whoever, they all seemed to glide about while giving no eye contact. Apart from one or two obvious exceptions, most of the people in that church struck me as robotic and zombie-like. Although our choir at St Hilda's isn't anything special, at least they try putting some expression into their music. All Saints' choir seemed to be automated, not animated. In fact the difference between the two choirs struck me as quite startling.

'Maybe they're still traumatized over the loss of Stacey Witcombe,' he went on. 'But it was the lack of any expression that got to me. There seemed to be a presumption that the service would somehow run itself, a bit like a flawless Songs of Praise but without any of the feeling. I know that many churches, especially our cathedrals, can pride themselves on their performances, but the performance at All Saints had a particularly *nasty* feel to it.'

And then Ben added, 'Things happened on cue but on this occasion the puppeteer was absent.'

Having sensed the same thing, Angela wrapped it up in six words. 'It's the *control freak,* isn't it?'

'It has to be,' he agreed. Pausing for a moment he resumed, 'I get the feeling that in some way, consciously or otherwise, Christopher has sort of hypnotized them. He's certainly got them where he wants. Do you remember in the late seventies that merchant of death, the so-called Revd Jim Jones? Was it in Guyana or some place in South America? Having created a jungle community called Jonestown, he then got some 900 of his followers to swallow poison on his say-so! Parents, children – they all succumbed to their maniac of a leader's command to drink poisoned fruit juice.

'What's to say that if All Saints were transported into some rainforest in Latin America with Christopher as its pastor, he might just as easily create his own settlement of *Wilkestown!* I've been thinking about it all afternoon, Angela, and I honestly don't feel that I am exaggerating.'

It was from any sense of mirth that she wanted to giggle, but out of fear. Angela knew all too well about mind-control, of how the miniscule Mother Superior, tiny as she was, held St Juliana's in thrall. Hers was the power of a despot. Scarcely a glance was needed to reduce the sisters into groveling servitude. Weird, wasn't it, how in her case even the scrawniest of figures could induce such fear? With the greater advantage of his height and good looks, why couldn't Wilkes do the same?

'But as though to confirm my misgivings,' Ben went on, 'I had two phone calls this afternoon from two of the folk from All Saints, one being – guess who? – Christopher's wife, Frances, and the other from that decent chap Di Hagan who's due to retire as churchwarden.

'I'll tell you what Ange, they're both shit-scared for different reasons, but on account of the same man. Frances came close to admitting that she has no idea as to the man she's married to. If that isn't bad enough, she's got a daughter – wait for it,' he paused, 'up to her eyes in a coke habit, and for whom her father shows not the slightest degree of concern. And then I heard from Di Hagan. Having been in the CID at one time he would appear to know things about Christopher, which might just nail our Canon Wilkes to the disappearance of Stacey.'

Involuntarily putting her hand to her mouth and with the colour draining from her normally rosy cheeks, Angela could only say, 'You've got to be joking!'

Shaking his head glumly, Ben said, 'Hagan more than hinted he has reasons for suspecting Christopher, despite the police appearing to have discounted him as a suspect. My sense – more like a premonition – is that he's right. You know, ever since our pilgrimage I've had this feeling about Christopher. Despite being a withdrawn type, he has a knack for winning people over with his charm. Deep down my gut tells me that *he's seriously bad news!* I don't want to scare you but I believe that he *is* scary big-time. In fact just talking about him makes me feel cold.'

Angela felt *herself* go cold.

Ben continued, 'Di Hagan wants me to meet Christopher as soon as possible. I know tomorrow's Bank Holiday Monday, but I'll have to see him and reckon it would be no bad thing if you came with me. I'd value your support and besides you're probably the best person to help Frances. Putting it at its kindest, Christopher is clearly in need of help.'

She nodded. Despite hoping to have spent the bank holiday relaxing together, the forecast was for rain and nothing would deflect them from the urgent matter in hand.

Eating in glum apprehension, they couldn't enjoy their supper, grateful only for their respective strengths which made them that much stronger. The Chateau du Basque remained unopened. Nor could Easter night be spent together with Ben choosing to return to his vicarage to reflect more on the problem.

Both needed clear minds for the day ahead.

With the area dean returning to his vicarage later that night the phone rang with Christopher at the other end.

'Ben?' said the ever-urbane voice.

'Yes!'

'I'm phoning really to say thank you for taking this morning's service.'

After Ben's 'Not at all!' there followed a short pause.

'However, I have to say it seems as though you have upset quite a number of my parishioners.'

'Oh, how might that be?' asked Ben lightly.

'Well, you appear to have been saying such things as it doesn't matter what they believe about Easter, and that sort of thing.'

He found the piety behind other man's tone cringe making, as he replied, 'Well, quite the contrary in fact, Christopher. I told them how crucial it is to know *what* we believe, rather than just saying things that we don't understand or haven't properly thought about.'

There was a longer pause, as though Christopher didn't know what to say next, which he didn't.

'Well, I think it's a great shame when one brother, especially the Area Dean, comes along and upsets people's thinking.'

'Well that's just it,' interrupted Ben. 'Most of us are *not* thinking!'

Christopher then chose to pontificate: 'Well more to

the point surely was that we had an excellent opportunity this morning for strengthening the bonds between our two churches, and on Easter of all days isn't our task to declare the faith and to preach the good news? It's not *our* job to upset people, especially when Easter gives us an opportunity for welcoming outsiders.'

God, I really can't stand this man! Ben bit his tongue, before retorting: 'We've got a perfectly good precedent for upsetting people!'

Christopher's voice carried an echo of those other pious types who seemed to proliferate these days. It wasn't the Church of England that Ben had known and loved as a child. Secretly he damned this new breed saying more than once: 'These evangelicals and their equivalent can be *such a bloody pain!*'

'Anyway what are you wanting to say, Christopher?' he tried to stay civil: 'if you're phoning to thank me for helping you out this morning then I accept your thanks! And I trust that you had a worthwhile morning at the Cathedral.'

Given his obsession with good manners and the fact that little ever appeared to rattle him, the vicar of All Saints then did something wholly out of character. Where normally any discourtesy shown on the telephone was anathema to Christopher, it was he who then put down the phone without uttering another word.

Ben felt numb. Not only had Wilkes begun to sound all-pious and obnoxious, clearly someone from the All Saints' had 'snitched' on Ben at their Easter Eucharist. Had one of his own flock informed on him, he wondered. Nor was he to know that the two women who'd seen the area dean arm in arm with some strange woman had passed this further detail onto Christopher. But none of that much mattered. What spooked Ben far more was the way Christopher had just behaved on the phone.

*'Jesus!'* thought Ben. 'We've got a problem.'

Possibly by putting the phone down as he had just done, Christopher came as close as he'd ever done to identifying that 'the problem' was himself. There was no denying that the area dean was a man who enjoyed a natural rapport with many. Furthermore he had the courage to deviate from the safe, pre-packaged conformity into which *he* Christopher had moulded himself. Not only was Fr Ben prepared to be outspoken the canon had observed, perhaps even with a twinge of jealousy, the growing friendship between Ben and the nun Sister Angelique whilst on pilgrimage.

The wholeness – was it even holiness? So manifest in Ben's life highlighted everything that *he* was not and never would be. The contrast did appear to point to contradictions in him. But if thoughts of his being a counterfeit where he felt nothing and believed nothing surfaced for a second, Christopher's disguise remained his most formidable weapon. For even if behind the mask he caught a glimpse of the consummate operator who feigned both piety and false affection for those whom he despised, such glimpses were not to be dwelt upon.

For it was his lust to control others that felt good and real. Any other insights and the shutter of his mind would close with a snap - his being a pathological dread that any natural light might invade his preferred world of darkness. For Christopher's inner world remained as black as the interior of a camera, and it was his choice to keep it so.

'Mum, are you sure you don't want me to stay on for a bit?' he'd asked, ever considerate.

'Dom I'll be fine, don't you worry. You need the break,' she reassured him.

With Christopher having been invited to dine with the bishop, mother and son had had their lunch together on that

Easter Sunday. But now she insisted that he enjoy the brief backpacking holiday planned with two of his chess-playing friends, even if it meant his departure taking place after lunch and not returning until Thursday.

'If you had a mobile I could text you,' he teased.

'Stop fretting! As I told you I'll be fine.' Her reassurances came with difficulty, With Katy in her sheltered detox unit, her slow progress further hampered by an eating disorder, Dom was the only family she had. The prospect of spending that Easter evening and Easter Monday with Christopher filled her with foreboding.

The relationship between husband and wife had become non-existent. Sexually there'd never been intercourse to speak of. Socially it was the same. She would sit and iron in the kitchen, usually listening to the radio or watching the portable TV; he'd either be out or stay cooped up in his study. Along with its pine furniture and the cat spending many hours curled up in a fruit box, plus the steady ticking of the old station clock, Frances found the kitchen with its warm boiler the most comforting room in the vicarage. As for their well-furnished and richly decorated 'living room', it was given the absence of Dom and Kate more lifeless still.

In desperation, one or other of the estranged spouses might have coaxed something from the other. But beneath any wish to conduct a veneer of civility with Christopher lay the deeper truth that she was now *very* afraid of him.

More than anything it was his remoteness. For despite still cooking his meals, he would eat them with mere snippets of conversation being exchanged. Then wiping his mouth with his napkin, he would depart. Nor could he see how through the enactment of this ritual he replicated the exact characteristics of his late father back in Kenya. During meals Harold Wilkes too had repeatedly dabbed at himself with a napkin without scarcely uttering a word.

No offers were made to do a few household chores like clearing things away or stacking the dishwasher. Childhood memories of Kenyan servants attending to his every need remained entrenched, and given that his wife had acquired the services of a home help, it never occurred to him that by sharing in a few of the chores he might make himself more agreeable or home-loving. In his mind the home help and his wife operated with the sole purpose of serving *him*.

Having had things all his own way for so many years, Christopher couldn't see how the tyrannical father was busy reclaiming the soul of his son.

For Frances, it was like she'd been some outsize butterfly artificially restrained within its pupa. Only now through a set of circumstances – good as well as horrific was the pupa beginning to stir. More than anything, her stirrings came from the moral support given her by Di. Also that morning she had been amazed and excited by the extraordinary sermon preached by Fr Ben. Now beyond the darkness it was like a sunbeam had managed to pierce an exposed part of her retina.

There was little to stay up for on that Easter night, leaving her to retire early to read in bed, even before Christopher had put his phone call through to Benjamin Carter. Having then fallen asleep for around two hours, she was awoken by a series of scraping sounds coming from Christopher's bedroom. For some unaccountable reason the sounds suggested that he was moving the furniture about, almost certainly opening and shutting drawers. Hearing vocal sounds also, he seemed to be muttering to himself.

She then heard him go downstairs, at which point she couldn't be sure whether she dropped off to sleep again. But if she did so it was to be awoken by further sounds emanating from the kitchen. This time he seemed to be scraping something, as though the kitchen table was being moved or some domestic unit such as the fridge or cooker was being heaved about. There then followed a series of thumps, the sort of sounds she associated with the tenderizing meat in order to make schnitzels. It then sounded like he'd switched on the food mixer.

If the sounds weren't so incongruous, they might have been almost funny like some sort of party game like audible charades. Next and not so funny at all came the distinctive rasping noise of a knife being sharpened. Now Christopher was talking to himself, his voice getting louder, wholly oblivious it seemed to any distress he might be causing her. Finally there came the shattering of glass.

She lay there terrified! Had he been sharpening a knife to cut some cold meat in the fridge? Was he about to do mischief to himself, or to her, or to both of them? Did he have some sort of premonition – some awareness perhaps that whatever the game he was playing he was running out of time? Was someone pointing the finger of guilt at him over Stacey? One thing Frances knew for sure: She'd never experienced such deranged antics from him before. Perhaps he was intending suicide. They had an airing trestle suspended from the ceiling. By moving the kitchen table was he planning to slit his wrists and launch himself from the device? Her imagination was running away with her.

Nor had she any telephone in her room with which to make a hasty call to the police, or even to her trusted friend Di. She was in the guest bedroom. The upstairs phone remained in the master bedroom, the domain still occupied by the ranting 'master' downstairs. With the manic pantomime continuing downstairs she felt petrified and immobilized.

But she had to do something.

Maybe he intended taking her with him; abducting her in

some way What if he tried coming into her bedroom? Having shown no interest in her sexually, she assumed that it was unlikely for him to change now. But then again, he was acting in a way that was completely unfamiliar. Was he planning on entering her room to knife her, or even make an attempt at raping her before committing a double murder maybe?

Her line of defense was flimsy, futile even. But anything was better than nothing. In the event of there being a literal murder at the vicarage, her feeble gesture to use an upturned chair might hint at the semblance of a struggle. Creeping out of bed, she walked a sturdy upholstered Victorian prie-dieu, which she pulled up against the doorjamb while yanking it under the doorknob. Of course in resistance to the shoulder of a strong-minded man, let alone one as physically strong as Christopher, the chair presented a pitiful barricade. Yet even as it had once served the purpose of being a praying chair, it now became a desperate implement of prayer.

Whether Christopher was aroused by an echo of the sounds he'd been making earlier, that of some furniture being shifted in his wife's bedroom, it didn't seem long before he was coming upstairs, still talking to himself as well as making obscene laughing sounds. Then using the absurd singsong voice of a father playing peek-a-boo with his child, he came to her door, 'Frances, are you there-ere?'

Gently, he coaxed further. 'Yoo-hoo, can you hear me darling?'

Only occasionally had she seen her husband's countenance alter. Normally it could manufacture at will a ready twinkle in his eye that few might interpret as being near manic. But every so often she'd seen it; the twinkle morphing into a steely glint and the smile distorting into a twist of his mouth, where the lower lip could bare itself with bloodied fangs.

Like Little Red Riding Hood she could now see it. The wolf at her door!

Retreating to the far corner of the room near to the windows with their full-length curtains might provide temporary concealment. But it was pointless trying to hide. He'd find her in an instant. Nor with the sash windows designed to open no more than six inches, could she make her escape from the window.

He tried the door handle, teasing it open without effort. No more than a well-placed kick would put paid to the chair's feeble resistance. But for the moment he was seeking admission to her room like he was the soul of discretion - the considerate spouse under instructions to arouse her with an early morning cup of tea.

'Are you there-ere?' he repeated with a mocking sneer.

*'Go away!'* cried Frances. She sought to give an impression of being in control.

'I'm coming i-iin.'

She tried to think logically, when suddenly a voice of strength spoke to her from within. It was a voice that startled her even as she heard its power and authority. 'Do not hide!' commanded the voice. *Never show him that you're afraid!'*

Any moment the wolf might let out a piercing howl.

'I'd like to talk, darling,' he said.

Why he chose to use the singsong voice was a complete mystery.

'Please go away. We can talk in the morning.'

*'Don't be so polite!'* commanded the voice once more.

'But it's urgent, I need to talk,' he said pushing harder against the resisting door.

It was then that Frances surprised herself. She went on the offensive, came out from behind the curtains and spoke to him like a naughty child,

'Christopher Wilkes, go back to your bed immediately!

You've woken me up and it wouldn't surprise me if you haven't woken up half the neighbourhood. Goodness knows what you're playing at! Go back to your bedroom right *NOW!*'

She emphasized her order by going to the door and shutting it, even with his weight still against it

For a few moments she could hear him standing there, breathing heavily.

But then she could hardly believe it when, as though faced with a fiery brand, the wolf did as it was told, turning tail and slinking back to his bedroom. When he'd closed his door and she'd heard him getting into his own bed, everything became quiet leaving her to assume that he had fallen sleep.

In that nightmare episode the hitherto demure vicar's wife had transformed herself. Even as she marveled at that other unknown part of herself that had spoken so boldly, delivering her from God knew what, she shook violently. First thing in the morning she would leave the vicarage for good.

Wild horses would never bring her back under the same roof of the man who would shortly be her ex-husband.

Next morning there was no need for her to creep out of the house because Christopher had already driven off somewhere in his car. Briefly, she tried making sense of the disarray in the kitchen – of the table shifted across under the airer, and from where strands of washing line now hung. Why too had one of her large kitchen knives been thrust into the pine table where it remained embedded? The glass of the station clock had also been smashed, although remarkably the timepiece kept ticking. Coolly removing the knife and putting it back into the drawer, she heaved the table back into place. The dangling cord from the airer could stay where it was. Although none of it made sense she felt sufficiently in control not to flee the house, even managing to eat a bowl of cereal while downing a cup of tea.

Methodically she set about collecting a small suitcase of belongings, along with other essentials such as her savings book, bank and credit cards. She then left a note on the outside door for the home help telling her not to trouble herself that morning, or for the foreseeable future and that she'd settle up with her in due course. With their stray cat having disappeared, she left some dry biscuits outside while choosing to lock the cat-flap.

Writing a further note to Christopher, she told him that she was going away indefinitely. By way of emphasis she used a small kitchen knife with which to secure the note into the same crevice left in the kitchen table from the night before. Nor did she inform him that she would be contacting Dominic and Katy later that day, to let them know of her decision. Before leaving the house, she telephoned Di Hagan and Fr Benjamin Carter. Told by Di to go straight over she learned that Ben Carter was planning to call that morning as well.

Flinging her few things into her car, she drove directly to her friend's house.

Snap was relegated to the kitchen once more, although Sleuth was allowed to stay in Di's living room, presumably to offer some therapeutic aid to the deeply troubled visitor.

'Thank you Di,' she whispered, returning his tight hug as she stepped across the threshold. Still standing she regaled him with her nocturnal horrors, ending with: 'from what I saw of the kitchen this morning it looked like he was threatening suicide. At least instead of plunging a large carving knife either into himself, or me he'd rammed it into the kitchen table where it had been left. I got about two hours sleep last night.'

'Sit you down,' said Di. 'Have you had anything to eat?'

'Yes, I had some breakfast because unaccountably he'd driven off in his car before I woke up.'

He commended her for standing up to him, describing her courage as 'a sort of primordial spirit coming to your rescue and one which may well have saved your life.' As her story tumbled out Di could see that she was worn ragged. Yet she wasn't so exhausted not to notice how he too looked anything but well. There was a part of her that hated having to trouble him at all.

Holding her tea with one hand she stroked the cat with the other. Sleuth was already on Frances' lap purring vigorously whilst apparently sound asleep. Just then the doorbell rang and Di stood up to announce that that would be Fr Ben.

With Snap in full voice, Di found himself greeting not just Ben but the woman whom he saw in church only the previous day – Angela.

'Good morning, Di! Do you know Angela? Angela's become my close friend and companion. We met on pilgrimage and, as she knows Christopher, Ange will have her own insights.'

'Delighted, come on in,' said Di warmly. 'There have been further developments as I think you know. Frances has just arrived here after spending a terrifying night at the vicarage.'

Tail wagging; Snap went up to greet the two new arrivals before going off to chew on a bone.

Trauma and pain brought them together by way of hugs and tender embraces with Di then giving a summary of what Frances had told him.

'There's no way I can go back there,' she told them. 'In fact I've left a note for Christopher to say that I have no intention of returning . . . ' before adding the word *'Ever'* for emphasis. 'So although I want nothing more to do with him, I am concerned about what he might do, or what's he's doing right now for that matter. I shall be contacting Katy and Dominic to tell them what I have done. Dom's on a short walking holiday right now, and the last thing I want is for him to return to the vicarage only to find a father who's completely unhinged.'

Angela then asked Frances where she intended staying.

'To be honest, I haven't even thought about it yet,' she answered.

'There's no problem about you staying here,' said Di. 'The only problem, if one wants to call it that, is that word will get about and tongues will wag.'

It was more a case of placing no further demands on him that she replied, 'don't worry Di! I'll find somewhere.'

Looking at Ben, Angela said. 'I'm sure we can arrange some emergency accommodation at the hostel.

Ben nodded, 'No worries on that score!'

'Take that as definite then!' said Angela touching Frances' arm reassuringly.

Frances gave a wan smile of thanks.

'But what should we do about Christopher?' asked Ben. 'I knew something was seriously amiss last night when he phoned to say that I'd upset some of his parishioners with my sermon, and then refusing to hear what I might have to say he put the phone down on me without another word. Normally he'd *never* do that!'

'That was a tremendous sermon by the way,' said Di. 'I've never heard anything like it! Small wonder that the canon wouldn't have liked it. It gave us sleepy heads a real wake up call and not a moment too soon. In fact it made more sense to me than anything I've ever heard preached before.'

'Thank you,' said Ben. 'I had a feeling you might be

enjoying it – even that you wanted to laugh when you ended up coughing?'

Despite everything else, Di couldn't help smiling his agreement.

'Anyway I did have it in mind to go and see Christopher today,' continued Ben, 'maybe to see if I can get any idea of what's happening to him.'

'You must *know* what that is!' interjected Di, glancing at Frances and then at Angela before continuing, 'Christopher knows more about Stacey's abduction and what we must assume to be her death. Ben and I spoke yesterday and we both believe that he's living with some terrible secret and it's probably that which is sending him mad.'

Following a short silence it was then that Frances told them about Christopher's interest in Philippa, Stacey's sister.

'Unfortunately that piece of information has become common knowledge, certainly in the Magpie, courtesy of our friend Mr. Zbierski,' said Di. 'Christopher's obvious interest in Philippa was pretty apparent in church as well,' he added.

'*Good God!* I didn't know anything about *that!*' said Ben.

'Well, it appears,' continued Frances, 'that he's bought her a flat and meets with her quite regularly to see how she's faring. What's especially alarming about that is how Philippa looks almost identical to Stacey.'

'What on earth do her parents think about that?' gasped Angela.

'It seems that like so many others who think no evil about Christopher, they're just plain grateful,' answered Frances. 'The Witcombes are very trusting folk who can't get over how caring their vicar's been, whether in giving them his support over Stacey or more so, now that he's helped Philippa get her own place.'

'You'd better tell them about the photograph,' said

Frances to Di.

Di duly told Ben and Angela about the photograph of Stacey found some months back in the pocket of Christopher's cassock. In the circumstances Di still declined to tell them of his other hunches, relating to the oak coffer and of the vicar's unaccounted for mileage.

'I can't see how the photo gives him a leg to stand on,' confessed Frances.

'Well, he did offer you an explanation, however implausible,' replied Di, telling the others what Wilkes had said.

With that disclosure they fell silent for a few moments.

'I wonder where he's gone to,' mused Ben. 'I think that Ange and I should go and see if he's returned home, and tell him that we know about Frances' decision to leave. You don't think he's gone to pay Philippa a visit, do you?'

They checked out this worrying possibility by phoning Philippa straightaway.

'No,' Her tone sounding mystified Di told her not to worry: 'It's just that I need to speak to him somewhat urgently, so could you please contact me immediately if you see him.'

Having double-checked Di's number, she'd replied simply that she would.

Around midday, Ben and Angela left Di's house to call in at the vicarage, on the off chance that Christopher might have returned.

But had they known it, he was miles away.

## Chapter 17

Despite some build-up of holiday traffic, his drive to the Lake District was steady enough, the Bank Holiday forecast delivering what it had promised - gray cloud turning to rain. Despite it being a journey of anxiety with part of him wanting to forget everything about the girl, now he had to make sure.

So strong was his wish to forget that he'd have willingly sacrificed their sacred dream, for it was now that dream that so disturbed him! For no longer did she smile up at him in circumstances intimate and uninterrupted; no longer did she offer her neck in loving submission. Interlopers had begun to appear as though chaperoning her, leaving him powerless in knowing how to banish them. For in her shadow there they would be, dark presences like Officer 331 or Di Hagan or, worse still, Zbierski the Pole mouthing his obscenities. Sometimes Stacey's face might also contort - the smile changing into the expression of his long-suffering wife, as though even Frances had begun to see things differently.

Worse was to follow. The face of Stacey would then morph into that of his daughter! Through an ulcerating expression of sores, it was *Katy* who began leering at him through the eyes of Stacey. Had Stacey broken faith with him in some way?

That night had been the worst. For with his mind full of Easter images depicting Christ's resurrection, might the girl too through some supreme act of willpower have cheated death, - disinterring herself from her grave of bracken and nettles to call out for help? For one of the Bible's great Easter readings spoke of the graves disgorging their dead, and where in the grand finale of Christ's Passion all departed souls would along with the saints rise back to life.

What maybe if she had never died, or been blessed with an Easter resurrection in some way? Such nightmarish thoughts had led to his terrifying antics in the vicarage the night before, and where to restore his peace of mind, he'd got up early that morning to revisit the Grizedale Forest – the place that up until had seemed so effective as a place of concealment.

With the intermittent rain starting to fall more heavily, he arrived at the lay-by adjacent to Coniston Water. It was around lunchtime with a few other drivers forlornly eating in their misted-up cars. Having bought some sandwiches on the way and with a flask of coffee, he too sat there quietly eating and reflecting at the scene of the improvised grave. Then with his recent insomnia and the drive having exhausted him, he crashed out for over an hour. Upon awakening and with the rain cascading in windswept gusts, he saw that the lay-by was empty.

By pulling the car a foot or so closer to the dry-stone wall, and counting the whitewash markings painted along it every few yards, he knew the exact spot. Wasting no time and donning some waterproofs, he took out a length of rope, which although now reserved for towing purposes, had once done service as double nine millimeter climbing rope.

Tying the rope around the front axle of the Volvo, he abseiled over the wall with the agility of a man familiar with a skill learned from childhood. His descent took him some forty or fifty feet down the near-vertical edge of bracken and undergrowth, to where the ground flattened out and where, as he remembered, the corpse had come to rest.

Immediately the dull hum of flies and mosquitoes reassured him, although just to make sure he cleared the ferns and bracken with his feet. The joint effects of weathering and decomposition had ripped open the old linen covering, exposing what through the completion of larvae activity was no more than a skeleton. A rib cage and a head all but bereft of its flesh and hair exposed her skull. Despite giving an involuntary shudder, his nausea was overcome by the relief in knowing that the girl's remains lay where they had fallen.

There was no need to linger, so ensuring that the ferns and bracken were all restored back in place he prepared to leave. Above him on the road the traffic passed with the tired tedium of bank holiday motorists, welded to their seats along with car tyres hissing their frustration at the weather.

Unlike the rest of them, Patrolman Sgt Robert Dench was driving not in the comfort of his patrol car, which was in for an extensive service, but on a large BMW motorcycle. If nothing else, being on two wheels brought home to the sergeant that he was getting too 'soft' for his own good. Having once been a keen fell walker and rock scrambler, he'd always been an out-of-doors fellow, and where a few years back, he'd done a civilian survival course run by two retired members of the SAS. Over ten-days in his native Lake District during mid January, the course had taught him how to forage for berries, fish using an improvised line, and to sleep rough whilst adapting the most inclement of circumstances to his advantage.

Now with the landmark of his fortieth birthday pending and married with two teenage daughters, the outrider was giving serious thought to getting himself back into peak fitness once more. 'The last throw of the dice' was how he'd put it to a wife; sympathetic to her Bob's mild panic attack that life was passing him by.

Noticing the Volvo parked in the lay-by he thought no more about it, other than the fact that it was unoccupied. Mildly curious, Sgt Dench made an instinctive mental note of the car's registration. Having a photographic memory he did this as a matter of course. Test match scores, car registrations, mobile telephone numbers, he seemed to remember them all. Memorizing numbers had become a sort of obsession for him - not a particularly useful talent, although as a police officer it had occasionally proved useful.

Presuming that the car's occupant or occupants belonged to that group of mad dogs of Englishmen and women who go out in all weathers, he drove on. Sightseers exploring the Lake District even as the heavens opened were common enough. Anyway, being out of condition at that moment Dench felt cold, wet and disgruntled, knowing that spending a bank holiday in the family's snug home would have been preferable any day.

To Christopher making his steady hand-over-hand ascent on the rope tied to his car axle, this brief mental appraisal by the officer cruising past left the climber in blissful ignorance. With the patrolling officer gone, the climber appeared over the lip of the wall, deftly untying the rope and shedding his waterproofs. There being no further need to stay and with the bad weather persisting, he decided to return home.

Knowing that Stacey was 'safe' reassured him greatly.

Unaware that Frances had now left him, he had resolved to talk candidly with her upon his return, even mentally planning ways and means by which they might sort out their marriage. He could explain to her how he'd not been himself at all of late, what with Stacey and now Katy.

Driving home in the knowledge that the body remained undetected, and that the ramifications of Christ's death in Palestine bore no relevance to an unmarked grave in the lakes, Christopher felt a surge of confidence. In fact he felt more like his old self than he had done for months.

The rest of that Easter Monday became wretched for Di Hagan. He fretted about Frances who had gone with Angela to look at her new temporary accommodation. He had serious misgivings about not having contacted the police, or of drawing their attention to the missing items from the coffer. Nor had he told anyone either about the unaccounted-for car mileage or perhaps more crucially the photograph. Viewed separately each hunch was speculative, of course, but as an accumulation of details they had to be significant.

He knew that Frances had taken his advice to contact the police about Katy's drug problem and to report her lowlife of a boyfriend. But was there more he could have done? Had he been more proactive, Christopher might by now be in custody or at least be under constant surveillance. Nor was it just worries over Frances and daughter Katy. On top of all that he feared for Philippa and her young daughter Rosamund. For like her parents and sister, being trusting to the point of naivety might Philippa yet offer Christopher sanctuary in some way?

Challenges were presenting themselves for Di from all quarters. Ben's Easter address made him want to have a serious chat with the area dean about life and, more importantly, about life after death if not just *death* itself! For a man with progressive angina, he knew he was pushing it. Although the stress from eight years of widowhood had been controlled with medication, the concentration of all his other worries could act as a dangerous trigger, health-wise.

At around ten p.m Frances had phoned him to say that she was in her 'safe' house, an apt description given that at least Christopher would be denied any re-enactment of his antics from the night before. She also informed Di that she'd left a message at the Youth Hostel where Dominic would be staying, and that she'd spoken to Katy even though her daughter seemed uncomprehending. Having rejected her father long before, it seemed that any similar initiative taken by her mother now left Katy cold and unsympathetic.

Falling into a fitful sleep, it was to be his last night spent at home.

Around three thirty in the morning and the shooting pains in his chest told him that the Damoclean sword he'd always feared had now fallen.

Gripping his chest while grappling for his bedside phone he managed to dial for an ambulance, which thanks to their rapid response got him into Intensive Care in time to save his life. Sometime later he was informed that on the Richter scale of heart attacks, his had been a big one. But prompt action and some first-rate treatment in the A. & E. department had sufficiently revived him later that day to allow him to make two telephone calls.

His first concern was to ensure the welfare of his pets. His sprightly neighbours, having been awoken in the night by the ambulance, and holding a key to his house, had assured him that they would take care of Sleuth and Snap for as long as was necessary. He then telephoned Fr Ben and asked if he would let people like Frances know, not to worry her of course but just to keep her in the picture. Ben promised both to get in touch with Frances straightaway, and keep himself up to speed with Di's condition.

As the sole parishioner in whom she'd expressed her trust, a devastated Frances was allowed to make a brief visit the following day.

'Oh dear Lord, *Di!*' she tried putting on a brave face, 'What has happened?' Not so much a question, it was more a forlorn comment on their shared misfortune.

'I don't know, to be honest. Guess I must have overdone it of late.'

He knew how the experiences of the last nine months were the worst-case scenario for a man in his condition. Yet knowing how readily she heaped blame on herself, he had no wish to tell Frances as much.

'These past months won't have helped you at all,' she acknowledged.

'Well, the bad news, Fran, is that I've had a heart attack and not a tiddler either. But the good news is I'm in here and feeling much better!' Di mustered a smile. 'Besides I'm really glad you've called because we need to talk.'

'Another time, surely. You're not up to it now!'

Looking at her directly, Di replied, 'the truth is that there may not be *another* time or at least not *much* time. I'm a lot more "up to it" now than if the bell rings unexpectedly!'

For a moment, she chose not to understand the metaphor, even as he pressed her hand and smiled.

'Frances, you're going to have to be strong, stronger perhaps than you've ever been. You've got two children who need you desperately. They may be in their late teens but I would guess that Dominic is traumatized, not obviously like Katy, but in a serious way nonetheless. In fact I have a hunch that Katy will be all right but it's going to take considerable time. Both of your kids are going to need you, particularly in view of what might come to pass regarding Christopher.'

'You believe that he killed Stacey, don't you?' The question was stark, one of many that she'd begun to ask where answers, if made at all, were done so with short glances and gestures.

After a pause, Di said, 'My detective know-how as well as my instincts make me almost a hundred percent sure.' Again taking her hand, he went on: 'but what I may have found needn't worry you right now. You're not supposed to be the one to suspect your husband. That's a job for the police, and until they discover the body there's not a lot that they can do. They've interviewed Christopher twice, and clearly he never gave them anything to charge him with.

'But that isn't really what I want to talk to you about. I'm a bit of a man with hunches. The heart attack I had on Monday night means I can't possibly be the same again. I've not lived very responsibly for the past few years. Too much booze and tobacco and not enough exercise – all against the doctor's advice! I have to admit that since losing my wife Alice, there was a part of me that had given up.'

Catching his breath, he added, 'And then you appeared, notwithstanding your own troubles,' he smiled. 'You helped to restore my faith, when my own faith in humanity had started to lapse once more.' And here looking faintly embarrassed, he added: 'You're nearer to being the good soul that Alice was than anyone else I've come across.' And then with a quiet smile he whispered, *'Thank you!'*

*'Don't!'* whispered Frances in turn.

She, who had had a largely loveless childhood and supposed that love was more a matter of externals, had all those years back mistaken Christopher for her knight in shining armour. It had taken abduction, probable murder, a drug-doped daughter and the demented behaviour of her husband to make her realize that the homespun retired detective, now on his deathbed, was her true Galahad.

Sedation was making his eyelids heavy with sleep. Struggling for composure, she leant across the wires of his ECG monitor and the drip tube to tenderly kiss him, her lips brushing his ear with the whispered message that she loved him.

Rallying somewhat the following day he received a number of visitors. In fact he negotiated with the staff nurse to inquire who was calling, before he saw any of them. One or two of All Saints' more dutiful parishioners were told by the staff nurse, as were a number from The Magpie, that he wasn't quite up to seeing folk just yet but he thanked them with his best wishes.

One of the visitors to be given a ready audience was Philippa.

The sweet-faced woman, so reminiscent of her younger sister and with a radiance startling enough to rouse a man even in his death-throes, brought him a lovely spray of daisies, carnations and wallflowers. She was solicitous to know how he was and whether it was all right to stay.

'That's really kind of you, Philippa,' he said weakly. 'I'm so glad that you've called since I need to talk to you. First of all, how are you getting along?'

'Quite well now, thank you,' she said giving a concerned smile. 'I've still got to get my decree absolute through but thanks to Christopher I've got a place of my own, as you know, and am beginning to get my life and Rosamund's together. But can you tell me what's happening to Christopher? I've heard stories that his wife has left him.'

'*That's* what I wanted to talk to you about,' answered Di, measuring his response. 'I don't want to go into everything now but Christopher's marriage was far from happy, and it's as good as over. It's important for you to know that. Perhaps you also know about their daughter Katy?' he said gauging her reaction.

'I've heard something about her being on *drugs?*'

Di nodded. 'Well, life at the vicarage had got out of hand, and Frances Wilkes has left fearing for her safety.'

Philippa looked shocked. If it weren't for the solid and responsible former policeman and churchwarden telling her this, she'd not have believed him.

'But he's been so kind to me, as well as to mum and dad . . .'

'Do you know something I really hate doing?' Di interrupted, even as his voice faltered, 'It's telling someone that a so-called friend is *not* a friend at all. In my police work of over thirty years I saw people let down over and over again by so-called friends.'

He paused to catch his breath. 'Often so-called friends could turn into out and out con-men, often they would be two-timing, sometimes they were murderers or close to becoming murderers. Invariably although not always, it was the women who were being victimized by the men.'

'Well, I know that I was the victim from my first marriage,' she replied. 'I never suspected my husband for the man he was, until he showed his other side. He was a promise-breaker all right. But Christopher . . .' she almost whispered it, 'Christopher has always been so *good,* so. . . '

. . .'He's always been so *considerate*, so *generous!*' Only with effort could he complete her sentence.

Di hated having to remind this lovely but naive woman of her deceased sister, and with whom she'd last been before her disappearance. But Philippa's eyes had glazed over, reminding Di of those sightless underwater swimmers he'd seen in church, and as Ben had so aptly described them both to Angela and later to him. 'Wilkes seems to have mesmerized them all' was also how Ben had put it.

'Wake up, Philippa!' he took the plunge to speak his thoughts. 'Who was the last person to have seen Stacey alive? Do you want me to tell you some facts about Christopher, that make me suspect him of her abduction, if not of her murder?'

Only the brutality of these remarks seemed to remove the film from her eyes.

'Do you want me to tell you where I think he put your sister's body, even though I don't know where it is now?'

Her hands knotted into fists. Was the patient on his sickbed delirious?

'NO, *PLEASE* don't tell me such things. I don't want to hear them. *Nobody knows* what happened to Stacey.'

'Well, I won't tell you if you'll make me a single promise.'

'*What?*' she whispered.

'That if Christopher ever comes to your flat, you'll refuse him entry point-blank.'

'But I've invited him in several times already.'

For a moment Di was incredulous: 'Philippa, the vicar's wife has left him because she's *terrified* of him. If anyone should know, she should. I have evidence to prove that he's bad, that he's a consummate liar and that he could well turn violent even if he's not been violent before. The man who specializes in charm, especially with beautiful young ladies like yourself isn't what he appears to be. Believe me, until you've met such people and seen their other side, you'd never credit that they could be so different!'

With his remark applying, to no small extent, to her ex she couldn't refute his observation outright. But surely not *Christopher!*

The patient was visibly tiring: 'Philippa, for Stacey's sake, have nothing to do with him!' He was forcing himself to stay awake.

Had the luminous glow that had come into her eyes when first speaking of Christopher faded somewhat? With his own failing eyesight it was difficult to tell, leaving Di only to pray that this heavenly but starry-eyed woman might be blessed with a new sense of reality.

'*I'll try!*' she said.

He knew that he could do no more to persuade her.

The days and weeks that followed were eventful. Despite predicting the imminence of his death, the bell tolled for Di peacefully on the Friday of Easter week. With many in the community shocked by its suddenness, Frances was left desolate. The deceased had had his much requested talk with Fr Ben, and Ben, with his experience of counseling the dying through his hospice work, gave Di the peace of mind that he sought and deserved.

The large crowd at his funeral was testimony to the respect in which the former police inspector was held. Among the mourners were a number of police officers including an Assistant Chief Constable, many members from All Saints along with most of the regulars from the Magpie, including Nick Cocheron the landlord.

How often are the dead grieved by so many, whilst in life they can feel so alone!

On the night when they learned of his death, The Magpie clientele were greatly subdued. Everyone, including Granville Zbierski, thought well of the retired and retiring man who, despite keeping himself to himself, was 'one of de very few honest coppers I ever met.'

'As honest as the day is long' echoed Nick Cocheron.

'Straight as a die like his name!' Nick Crooks spoke for everybody

Having made his final wishes known to Ben Carter, there had been a full funeral service at the local crematorium. Less to do with any relapse into his former agnosticism, a funeral at All Saints would have been unthinkable - more so in the of Canon Wilkes offering any eulogy!

With no family to pass his estate onto, Di had originally planned to offer the proceeds from the sale of his house and furniture in equal parts to the heart foundation, and to the

*A Candle For Lucifer*

RSPCA on the proviso that they'd look after his cat and dog. But whilst in hospital he'd altered his will, with his bungalow being passed over to Frances, whilst other sums raised from the disposal of any furniture plus a savings account of several thousand pounds be given to Philippa. With the residue of a Life Assurance claim going to medical research, he'd further requested that between them Frances and Philippa were to take care of Snap and Sleuth.

Clearly Frances had never explained to Di the extent of her private means, and that she could have easily bought such a property for herself. But he'd been thinking in terms of Frances' immediate needs and had, for strong emotional reasons, wished to bequeath his home to the woman whom he'd grown to love. His generosity touched her deeply and with everything else going on, it seemed fitting for her to respond by moving into his bungalow.

Furthermore with the vicarage cat having disappeared, Sleuth was a happy substitute indeed. It was also reassuring to look after Snap for the time being.

Philippa too felt indebted. To be receiving a tidy cash sum from a man whom she'd hardly known, and with whom she'd become angry so near to the hour of his death felt strange indeed. But having told her things about Christopher that she had no wish to hear, Di's generosity at least gave her some perspective on the other man's largesse. For it was true that Christopher's generosity always seemed to necessitate a fuss being made of him whenever he called. Not that she minded over-much. It was just that alongside Di's warning, a small part of her would from thereon grow weary if not *wary* of him.

Returning from his day-trip to the Lake District, Christopher arrived at the vicarage to find the note from Frances. 'I have no wish to see you anymore. F.' was all that the note said, but it was quite enough. With the manic euphoria felt at having checked out Stacey's 'safety' evaporating, his mood reverted to a sudden paroxysm of fury. To think that his wife had made taken such a bold initiative infuriated him, and what possessed her to pin the message to the table *with a knife?* Flailing about in the kitchen, he wondered where she might be and, more to the point, how was he going to explain her absence to the parish?

'What's the bitch playing at?' he found himself yelling at the top of his voice, only to be interrupted by the telephone.

'*Yes!*' he snapped into the receiver, before he could regain his composure.

'Christopher, it's me – Ben!'

'Oh, hallo.'

'I tried calling you earlier today. Not only was I disturbed by your phone call last night but I'm very troubled for you and Frances. She's told me of her decision to leave you.'

Christopher's mind went blank over the phone call made the previous night, the one complaining of Ben's Easter day sermon.

'Well, I'm sure that my wife will return. She's done this before,' said Christopher seeking to make light of it on the one hand while telling a lie on the other. For Frances' problem was that she'd *never* run off before, not so much as even addressed the problem of the man she was married to.

'I think you'll find that she's determined to leave you, Christopher. That's why it's important for us to talk. Can I come over first thing tomorrow?'

It was agreed to meet in the morning.

Having just received details of Di's heart attack that night Ben had no wish to impart this information to Christopher. For her part, Angela felt it necessary to support Frances who would be even more vulnerable given what had happened to

Di.

'Come in,' said Christopher flatly. There being neither a housekeeper nor wife to perform the duty for him, he was obliged to answer the door himself.

For once the vicar did not look his smooth urbane self. For one thing he wore no clerical collar. To Ben this made Wilkes look curiously exposed – a bit like someone who'd recently shaved off his beard without warning. Contrary to which, his facial stubble revealed that he hadn't shaved for two days. And with the bags under his eyes, he was clearly short of sleep.

Ben decided that Christopher had to be given an immediate discharge from all duties and that the parish be appraised of the situation. There was to be no beating about the bush. Tell it how it was: The vicar was having marital problems and had been advised to go on indefinite leave – for fear, it might be added, of having a nervous breakdown.

'Christopher, you're struggling on two fronts here,' Ben advised him. 'The Stacey Witcombe mystery hasn't gone away. You may have imagined that her disappearance would be forgotten in time but it would have taken a good five years for that wound to heal properly. And for that to happen, you and Frances would have had to be seen as blissfully happy. Not only is that *not* the case, you have all the problems concerning Katy. I'm sure you are aware that people know about her drug problem.'

All the time as Ben was eyeing him, Christopher chose to look blank.

'Marital breakdowns for vicars are unfortunately always the talk of the town,' he continued. 'There's no way to keep them secret. If you tried to stay here as the vicar working on your own, you'd have the press on your back, as well as people whispering and saying all manner of things. In short, life would become unbearable.'

It was only then that Ben realized he was giving himself a warning, albeit from a happier perspective. The fact that he and Angela now lived together never struck him as anything other than reasonable and sensible. But being a vicar as well as the area dean, his affair with Angela was in another way just as sensational! For in the event of discovery by the media, they'd be as much fair game for a salacious story as anyone else! Although Wilkes' crisis was infinitely direr, Ben recognized that he too would soon have to take stock of his own position:

'Christopher, we must go to the bishop over this. I'll call him and arrange either for you or both of us to meet with him as soon as possible. My advice, indeed my directive is that you suspend all parish duties forthwith. You can abort your emails and leave a message on your answer phone to say that you are on indefinite leave. I will contact your two churchwardens. The parish must go into an unofficial interregnum and although you might like to stay here in the vicarage, I would urge against it. I'm sure that the diocese can fix you up with some temporary accommodation, if you'd like that.'

Having no idea as to what he 'liked' at that moment Christopher's inner turmoil had for once left him speechless, for he too realized that he could no longer continue at All Saints. More than anything there'd be the loss of face over losing Frances, she who'd been such a crucial prop in his subterfuge.

Meekly acquiescing to Ben's instructions, he arranged to meet with the bishop later that afternoon.

## Chapter 18

Fordham diocese had turned out to be a huge disappointment. A flop in fact!

As a millennium experiment seeking to provide a sort of ecclesiastical 'Enterprise Zone', everyone was laughing, or rather despairing. For while some had prayed that the new diocese might be relevant for the twenty-first century, quite the opposite had come to pass.

It was through the convergence of four surrounding Midlands dioceses that an area had been designated to produce a fifth. But the experiment to thereby create Fordham diocese had been a disaster due solely to its new bishop, the Rt Revd Duncan Letharge. For rather than being someone to provide new ideas and offer fresh impetus, Letharge was an arch-traditionalist. In their wisdom, or arguably their total lack of, the Church Commissioners had compounded this absurd choice through the purchase of a six-bedroom Georgian property which, despite the Church's cash-strapped times, suited his Lordship admirably.

These days it being unfashionable for bishops to refer to their residences as 'palaces,' or to be addressed by their formal title of 'my lord', Duncan Letharge chose to resist both trends. He lived in a palace, his title was to be that of 'my lord' and all other abbreviations such as being addressed merely as 'bishop,' or still less desirable as 'Bishop Duncan' were anathema.

Letharge chose to operate like the revival of some Barchester Towers caricature.

Having learned from the area dean earlier that morning that a tragic domestic problem had arisen between Canon Wilkes and his wife, the bishop rearranged his diary for a 3 p.m. appointment with the beleaguered vicar of Ketborough.

Timing his arrival to coincide with the striking of the cathedral clock, Christopher knocked on the heavy paneled door of the 'Palace'. He had tidied himself up beyond recognition from how Ben had seen him earlier that morning. And now that he was washed, fresh shaven and dressed in a gray suit with black clerical stock and collar, Wilkes felt more like his old self. He was also quietly confident that the bishop would offer him the same civility he'd been shown on earlier occasions.

Invited into the downstairs hall by the bishop's housekeeper, and in the few moments that he had to sit and wait he appreciated his surroundings once more. On the occasion that he'd taken lunch with the bishop over Easter, he'd caught sight of the opulence then. Now he could do so undistracted. Italian wallpaper and silk curtains were clear signs of gracious living, as was the Chippendale armchair where he sat. Then there was the gleaming parquet flooring surrounded by four Regency rope-back chairs set opposite each other, all immaculately polished. In the middle of the hall the eye focused on a Cuban mahogany tripod table on its birdcage support, with a Gallic glass vase in the centre filled with tulips, the table itself standing on an oriental Ghashghai rug.

Magnificent! Even Christopher was taken out of himself.

He appreciated that his lordship's collection of antiques had to be way beyond the means of your everyday bishop, even for one who was unmarried. Forty or fifty grand a year wouldn't begin to buy what was on display in the hall alone. Such treasures could only be acquired by a man of considerable private means, his being a case of old money' in other words.

Notwithstanding rumours as to where the bishop's other affections might lie, the undisguised love of his life was that of his antiques. In this splendid residence, apart from having a live-in housekeeper and two secretaries (one full-time, the other part-time), the bishop lived alone with his treasures - his treasures, so to speak, being his family.

There was hardly time to admire the framed gilt painting of an eighteenth century landscape, before the study door opened and the bishop came across to Christopher, all solicitous. A short, somewhat plump man with sharp eyes and flushed complexion, it was as though his unprepossessing appearance served only to heighten the emblems of his Episcopal power: The dark bespoke suit with the diamond encrusted cross over the purple stock. Impossible too to ignore the fisherman's ring with its garish amethyst, as worn on the prelate's right hand.

The diocesan joke was that if he could have got away with it, Bishop Letharge would have worn a berretta, frock coat and gaiters.

Christopher's attire suitably understated that of his host. Yet the high quality black brogues worn by both men seemed to gleam as though in acknowledgement of the other's affluence and good taste.

'Hallo dear boy, do come in!'

'Thank you for agreeing to see me at such short notice, my lord.'

'Nonsense, nonsense – not at all! Do come in.'

Christopher was ushered into his study and directed to one of a pair of Georgian mahogany library chairs. The bishop sat opposite him.

'It seems only like five minutes ago that we were chatting at our Easter Festival, doesn't it? By the way, I thought your sermon was first-rate dear boy. *Just right* for the occasion.'

'Thank you, my lord, it was a privilege to be there.'

The paternal affection proffered by bishops to their clergy is well known. But when it is preceded by a summons from the bishop to have a little chat, the immediate outcome as to where such a chat might lead is often unclear. Would the outcome be good or bad? Often an opening gambit of friendship might steer itself into a consultation about the priest's private life or worse that, at short notice, a decision had been made to move him or her on. It was far from unknown for the velvet glove of a bishop to deliver many a knockout punch.

So ushered into the bishop's lair, even Canon Wilkes wasn't quite sure what might transpire. Yet he remained confident that Bishop Letharge liked him, this being affirmed by his lordship's suggestion that they enjoy a glass of port: 'I would imagine that you could do with it, Christopher, after all the goings on in your parish.' His host sounded almost jocular.

Although not a heavy drinker, Christopher knew it would be rude to decline the cut-glass goblet of vintage Taylor's being held out to him.

What he didn't expect to hear next was that his former churchwarden, Nicholas Hagan had been taken ill with a major heart attack. 'Apparently the prognosis looks serious' he was told. Although visibly affected by the news, Christopher concealed his feelings skillfully, since he'd never much cared for Hagan. Known to others, as 'Di' the man was too much of an unknown quantity for Christopher's liking. Being a retired police officer didn't help either, given that perhaps he knew more about Stacey than he let on.

Yet with Christopher's other calamities, the news about Hagan only seemed to make the bishop more solicitous, Letharge making it clear to Christopher that he'd always seen him as a hard-working, no-nonsense fellow, who operated a well-run parish. He also cut a fine figure of a man, which made him a credit to the institution of Mother Church. Furthermore the bishop's physical inferiority to Wilkes seemed less to vex the other than might have been supposed.

So despite 'all that wretched business about the disappearing choirgirl,' and now 'this unfortunate matter of Mrs. Wilkes running off,' the bishop remained warm and friendly, putting it to Wilkes that he'd lost none of his faith in him.

Nor did the bishop seem unduly concerned over the saga of Mrs. Wilkes. The rumour of course was that Letharge was a clandestine misogynist – who having never contemplated his own marriage remained hostile to women generally, even when pretending otherwise. His next remark was audacious: 'It might go easier with you Christopher, in terms of winning people's sympathy, if your wife had been seen to have gone off with another man,' mused the bishop. 'Was there by any chance, or *is* there anyone with whom she might have been having an affair?'

Insofar as he had no idea as to what may or may not have been his wife's desires, the question shook him. Yet seizing upon this as an excuse he replied. 'Well, I never wished to think along those lines, my lord, nor do I now. But I suppose I do have my suspicions. In fact the man whom you've just mentioned – Mr. Hagan has over the last six months or so become unduly friendly with Frances. Whether it became intimate, I cannot honestly say. But they were known to see a lot of each other. In fact I know she went to see him only yesterday, the night before he had his heart attack. But I hate thinking in this way, even if I have been too trusting of Frances.'

He caught himself putting his relationship to his wife in the past tense. Did 'have been' mean that it was over? Was that what he wanted? Although it might go better for him if his wife was known to have been unfaithful, there was still the stigma of a divorce to damage his future prospects.

Having drunk their port Duncan Letharge got up, suggesting that they might share a pot of tea. He went out to have a quick word with his housekeeper, allowing Christopher time to reconsider his thoughts. Did he want to get rid of Frances? Perhaps he'd be better off without her? After all, his family seemed to have brought upon him a fair degree of misery of late.

His eyes scanned the lovely oak-paneled study, cosseting the Regency gesso and pine mantelpiece with its burr-walnut Georgian bracket clock, above which hung a gilt wood wall mirror. He reflected on how the bachelor lifestyle could provide benefits and who knows, with Letharge in charge, might in due course enhance his career rather than hinder it.

He came out of his revelry.

'Mrs. Deekes won't be a moment,' said the bishop affably, returning to his chair.

'There is another matter concerning your church, Christopher, but which perhaps has nothing to do with you. You sure you won't have another port?' he interrupted himself as he proffered the decanter. With Wilkes declining, the bishop replenished his own glass before resuming: 'Quite out of the blue this morning I had a phone call from the Ketborough Herald, asking whether I had authorized area dean Ben Carter to say all the sweeping things that he apparently said at his Easter address at your church for Easter Sunday!'

'Dear, oh dear!' responded Christopher, shaking his head: 'I feared as much. A number of my parishioners phoned me on Sunday afternoon to say how appalled they had been upon hearing the area dean's sermon. As you know we were holding a shared Eucharist to commemorate our January pilgrimage together and I had asked Fr Ben to preach, this being after you'd so kindly invited me to the cathedral. Apparently in my absence he said a lot of, dare I say it, *heretical* things about our beliefs, not least concerning Easter. I was so upset about it that I had to phone and tell him so. Over the phone he sounded, if I may say so, not contrite at all, if anything rather pleased with himself!'

'Hmm,' said the bishop who to the cognoscenti aware of what were good and bad sounds emitted by his lordship, augured ill for Ben Carter.

'Well between you and me, there are a number of things I'm not happy about concerning Ketborough's area dean,' murmured his lordship thoughtfully.

Despite his inward glee, Christopher showed no sign of gloating.

Making the inevitable temple with his fingers, a mannerism adopted as though by patent to the clergy when they are being thoughtful, the bishop said: 'I am going to propose this, Christopher, that you take a period off work immediately, say four to six months. You are going to have to sort out your marriage or if the worst comes to the worst, you must part from your wife as amicably as you can. It won't be the end of your world if that happens. On that, I'm prepared to give you my word.'

In the light of such unexpected encouragement, Christopher felt able to contemplate divorce proceedings in a more favourable light.

'So I would advise this, dear boy. Take your break. The area dean, what's his name – Carter? We can leave it to him for the time being to take care of everything at All Saints. I'm sure that he'll explain tactfully to the congregation that you have some domestic issues to sort out, and that your leave of absence has been authorized by me. I think 'leave of absence' sounds preferable to sick leave, don't you? Although we can let your flock believe that you may return, the probability is that we'll have to move you on. But rest assured this diocese values your gifts and something will be made available for you in due course.'

'Thank you, my lord.'

A bustling Mrs. Deekes brought in the tea tray, and placing it on a satinwood sofa table behind them poured out two cups. After jaffa cakes and biscuits had been presented and she had withdrawn, the bishop said with an affable wink. 'Mixed blessing these women, you know, Christopher. I mean, they're indispensable in some ways, as it were, but they can be an awful handful at times, wouldn't you say? As you know, I wonder about their usefulness in church, quite apart from what they get up to at home.'

Clearly the second glass of port had loosened the bishop's tongue.

'Anyway, you know my views about that,' he added cryptically, 'and I don't wish to bore you.'

'Not at all, my lord,' replied Christopher, quick to appreciate the sort of 'nudge-nudge-wink-wink' repartee of his host, and where collusion with the bishop's cause could do no harm to his own. By responding in the 'You're absolutely right' sort of mode, he and Letharge bonded further.

Both picked up from the other that each of them was, if not a self-declared woman-hater, then a man with distinctly ambivalent views about women in general.

What would have appalled more astute clergy like Ben Carter was that the bishop showed neither pastoral interest towards nor insight into Wilkes himself! It was as though Letharge regarded Wilkes as someone with no obvious 'problems,' except perhaps for having a hysterical wife. Far more importantly Christopher had those admirable qualities of flair, modesty and charm that bishops as a group tend to covet. Also being akin to each other with their obscure sexual orientation Duncan Letharge and the canon, consciously or otherwise, cemented their alliance.

So it was that the formal part of their meeting was concluded. Over a second cup of tea further pleasantries were exchanged concerning Regency furniture, along with another of the bishop's passions – cricket.

It was hardly surprising when an hour later and upon leaving the Palace, Christopher felt greatly heartened.

A few weeks later Frances moved from her temporary lodgings into Di Hagan's home. Despite the lingering sense of sadness, she liked the atmosphere of the bungalow, which despite its need for many improvements she'd attend to after a respectful interlude.

Choosing to have no further contact with Christopher, the grounds for her divorce were simple. Although 'unreasonable and threatening behaviour' felt like a grievous understatement, it facilitated the process to go through that much quicker. She was further relieved that Christopher, now living elsewhere, chose not to contest the writ.

Although by moving into her deceased friend's bungalow she still resided within the parish of All Saints, from thereon she would no longer attend church or at least not *that* church!

While these experiences felt liberating, her children remained uppermost in her mind. Now that he was at Cambridge, Dominic came to live with his mother during the vacations, and although she'd not seen her daughter recently she liked to think that Katy was making slow but steady progress. What was clear was that neither Kate nor her brother wished to have anything further to do with their father, both of them harbouring growing fears that he was responsible for Stacey's disappearance.

As a result of Di's generosity to both Frances and Philippa their friendship had grown closer. In consideration of his pets Snap was also to stay with Frances for an indefinite time so as to allow Philippa to sort out her plans. Nor had Frances appreciated before how much of an animal lover she was, the bonding between the old gnarled hand of Di and this softer hand that now fed the tabby and the collie being almost seamless.

Using the lump sum given to her by Di, Philippa had by leaving her infant Rosamund with her parents started an afternoon college course of upholstery and soft furnishings. She'd also invested in a comprehensive tool kit for sewing, knitting, pattern making and for the purposes of doing general upholstery. Her most expensive item for this enterprise was a fully automated sewing machine.

Even before the completion of her course, she'd begun working from her one bedroom flat. Two small advertisements placed in the local newspaper surprised her with an on-rush of orders to make up curtains, embroider cushions, even to restore back to life a small old Edwardian settee. Her enthusiasm for her new livelihood was infectious enough even to get Frances interested.

Of course, what with plans for doing up the bungalow and cultivating the garden, Frances too had more than enough to be getting on with. But in her endeavours to help Philippa, Frances sometimes took charge of Rosamund - the infant always looked forward to seeing her Auntie Frances while playing with the long-suffering cat and dog.

# Chapter 19

In wanting the best for her daughter Frances went into denial, refuting just how serious Katy's situation had become.

Following Christmas and through the months leading up to Easter, and with her marriage having gone from bad to non-existent, she liked to suppose that through her admission to a detox-unit, Kate had turned a corner and things would improve from thereon.

In reality even as she underwent treatment, Kate had got her hands on another Class 'A' drug, smuggled in by a so-called well-wisher. Having been told that E's or ecstasy didn't have the same toxicity as the other stuff, and that the new drug seemed to re-vitalize her somewhat, she wasn't complaining. Yet this 'change of gear', so to speak, fooled no one except herself, merely accelerating her demise into deeper addiction.

With the one immutable rule being that rehabilitation was terminated in the event of other drugs being taken, she'd been told unceremoniously to leave. Any re-offending with drugs and the contract was broken, and while she would be allowed to visit the centre she was no longer eligible for treatment. Thus were two months of treatment thrown to the wall.

Only when the detox center informed her of this development did Frances grasp the full picture. But how in God's name was her daughter continuing to find the funds? Given that Dom had told his mother a £10,000 legacy would be peanuts in junkie currency, presumably her savings were all but depleted.

Having had his fun with Katy long ago, her boyfriend-come-dealer negotiated less favourable terms shortly after a week, concluding with no terms at all. Not only that, Pete's departure out of her life had been swift and sudden. One of the reasons that she'd been arrested ('for her own protection', as she'd been told), and passed on to the Drugs Unit was due to the Staff of Life having come under some serious scrutiny. However, thanks to their own informants, her supplier and his cronies had got out in time, 'doing a runner' to Amsterdam.

Before going their separate ways, Pete had divulged to Katy another wheeze for 'keeping you up to speed with the readies'. She'd hated how in toying with her future, he treated any ventures into crime so matter of factly; the two choices having been either DSS fraud or credit card fraud. With the credit card scam appearing simpler, he put her in touch with someone who specialized in acquiring chip and PIN numbers, which through the use of appropriate software could then be encoded onto a blank plastic cutout. 'The other person's got no idea that their card's being used, since they've still got their original,' she was told, as though the small matter of that 'other person's' hugely inflated monthly bill was inconsequential.

To ensure that the fraud worked, she'd performed a simple experiment. Having had her own bank 'Connect' card copied, she made a withdrawal using the counterfeit card.

Out came £20 of her own money, by way of the blank card, which had nothing on it except her encoded PIN with its magnetized strip. Clearly the chrome hologram on her original card offered no protection whatsoever. So the only advice worth heeding, she was told, was to scrap each card after a sum of around £1,000 had been extracted.

'Easy, peasy!' she thought to herself and had indeed made a clear net profit of around £2,000 in this way before her supplier dried up. Or more to the point the forger of PIN numbers wanted 'a little something extra' than the £200 commission on each number supplied. Like her drug-pushing boyfriend he wanted further payment in kind, making Kate realize that, as with Pete, this too would become a contract with diminishing returns.

Hole in the wall card fraud was reluctantly put to one side.

Like other attractive female addicts her final standby became obvious. With desperation taking care of all moral niceties, going on the game was far easier than she supposed, more so within the anonymity of London where she'd become just another face.

Once she'd established a routine and paid off her pimps, £400 or £500 could be made a night without undue fuss or bother, her improved income allowing her to return to crack cocaine with full-blown intensity. Furthermore, with London prices being cheaper, better deals could be struck allowing her to stay high for 'as little as' £800 a week.

Just so long as her looks and health held out, Kate could make some half decent money while meeting all her other overheads.

Following her parents' bust-up, there were occasions when she felt some sympathy for her mother. Yet while the cocaine offered some respite for her to think more rationally, her worsening addiction ensured that the gaping fissure between mother and daughter would remain so. Only in a solitary postcard postmarked central London, could any sympathy be expressed, and even that was heartbreakingly brief:

*'Dear Mum, try not to worry about me. I've gone to London to find work and to try and sort out my life. Will be in touch, Love Kate.*

*P.S. Say Hi to Dom for me and tell him I'm OK.'*

'We're going to have to work out where we're going, darling,' he told Angela one evening in early May when they had been celebrating his birthday at her flat. 'Something's got to give and I don't want it to be our sanity!'

Ben had insisted on showing off an excellent sample of his home-cooked Indian cooking – Tandoori-chicken marinated in spiced yogurt and herbs. Through misty eyes softened further by a shared bottle of Niersteiner, Angela asked, 'so tell me what you really want Ben! I know that we want to be together. That's not the issue! But do you need to stay in the church out of some self-preservation? Is it the security you're after? I'm not blaming you for that. But be honest, how true to yourself are you being by remaining in an institution where you feel so much conflict?'

Despite their wish to live openly together without shame, the Church had never been well disposed towards those who, to use that horrid expression, commit 'the sins of the flesh.' A summons out of the blue from Bishop Letharge might easily present them with the stark choice of staying together, or of him having to give up the Church.

'A nun who reneges on her vows is scandal enough,' she went on. 'But don't forget up until now a number of the faithful have looked up to you as a sort of role model; a shining example of all that's best about the celibate priest!'

She couldn't help winding him up.

'Hey, I've never tried to be that,' he exclaimed. 'Just because I signed up for the single life is no excuse for others to put me on a pedestal!'

They both laughed as he went on: 'you're completely right of course, darling. But being practical for a moment how would you and I survive, if I jacked in the church or at least quit the job I'm in now? You've got no salary to speak of, Angela, and part of me asks, Why the hell should I have to contemplate leaving the church just because you and I are living together? Nobody's getting hurt; we're not cheating on anyone! Perhaps we should just live together at the vicarage and see what happens. As it happens that idea quite appeals to me!'

'Me, too!' laughed Angela. 'At least if someone told tales to the bishop, we'd probably get to find out who it was whose moral sensibilities snapped first!'

'It's all so hypocritical!' said Ben raising his voice. 'Here we are, you and me having to live like a pair of fugitives because we love each other, and express that love in the obvious way.'

'Which ought to bring us to another point,' said Angela. 'We've been having unprotected sex now for nearly two months. Don't be surprised if before long . . .'

Unfazed, Ben replied, 'Good, can't wait for it to happen.'

'But we must make some plans.'

'Yes of course. If I'm asked to leave the church or find it too uncomfortable to stay, I could probably get some work in one of the two charities I'm responsible for. That would free us up to move. Or else maybe we could work jointly administering an old-folks' home, or some such thing.'

'I've been thinking about what I might really like to do,' said Angela looking wistful.

'Go on.'

'Well, I've looked long and hard at the church and all I see is a large institution shooting itself in the foot so many times, it'll probably end up shooting itself in the head. That's not to say that a lot of people won't cling on to the carcass so to speak, but it seems to be losing all relevance in the modern age.

'I mean just look at Christopher Wilkes!' she continued. 'The man's a visible *wreck*. Anyone with eyes can see he's out of control. And yet he seems to have conned his congregation. It seems that with Frances having left him, most of them would *prefer* to suspect something bad about her, than to think anything bad about their beloved vicar! After all, Christopher has already made it appear that *he's* the injured party. Yet it's only been by Frances walking out that he'd been stopped from staying on at All Saints and getting away with . . . *murder!'*

'Or *another* murder perhaps' added Ben: I wouldn't be at all surprised if he hasn't conned the bishop, or more precisely whether the bishop and Christopher haven't conned each other.'

'I agree. But what are you saying about yourself, Ben?' asked Angela.

'Well, I'm wondering whether I can somehow transcribe my Christian experiences into something useful.'

'Such as going to Iraq or Darfur maybe?'

'Well of course you've got to admire anyone who get off their backsides and tries to do *something*. But I'd like to reach people in this country, strike a few chords with thinking and serious-minded people here in England!'

He continued, 'Working for the Citizens' Advice Bureau is, for example, an obvious way to express Christian love.'

'Well but for myself *I'd* prefer to do something more mystical in some way,' she replied. . . . 'Do something more unusual, more esoteric if you like.'

'Astrology, for example? Or regression therapy into reincarnation perhaps?' asked Ben, knowing of Angela's newly acquired love for such things.

'I think so. In fact, from my research into astrology so far, I'm persuaded that it *does* represent a vital source of knowledge. Of course in countless ways it's still in its infancy, and gets trivialized in a load of different ways. But who knows in twenty-five years from now, doing one's natal chart could become a perfectly acceptable way of learning more about ourselves, as well as helping us better understand our children, or whoever.'

'You should go for it then!' said Ben. 'But in the meanwhile I think that we had better continue living in sin, ho, ho, but doing so in secret for as long as possible. There's no point in jeopardizing my job just so as to keep the bigots happy. Discretion remains essential. However if we *do* get found out, we'll just weather that storm as and when it happens.'

With it being agreed that they would continue only to liaise there for the time being, her 'safe house' was aptly named.

'I used to believe that not being found out for wrongdoing was a mortal sin,' said Ben. 'I now believe that there are some so-called sins, where *not* being found out has the whole-hearted support of God!' chuckled Ben.

'Do you remember the one about the child's misprint of the seventh commandment?' reminded Angela, 'Thou shalt not *admit* adultery!' As they creased up with laughter Angela added, 'children can be so wonderfully innocent.'

'Or yet again what about the *eleventh* commandment?' answered Ben. 'Thou shalt not be *found out!*' Which reminds me,' said Ben, 'did I tell you the one about the nun who went to her doctor complaining of hiccups and who rushed out shrieking hysterically?'

Grinning broadly, Angela shook her head.

'Well by telling her she was pregnant, her doctor at least sorted out her hiccups!'

Laughing again, Angela advised, 'But I'm warning you reverend sir, there may come a time when a certain 'bump' will have nothing to do with hiccups with this ex-nun. You have been warned!'

'Can't wait' said Ben, slapping his knee with mirth.

'Well, if that's the way you want it!' she replied. Pushing aside her plate, she got up and stretched out on to the bed to look instantly ravishing.

The charm of Ben and Angela's love was that they were like two children, who while loving the *mischief* of their love had no intention of behaving dishonourably.

And the bump arrived no later than expected.

Christopher began his leave of absence by moving into a flat provided by the diocese and useful, if for no other purpose, than for the privacy it afforded him.

But little else actually changed for him. Devoid of any feelings for his estranged wife, he remained wholly indifferent either to her welfare or to that of his son at university, let alone to the more serious plight of his daughter. His re-adjusted lifestyle was more a case of re-embracing the bachelor he'd always been at heart.

Of course there were incidental matters like laundry and cooking to consider. But shirts and underwear could always be cleaned and ironed professionally, and he could eat out as often as he chose. So rather than feeling despondent with a marriage on the rocks and his career in temporary suspension, he took to his new life with not a little gusto.

Indeed with solicitors sorting out his domestic affairs, he chose to launch out on a spending spree. From his underused inheritance and all but ignored for so long, he purchased without difficulty a small fashionable London flat in a Chelsea Mews. He'd always fancied having a bolthole in the metropolis, and it would provide him with further anonymity during his leave of absence. He bought the mews, confident that Frances would make no claims upon his inheritance given that she, like him, had inherited a significant legacy of her own. Shortly before his death her father had sold up a small engineering business in Surrey, passing on the proceeds to his only daughter. In this one respect Frances and Christopher had resembled each other, with both being wealthy in their own right yet living frugally up until then.

Following the purchase of his London property, he also chose to treat himself to an extended climbing holiday in the Alps.

Although he'd lost none of his climbing expertise, he wanted to get back into a peak of climbing fitness, applying for and being accepted to join a party of other middle-aged climbers at Courmayeur in Northern Italy. From there, he'd been singled out to join a select all-male party to climb Europe's highest peak, that of Mont Blanc. Of the group of six, two were long-standing members of the All-Alpine Club.

Mont Blanc provided an exhilarating antidote from his other distractions and, as it happened, an unexpected fillip to his self-esteem. With their state-of-the-art mountain gear, he and his small group of climbers had set off in high spirits. Despite their climb being hampered by loose rocks, they reached the peak by way of the standard route up the mountain's 'tunnel' without mishap. From all those years ago, when he had scaled and bivouacked on Mount Kenya, the crystal air and a night sky peppered with a myriad spangled lights thrilled him once more. Having made their successful ascent of Mont Blanc in the light of a full moon, the same mood of invincibility now swept over him.

It was in the early hours next day that they descended by the glacial track known as the Glacier du Dome. Owing to the difficulties they'd had with rocks and loose scree on the way up, they chose this alternative route in preference to the narrow ridge used earlier.

With a rising temperature and the surface snow starting to melt, the Glacier Du Dome was a familiar enough route, although in melting conditions it was known to be hazardous. In two groups of three roped together, they made their descent. With each climber being spaced some four meters apart, Christopher was in the first group, although as the heaviest member of the trio was third in line,

Having already negotiated several small crevasses was when the accident struck. Estimating that most of them were but no more than a few feet in depth, the front climber then plunged into what was in fact an ice cliff. Unable to flail his axe to find a crude ice hold, the first man had vanished over the edge leaving the second climber clawing frantically in an effort to save the other. But with his axe buried in ice dangerously close to the lip of the abyss, the two stood to crash to their deaths, but for the quick action taken by Christopher. Blessed with a speed of balance and reflex cultivated in childhood, their anchorman had locked himself into a prostrate stance with his axe buried over his shoulder. This move known as a 'deadman' gave them some precious extra minutes, in which to be rescued by the second trio of climbers following behind, and who quickly helped to take some of the strain.

After radioing for assistance, while locking additional ice axes in place along with their securing lines, Christopher and his party were all duly airlifted to safety. The first climber, having been suspended over an ice-cave around 200 feet deep, sustained no more than several cracked ribs and severe bruising.

Once the team had been returned to Courmayeur, Christopher found himself feted as something of a hero, his quick responses having saved his group from serious injury if not death.

Yet his heroism although briefly applauded by the mountain fraternity drew no further attention - no mention of it having been made in the media.

# Chapter 20

'I wanna do a weewee,' said Jonathan.

'So do I,' piped up his older brother Martin.

'All right, I'll pull up at the next lay-by,' said their father. The pleasure of two parents on holiday was being sorely tested not just on account of the demands of their two youngsters, but more so because of the weather. Dan and Diana Westward had first met on a climbing holiday in the Lake District. Having returned there with two sons aged four and one, any strenuous exercise these days was way off their agenda. The rain didn't help either. Nonetheless the Lakes were a convenient hop up the M 6 from their home in Preston, and they were consoled with happy memories.

Besides it had been memories of a blissful holiday taken there the previous year that had prompted their return. Having had wall-to-wall sunshine from June through to September then, they had enjoyed a fortnight's rain-free holiday, exploring the Derwent Water area and the lower reaches of the Langdale Pikes. It had been an exceptional year weather-wise and all in stark contrast to summer *this* year, which with its wind, rain and sun felt more, like a prolonged April.

'This looks as miserable as anywhere!' said Dan trying to

# A Candle For Lucifer

humour his wife. The lay-by in the Grizedale Forest overlooking Coniston Water was empty, leaving latrines to be found at the side of the road.

'You go with daddy while I'll get the lunch ready,' said Diana as Dan struggled to get their children into their kagouls.

What a way to carry on! Trying to remain philosophical, he assisted his youngest in relieving himself. Rain always made everyone want to take a leak, as well as putting the kibosh on everything else!

'Race you back to the car,' he said to two children readily amused by the distraction of splashing in puddles as they made their way back to the family's secondhand Isuzu Trooper. After eating their sandwiches, crisps and apples, which always made everybody feel better, plans were made to go to Ambleside for a swim in the public baths.

After lunch, with the car growing airless Martin had wound down the rear window, even as Dan still in his kagoul declared: 'I've got to stretch my legs again.'

'Me too, said Diana. 'My turn to want a loo.'

'Not much privacy, I'm afraid love.' As both parents got out, Diana instructed her sons, 'be sure to stay in the car. I won't be a mo!'

Martin their four-year-old had one of those simple but curious little toys called a 'helicopter.' In fact it was a toy that his father had dug out of an old trunk in the attic. Still in its original wrapping it was a toy that he'd clearly looked after in his own childhood. By pulling a string on a retractable spring located in a plastic post, a small plastic rotor could be made to whizz round and ascend skywards. As long as Martin played with the toy where he was, the rotor could only spin upto the lining of the car's roof, sticking there for a few moments before floating back down.

But with his window half open Martin chose to let fly

with his helicopter to see it sail from the car across the drystone wall and into apparent oblivion. Dan who was already standing outside and staring out across the wall saw the object pass him before drifting down towards the undergrowth below, where it alighted on some ferns.

'Look what you've done, silly boy,' he said, aggrieved that toys in his family had a life expectancy of about five minutes. He'd always managed to hold on to his, as was proof with the said toy handed down to Martin.

'It just flew off,' said Martin as though the rotor had suddenly assumed a mind of its own. 'Dad, can you get it for me?'

'*No way,* you've lost it! Who do you think I am – Superman?

Diana returned and said. 'You've lost it Martin and you've only just had it.'

'*I want it back!*' They hated it when the four-year-old went into sniveling mode.

'I'm afraid it's gone,' said his mother. 'Come on, let's go and try and make some sense of the day.'

'*I want it!*' Martin was starting to kick out in the direction of his younger brother.

'*God!* These holidays drive me spare,' she muttered to herself, not helped by the fact that she couldn't find a suitable loo.

'Actually I can see it just resting on top of that undergrowth,' said Dan who was still standing near the wall. 'The red stands out quite clearly.'

'You can't get down there,' said Diana. 'Come on, we'll try and buy another. It'll hardly break the bank.'

'I told you, you can't get them *anywhere* these days,' replied Dan.

He'd been looking to buy a replica of the toy for Jonathan, so that there would be no arguments. But like many good, simple toys from *his* childhood, these days what with everything being electronic the old toys were no longer obtainable. He began to feel an absurd nostalgia for the little rotor.

'I'll tell you what. Time me to see how quickly I can get it if I abseil down and climb back up. Anyway, I need an excuse just to shin up and down a rope, even if it is only for five minutes.'

Diana complained briefly, but with Martin's worsening mood and a husband suddenly set on doing something there was no point arguing.

He liked to keep a couple of reels of eleven millimeter Kernmantel climbing rope in the back of the family jeep, even though present circumstances only allowed him an occasional weekend's climbing. Extracting one of the coils he tied a standard figure-of-eight belay through the towing bracket of their vehicle, while shrouding the rope in some cloth to stop it fraying against the edge of the wall. It then took no more than thirty seconds for him to drop down the fifty or so feet, moving across the less steep gradient to where, like a colourful butterfly, the rotor had come to rest on some large ferns.

'That was easy,' he shouted up. Diana was holding Jonathan and the three pairs of eyes peering over the wall looked pleased, with Martin clapping his hands.

'Dad to the rescue again!' she thought.

For Dan, it felt good just absorbing the scene of moss and woodlands that now surrounded him. Steam rose from his kagoul and, despite the family upon whom he doted, *any* excuse to revisit the silence of nature always thrilled him. So just standing among the wet ferns, however briefly, renewed his sense of well being.

But as he prepared to move away his foot stepped on something brittle, sending up a shower of small gnats and flies. His feet went wobbly as though standing on a gradient of shingle obliging him to clasp his rope more tightly so as to keep upright.

'*Sweet Jesus!*' It was then that beneath his feet he saw the detritus of what looked like a pair of jeans and trainers, a ribcage and a skull. Furthermore, the strands of blonde hair around the skull and the tapering fingernails on the skeletal hands were, to Dan's inexperienced eye, enough to tell him that the remains were probably those of a young female.

'*Sweet Jesus,*' he whispered once more. His first instinct was to check if the peering eyes from the parapet above had seen what he'd just had to witness. But with interest lost once it was realized that dad had got hold of the rotor, nothing untoward had been noticed, and for that he could give thanks.

If his descent had been swift, a wave of adrenalin propelled him to the top in almost record time.

'You're still quite fit for a father of two then!' joked Diana leaning out of the window as he unhitched the rope and stowed it into the back of the car. She was surprised to see him quite so soon.

He'd left his mobile at home. '*You drive!*' He gasped. 'The nearest phone-box, *quick!*'

'Are you OK? You look as white as a sheet!'

'No, please. Just drive!'

Where's my 'copter?' asked Martin.

Having stuffed it into his pocket, Dan passed it over to him wordlessly. They managed to find a payphone and 999 having been dialed, the police were summoned to the scene at the lay-by immediately. Dan promised to return to the scene once he'd delivered his family to Ambleside swimming baths.

It was a difficult location for the police to reach and still more so for the forensic scientists. None had the agility of

Dan Westward, and viewing the skeleton without disturbing it required having to work at a difficult angle. Nor was it practicable to make a full investigation of the skeleton where it lay and so, after extensive photography and a scrutiny of the surrounding area, the remains were eased into an unzipped body-bag and stretchered up, keeping it as much in place as possible.

Naturally with earlier decomposition a path lab can learn considerably more about a person's injuries than when dealing with a skeleton. Yet even when reduced to it's two hundred or more bones, nail and hair particles plus all or some of its thirty-two teeth a de-fleshed corpse will, with patience, still tell a story. Through their mutual co-operation osteobiologists, forensic anthropologists and odontologists can, assisted by dental and medical records, usually establish a victim's identity as well as confirm the nature of death. Here it became apparent that the victim had been strangled with a ligature. For although such a death does not require the fracturing of the small hyoid bone at the base of the neck, this invariably occurs due to the rage of the assailant.

Further investigation showed that the basilar joint at the base of the skull had not yet fused to the skull's underside, signifying that the skeleton was that of a girl probably still in her teens. Dental examination revealed that two molars had been removed, with a further procedure of two small fillings having been performed. This minor surgery, along with profiles of the girl's upper and lower jaw, could soon be matched up with the dental X-rays of other missing persons. A calcium build up in the girl's right forearm also suggested that she would have enjoyed racquet sports, such as squash or tennis.

Stacey Witcombe's identification proved itself relatively straightforward.

The fine strands of white nylon cord found embedded in a broken fingernail would also be carefully examined.

# Chapter 21

'It's going to have to be make-up-your-mind time,' said Ben. 'You're four months pregnant and to put it bluntly, I'm pissed off at having to pretend any more.'

'You're probably right,' replied Angela. 'Just so long as we know *why* we're doing *what* we're doing! Let's be clear about it once more. Most people who know I'm expecting are either pleased for us or aren't in the slightest bit bothered, at least not bothered in the sense of our being unmarried.'

'True,' responded Ben. 'It just goes to show that the moralizers are in the minority and a very small minority at that.'

'And,' interjected Angela, 'given that we don't have any problem about "living in sin," we'd better do what we've gotta do and visit *His Holiness.*'

'You mean His Defilement!' said Ben.

And for good measure, she added, 'and I still say, damn his eyes!

Ben knew that whilst only a few of his clergy contemporaries might applaud his lifestyle, he was popular with the public at large. In addition to that having recently taken Di Hagan's funeral, many folk admired his skill in conducting such a solemn occasion with great compassion but also humour.

'So, how shall we play it?' asked Angela.

'I'll ask to see the bishop and tell him straight that you and I are having a baby, that we love each other and that in due course we plan to get married,' replied Ben.

'The trouble there, my love, is that you've got the problem and the solution in exactly the reverse order as to how the bishop would want to hear it!' she said half-smiling.

'Well, we know that! But we might as well know where we stand with him and take it from there.'

'Well, what we know about His Worthy Lordship,' said Angela, 'is that considering he made no effort to get to the bottom of the Christopher and Frances bust-up, he's unlikely to take kindly to our situation. The man's a confirmed bachelor, quite possibly gay and as likely as not will pontificate that if women have to get pregnant, then they should do so only within marriage.'

'It's a classic Catch 22,' Ben admitted. 'Keep you hidden during your pregnancy and we make ourselves look guilty. Ask the bishop for his support and he'll request my resignation.

'And it's still a matter of keeping the security of a job,' he went on. 'What's more, I know that I'm a half-decent area dean and vicar.'

'That goes without saying darling,' said Angela, adding with a laugh: 'To my mind you're a bit like a modern-day Francis of Assisi, of whom it was said "nobody doubted he was a saint, but when among sinners he was one of themselves."'

He bowed at the compliment. 'Ah, but there's a difference there,' he said ruefully. 'I've always suspected that old Francis could take kindly to poverty because as a retired prince he had private means stashed away. Had push come to shove he could have always reverted to the good life, if he so chose. This modern-day Francis,' he jerked a thumb at himself, 'has no hidden pot of gold. What's more, my love, despite your being halfway through an astrology course, you'll soon have the heavy duties of motherhood thrust upon you.'

Looking her straight in the eye, Ben said, 'we have no choice. I have to see the bishop. We can't stall any longer.'

An appointment was duly set up to meet with Bishop Letharge.

No port was forthcoming from the bishop whether by way of liquid refreshment or, more desirably, as a protective harbour from a stormy sea. For as long as the area dean did his job without rocking the boat, then the bishop would offer him token sanctuary as a 'caring' employer. But now, the long and the short of it was that, having rocked his little coracle with suicidal intent, his Lordship wouldn't have minded if Father Ben Carter had sunk without trace.

'Area deans don't normally go around making former nuns pregnant. This is a serious breach of moral probity!' was his opening gambit. Nor did he have any time whatsoever for the antics of breakaway sisters like Angela; his unspoken view being that any nun reneging on her vows only to start living with a man was tantamount to behaving like an adulteress.

'I really am at a loss as to know what to say,' added the bishop who in fact could have said a lot more, most of it unprintable.

As someone who had no time for women, or for men who got carried away by them Letharge could be a lethal adversary. Play by his rules and he could be charming and supportive. Breach those rules and he could become icy and remote as he was now demonstrating. For if he'd feigned any affection towards Ben as a fellow bachelor and celibate that had all now vanished. For clearly Ketborough's area dean wasn't just heterosexual; he was a *womanizer*!

With no friendly housekeeper summoned to bring in tea and jaffa cakes, or of small talk about furniture or cricket, the interview was kept to a few preliminaries to forewarn him of what was intended:

'The first priority is to consider the people and clergy of this diocese,' said the bishop with that sort of clerical reasonableness, which became instantly unreasonable when it came to his victims. 'People and clergy' were for the convenience of the moment supposed to include everybody *except* Ben and Angela! For the greater good of the whole, it was they who'd be required to become the sacrificial lambs.

It was obvious what the bishop would say next. 'I have to tell you, here and now, that I must ask for your resignation, both as area dean and as vicar of St Hilda's. This is not a decision lightly taken. Rather it is one I have deliberated on for several weeks.'

With scarcely a pause to test Ben's reaction, Letharge went on, 'I don't know whether you are aware of it, but a number of your parishioners are of the opinion that you've lost your faith.'

Ignoring the insensitivity of this latter remark, Ben couldn't disguise his look of panic as he asked, 'But what am I to do for work, Bishop?'

'I shall make inquiries,' replied the other, unable to disguise his look of annoyance at having been addressed by the less formal title. 'There are one or two people in the diocese who may be able to help, and you are at liberty to place yourself on the National Appointments Register.'

This latter suggestion was futile, as both men knew. Without a bishop's license questions would be asked, thereby making it impossible for Ben to exercise a ministry elsewhere. Ranks would close, the drawbridge of Mother

Church would be pulled up behind them, and by being placed on the archbishop's cautionary list - an automatic procedure that accompanied any sacking - the ostracized priest didn't, as the phrase would have it, 'stand a prayer.' By making the inevitable temple with the fingers of both hands tapping together, the bishop conveyed to Ben a piece of body language akin to Pontius Pilate washing his hands.

Before closing their meeting and as though he were the fount of pastoral concern, the bishop suggested, 'I would urge you, Father Benjamin, to sort this matter out as a matter of priority. I presume you intend keeping the child, and although marrying this lady would be one way of sorting out where to go from here, there could be alternatives.'

'Such as?'

'Moving to another part of the country and resuming your ministry in a completely new sphere of work.'

Ben was mindful of the large number of Catholic priests - was it in excess of 100,000? - Many who had been lured by similar advice. After making so many thousands of women pregnant, *'Fathers'* were allowed to hush things up simply by walking away as parents and partners. Ben couldn't conceal his look of disgust at what the bishop seemed to be proposing.

'Anyway I shall remember you in my prayers,' oozed his lordship, getting up from his chair. He was about to offer Ben a handshake but thought better of it.

Returning to their flat, Ben felt sure that his career within the church had hit a wall.

*'The Bastard!'* was all he could say to Angela.

'What did he say? No, don't tell me, I can guess!'

'The usual sanctimonious claptrap, making out he had everyone's interests at heart, when he had none,' said Ben. 'At least, no-one's interests but his own! He wants me out, while making a strong hint that I had an alternative by walking out on you!'

'*Good God!* I don't believe it! Damn his eyes!' For a moment Angela really lost it. 'He's a complete *arsehole!* A total fraud! Did he give you any time limit?'

'No, but I'll try and press him for as much time as possible, like a full year's salary with effect from my resignation date.'

Ben was in that hapless predicament, experienced by a few clergy, told to vacate their living with little or no fair redress against constructive dismissal. Many clergy remain subject to the near-feudalistic power still exercised by certain bishops over them. A disenfranchised vicar, whose living is in the gift of the bishop, as it was in Ben's case, has no effective comeback through a court of appeal; still less through any European Court of Human Rights.

'That bugger gave Christopher Wilkes a fairer deal than he gave us,' exploded Ben. 'In fact there's no comparison! I know because Wilkes, told me that if he took six months' paid leave, the bishop would find him something suitable in due course. You've got a complete psycho like Wilkes who looks like he's committed murder and who's treated his wife and family like shit, and the bishop's prepared to offer him something after a respectable interlude, and all the while keeping him on full pay. It's *unbelievable!*'

'All it proves is that the bishop's a psycho too!' replied Angela. 'It also brings home the fact that even if you stayed in the stipendiary ministry, you could never work properly with the likes of Letharge at the helm.'

Having had his hand forced by the bishop, they needed some secure employment. Perhaps he could be employed as a field worker with the homeless charity, for which hitherto he had been an unsalaried director. Before long, Angela might work at home as a semi-qualified astrologer, with consultation fees in the order of £25 an hour. But their options were further limited with Angela's pregnancy.

The people attracted to the vocation of priesthood are often, if not 'loners' then individuals, who can enjoy their own company. This is a normal state of affairs, since men and women called to holy orders need to be able to stand apart and who, by so doing, can more easily fulfill their calling. But Christopher Wilkes was not only a person who stood isolated, he lived in his own world sensing that if he had friends at all, they dwelt in the mists of time.

Commonly our friends are those with whom we can identify over some shared experience in our past - friends from school or college perhaps; friends with whom we may have shared some adventure or danger, or more importantly friends who've just stood the test of time. With the passing of the years old friends may appear more enduring than many of the acquaintances we make in later life, given that cynicism can too readily choke off the potential for developing friendships as we grow older.

Following his climb in the Alps and upon returning to England, Christopher was on something of a 'high.' Mont Blanc had exhilarated him, reminding him of his earlier experiences on the mountains of Kilamanjaro and Kenya. Purged by the clean alpine air and having put his life literally 'on the line,' he was elated to have done something 'right' at last, something that in fact had been truly gallant! Having saved three men's lives including his own, he could turn his back on his past. As well as making a clean break from All Saints, he could forget everything - his ex-wife and family along with any other unfortunate memories.

With money to spend, a new chapter in his life beckoned.

Having just saved the lives of two fellow climbers, one a Frenchman and the other an Italian, conceivably new friendships might have been forged. Yet despite the effusive backslapping immediately afterwards, their camaraderie had been only of a functional nature, lifesaving for the duration of the climb but now like the unhitching of their ropes laid to one side.

Perhaps it was this that made him more conscious of being friendless. Nor is friendship secured necessarily even by decades of time, as was all too evident from his failed marriage to Frances. For with divorce proceedings underway, it felt as though he'd *never known* his wife.

So much of a stranger did she now feel to him that he wondered whether he'd even recognize her, if he saw her. The same was true of his children. Dom, Katy – just who were these people? Such estrangement reminded him of his own non-existent relationship with his father; the sadistic ex-missionary turned coffee-planter, whose only legacy to his son had been to pass on his considerable wealth. How easy it is for perfect strangers to live under the same roof. Now perversely it even felt easier to conjure up the face of his long departed *father*, than to visualize those of Frances and their children. With Frances, Dom and Katy out of his life, they bore about as much 'reality' to Christopher as the deceased Stacey.

All this gave Christopher cause to think about would-be friends from his past. There'd been his childhood friends from Kenya of course – Samja, Namdi and Okutu nicknamed, 'Little Snake.' Maybe it was the innocence of youth that brought back such evocative pangs of, was it *love*? Was it his soul that somehow unsullied by childhood memories made young love seem so much more *real*? He thought of friends from his time at university, those he had run against at athletic meets. Were they friends, acquaintances or no more than past shadows?

Casting his mind back he wondered whether there was

anyone, any friendships salvageable from the past whose friendship he might rekindle.

His mind alighted on a contemporary from theological college. After three years of training Mark Tipperary had decided to withdraw from the church, choosing a career in the theatre instead. Since making that decision, all that Christopher knew about Mark was that he'd become quite an acclaimed playwright, living at Camden Town in north London.

Part of Christopher's planned rehabilitation was to do some further climbing for the remainder of his leave of absence. Remembering that Mark too had been an enthusiastic climber, Christopher planned to look up his old acquaintance with the suggestion that they reconnect by going on a climbing weekend in the Lake District.

Before Ben resigned, it was more than the bishop's life was worth to prohibit him from fulfilling one last painful duty. In his capacity as area dean but particularly at the request of Mr. and Mrs. Witcombe and Philippa, Ben had been asked to conduct the funeral of Stacey. With forensic examinations and her autopsy now complete, the remains of her body were at last released for burial, with the funeral being held at All Saints.

Compared with the funeral of Di Hagan this was a yet more searing challenge for the outgoing area dean. With the vicar of All Saints suspended and suspected by some (more so now by virtue of his failed marriage) of being implicated in Stacey's murder, Ben had to call on every ounce of his moral fiber.

Given that the murdered girl had been an active member of the church where she was now being laid to rest, there were so many hurts. Martin her boyfriend was present along with many of her old school friends. The choir had also bravely presented itself, as did Frances Wilkes and her son Dominic. On top of that, of course, the funeral was being conducted within the deanery where he, Ben Carter, had lost his job! Yet he still managed to speak movingly about the young girl, who, despite her wickedly foreshortened life, had given so much to others, eulogizing her for her pretty outgoing character.

'She was a person,' said Ben, 'with everything to live for who, although now dwelling in another place, would remain constant in her love towards all those who loved her.' And he concluded his address almost with a shout, *'LOVE IS A FORCE THAT CANNOT BE EXTINGUISHED BY DEATH!'*

The packed congregation had been consoled in a powerful way. For despite the horror of it all the disposal of Stacey's remains had through a loving Christian burial been given dignified closure.

And if the penny hadn't dropped earlier, it dropped now. Slowly the Witcombe family was coming to suspect Canon Wilkes over the murder of their beloved daughter. Mindful too of Di Hagan's deathbed warning, Philippa felt increasingly uneasy in allowing herself to become so beholden to the former vicar, over the rental arrangement for the flat. Although finances continued to be tight, she was determined to pay her way at the earliest opportunity.

Having a nasty hunch that he might call in his debt some day soon, her intuition was at last functioning along the lines that Di had long hoped and prayed it would.

# Chapter 22

Financially Christopher Wilkes hadn't a care. For whatever the market trends, his portfolio of blue-chip shares and other long-term investments left him lacking for nothing. Despite his mews having set him back by over a million, there was a similar sum again left over. Not only that, his incumbent's stipend was still being provided, like it was some ex gratia payment for taking an extended holiday. So notwithstanding the major acquisition of his London property, he indulged himself further by trading in his Volvo Estate for a new LandRover Discovery. The new vehicle would be more practical for some of the off-roading he might plan to do, when visiting the Lake District or elsewhere.

With few other significant outgoings, a mild irritant persisted that he was continuing to pay the rent on Philippa Witcombe's flat. Part of him didn't mind at all of course. It was more a case of being reminded of Ketborough, a place which at least for the time being, he'd rather forget.

Nor was he to know that Di Hagan had left Philippa a legacy of several thousand pounds in his will, or that the DSS could have paid her rent once her legacy fell below a certain amount. Yet sensing that she might have grown a mite casual over his generosity, he decided to pay her a visit in mid-August whilst on the way to another climbing trip to the Lake District.

'Who's there?' asked the voice in response to the bell which rang just after 8 p.m. Hearing the sensual voice reminded him so much of her sister, not just in looks but by the way she spoke.

Yet Philippa had no wish to convey sensuality to anyone, least of all to a man. A failed marriage to someone who'd shown no further interest in her, despite having fathered their fourteen-month-old toddler, meant that right then men didn't figure at all. All she wanted right then was some independence.

'Pippa, it's me, Christopher!' She felt shocked to hear the familiar voice, and relieved that she'd not opened the door outright.

'What are *you* doing here? I thought you were supposed to be in London.' She also resented the familiarity with which he continued to address her as Pippa.

'I was passing through and wanted to come and see you. I hope that it's convenient since I thought we might have a little chat.' She reacted further to the phrase of 'having a little chat,' like he sought to perpetuate some parental role, and where she knew clearer than ever that none now existed.

'What about? I don't think that's necessary,' she replied guardedly.

'Well, I wished to see how you were for one thing.'

'I'm fine. There will that do?' She was surprised at the sharpness of her tone.

He half-expected her to be wary. Knowing that her sister had been murdered and that her killer still remained at large, Philippa was bound to be uneasy.

'Please do let me in!' the voice pleaded.

It was as though beyond the door she could see the soft

eyes of a slightly differing shade of brown, eyes that had beguiled her before and, had she known it, beguiled others also! For Stacey had been transfixed by those eyes when he'd asked her so endearingly for a photograph of herself, and whether she'd accept him like he was some father-figure.

Two new mortise locks plus a security chain were as much to protect her equipment as herself. There had been a spate of break-ins of late, and although it hadn't been practicable to acquire the late Di Hagan's Border collie just yet, she looked forward to the further protection of Snap in due course.

But was it a lingering sense of guilt and gratitude that then allowed doubts to creep in? For she couldn't deny how kind and thoughtful he'd been in the past. Of course had he phoned beforehand, she might have felt better disposed towards him, or even found some excuse not to be there at all. So despite remaining nervous and annoyed by the interruption, she chose to unlock the two mortises while leaving only the security chain in place.

Her evening hours were precious. For with Rosamund safely in bed she could round off household chores, before returning to her latest project - the re-upholstering of a small Edwardian sofa, brought to her by one of her newly acquired customers. The bell had rung just as she was preparing to staple an undercover of calico in place, before completing the task with a top cover of dark blue embossed velvet.

Nor, however, if she were totally honest could Philippa deny how the man paying her rent might yet be useful. Money remained tight, and there was nothing to prove conclusively that he wasn't the innocent, if not hard-done-by, cleric and husband. Perhaps she shouldn't judge him too harshly. He'd not been arrested or anything, and she'd not heard his version of what lay behind the break-up of his marriage.

But nor could she forget Di Hagan's words spoken as he lay dying; of his warnings over Christopher's apparently weird antics at home, of his treatment of Frances or, for that matter, the total indifference he'd apparently shown towards their daughter Katy and now on drugs. Worse than anything, of course, was the fact that he'd been the last person to see Stacey alive!

Yet she had to arrive at her own conclusions, form her *own* judgment. True, she'd been far too trusting of her ex-husband who'd left her with no more than 'sweet-nothings' whispered in her ear, while proving himself to be 'good for nothing!' But from her experience of him, Christopher Wilkes had been kindness itself, merely wishing to lift a load of worry off her and her impecunious parents.

She decided to test him out. Trying to look at him while talking through the door space, she asked. 'You will have heard of course about Stacey. That she was found in the Lake District. They say she was *murdered* around the time of her going missing!'

'Yes, I heard,' replied Christopher. 'I'm desperately sorry to hear about it. Your parents must feel devastated.'

'They are! We all are! Revd Ben Carter took her funeral and somehow despite everything, he seemed to help everyone.'

She wasn't to know that any admiration expressed for Ben's ministry pierced Christopher like a dagger, it being a reminder of the other's guileless sincerity.

'He also said something very unusual; what's more he said it in your old church,' continued Philippa. 'He admitted to an interest in reincarnation! He even suggested that Stacey might have reincarnated as someone else already and that because we each have an immortal soul, we have to live with who we are, for good or ill!'

With her words welling up in an emotional torrent, she

then began to speak very quickly: 'He also said that Stacey had no problem because she was such a good person, and could reincarnate further up the ladder or some such phrase. He said that the murderer is the one with the problem, because *God knows everything* and even if the killer evades capture now, *he can't run forever!*'

What had become a one-way conversation was being conducted through the safety chink of a door on its security chain. Where was her unaccountable rage coming from? *'Who do you think did it, Christopher?'* She didn't so much ask as hiss the question as she looked directly at him through the narrow gap. Even as he glanced downwards when she put her question, she noted how well and rested he appeared. Either he was someone without a care in the world because his conscience was free, or a man who had no conscience!

Making to say something like: 'I've no idea,' she interrupted any response. 'Do you think that he'll get caught? Apparently the police can discover just about anything these days with their DNA and other tests,' she said. And then, loading the dice further she asked: 'Do *you* believe in reincarnation, Christopher?'

In much the same way as Stacey's question had 'got to him' in the vestry, her sister's rapid-fire interrogation suddenly incensed him. For without answering her, he had in a trice seized her hand that was resting on the wall by the door, to shackle her wrist and forearm.

Only then did she see the expression *beyond* hate.

Shock and pain coursed through her arm to bring an incongruous image to mind. Somewhere she'd read how badgers, if cornered, might bite their adversary until their teeth met.

*'Let go, Christopher! I'm in agony!'* she said between clenched teeth. Was this how a victim of prey might feel when weakened in the pre-numbing stage of poison or

suffocation?

'*Not until you let me in!*' he snarled, his upper lip curling visibly. Pinioned by his large talon-like hand, the absurd line from Little Red Riding Hood ran through her head, 'What big hands you've got grandmamma!' With his upper torso clad only in a short-sleeved shirt the hirsute arm bulged obscenely.

In the few seconds before her death, Stacey had seen the same terrifying transformation. Now after the brief fusillade of questions from her elder sister, the snarling alter ago had been released once more. If Philippa had had any doubts up until then, they were dispelled in an instant by the baleful intimacy now uttered. 'Pippa, I want to be your *friend!* You remind me so much of *Stacey!*'

Her mind was racing. To scream might help but it would also terrify Rosamund, if not provoke him into injuring her further. Such was the right hand's manic strength that it would take no more than a split-second to crush her forearm.

At least the piece of furniture she'd been restoring was fortuitously placed almost up against the door, should he try to break in. Dangerous equipment, which couldn't have been left lying about during the daytime also lay scattered near to her upholstery box. Curved needles, a twelve-inch steel regulator, tack remover, screwdriver, and hammer were all near to hand. Only the large scissors, possibly her best weapon, had fallen to the floor.

It was then that she saw her other weapon. To upholster an Edwardian settee properly, she should have been using tacks. But out of convenience and consideration for her neighbours where repeated hammering would have been tiresome, she'd been using a staple gun. By depressing the trigger, a staple would discharge itself into the material securing it to the piece of furniture being re-covered. Like a paper stapler an upholstery stapler works on the same principle, only using larger staplers and firing them with greater velocity.

As though making to open the door she then made a grab for the tool. Having recently reloaded it, she had plenty of 'ammunition' with which to direct a salvo of staples directly into his right forearm, the arm that was choking the life out of her own.

With no protective clothing the exposed flesh now perforated with wire stitches began to cascade blood, even as his grip hardly lessened. But this only enraged her assailant to twist their interlocked arms around so that it would be her arm, now awash with rivulets of his blood, which she would injure should she continue firing.

'Mummy, I can't sleep!' came a muffled little voice from next door. Maybe it had been the crack of stapler firing that had awoken Rosamund.

'*Dear Christ,* what do I do now?' thought Philippa.

For a moment Wilkes hoped the distraction might give him back the advantage.

Philippa could do little more than half turn her head, as she called, 'I'll be right there, darling!' Trying to sound as normal as possible, she added, 'Go back to sleep, there's a good girl!'

She was now defending her daughter's life as well as her own.

'Aim for the eyes!' she told herself leveling her weapon like it was a real firearm, lethal enough to fell the beast and bring it crashing to its knees. More staples then struck him across the bridge of his nose, and which although failing to penetrate to any depth produced more bleeding plus a flood of involuntary tears. With blood and tears flowing down both channels around his nose and into his mouth, he turned his head, all the while trying blindly to wrestle the stapler from her with his free hand. This resulted in a further discharge of the two-pronged needles fired into his left cheek and temple.

'*Mummy!*' the small voice persisted.

'I'm just coming darling. Go back to sleep. There's a good girl.'

Still he clung on with the blood now coursing down his arm, great drops starting to saturate the doormat outside. Perversely the coconut matting was inscribed with the word 'Welcome.' With more of the darts searing his flesh while having failed to disarm her, he sought to protect his face by using his open palm.

'Mummy' the voice was growing quieter.

*Please God*, let Rosamund go back to sleep, she found herself praying.

Even as his grip started to slacken, there was a side to her that wouldn't abate; molten lava that continued to flow long after the first volcanic explosion. For it was *she,* who now sought to prolong the contest, she, who wished to both mutilate if not destroy. For he'd become the target not just of her loathing or one for avenging Stacey's death, but as the embodiment of male depravity. In her teens Philippa had met boys who'd tried to seduce her while showing no overtures of affection. Shadows emerged from her past to include the ex-husband, who'd simply used her only to become the non-existent father of their daughter. As for this one time vicar whose earlier kindness had been no more than veneer for his own depraved behaviour, her rage felt insatiable.

The left hand he'd been using to protect his face now stood open, bloody and perforated like a paper target from a rifle range. Still he held his hand up almost invitingly, allowing her the savage pleasure of inflicting further pain, even as the repeated pulling on the trigger caused her hand to throb violently.

The wolf was dropping on its haunches; the predator now himself run to ground was cowering if not whimpering. Literally she had the upper hand but as long as he clung to her wrist, limply now, she struggled to keep discharging more staples into any exposed part of his upper body. Only her exhaustion thwarted her from prolonging his torture.

It was then that with icy detachment she said, 'Stay in my line of fire for as long as you can stand it, *you fucking bastard!*' No longer the gentle creature with doe-like impressionable eyes, she'd become feral, demented even. What might have been the gruesome foreplay of murder preceded by rape had been reversed into a sadistic wounding by the victim upon her attacker. Going down to meet him on his knees, Philippa hissed at Christopher, 'Go now, before I scream and call the police. Stay out of my life and never *ever* return!'

Not wishing for a stream of blood to be traced to her door, she flung him a piece of discarded upholstery material with which to mop himself up. Neither the material nor his shirt, crimson on his left side, would staunch the bleeding. But she was thinking coolly in terms of keeping the landing outside her flat as free from bloodstains as possible.

With his grip little more than the pleading clasp of a beggar on his knees, she pulled her arm free leaving him to roll away from her door, which she immediately made secure once more. In the near darkness outside she could hear him groaning quietly while bumping against the metal handrail of the stairwell, like he was a drunk.

'What if someone sees or recognizes him?' she thought. But he would have been as anxious to retreat into the shadows, as she was in seeking not to draw attention to herself. With the bile surfacing in her mouth and slumping onto her upholstery stool, she put her head between her knees. Despite the night's warmth, her left forearm blood-soaked and bruised caused a wave of cold perspiration to wash over, only to leave her whole body shivering violently.

A full five minutes passed before she rose unsteadily to her feet first to wash off the blood, *his* blood! Bathing her face and neck with warm water, she then rinsed her mouth and swallowed two cupfuls of water, before going to make some strong sweet tea and checking out Rosamund. With her sleeping form untroubled, it seemed that the infant had done no more than been calling out in her sleep. Brushing her hair with her undamaged hand she kissed her goodnight.

Warily she then half-opened the front door in order to retrieve her doormat, which she later soaked thoroughly in the bath. Then opening the door once more she wiped clean all traces of the blood that had splattered in and around the doorjamb itself. Mercifully everything seemed quiet outside. With her immediate neighbours rarely being in before ten, she could see no obvious blood splashes leading from her door to the stairwell.

Although she should have reported the attack straightaway, insisting that Ketborough's former vicar was, beyond doubt, her sister's killer she had an almost morbid dread of *not* being taken seriously. Some irrational fear told her that the police might be more sympathetic with her attacker than with herself. For despite any allegations made against Wilkes, the law might take a perversely different point of view - that he'd not intruded, not so much as even crossed her threshold and that it was *she* who'd engaged him in conversation; she who was in receipt of payments made by him for her rent, and that it was she who had committed a serious assault upon *him!* She was aware how the law could sometimes argue that black was white by turning things around entirely. For instance had she not cleaned up the blood around her front door, an argument might have been presented that it was her visitor who'd suffered a malicious wounding, and not the other way about.

With whom might she share her woes? She dared not tell her parents. There was no longer the wise and sadly all-too-perceptive Di Hagan to consult with. She decided to contact Frances there and then. Although this would mean giving her further terrifying information about her ex-husband, she - Frances needed to know the full picture, reasoned Philippa. It would put her more on her guard than perhaps she was at present. For if Christopher could sneak up from London and make a surprise call on her, he might well do the same to his ex-wife.

Nor had she any idea where he might have escaped to that evening.

The tragedy was that by not going to the police, Philippa failed to understand how supportive they would have been.

With his upper body and face wracked in pain, he knew there was no choice but to return to London. Despite his intention of visiting the Lakes, too many questions would have been asked about his facial appearance. More to the point all climbing would, for the time being, prove to be impossible. Better to hunker down in the metropolis for a week or two and lick his wounds, and where if he had any explaining to do it was easier doing so within the anonymity of London. He could always make out that he was recovering from a climbing accident or some such story. More positively, despite the pain, he sensed that his injuries were relatively superficial. He'd not been blinded and had he been wearing thicker clothing, he could have easily snatched the stapler out of her hand.

With no intention of visiting any Casualty Department, he clearly couldn't drive in his present condition. Fortunately climbing had taught him the rudiments of First Aid, as well as ensuring that he always kept an ample medical supply close to hand, with bandages, splints and antiseptic all stored in the back of his LandRover. Having no wish to leave bloodstains on the upholstery of his new vehicle, he sought to patch himself up somewhere close by.

He'd left his car in a quiet part of Ketborough not far from where Philippa lived, and from where he chose to walk to one of the town's small public parks near by. In the late dusk and having gathered some medical kit along with a spare tank top and a pair of tracksuit trousers, he reached the park. One or two couples lingered in the near darkness, but whom he avoided by entering a dense area of lilacs and rhododendron bushes. Gratefully he fell to his knees in the soft peat.

First, he had to remove the embedded shards of wire. Working by feel and with the use of a pair of tin-snips, which he'd retrieved from his toolbox, he used his right hand to sever and remove those staples in his left arm and some around his face, doing so with relative ease. The removal of staples embedded in his left hand was both more painful and difficult, as then it was to use his left hand to remove the staples in his right forearm.

The whole exercise grew more difficult as his blood began pouring profusely once more. He had further difficulty with the dozen or more staples that had entered his temple and right cheek, opting to use a pair of nail scissors. This was where a visit to Casualty would have been so much easier, for by prizing the scissors outwards rather like circlip pliers, they were only partially effective. Some staples had to be torn away rather than smoothly extracted now that blood, slippery as oil, was running everywhere. He then struggled to dislodge a further cluster of staples that had harmlessly enmeshed themselves in his thick head of graying hair.

Desperate to wash off as much of the blood as possible, he was fortunate to find a men's toilet in the park, which despite its rundown character was both unlocked and provided a sink with running water. Washing off the surplus blood, he then dabbed his wounds with TCP, the antiseptic's excruciating sting reminding him of a time back in Kenya when he'd been attacked by hornets.

Having washed as best he could, he returned to the bushes to wait for a further fifteen minutes to allow his wounds to congeal. He then swathed his right arm in a crepe bandage, whilst applying more antiseptic using cotton wool swabs and melolin patches where necessary. Removing his bloodied shirt and trousers he stuffed them as far into the bushes as he could, before pulling on a tank top and tracksuit bottoms.

Now in total darkness, he slipped away from the park back to his vehicle. Before driving back to London, he restored his strength with some mint-cake and high-energy glucose tablets. Fortunately with the LandRover having an override facility driving was fairly straightforward where, without the need for changing gear, he could spare the use of his left hand.

Sensing that nobody except Philippa would have known of his visit to Ketborough, he suddenly felt elated. It was the same sensation as when he'd scaled the peaks of Mount Kenya and Mont Blanc, or more recently when he'd checked to see that Stacey's skeleton had remained undetected. But goddamit she'd now been found. And there was, of course, another part of him felt enraged: Enraged that along with his wife, a second woman had had the courage to resist him. Yet in manic-depressive mode, by the time he'd driven eastwards on to the M40 from the M5, so a degree of his old swagger returned. Furthermore, he could get one over Philippa by cutting off all payments towards her rent from thereon.

For a moment in the cosseting comfort of his vehicle he smirked, only then to let out a terrible and mirthless laugh.

In the belief that no one other than Philippa had seen him, a further fleeting thought crossed his mind.

Did he perhaps, just possibly, have the luck of the devil?

# Chapter 23

'I probably shouldn't feel pig-sick that the Church wants to get shot of me. I've hardly toed the conventional line,' said Ben before adding. 'But I'm still gutted!'

The four of them were seated in the living room of the area dean's rectory and, although given three months' notice, he was now officially sacked. Despite the house being too large for a man living on his own, it being a large well-modernized Victorian structure standing in nearly an acre of walled garden, it was nonetheless *home*. But such being the ways of the Church of England where the job and the house go together, dismissal for any parish vicar always meant eviction.

'You've every right to feel gutted,' replied Angela. 'In terms of your livelihood and home being taken away, that is! Whether or not you want to *stay* in the Church is a different matter entirely. But what makes it so much worse is that our highly-favoured Canon Wilkes can enjoy leave of absence on full pay, presumably to be welcomed back into the bosom of Mother Church in due course.'

Frances and Philippa nodded in glum sympathy, the occasion for their meeting being the day following Christopher's lethal attack on Philippa.

Angela continued: 'such are the ways and means of Anglican justice when you've got a despotic bishop in charge. So much for 'human rights! One man pilloried for his gifts whilst another, who at the very least should be under twenty four hour surveillance, goes on being pampered and provided for.'

Only then did Ben suddenly look contrite:

'Dear Lord, Philippa, I'm so sorry! We've met specifically to hear your problem, and here I am rabbiting on about *my* own woes. Tell us what happened, if you're up to it. Like so much else it sounds beyond belief!'

'It's OK,' answered Philippa, who had asked her parents to look after Rosamund for the day. Looking wan and drawn through lack of sleep she spoke very quietly, 'We've all got huge problems right now and having phoned Frances earlier, she's already helped me off-load some of mine.'

'What in God's name happened?' asked Angela.

'Well, you have to know, that's for sure,' replied Philippa. 'I'm sorry to repeat most of this, Frances.'

'Go ahead, we all need to hear it.' Frances sounded totally desolate.

Philippa paused: 'Well, he, *Christopher* arrived completely out of the blue last night, making out he needed to talk with me and that it was urgent. By paying for my rent he tended to do this as an excuse for laying claim on my time. He'd done it before. Anyway at least I held out from letting him in, keeping the door on its chain. Not only was his call inconvenient, I was in the middle of restoring a sofa and had no wish to talk to him. I didn't want to awaken Rosamund for one thing . . .' She paused, 'and of course it was so soon after Stacey's funeral; that along with the fact that just a few days before he died, Di had warned me to be on my guard.'

'Have *nothing whatever* to do with him'! She could hear his tired warning more clearly than ever now.

'But the next thing I knew,' continued Philippa, surprised at how calm she sounded, 'was how when he grabbed my arm through the space in the door, he looked totally completely mad in a way I've never seen before! And *God!* The pain from his grip was unreal! It was then that he told me how much I looked like Stacey and that he wanted to be my friend!'

'Holy shit!' Ben needed to watch his blood pressure already.

No further proof was needed to attest to Wilke's insanity, even as Philippa then rolled up the left sleeve of her summer cardigan. There were the blue and black indentations of her assailant's thumb and four fingers around her slender forearm.

*'Jesus wept!'* was Ben's next expletive. The bruise looked like the shadow of some giant tarantula.

'Don't ask me where the image of little Red Riding Hood came into all this, but it was like being in the grip of some monster,' said Philippa.

Aghast, Frances concurred how on that Easter night at the vicarage, she'd experienced something similar. The dark outline with its curled lip and wheedling voice returned to her in a terrifying flashback.

Recalling the sight of Christopher's hands in prayer at their Chapter meeting, Angela too was reminded of her premonition. 'Talk about having cruel hands,' she said as though talking to herself.

'*Christ Almighty!*' exploded Ben. 'If the man did that to you, he's truly dangerous! Talk about the mark of the beast!'

Frances flinched that so terse a description of her ex-husband said it all. For how easily it might have been *she* who'd been 'marked,' if not murdered.

'Yes, but that's as nothing compared to what I did to him!' replied Philippa. 'Because I was upholstering at the time I managed to grab my staple gun and lacerate his arm, face and hands with it. In fact it was like I got completely taken over, shooting at him for as long I could. I just didn't want to stop. I wanted to paralyse him, blind him, although I didn't!'

'What happened next?' Angela's jaw had inadvertently dropped a full inch.

Despite having told Frances the story already, it seemed to help Philippa having to repeat all the details:

'Well, he eventually slackened his hold and let go, hardly surprising in the circumstances. His blood seemed to have gone everywhere, and eventually I was able to push the door shut on him. I then heard him lumbering off, a bit like a wounded animal. Looking back I'm amazed at my own reaction, fearing that I might even have *killed* him.'

'Fat chance,' said Ben. 'I wouldn't much fancy having staples fired at me at point blank range, but the wounds would have been largely superficial even though he'd have bled profusely. Besides, given that we suspect Christopher of having killed your sister, you'd have been fighting for your life, as well as being consumed with revenge in some way. Your rage and fear were probably the things that saved you!'

'What should I do now?' asked Philippa.

'The first thing surely is to have your arm looked at?' asked Ben.

'No, I don't believe that anything is broken in fact. But if I feel that there's anything wrong other than just the present bruising and soreness, then I'll go to Casualty,' she answered.

'You have to go to the police, surely?' asked Ben.

Although they respected that she needed to handle things her way, the others found themselves somewhat confused as to why Philippa hadn't gone to the police already.

Turning to Frances, Ben asked, 'At a practical level, Frances, have you made sure that your bungalow secure?'

'He may have some notion as to where you're living,' added Angela.

'Don't worry,' Frances replied. 'Improving the locks was one of the first things I did when I moved in.'

Promising to give each other their full support, they got up to leave.

'Oh, I nearly forgot to tell you,' said Frances, 'our friend Mr. Zbierski has been making his observations again. I spoke to him briefly this morning and apparently he saw Christopher driving a new LandRover yesterday evening, presumably only a short time before he attacked you Philippa. Mr. Z said he was positive that it was "dat bloddy vicar, thou's ex!" – as he put it – and wondered what was going on. Z had been in somebody else's car at the time, so he couldn't tell me any more.'

Despite everything they had to smile at Frances' attempt at imitating the Pole.

'All the more amazing then that he saw anything,' mused Philippa. 'They all say the man's got eyes like a hawk.'

'And here's another thing,' said Frances, 'everybody's saying how much kinder Mr. Zbierski seems to have become. He struck me as being quite different - not his old rude self at all. In fact I got the clear impression that he was genuinely concerned and wanted to help.'

'Did you say anything to him?' asked Ben.

'I didn't know what to say,' answered Frances. 'I was scared more than anything. Of course Philippa had told me about the visit, so I knew that Zbierski must have seen Christopher, although that's the first I heard about him driving a new car.'

'Living it up on his freebie holiday, all paid for by the Church.' Ben couldn't resist the bitter jibe.

'Well, at least Mr. Z's a witness if we need him,' said Philippa. 'I wish someone like him had actually seen what took place outside my front door. I've never been so terrified in my life!'

'And yet you were given some supernatural strength to see him off,' suggested Angela, before adding, 'we've got to stand together. Not just against *him* but against the *bishop*. Surely it can't be long before we have the devil on the run.'

'I tell thee, I saw him, plain as a bloddy pikestaff! He was driving a great big LandRover or summat. It had got a new number plate,' said Zbierski.

'Well, how do you know it was a LandRover?' asked Nick Crooks. 'You've always said you don't know one car from another.'

'I know a LandRover when I sees one,' replied the Pole. 'You see enough of 'dem big boggers at the Races. Big posy things with bull-bars on the front and all them fancy bits inside.'

There followed some debate as to whether it might have been any one of a number of off-roaders, with Crooks observing: 'There's Mitsubishis, Toyotas, Nissans Patrols and a whole load of SUVs so that if you don't know what you're looking for they all look alike.'

But Z remained adamant. 'I tell thee, the bogger was in a LandRover.'

Over the past months life had returned to something like normal at The Magpie. But now with the girl's body having been discovered up in the Lake District, and of her recent burial the pub's gossip had been revitalized; in fact put back on red alert with Zbierski's recent sighting of Canon Christopher Wilkes in the neighbourhood.

Even Mrs. Myers, who still sang in All Saints' choir, and while having a quiet drink with her husband, couldn't stop herself declaring, 'I think it's a crying shame that they've got rid of that area dean chappie, what's his name? Ben Carter?

All right, I don't necessarily agree with him and that ex-nun living together, but these days what's the harm? I mean it's not as though he's run off with someone else's wife.'

'So what if he had,' chipped in Lech. 'He'd be a bigger Christian still if he ran off with my missus!'

The comment hardly raised a laugh, knowing that Lech was in fact as happily married as anyone had a right to be.

'It's got to be all wrong,' said landlord Nick Cocheron, 'especially when Wilkes is being given time off on full pay *and*, so I'm told, looks likely to be given a new job once he's got his divorce over and done with. After all, if he can get a divorce and still stay in favour, where's the logic over this Carter chap getting the push?'

Leaning on the bar and rubbing his chin, the landlord went on, 'Speaking of which, how's his wife doing, *ex*-wife I should say?'

'She's in Di's old place,' answered Z. 'He gave it to her in his will. 'Sides she looked all shook up when I asked her as if she'd seen her old man, because I told 'er I 'ad.'

'What did she say?' this question coming from Mr. Myers.

'She said that No, she didn't know he'd been in town. But I'll tell thee what. My question got her frit big time. She started shaking and didn't seem to know where she was. She's a nice lady but I reckon she's in a bad way. He's a bad bogger that Wilkes and I don't give a sh… Kraut sausage who knows it.'

Scrunching their eyebrows while jerking their heads back, Lech and Crooks looked at each other. 'What's got into Z that he's trying to mind his language?' was their unspoken question. Nor were they the only ones to have noticed how Zbierski seemed to be cleaning up his act.

'Well, as I say, I think it's a crying shame that they should get rid of that Reverend Carter,' chipped in Mrs. Myers.

'He's a real gentleman and he took a beautiful service for that poor wee lamb Stacey.'

There was a strong murmur of assent. It seemed like most of the town had attended the funeral and from all accounts, the area dean had done magnificently.

'I'll tell thee what we can do,' said Z, 'we can hold a protest. Ask the bishop what the f… what he's up to, getting rid of a good man like dat, an' 'olding on to that other bloddy creep.' Z's language could only restrain itself so far.

'Who's going to organize it?' asked the landlord.

'Why, thou can do it,' said Zbierski.' Get thee out of thy cabbage patch for a bit. Do thee some good!'

Nick Cocheron's obsession with his allotment did tend to make him something of a loner, if not actually antisocial. He'd become besotted with producing record-sized marrows, huge unsightly objects which although hardly edible were said to be worth upwards of a £100 a specimen.

By taking a swig on his shandy, the landlord signaled that his resistance, while bouncing back with the retort: 'I reckon Granville's our man for getting things done!' Like Crooks, the man behind the bar saw himself more as a follower than a leader.

Nor was Z unaffected by the flattery, with Crooks further endorsement: 'Sides, you know how to fight, Z. I'd back you up all the way. You've got what it takes. Look how you got everyone behind you over that pelican crossing! The Council had no choice in the end but to put it in place. People are starting to sit up and listen when you speak, Granville. You're the man for the job!'

'We'll back you up one hundred percent,' chorused Mr. and Mrs. Myers. Having always been a filter for the latest church gossip, she knew that there was a growing number at All Saints starting to see things differently. Now that their vicar had left, some in the congregation had begun to express doubts, not just about Wilkes but about the way the bishop had treated Ben Carter. She felt emboldened to add: 'After all, people from All Saints are beginning to ask questions, like, "Mrs. Wilkes can't have just walked out on her husband for no good reason. She was always such a nice person. Something must have pushed her to do such a thing. Besides there's nobody else involved . . ."'

Spurred on by the new mood of simmering anger, Cocheron helped to make up everybody's mind: 'you know something else? Our friend Di Hagan would, to my mind, be the one up front leading the petition, if he were still alive. I know for a fact that he couldn't abide Wilkes, and they say he was one of the best damn detectives on the Force in his day. He knew more than he was letting on. I agree with Crooks that Granville's our best man to put the bishop on the spot. Besides ol' Di would be the first one to give you the thumbs up, Z'

That was the clincher! It was taken as read by the patrons at The Magpie, along with what was felt to be Di Hagan's backing from the grave, that the fiery Pole should get a petition underway and God help anyone who objected.

'Righto, everything's got to go that you can see, except *that,*' said Frances pointing to the large desk in her living room.

Much as she had loved Di, the purge on his property provided a much-needed distraction. Having lived in her new home for nearly three months, she felt the time had come to make changes. With the bungalow having been left in a sorry state for too long and with Frances seeking to make a clean break from the past, the clear out was therapeutic as would be the decorating she planned to do later.

There were weighty lumps of furniture to dispose of, these including a cumbersome three-piece suite, an unpretentious oak dining room table, plus four late

Edwardian chairs, a winged armchair, a mock Victorian dresser and an upright piano. Old carpets, tired bedroom furniture along with two G-Plan wardrobes also just made it to the auction in preference to the dump. Along with these there were items of furniture brought across from the vicarage that she also wanted to be shot of.

She's suggested to Dominic and a student friend that they'd come over to help her sort out the bungalow. 'Better to pay you than the removal men' had been the incentive for them to hire a van to visit the auction with any saleable items, while going to the local dump with what was left. 'Oh, and one other thing,' she shouted from the kitchen. 'Please go through any drawers or cupboards to check for any papers which I may have missed.'

She said this because, despite going through everything meticulously, she remained perplexed as to how one item in particular still eluded her.

'There's some papers at the bottom of this tin box,' said Dom's friend as he staggered out with a medium size trunk mostly full of crockery.

'No, that's okay,' replied Frances. 'Anything that's packed up, I've already gone through with a fine toothcomb! That goes for all the magazines in boxes along with the pile of old music scores on the piano.' (Di's wife had played the piano for many years). Poor old Di! He really had taken to living in a time warp. Items of his wife's clothing had appeared, all suffering from years of moth and decay. These were all scooped up as were potted-plants, a number of landscape prints that had hung on tobacco-stained wallpaper along with a rack of meerschaums and other curly pipes.

Restoring her new home throughout was a further way to pay her respects to Di. For he deserved better than the treatment that, in grief and in retirement he'd meted out upon himself for too long.

'But that desk must go absolutely nowhere, except to stay where it is,' she repeated her instruction to Dom. 'It's written down in black and white in his will.'

The desk was a large roll-top Edwardian bureau in which Di had kept all his papers and which had, to all intents and purposes, served as his filing cabinet.

'Why would he want to keep it?' asked Dom. 'After all, it doesn't look much better than the other stuff and you've been through all its contents.'

'Ours not to reason why,' answered his mother. 'It's down in the will to stay and stay it must!'

In the same way that she felt constrained from decorating too soon, she had hesitated about going through his papers and other memorabilia. Yet as the sole executor along with Di's solicitor, as well as being the principle beneficiary of his estate, Frances had been obliged to make a painstaking inventory of all his personal effects. For despite the run-down condition of his home, Di had been fastidious when it came to keeping important documents, these all having being kept within the confines of the desk.

She decided to hold onto his old photographs, especially those of him and his late wife, as she did with a number of his other records. What he'd kept was either precious during his lifetime, or might yet be of further importance. Frances chose to hold on to these plus other documents, 'just in case.'

It was because of his thoroughness that she was all the more puzzled to find no trace of the photograph of Stacey Witcombe, which she'd given him for safekeeping all those months back just after she'd disappeared. She also recalled Di mentioning that in the event of the girl's body ever being discovered he had some further 'evidence,' which should be reported. Yet having scoured the house from top to bottom, looking in every nook and cranny including an old chest of drawers in the garage, full of tools, she'd found nothing.

'Mum, are you *all right?*' Dom had come into the kitchen where she'd been scouring the tops of old Formica shelves now empty, but where deep in thought she'd been doing so absentmindedly.

'I'm fine,' she said. 'It's just this clearing out's a lot of hassle. Let's all go out this evening and enjoy a Chinese or something.' She mustered a smile. 'Besides which I mustn't put too much strain on my chess-playing son.'

'Bollocks!' said Dom who disliked any suggestion that likened his chess skills to wimpishness. Then adding with a smile, he asked: 'So when do we get paid?'

'After we've eaten' she dug him in the ribs.

Their laughter aside, he didn't mind his friend overhearing when he said: 'but mum, something's on your mind. I hope it's not dad. You're freer now than you've ever been to be yourself and we know that Katy's getting some proper treatment.'

She hadn't had the heart to tell him of Katy's relapse.

'Don't worry, Dom, I'm just a bit overtired,' replied his mother.

'If you say so,' he replied, unconvinced. 'Anyway, we'll just slip down the road for a quick one. See you in about half an hour.'

She gave thanks for the brief respite. For rather than helping her to forget, it was as though having Dom around only sharpened her thoughts. For not only were there all the worries for her son and more especially for Katy, where on earth was that mislaid photograph as found in Christopher's cassock? Not only that the ghastly episode with Christopher back in the vicarage some months back had re-surfaced in the light of his recent attack on Philippa. And with Stacey's body, so recently discovered in what was one of *his* favourite climbing haunts in the Lake District she longed for the companionship of Di to help her. Whilst other pieces of her broken and jagged jigsaw were fitting together with frightening precision, all that seemed to be missing was the other 'evidence' he'd once spoken of.

Seeing now all too clearly how Christopher's fixation for Stacey and her elder sister revolved around violence and his penchant for impressionable young women, Frances felt waves of guilt wash over her. Why had she been blind for so long?

She wanted to go to the police. Yet like Philippa, she had had misgivings. She had no evidence as such against Christopher. Harking back to some domestic altercation at the vicarage would have proved next to nothing. Nor would some reference to a photograph of Stacey found in her husband's cassock mean anything if it couldn't be found.

In a court of law, without corroborative evidence, Christopher's defense could have embroidered an argument to suggest domestic spite, dismissing her for being vindictive. 'Hell hath no fury like a woman spurned in marriage,' would have been a central plank of their argument. 'Such was her desire for revenge that she'd stop at nothing, even if it meant seeking to entrap her former husband for murder'!

It was as though she could hear his defense lawyer speaking, even as she thought how to incriminate her ex.

# Chapter 24

'So what's your preference ducky. Fancy a good time, do you?'

If the girl in the red boots and matching leather skirt with a slit either side up to her waistband fancied any of the older men, this one looked better than most. In his cavalry twills, Daks jumper and tooled leather shoes, and notwithstanding the tight facial expression he was an improvement on those fat slobs who still liked to imagine that they were God's gift. Besides he doesn't look short of a bob or two, she thought.

'You looking then?' she persisted.

Although not familiar with the proposal, the words registered a cliché as old as the hills.

'No, thank you!' Christopher's air of aloofness contradicted itself as someone not interested, yet morbidly so.

'Another time, ducky,' scarlet lips pouted him a kiss as he walked on. She felt pity as much as anger at so many typical of the last the last gent who failed to stop. 'Trying to come to terms with themselves, getting their jollies by window shopping but not buying.'

Three weeks had passed since his ill-fated trip to Ketborough, allowing his face and arm to heal remarkably well. The scabs had cleared and the effect of taking runs in Hyde Park in the midday sun had largely coloured out the red welts around his forehead and left cheek, welts that would duly fade into insignificant scars. Thanks to the city's anonymity he was also spared having to explain how his disfigurement was the result of a climbing accident. For those with sufficient funds, London was a great place in which to hide one's identity.

The night was warm, and confident enough to show his face in public, he'd been to see a play in Shaftesbury Avenue. But the production had been disappointing and he chose to walk up to Charing Cross Road. On several occasions earlier, he'd visited the phone booths around St Giles Circus, intrigued by the lurid little cards left there. Previous curiosity as to the sexual favours being offered now turned the vagaries of his walk into a more purposeful venture into Soho.

Yet for all the dangers he posed at one level, he was at another sexually naive. A closely guarded secret was that from late adolescence he'd suffered from a severe form of erectile dysfunction, a serious bout of malaria contracted in childhood having been diagnosed as the cause. For someone so apparently virile his dysfunction was both a contributor and consequence of his damaged personality and one, needless to say, aggravated further by his loveless marriage.

Indeed the secret, still withheld even from their children, was that Dominic and Katy had been conceived through the services of a private clinic offering artificial insemination. Long before the liberating era of in-vitro fertilization treatments and frozen embryos, A.I. was considered if not morally questionable then certainly weird. It was this parental shame as to how his children had been born in the world that never left him nor, to a lesser extent, Frances.

Nor could he deny how his dysfunction was a problem,

or how the sado-masochistic invitations on the calling cards might arouse him in a way that little else could. Of course he knew that 'S & M' was not new to him as a 'turn on,' there was something of the Harold Wilkes in him. Nor could he deny that the murder of Stacey had in some way been sadistically pleasurable. Yet despite the killing itself having excited him he'd not physically molested her, recalling how his dysfunction had existed even then.

Before he could check himself, and as though his leave of absence from the church destroyed his inhibitions in some way, a quick phone call had directed him to an address five minutes away on foot.

To outward appearances the brothel was a massage parlour. Taking his £110 (£200 for the full hour), the Madam in charge stated, 'Half an hour to go with whoever you choose, depending on who's available.'

She pointed him to a wall on which were fixed some ten black-and-white photographs of girls in suspenders and micro-skirts, under which were printed their names plus specialities rendered.

'I'll take her,' he muttered, pointing to a Danish girl called Brigid, motivated by the further anonymity provided by seeing a European girl.

Brigid turned out to bear little resemblance to her picture for the simple reason that she was dressed from head to toe in a black leather catsuir zipped up to her neck, and topped with a black facemask. The thick dark brown belt, flexed in black leather clad hands, was clearly her talisman. If he sought his own anonymity, it was as nothing compared to the faceless woman who spoke only in whispers, as though even talk wasn't part of the deal.

It was the absence of preliminaries that appealed, along with the fact that she appeared to take actual pleasure in lashing at him with her belt. With no questions asked, theirs was but the encounter of two damaged psyches meeting in a loveless alcove of pain. For, like his assailant, he was but one of so many for whom erotic pleasure had declined into a sadomasochistic exchange. With no warm parental cuddles in childhood, he would no more divulge to this Brigid bitch his father's beatings of long ago, than she with him over a drunken stepfather who'd constantly hit and abused her. Only the catharsis of laying into a man of middle age brought her any respite.

Upon returning to his Chelsea mews he felt purged and elated, excited that having visited a prostitute he felt so little *guilt!* It was like crossing some chasm of which hitherto he'd been terrified. Now if he admitted to any need for therapy in years past, he saw his newfound experience as compensation for the violent urges he'd fantasized about before. In Stacey's case it was just unfortunate that through her 'innocent' question, she'd shattered the fantasy thereby inviting her death. Had the girl played his game better, all might have been well. But she'd died as very nearly had Philippa, because both young women challenged with a reality from which he'd long detached himself.

From thereon he knew his fantasies, his world of unreality, would take him into a deeper and darker place. Destiny would decide to where those fantasies might lead. But for the time being his monthly pay cheque from the church would be used as a form of mischief currency, allowing him to visit Brigid on several further occasions before seeking new areas of excitement.

It was in looking up a pricier dispenser of pain who went by the name of 'Paratroop Sade,' that he ran into serious trouble. Sade, short for Sadie, preferred S & M on account of the fewer risks involved. An intelligent woman who, despite acting the part, liked to treat kinky sex more as a laugh than something to which she was naturally predisposed. More to the point, Sade could select and retain a carefully chosen clientele.

Self-employed for almost ten years she had, all things considered, worn well. Yet tiring of the unending customers who came to her for straight sex, S & M felt like a welcome relief. For one thing her customers tended to belong to a higher class of punter. These included a retired barrister, various politicians and a number of high-flying businessmen, most proving that they were mere pussycats as to what they required by way of chastisement.

Exercising her guile, she walked the thin line between treating her customers as clients only interested in 'getting their rocks off,' and trying to touch them as human beings. Often she succeeded in getting otherwise respectable professional men to open up, telling her things that they'd have never told their wives. She even got them to treat their perversions with a matter-of-fact directness, as though 'everyone's kinky, darling, in one way or another.'

'Might easily have become a psychotherapist if I had my life back over again!' She joked to the other girls: 'or one of those agony aunts in the tabloids.'

Where possible Sade liked to share humour with her client. But then she had to be careful not to let humour sabotage her business acumen, recognizing that most of her clients preferred not to have their punitive delusions undermined by laughter.

Christopher had been 'introduced' to Paratroop Sade by Brigid, unaware that he was in effect a 'hand me down' from the Danish woman, who was always on the lookout for new elderly men to thrash.

'Come in luv,' she said to Christopher. 'You look a bit nervous, there's no need to be,' was a common enough ploy for breaking the ice when greeting new clients.

'Have I come to the right place?' was his admission to

nervousness.

Although in her late thirties, her large physique fitted her well. She wore her long hair in a bun and had a cultivated maternal manner.

'So what do you think of my place?' she asked, as though almost house-proud.

When he made no response, it was she who then felt a touch nervous.

'Watch out for the quiet ones!' was advice she and the other girls repeatedly gave to each other.

Her den in South Kensington consisted of a downstairs cellar decked out with the special effects of whips, straps and ropes held in racks and pinions shackled to the walls. To the cognoscenti of S & M, the cellar provided an immediate turn-on, three of the walls being covered with brickwork wallpaper, while the fourth was one of exposed breezeblocks, all of which in the half-light created the desired effect of being in some sort of torture chamber.

Paratroop Sade's rates were set at £180 an hour. Being her personal boss was so much easier. No pimps for one thing, while working free-lance meant she could plan her engagements accordingly. Absurdly a number of her regulars were so docile that they wanted nothing more savage than a few taps on the behind. Some wanted toe massages, with the occasional toe pulled back to induce mild pain. Most seemed to prefer the vicarious thrill of just being in a room where 'torture' could be fantasized over, rather than actually applied.

Sometimes while some of her clients enjoyed the privacy of her den to view pornographic material, she might even glance through a paperback. 'A bit like putting your kid in front of the TV' she shared in her off-duty moments. 'Give them some porn to watch and get paid for it! I tell you girls, my life's a great deal easier than your line of work!' Whilst of course her doing 'blow' jobs and talking dirty as and when requested might be called upon, adapting to the proclivities of her clients often seemed more silly than ever seriously endangering her comfort zone!

There were of course exceptions, with a few hard-core bondage merchants bringing their own fetishes with them. But only rarely did she come up against a real psycho, a danger-man to warn the other girls about, if not to tell the police. Most of the time Paratroop Sade counted her blessings. Hers was a niche market; way better than the life of most hookers who, apart from working for lowlife pimps, had to work the streets meeting God knows whom.

'Those who claim to want straight sex out there can be a lot kinkier than my select little bunch!' She'd come to appreciate that from personal experience.

After their first meeting, Sade could tell that the tall man in his nice clothes veered more in the direction of her serious bondage types than most of the clients she'd got on her books.

'No matter,' she'd told one of her friends. 'He's polite as far as it goes, always pays cash and seems harmless enough. What with his posh accent, he's probably got loads of dosh like most of them.'

He did strike her as a bit weird though, especially the trouble he seemed to have with an erection. 'Nervous first time,' she thought, 'I'll try and put him at his ease next time around.'

On a subsequent visit Christopher required that she turn up the heat somewhat. He wanted her to change out of her regalia, as a paratrooper dressed in fatigues, and don the outfit of some mediaeval knight with helmet and whip. It was as though he wanted better value from Sade who, within the 'trades descriptions act' of her profession didn't, by her own admission, always give 'value for money.'

Then she was required to produce all her special effects, whips, leathers, straps, boots, masks and chain, some of the paraphernalia that in a twisted way reminded him of the terrible enigma of his sadistic father. He didn't know why the fetishes helped or why he was drawn back to this childhood memory. Yet in some twisted way there seemed to be a part of him that even admired Harold Wilkes, a flogger of anyone less powerful than himself. And then there was Christopher's mother Ivy, whose religion purported to make her so saintly but who in truth was another masked colluder, silently compliant over her husband's perversions.

Towards the conclusion of one of their sessions, Sade tried to find out something more about Christopher. But having told her that his name was Nigel and that he lived in Leeds, he disclosed nothing more. She, for her part, told him of a Dutch girl called Roxanne who living in Leeds was into S & M, and that he could tell her he came with her reference.

Another time Sade tried to reassure Christopher that he wasn't that kinky to want to do what he did.

'There are thousands and thousands of fellows in London alone who can only get satisfaction by pain. Many of them are respectably married or have high-powered jobs in the City. They feel embarrassed or ashamed to tell anyone but I try to put them at their ease, saying it must be normal because there are so many like them.'

It was more than her job was worth to suggest that such men were damaged goods who'd do well to consult a trained therapist.

On this occasion Sade seemed to be getting through to him. Listening to her comments with a measure of interest, he told her: 'At least I can be myself here, not having to pretend I'm happily married.'

Sade continued, 'There you go then! My clients come

from all walks of life. Bankers, civil servants, commodity brokers, bookmakers, doctors, lawyers, chaps from Whitehall. You name it. I've had them all or know others who have. I've had several Catholic priests and an archdeacon, never a bishop, mind,' she sniggered.

It was then that he lowered his guard further: 'I'm a vicar, or rather *was* a vicar.' The admission slipped out before he could check himself.

'As I told you! It takes all sorts to make a world,' said Sade solicitously.

This last conversation was in fact the most amicable one to be shared. On a subsequent visit she'd gently teased him that although he was surrounded by every conceivable erotic aid he couldn't on that occasion get an erection, being more dysfunctional than usual. So she'd tried coaxing him, 'Can't little boy get it up then? Here, let mumsy hold it for you.'

This time she had dressed like a teacher. Her hair done up in its usual bun she wore the severe clothing of starched blouse and pleated skirt, with low-heel platform shoes. Up until then she'd tried to arouse Christopher through simulated stern threats of discipline and the swishing of her strap. 'Who's been a naughty boy then? Will I have to use the whip on you?'

Christopher's dysfunction was of course both of a protracted physiological kind, as well as psychological. On this occasion neither through the chiding of 'teacher', nor through the use of some viagra taken earlier could his problem be sorted, thereby making Sade's little taunts feel unduly provocative. Out of nowhere he remembered how in childhood he'd lash out at anyone who laughed at him, doing whatever it took to stop them laughing and shut them up. It was that memory which suddenly caused him to jump up, to seize one of the whips that she kept on a rack and flex it around her neck in an instant.

*'Don't ever laugh at me!'* he hissed, pinioning her throat with her own instrument of torture, before adding with a low growl, 'You laugh at me and you're *dead*, do you hear?'

It was then that Paratroop Sade showed she was made of sterner stuff than the fluffy maternal exterior she preferred to display. Trained in martial arts, partly on account of having done some voluntary national service, and because it was in every professional girl's interests to know the rudiments of self-defense, she reacted.

She slammed her school marm's heel down hard on his exposed right foot (he had removed his shoes), and then elbowed him in the stomach to wind him. In a flash she had freed herself from the grip that had clearly expressed murderous intent. She then spun around to kick him so hard in his dysfunctioning groin that he collapsed faint and nauseous with pain.

'Get out you *fucking scumbag!*' she snarled. 'Don't ever dare to show your face again. You're finished with me, Nigel or whatever your bleeding name is.'

She then kicked his clothing towards the door, and for good measure wrapped one of her whips around his throat dragging him out into the hall, where for a full five minutes he remained semi-naked while gulping in large breaths of air. All sympathy dissipated, she continued to stand over him with undiminished menace. Doing no more than allowing him to dress back into a disheveled mess, she ejected him on to the street.

Slinking away from a den in which he'd been subjected to real pain and well beyond the province of any services requested, he limped back to his flat to lick his wounds.

This was the third time that the wolf had been beaten back. The third time in fact when he'd lost control only to be repelled by *another woman!* Three women had taken care of a man more than usually capable of taking care of himself. Frances had ordered him back to his bedroom on the night of his ravings in the vicarage. Philippa had felled him with a staple gun and now Paratroop Sade had shown him who the boss was in a real fight.

Lying on his bed with a severely bruised foot and groin, he seethed with anger. The wolf was shaping up for a fight where he refused to be beaten again.

Yet despite his last experience with Sade, Wilkes remained tantalized by the twilight world of prostitution. A whore provided the tariff both for fantasies and anonymity - value for money surely for someone with money to burn and a twisted passion to expend.

It was as though his 'old life,' if he could call it that, had never existed. He was free to roam, unchecked, and reprieved from all worries whether over his ex-wife and family or his job. With grounds for his divorce having been presented there would be no settlement to contest, thereby ensuring that a decree absolute would be a formality in the near future. As for all the hassle of running a busy parish church that too was at an end.

He felt no grief.

Nor would he have ever guessed that Katy his daughter had become embroiled in a profession to which he, as a client was now drawn, or that they were both doing the rounds in London's central red-light district – he as punter, she as hooker.

# PART TWO

*Andrew de Berry*

# Chapter 25

'IF YOU WANT TO SIGN A PETITION REQUESTING TO KNOW WHY REVD BEN CARTER, RECENTLY VICAR OF ST HILDA'S, KETBOROUGH HAS BEEN SACKED, THEN CALL IN, OR PHONE THE MAGPIE PUBLIC HOUSE, KETBOROUGH.'
Phone, Ketborough 413822

Zbierski hadn't been so much busy, as demented, copies of his handbills having been circulated far and wide not just in the town, but also throughout the neighbourhood. The fliers had gone up everywhere - pubs, shops and local post offices, as well as in bus shelters and public toilets just for good measure! A further batch had gone out with photographs depicting Ben in his dog collar alongside Angela, asking in bold capitals underneath,

**'WHY SHOULD THIS VICAR LOSE HIS JOB?'**

With the scandal of Ketborough's two vicars hitting the media, The Magpie was quickly overrun with reporters and their ring-tones and where with Zbierski attempting to field all the inquiries, the interest only accelerated.

With so much media hubbub, the pub regulars had a ringside seat, more so when the cause of Ben Carter was being aired. In fact, with Z's phone amplifier switched on those present could, by lowering their voices, hear the entire gist of a conversation. One such occasion was when Z was responding to a call from a national daily:

'Excuse me, Mr. Zbierski, but can you add anything regarding the petition that's in circulation right now?' The female accent sounded ever so posh.

'Bloddy right I can,' responded Z, who having stirred up such a commotion was in his element. Any attempt to clean up his language had for the moment disappeared: 'What I want to know is how come a bloddy decent vicar like that Ben Carter chappie gets sacked just for shagging an ex-nun while that focking Wilkes, last seen with that choirgirl Stacey before she get's mordered, *still gets to keep his job?* What's more, Wilkes' missus has left him because she can't stand the bogger and yet 'e's kept on full pay, and chances are 'e'll get 'is job back.'

'So you feel that Reverend Carter has had an unfair deal?' Surely the reporter was winding him up for maximum effect.

'You tell all thy readers 'dat man Wilkes is a baddun' through and through,' His slightly more tempered response was given only on to remind himself of doctor's orders about going easy on his blood pressure. Yet for good measure Z added, 'Thou wants to ask that baddun of a bishop what 'e thinks 'e's playing at!'

'Thank you, Mr. Zbierski, you've been most helpful.' Nor could she prevent an audible chuckle. Remembering the Stacey Witcombe story, the lady interviewer had ample material for the modest print space she'd been allocated. As he put down the receiver, Granville said, 'you should get me a bloddy secretary at 'zis rate.'

Secretly the drinkers wanted Zbierski to field *every* call because he just cracked them up, more so whenever he spoke to the media. The landlord too came to appreciate that second to the Staff of Life up the road, his place was becoming the best entertainment in town.

'My lord, we shall need to do something about all these press inquiries.' The Bishop's two secretaries were in a flurry of activity, quite out of keeping with their normally calm and dependable manner. The more senior one had come to his study door to speak to him.

'What do they want?' he replied without looking up from the Regency desk where he was busy signing letters. He hated it when his women staff got all in a fluster.

'Well, in short, they want to know why Ketborough's area dean has been sacked and why in similar circumstances, Canon Wilkes remains on full pay?'

Did he detect a whiff of disloyalty from his normally dependable secretary, herself half hinting at the possibility of an injustice?

The bishop still didn't look up. 'Tell them that the Revd Benjamin Carter has been given three months' pay and that since the matter over Canon Wilkes is confidential, there's nothing more to be said.'

He then added, 'If you find the press becoming too intrusive, then feel free to use your voice mail for a time so that we can put out a general press release later.'

'Thank you, my lord.' The woman had re-composed herself, before adding, 'just one other thing, this was delivered by hand earlier.'

She presented him with an open package before closing the door. He glanced up. The package revealed several pages of signatures; others downloaded by email, which in all appeared to run into several thousand, each petitioning that Revd Ben Carter be given his job back.

Pausing for a moment, he put the package to one side. If

he reflected on the list at all, it was only to mutter that people who sign things rarely take matters any further. Then with a dismissive shove he sent the list tumbling into his waste paper basket, before muttering *'Damn him!* I bet that cohabiting priest put the press on to this so that everyone can have a good stir.'

The petition only heightened his anger towards Carter.

'Have you any idea what might be happening to her?'

Frances now spent a lot of time with Ben and Angela. If she had a distraction from thinking about her ex-husband, it was over the churning anxiety felt for Katy:

'I mean they were saying on TV recently that young girl addicts are invariably into prostitution.'

'That has to be par for the course. Drugs and prostitution become inseparable.' Angela saw no point in soft-soaping Frances before adding: 'Some of the homeless mums who come to the Centre tell me that there are children as young as *ten* getting into drugs and sex.'

Of course they'd all heard about child prostitution in the wider world but somehow Kate's predicament brought it all so much nearer to home.

'It's getting horrific out there,' said Ben. 'Before long, there could be child prostitution and rampant paedophilia in *this* country. Binge drinking may be the number one social disease at the moment, but underage sex and all the rest of it are running it a close second, so much of it aided and abetted via the internet. There's already a feeding frenzy going on with sex tourism from this country to South America and Eastern Europe, all thanks to technology. Like pornography, paedophilia will soon get marketed as respectable.'

'So if Katy isn't properly off drugs, then in all probability she's into prostitution?' Frances was beginning to answer her own question.

'That, Frances, is I fear a *near* certainty,' said Ben. His sense of outrage for the mother and her daughter exploded on account of the more horrific scandal. 'According to the National Criminal Intelligence Service Index,' he went on, 'there are 10,000 paedophiles out there which in reality could be multiplied tenfold. *God, what's it all coming to?*'

'There's no let-up to this nightmare, is there?' said Frances.

'No, there isn't!' said Ben. 'You've probably seen all the hoo-ha about the community getting up in arms on my behalf. Although I'm truly grateful my situation is just a tiny fragment compared to the world's problems.'

'Well, at least there's a good crowd of people out there who *want* to help both of you,' said Frances.

'Yes, but just you wait and see who'll win this little tussle,' said Angela. 'The bishop sits in his castle, impervious to all slings and arrows from the press or whoever. No one will get him to change his views. He's a complete law unto himself just like most of our bishops. Pull up the drawbridge and sit tight.'

'They reckon that we in Britain along with them in Germany and the States are the main offenders when it comes to child prostitution,' interjected Ben. 'There's a huge undercover black market for sex tourism in this country.'

Such was their turmoil right then their conversations were going in all directions.

It was then that Angela made a proposal. 'Can I suggest that we *pray?*' she said quietly. 'Not in some stuffy way, but just so as to let our various thoughts and turmoil swirl about, and ask that *He* deals with them!'

Sensing that this was all they could do right then Frances, under the guidance of Angela, sought to rein in her thoughts. If she was to feel terror on behalf of her daughter, so be it. She tried to relax.

Visualizing the sweet ebullient girl who had grown effortlessly into a natural beauty by her seventeenth birthday, it was important to keep before her the image of how Katy had been before the terror of drugs had taken over. Yet it was also important not to halt the invasion of dark thoughts: Of how the once pretty and athletic girl who'd excelled at games like tennis and synchronized swimming, had morphed into someone emaciated and scarred. Frances had read enough to know of the disfiguring effects produced by hard drugs.

Bravely she tried holding the apparition of Katy as she now appeared before her, the Katy embroiled in those other lethal all-devouring sports of 'playing with drugs', and 'being on the game.'

She was in no doubt as to how the girl's father had done much to turn their daughter into the disruptive pupil she'd been at the school, and from where she had been expelled. How different things might have been if he'd shown a scintilla of care. God, how she detested the man, who'd brought so much ruination both to her family and the community!

*'I loathe him, I loathe him, I loathe him!'* She literally spat the words out as they sat there in their confusion trying to pray. She'd never known such venom.

Across her abyss, she heard the voice of Angela. 'It's OK, Frances; you have to feel and know such rage. We're seething too! Dear God, who is worse,' she found herself pleading, 'be they the wreckers of the world like the warlords and terrorists and those who abuse our young, or those hypocrites who betray the faith entrusted to them? Small wonder that our Lord ranted and raged against the religious leaders of his day who were so bereft of compassion.'

The images of Katy persisted - sallow skin, ulcerating sores, plagued in all likelihood by parasites and pimps, low-lifes no different from he who'd launched her into cocaine -

that odious creature Pete in his flashy car.

But then as they remained seated in their desolation, Frances had an overwhelming sense of God, or the Holy Spirit or whoever it was, entering their world of shattered hopes and dreams. For she then had a picture of dear, caring Dominic. How she loved the donnish son who'd brought her so much joy. Dom was no goody-two-shoes, just one of those straightforward people with a lot of quiet self-belief and love. Despite every trauma, nothing had severed the bond between mother and son and she felt confident that nothing ever would. It was just one of those rare and uncomplicated mother-son things.

Something stranger still then happened. Katy reappeared and doing so with her beauty restored. Although marred and scarred by suffering, she had in a strange way grown more striking than even in her teenage years. For the suffering depicted so graphically in her earlier imaginings had mellowed her, and she radiated light.

When Frances came out of the scene a few moments later, a host of little voices immediately assailed her:

'Just in your imagination, dear! Your daughter's a *loser*, a *whore*, well on the way to being dead and buried. You've *failed* as a mother and your own life's a ruin! There's no hope for *any* of you.'

But before leaving Ben and Angela, Frances told them what she had seen. Amazed, Angela replied, 'Frances, you and I have just had the *same* vision. I saw Katy like that as well. And if you heard little voices telling you none of it was true, just tell them to *piss off!* They're only the devil's dwarfs trying to do their damndest to undermine you.'

They also noticed how Ben's face, which as though earlier had seemed engulfed in a black cloud was now totally transformed.

'I don't know what happened just then,' he said. 'The

problems haven't gone away and all the other horrors of child prostitution are still around us. But somehow, *He* has heard us and I *know* that we are not alone.' It was no exaggeration to say that his face shone.

'What's more,' added Ben, 'I had this vision, call it what you will and I saw that I had been reinstated in the church!'

'Then God help us all!' said Angela with feeling. Gentle laughter swept across them restoring in Frances a newfound sense of awe.

# Chapter 26

'Christ, I look a *wreck!*' Having dared to peer into the mirror, all she could add was, 'My God, I feel I'm done for!'

'Nah, you've still got some mileage left in you,' said her roommate and fellow pro. 'Just got to find a new method. Remember, in this game it's your body they look at first. Lose that and you're really fucked!'

In the world of whoredom she felt her marketability was close to free-fall. With teenage boys and girls flooding the market, fresh merchandise could easily carry away the older girls like so much flotsam. Homelessness, drugs and unemployment were offering a buyers' paradise out there, and rates were liable to fall for the likes of Katy and her room-mate Maxine, even when they managed to hold onto their looks. These days a pro could be *old* in her late teens.

'The main problem is not to reach our sell-by date too early,' said Maxine.

'Christ, you make it sound like we're athletes who peak too soon,' replied Katy, thinking of what might have been when she's shown promise as a swimmer.

'Same idea, darling, different game,' replied the other ruefully, dragging on a fag.

'*Some game!*' declared Katy. Funds weren't as good these

days necessitating a move from crack cocaine to an amphetamine substitute known as 'crank', cheaper but more adulterated. Along with the crank or the crack when she could get her hands on it, she persisted with her E tablets. With funds dwindling fast, the only sport she now engaged in was one with *no* winners: 'The end-game seems to be to fuck up your looks and you end up with zilch, or in the Thames.'

'Jesus, you're cheerful tonight,' Maxine was getting restless.

'So go on, tell me what's good?' asked Kate.

'Don't want to!'

'*Can't*, more like!'

Kate regretted pushing the other girl. Trying to tell it how it was wasn't such a good idea.

'Anyway I'm off,' said Maxine. She got up from the one armchair in the room. With tight pants, skimpy top and fashion boots, she was already in her working clothes.

Katy had got to the point where she wasn't 'game' any more, either as prey or pursuer. Her dry skin ravished with yellow and purple sores was the blatant giveaway, as was the septum around her nose, which was blotched and unsightly. Neither rouge, nor lip-gloss nor eyeliner could distract the punter from the ravages to her upper face. Drug users unable to disguise their habit were a turn off like they were HIV plus, which more often than not they were.

'And God knows what's happening to my hair as well,' she whimpered, fearing an onset of alopecia.

She was staying in cheap lodgings, courtesy of her pimp. In fact her upstairs bed-sit over another 'knocking shop' wasn't where she conducted her own business. Having recently 'gone off sick' on account of her general condition and deteriorating looks, she'd been struggling to earn a living in another part of the city. But when she stopped work altogether, her pimp gave her one more week to 'get her shit together', as he so kindly put it, or get out.

The few days taken off helped her to feel marginally better, despite not having slept or eaten properly for days. Popping a couple of Es, she decided to look up another of the girl-lodgers who'd been working the day shift.

Mandy was a South African who'd been on the game longer than most. For the short time that they'd known each other, she'd been kindly disposed towards Katy.

'Come in, my darling!' she called out, as Katy knocked on her door.

Half-sprawled on her bed, the other was absent-mindedly eating a take-away and licking her fingers.

'Here have some,' she held out a carton of *Kentucky Fried*, still half full with two chicken drumsticks and a quantity of chips. 'I bought too much anyway. Go on, finish it off.'

Realizing how hungry she was, Kate sat on the end of Mandy's bed and devoured what had been offered. They then each had a large mug of sweetened tea.

Mandy was quite a gal. Tall and together, she'd kept her good looks while still standing tall in herself. Balancing her tea on her lap, she put an arm around Katy. 'So what's doing? You look pretty beat up!'

'You can say that again! The truth is, Mandy, I've got to get my shit together, to use our pimp's little ultimatum. I'm here till the end of the week and then I've got to quit this place. The reality is that I'm dropping off the ladder. My looks are going and I can't score any more.'

'Sweetheart, let me tell you something,' Mandy gave Kate's shoulder a further squeeze. 'When I came from South Africa, I stopped off at Amsterdam and met an Englishman. He was charming and offered to marry me, saying that everything would be hunky-dory from thereon. As it was he was an evil bastard who took me to his flat where he raped me, only to hold me prisoner for the next three weeks. Can you believe it – *three weeks*! He kept me gagged and shackled to his bed. Eventually I escaped, taking off through an upstairs skylight and across some rooftops, nearly killing myself in the process.'

Lighting a cigarette and squinting through the smoke she looked hard at the other girl. 'Kate honey, don't ever say you're dropping off the ladder when you still have some sort of control over your life.'

Mandy's story offered some perspective to Katy's woes, even as she said, 'OK, but I'm scared shitless about where to go from here.'

'*Don't be!* Get some more sleep and come and see me in the morning,' advised the South African. 'And by the way don't worry about that little prick of a pimp. I can talk him into letting you stay longer if you want to.'

Mandy blew her a kiss, which in a strange way reminded Katy of her mother.

Up until then his offences were pretty much limited to a score or more of 'taking and driving always'. TDA's was how the Court jargon preferred to call them, along with 'TWOCs' - the taking of a vehicle without the owner's consent. The only other blemish on his record was when one such TWOC got linked to an ABH charge. On that particular occasion the car he'd stolen, having been spotted by its rightful owner, caused the thief to jab open the driver's door against the other man's gesticulating arm, as he sped off. The 'actual bodily harm' resulted in no more than a glancing blow producing a few bruises, not serious enough to have been designated 'grievous' or GBH. Abbreviations tended to summaries the story of his criminal career.

'Merv Costello's a bit of a lad, but he'll not do you any harm' was how the general banter went about him in his local Birmingham pub.

'That's if you're not in love with your motor, of course!' came the rejoinder. 'He'd not think twice about nicking it if he had a special order. What's more, being a bit of a lady's man, he might just grab a nice motor to impress the latest bit of skirt he's taking out!'

But generally speaking 'Merv the Swerve', as he became known, was shrewd enough to know that 'you don't piss in the same tent as your mates'! So generally speaking he'd avoid messing with his mates' cars, leaving them to consider him as being honest in a crooked sort of way! And no way was he bashful in talking about his line of work, making comments like, 'All this TDA and TWOC bullshit. It makes no difference to me.'

He had been giving his pub speel over a recent conviction where he'd escaped prison by doing a maximum stint of community service. 'Why not just call it TDA and have done with it?' he queried. 'All this talk of TWOC is crap. I've not yet come across the owner of any motor I've nicked give me his smiling consent, saying "Please Mr. Costello, be my guest. Of course I give you my *consent* to steal my car!" I felt like telling her, and here he mimicked the lady magistrate's voice: "TDA *is* TWOC, Twat"! But I kept my trap shut, and at least she didn't give me no bird.'

Breaking a quarter-light, or punching his chisel just above the driver's door handle to disable its central locking, or bypassing an alarm and hot-wiring an ignition, these little specialties were the story of his life. So TWOCs, TDAs, what the heck, he was a car thief and that was all there was to it. Times however were getting harder he had to admit, what with all the micro-chipped keys and ignitions. But he refrained from pinching car keys from people's homes, given that house burglars, although rarely caught, got stiffer terms of imprisonment as and when they were.

A nice-looking youth around five feet seven but always a bit on the wild side, his natural intelligence had been blighted by six years of unemployment after he'd left school. Two stints in a young offenders' establishment only taught him the refinements of auto theft and being of no fixed abode, his Italian father and Irish mother having long since split up, he was left to live by his wits. If he was domiciled anywhere it was in a grubby Birmingham bed-sit, and to which he'd return most weekends.

Despite the lady's-man tag, having no steady job meant no steady girlfriend. But pussy was always available and he enjoyed his independence, even if in a vague sort of way he wouldn't have minded a bit of sat-nav for his life, so to speak.

On the Thursday before August Bank Holiday, having stolen a near-new LandRover and driven it from Nottingham up to Leeds, his plan was to sell the vehicle the following day. No harm done then if for the evening before he used it to try and impress 'a piece of totty.' It was more by chance then that he'd ended up in Leeds' red-light area.

As a bit of a flash-Harry who'd drawn attention to his curb crawling, it was around midnight when he was told to move on by two patrolling police officers who, having done a routine check on the car's registration, promptly arrested him.

Returned to Birmingham, his rap sheet went no further than the Magistrates' court, where along with several other offences taken into account, his solicitor and probation officer once more negotiated an alternative to prison. With no other charges like dangerous driving being included, the magistrates decided to give Merv Costello what, outside a custodial sentence of six months, was a further maximum tally of two hundred hours' community service.

So having evaded prison once more, he didn't think he'd done too badly.

# Chapter 27

'I want you to meet a friend called Monica,' Mandy told Katy the morning after their shared KFC supper.

'How's she going to help?' asked Kate. 'I've told you I'm past it.'

'Not in this line of work, you ain't,' replied Mandy coyly.

The oldest profession operates at many levels. At pavement level there are the pretty young things who go out on the streets, displaying what their skimpy outfits are designed not to hide. Their so-called protectors or providers are the pimps who despite their claim to act as brokers are little more than parasites growing fat off the girls' earnings. Then there are the madams who run massage parlours, brothels by another name, usually seasoned pros who have bettered themselves to become managers.

Whether managed by a higher class of madam or more ambitious pimp, escort agencies provide up-market variations on a theme, where the girls having made it 'to the top', operate typically from penthouse suites. The same pecking order in effect works for the gay/transvestite scene, where it is known that kinky sex, although usually available as an extra with the conventional pros, can be had in specialist forms at all levels.

At the bottom of the heap come the hundreds of child prostitutes now proliferating and even being 'bussed' into some of Britain's major cities, like it was something normal. Such depraved commercialism even tries to argue that under-age prostitution should be *de-criminalized*, it being a last-ditch survival strategy for society's most vulnerable. Yet because they are deemed to be AIDS-free, these children become more vulnerable still, whether from being infected by sexually transmitted diseases or at the hands of their brutal 'minders'. Furthermore by being dependent upon these surrogate parents who initially shower them with gifts, there's little that these children *won't* do in order to retain their minders' affections.

Perhaps beneath the child prostitutes there exists one yet lower stratum – that of those derelict pros who, marred by the disfigurement of their drug taking if not of their STDs, have little or no marketability.

By sheer good fortune, Kate had not as yet contracted any sexual disease. But in describing herself as 'at the bottom of the ladder,' she'd only spoken the truth, before adding, 'Mandy, I don't know what you've got in mind but I'm good for nothing that I can think of.'

'Relax sweetie, just keep breathing,' replied her companion. 'We're nearly where I want to take you first.'

They had walked to a shop near Oxford Circus shamelessly advertising sex aids of every size and description. Taking Katy through some raffia curtains at the back of the shop, Mandy called out, 'Hey Dice shake a leg!'

'Mandy babe, how you doing?' Dice called through before arriving to plant an affected yet affectionate kiss on Mandy's cheek. 'And who's this you brought with you darling?' The shop's owner was so impeccably made up and dressed as a woman, that it wasn't until she spoke that Katy realized that she was a *he*.

'Dice, baby, this is Katy. She's got a problem. She's worried about her face and arms and can't score right now. She needs some gear to cover up with. What's more she's out of readies. Can you help?' Mandy blew her a return kiss.

The friendship between the two was clearly an excellent one. 'Sweetie-pie,' said Dice in her huskiest voice. 'You know I'll do *anything* for you and your friend – Katy is it?'

Katy nodded.

Disappearing behind another raffia screen, the androgynous Dice re-emerged a short time later with a large carton full of objects and outfits.

'Most important to try out one of these cat suits for size,' 'she' explained. 'Cover up and then you'll be able to show them your figure in all its glory.'

It was true that despite her other facial deterioration, Katy had kept her figure well.

Like so many toys the box with its paraphernalia was then emptied onto the floor. Phallic stimulants, chastity belts, steel and spiked bras fell about them, and all without embarrassment to the proprietor.

Encouraged to put on a red cat suit embossed from head to toe in a sort of link-fence pattern, she found the outfit surprisingly comfortable. 'Fits you like a condom, darling!' Dice put her at their ease. An assortment of different headgear was then presented. There was a mask-cum-half-helmet, which with its strange pointed metallic ears transformed the wearer into a sort of werewolf. Katy was drawn to the object because whilst it left the lower part of her face exposed, it concealed her lifeless, depleted hair and scabby forehead.

'You'll learn to love the cat suit, dear. Some of my customers prefer it to their own skin. Just like liposuction, once you've had it you'll wonder how you ever got on without it!'

Dice's humour was infectious leaving Katy surprised to hear the sound of her own laughter.

Rigged up in the cat suit and with the helmet in place, Mandy looked on triumphantly. Hitching a length of rope around Katy's arm and slipping a menacing rhino-handled whip into her other free hand, Dice sighed full of mock admiration: *'Fuck me gently!'*

'Da da, she who must be obeyed,' added Mandy.

'Oooh don't, you'll get me all excited!' teased Dice.

With herself half entering into the party spirit Katy asked: 'Yes, but how much is all this going to cost?'

'Kate darling, it's on the house' replied Dice. 'Or shall we say on indefinite saleable return. Pick yourself up first sweetheart and then we can negotiate.'

'Thank you precious,' said Mandy, giving Dice a hug. 'Come on Kate, next stop Monica.'

Katy echoed her thanks.

'Can I put your purchases in a bag, madam?' Dice mimicked a tone of voice as used by the nicest of salesgirls.

'As a matter of fact, you can,' replied Kate, before adding in a pretend posh voice: 'you're most frightfully kind!' Stuffing the helmet conveniently folded at two hinged ends into the bag as well, she realized how much she needed the laughter.

'What about the rope and whip?' asked Dice.

'Don't worry, Monica's got plenty of them.'

'Then hang on a sec,' said Dice. 'Why don't you take these?' She went to a rack of shoeboxes to select a pair of bright red high-heel stilettos in mock alligator.

'You don't have to wear them, love, but I'll guarantee that if you put them on view, you'll never go short of customers.'

'Thanks, again,' Katy placed the shoes in her bag.

She knew she was being taken down the primrose path to

what she considered to be the nadir of prostitution - kinky sex. But given her lost looks, it was a case of 'needs must' she told herself. Besides, her 'sod-it' mentality had kicked in once more, despite another part of her detesting what she was getting into.

'So, where are we going now?' she asked. 'And who's this Monica?'

'We're going to the Department of S & M, where Monica works,' replied Mandy, referring to S & M like it was some famous department store.

Walking along Oxford Street and back onto Charing Cross Road, Katy knew, even in her dull and stupefied condition, how the idea of whips and bondage repelled her. For if she felt self-pity by the enslavement of her own condition, she felt pity turned to nausea for those who were slaves to vicious sexual pleasure.

They came to a Striptease club near Soho where on a nod from the man on the door, they were directed to an upstairs landing with Mandy pressing an intercom to ask for Monica. With the electronic lock snapping back, the voice on the other side of the door was clearly expecting them.

Monica appeared to share less of Mandy or Dice's general good cheer. Youngish and of medium height, her short auburn dyed hair suited her good facial bone structure. Did the jaw and tightness around her mouth suggest a general distaste for what she was doing? Some twisted memory perhaps from her past? Knowing where she had now landed herself made Katy a whole lot less judgmental of others.

Leaving her with Monica, Mandy smiled and said, 'you're in good hands now, sweetheart. See you around.' She blew Katy another of her mother's kisses.

'Mandy, I really *owe* you,' Katy responded, feeling better that her mystery tour had ended in reasonably convivial surroundings.

Monica explained that as Katy would be part of a team answerable to her so she, Monica, was answerable for results to some faceless senior management.

'Keep them happy,' she explained honestly. 'If management stay out of our hair then I'm not going to hassle you.'

Having seen Katy rigged up in her gear, Monica showed her a number of red-padded soundproof cells. 'This one will be yours,' she pointed her to the end cell. Equipment in the form of straps, whips and ropes were already in place.

'Remember, first impressions count,' said Monica. The gravitas with which she picked up and flexed a nearby cane was a clear reference to the 'impressions' she would need to inflict upon demanding flesh.

'First impressions' seemed to work well enough for a number of clients, with several starting to insist on having 'the slim bitch in chain mail,' as they tended to call her, leaving Monica to keep her on full-time.

Katy discovered that she belonged to a much larger organization than just the small domain supervised under Monica. From time to time she got moved about servicing clients, some of whom were well-known public figures. Later in her red cat suit and with or without her high-heel shoes, she got given the name 'Stiletto' and where in her drug-besotted emporium, the one usually off Charing Cross Road, she found herself making good money.

'You're doing OK' meant that she was operating within her boss' comfort zone. But who were these clients from the anonymity of London's masses? She was tired of asking the question only to hear the same bored answer:

'They're all sorts, sweetheart - business executives, judges, doctors, priests, you name it.' The constrained public school accents that went with these high fliers were plentiful enough to remind her of the voice of her weird, and long-forgotten father.

Over men who helped to rule in the great Metropolis and beyond and who, by a word or gesture, could destroy the fortunes of others it was Stiletto who now ruled. Whilst in the cut and thrust of their public persona she was a 'nobody', here in the underworld of their tortured selves she parried with them on equal terms. As the erstwhile daughter of a Midlands vicar and one-time promising athlete, 'Stiletto' Wilkes was a Dominatrix administering the coup de grace, unless a stay of execution was begged for until next time.

Hooker and hooked were intertwined.

# Chapter 28

It was nearing August Bank Holiday and Ben and Angela felt down on their luck, not helped by the sultry afternoon.

'It looks like Letharge'll do bugger all about the petition,' said Ben. 'I mean the appeal ran to thousands of signatures, the media's got involved and everybody seemed to be jumping up and down. And what have we got? A measly extension on our three months' salary concession to twelve months!'

'That's where the Church of England is a complete law unto itself,' replied Angela. 'Can you imagine any other organization in Britain these days taking the line: You'll have to go because you're living together! They'd be shot down in flames by every tribunal from here to Brussels.'

'Yet Letharge *is* getting away with it,' said Ben, 'because as the patron of St Hilda's and by using some odious argument about our salary not being a salary at all, merely a stipend or 'voluntary contribution,' he's sees himself at liberty to withdraw this at any time. By twisting the stipend argument they dare to imply that the paid clergy are no more than volunteers and that when push comes to shove we have no rights or entitlements. Here we are now into the twenty-first century and they're still prevaricating about proper terms and conditions of service.'

He was livid.

Angela knew all about Ben's hobbyhorse concerning the employment practices of the Church of England, appreciating how things seemed to be trickier for the paid clergy than at any time in the past. Naturally she shared his outrage.

'True, you've never been well-paid in the past, but now nothing short of a conspiracy seems to be afoot to remove the paid clergy wholesale, either by getting you all on short-term contracts, or by appealing more and more to all those other mugs who'll do the job for free. Downsizing's got nothing with this little scam.'

The 'mugs' she referred to was the growing army of non-stipendiary or volunteer clergy, the SSMs or self-supporting ministers. 'Only volunteers wanted from hereon' she added.

'My guess is,' said Ben, 'that there'll only be a handful of paid clergy by the year 2020, by which stage all the SSMs will then start complaining that they'll need paying *themselves!* Thee whole present arrangement is grotesque, and what goes around comes around. Anyway, enough of all this garbage! If the clergy can't think this through for themselves, then stuff the lot of them!' he said affably.

'Come on, let's cheer ourselves up,' said Angela.

'OK, give me good news!'

'Weeell,' she coaxed. 'Here I am four months pregnant and my morning sickness has all but disappeared. You wouldn't believe what a bonus that is!'

'That's got to be good. Tell me something else.' Like a small child he was in need of humouring

'We've got a new double bed!' said Angela laughing.

'About bloody time,' he replied. 'Our one concession to luxury and to *sin,*' he added. He was lying on the bed of sin as he spoke.

'More like a concession to necessity,' said Angela laughing. 'That other crap bed-settee hadn't been market-researched properly.'

'You mean hadn't had enough bonking hours done on it by an overweight vicar and his concubine from the convent . . .

'Hey, look you here,' he interrupted himself. He'd been glancing through one of Angela's astrological books. Getting up from the bed to remove a wasp bumping stupidly on the casement side of the open window, he said, 'It says here, "The scorpionic personality is essentially a creature of darkness, secretive, hiding in the shadows. Its sting is out of all proportion to its size, and it can strike when least expected. Throughout the ancient world, Scorpio was cursed as evil with the Mayas calling it the sign of the death god."'

He was thinking of the scorpionic character of Canon Christopher Wilkes, whose birthday fell in early November. 'Remind you of anyone?'

'Yes, but hang on a minute!' replied Angela. 'Don't forget that each sign has its higher, more exalted side. Scorpios can either be base or beautiful. The pedantry of the Capricorn, for instance, that too can produce in its youthful counterpart of a trait of being wise beyond its years; the sly Virgo,' she said speaking of her own birth sign, 'can be honest to the point of self-torture. The Taurean bull who can be so stubborn,' she said looking at Ben, 'can be the life and soul of any party, giving a sense of purpose and well-being to others when they feel dispirited, etc, etc.'

'OK, OK, I know I'm new to all this, but it certainly sounds fascinating. Reading about what could be Christopher Wilkes' dark scorpionic side feels a bit like knowing the man without ever having met him. But to have met him and know that he typifies so much that is pinpointed within that negative description does feel uncanny to say the least.'

'You can see then why I'm so taken with the subject,' replied Angela. 'But of course it doesn't end there. Some sun-signs even have facial mannerisms, along with physical characteristics. A typical male Scorpio will often display an intense gaze; have aquiline features with deep-set eyes and be of a naturally muscular build. Often on account of his fierce competitiveness, he can be athletic and it is even possible by looking at him or her to tell what sort of physical ailments they may be liable to suffer from.

'Of course there's a clear danger in making all this sound too simplistic,' she continued. 'We need intelligent adversaries to present their arguments, to speak up if they think the whole thing's hocus-pocus. Yet I defy anyone who gives even half a thought to astrology not to make some connection between a person's star sign and their personality. But here, take a look at this.' Producing a clipboard onto which were a set of traced diagrams superimposed over each other, she sat alongside Ben on the bed: 'You know that I got to know Christopher, as well as anybody ever could know him during our pilgrimage. So I thought I'd draw up an outline of his birth-chart. He told me quite a lot about himself; that he'd been born in Mombasa and that his father had at one time been a missionary, changing career to become a coffee-planter. He also gave enough away about his father to disclose that he was violently sadistic. I also learned from Crockfords that he was born on November 4$^{th}$ 1946.

'He also took special pride in telling me he'd been born an hour before dawn. Apparently an old Masai chieftain had once informed his mother that anyone born during that hour would enjoy a charmed life, and that whatever they did, right or wrong, they would be protected. As it happened Christopher did mention to me on one occasion that he felt supernaturally protected; something about an old mountain god or some such.'

'Now that does sound to me too far-fetched,' complained Ben.

'Well yes, but he went on to tell me about how he'd once climbed Mount Kenya, making the final ascent entirely on his own whilst in a blizzard. When he got down safely it felt convinced that the old god, associated with that mountain, had somehow looked after him. For not only had he survived a three-night storm of sleet and snow on the mountain, he seemed to avoid a second violent death whilst up the mountain. Apparently also during his time on the mountain, a group from the dreaded Mau Mau tribe had ransacked his parents' house, as well as butchering them.'

*'Bloody hell!'* said Ben 'and he told you all that? You seem to have got a lot more out of him than most of us. From what you're saying it sounds like he saw his parents' death as proof positive of his charmed life,' said Ben.

'I think he did. It was obvious to me that he had no feelings for them. But this is what's fascinating. Here, take a look at his horoscope,' she urged. The tracings on her clipboard revealed a cat's-cradle of sharp angular lines, making no sense to Ben whatsoever.

'All the shapes have got different names,' explained Angela. 'Some are called spheres, others trines or semi-sextiles and so on, all dealing with the inner and outer aspects of the universe. The more I learn about this subject, the more I wonder whether or not our lives are pre-planned and that, like it or not, we're destined to conspire in some divine plot way bigger than us. Maybe we even have to go to hell and back to get there. For instance, here we have a scorpionic type, who in better circumstances or with a happier upbringing might, *just might*, have turned out very differently.'

With her Raphael's Ephemeris to establish where Wilkes' sun, moon and planet signs were in relation to his date and place of birth, she pointed to the diagram and to the symbols in his first 'house'. 'Here we've got the Sun and Venus in Scorpio. In another context, our subject might well have been a bit of a Casanova, a Don Juan well able to charm the ladies and seduce them. As it is, with his damaged personality and with Uranus opposite in Taurus, we have what we have - an irrational individual prone to extremes of mood. But then with Pluto opposite to Mars square to Venus we've got a real powder-keg, powerful enough to induce sudden outbursts of rage if not uncontrollable violence.'

'Struth! So you're saying that the story of his life is written in the stars, and there's nothing he or any of us can do about it?' asked Ben.

'Except learn and become more honest about who we are,' she replied.

'Presumably in Christopher's case it's all too late for that,' Ben mused. 'Or are you lighting a candle for Lucifer?'

'That's an interesting phrase,' said Angela. 'I'd say that he was too far gone until the next time.'

He was incredulous that this former nun, now his lover and the mother of their forthcoming child, had so readily launched into an exploration of the 'occult!' For what would have been anathema to her in St Juliana's and to her orthodox Christian background in general – her newfound love of astrology, alongside an open-minded attitude towards reincarnation – now appeared almost as second nature. In shedding the wimple and sister's cowl, it was as though a symbolic veil had also been lifted, whereby she spoke as she saw. Was she, Ben mused, some sort of Christian seer for the millennium?

She interrupted his thoughts by laughing: 'God alone knows what sort of harridan I might have become had I not met you! Who knows I might have ended up an out of control sister scaring to death even the likes of our Mother superior! Virgos can be vicious and deadly if they lose the plot.'

They had discussed it many times before, Angela saying as she always did: 'It's fear that keeps the Church so stubbornly opposed to what it likes to dismiss as the occult, failing to understand that, rightly used, such hidden forms of knowledge could well play a crucial role to rejuvenate Christianity and help it move on.'

'Yes, but we've been over this before,' said Ben. 'We don't need any more dark arts, surely? My only interest in Christianity is what Christ did and taught. As I see it the Church has got enough voodoo, obsessed as it is in diluting away from the radical teachings of Jesus. The Church has only one objective in mind – to hold onto its power. That of itself turns its so-called orthodoxy into heresy. By promoting other beliefs like reincarnation or astrology the Church would weaken itself further. And the powers that be *know* that.'

'I'm sure you're right,' replied Angela. 'I see the Church fighting to the death to oppose the sort of "heresies" I'm interested in. Self-preservation is why the Church would dismiss all other insights about life as simply misinformed and dangerous.'

'Yep,' said Ben resignedly, while brushing the swelling bump in Angela's tummy. 'I guess it'll fall to the likes of him or her in there to work on the new heresies.'

'Let's hope that *they* can show up the Church for the pagan institution it now is, so as to get society a bit more switched on to what life's really all about.'

'But we've still got an important part to play as well,' Angela insisted. 'We may be getting on but we're not out of the frame either! Both you and I are still seen as representatives of the Church. For even if we're "fallen" in the eyes of the Establishment, maybe we're seen by other more free-thinking souls as *trying* to stand for a sort of Christianity, a form of "Truth," with which others out there can identify. After all,' she added with a smile, 'you said yourself that you might still have a part to play in the Church.'

The remark stung.

'I must have been dreaming when I said that,' retorted Ben abruptly. And reverting to little boy mode, he suddenly yelled. 'I want *OUT!*'

He remained too hurt and angry to think otherwise.

## Chapter 29

'So that's arranged then, Mark,' said Christopher. 'I'll book a hotel and meet you at Ambleside station at 6 p.m. on Friday evening so that we can get in a weekend's climbing, and let you get back to London in time for the evening of Bank Holiday Monday.' He had just phoned to finalize their arrangements.

'Sounds great,' replied his friend. Mark Tipperary had to return on the Monday for the matinee of a new play he was directing at the Barbican. 'But just remember I'm not in as good shape as you, at least from what you've been telling me. I haven't done any proper climbing for almost two years.'

'Don't worry,' said Christopher affably. 'You're in good hands with me!' Still in the afterglow of having saved himself and two climbers from his adventures in the Alps, he spoke with feeling.

'See you on Friday – 6 p.m., Mark said.

'I look forward to it.' He put down the receiver.

It was the Wednesday before August Bank Holiday weekend. Fourteen months had now elapsed since the death of Stacey Witcombe and although her body had been exhumed and identified some six weeks back, he felt increasingly detached from her murder. Nor did he entirely regret that she'd been discovered, since it would allow her parents to give the girl a proper funeral and let everyone move on.

Of course there were times when with the body's discovery, he cast his mind back on things. Just how thoroughly had he covered his tracks? With forensic science being what it was these days, you couldn't be too careful.

But overall he felt confident enough. The passage of time would have made it all but impossible to tell the type of ligature used, or to reveal rope burns or scratch marks on flesh long since rotted away. As for his cassock girdle, he'd burned that shortly after her death along with her suede jacket and his tank-top. He'd even ensured when buying a replacement girdle that it was of a different thickness and texture to the previous one. And although fibres and hairs not belonging to the girl might yet be retrieved, time and weathering would have seriously eroded the validity of any further evidence.

More then it was a case of feeling euphoric about the climb ahead, and where impatient to leave the sultry atmosphere of London he departed two days before he was due to meet Mark. For although he enjoyed the city's anonymity, London's pollution levels in late summer could threaten to be on a par with those in Mumbai.

Like some getaway car, his LandRover ever fuelled up and well stocked with provisions, was there ready for him to drive up to the Lake District later that day. His plan was to pitch his tent in an obscure campsite near Ambleside for two nights, during which time he could make his detour.

His detour was by way of a re-visit to Leeds.

A month or so earlier he'd met up with Roxanne, the one recommended to him by the whore Sadie. After his murderous bust-up with Sadie, it seemed that the paratrooping bitch had made no mention to Roxanne of a certain 'Nigel,' 'who might just want to kill you darling, and who happened to mention that he was a clergyman'. So there'd been no need to tell Roxanne anything about himself, leaving her to assume that he was just another punter.

Yet despite liking the girl, at least to start with, his encounter with her had left him humiliated.

On that first visit to the Leeds, he asked for directions: 'Excuse me I'm looking for a Dutch girl called Roxanne. Do you know where I might find her?'

'No, but I'm Queenie and I'll surprise you, darling. What's your preference?'

Out there on the street and unfamiliar with the pressure tactics at the sharp end of prostitution, he didn't want to get done for curb crawling:

'Sorry, I'm not interested,' If she had been a police decoy, his response was exemplary. He then drove up alongside another pair of girls. They eyed him up in his expensive motor.

'Yeah, I know Roxanne,' said one in hot pants and see-through T-shirt, a skimpy shawl draped around one shoulder.

'You don't want her, love. You don't look her type. Me and Rachel here, we'll give you a nice ol' time and at half the price. Drive us off in your Land Cruiser and we'll take you to heaven and back,' sniggered Hot Pants.

'Well, actually it's Roxanne I'm looking for,' he said as though asking after the welfare of one of his parishioners.

'Well, fuck you then!' said Hot Pants' companion mimicking his posh accent.

'Can you tell me where I might find her?'

With pros obliged to help each other out, more so when it came to different departments of sex, bitchiness had to yield to the rules of the game:

'Straight up here past the Star and Garter and it's the second house on the left.' Then as a parting shot, Hot Pants added: 'and watch your back, darling. Roxy may look harmless, but she can be a vicious bitch. We don't call her Rottweiler for nothing.'

Driving on as directed and with a punter just leaving the house, Roxanne had invited him into her downstairs flat without ado.

Although her specialty was S & M, he'd felt an instant frisson for Roxanne given that she so much resembled sisters Stacey and Pippa. Her English too was flawless, despite its European inflexion to convey both intimacy and aloofness. Her deep-set brown eyes framed by her blonde hair they too made for an interesting contrast - adolescent and sophisticated at the same time. Given her slim physique and calm expression, there was no rottweiler as far as he could see.

In the world's oldest profession Roxanne would in other circumstances have made a companionable escort. Intelligent and charming she certainly defied what he took to be the stereotype of your typical street girl. More surprising still was the air of childish innocence, which he perceived behind the professional facade. Yet what he liked in the *girl* he still loathed in the *woman*.

Not that she divulged much, but Roxanne's story was one where with her upper class Dutch parents having split up, she'd turned to drugs only to find that prostitution was the easiest and most efficient way to indulge her habit, with London and later Leeds proving to be good venues. But having kicked drugs two years ago, Roxanne now stayed in prostitution so as to make enough money before re-establishing her roots in Holland.

While he wanted some sort of cloistered mistress, about

whom he could fantasize as he had sought to do with Stacey, it was naivety that blinded him into recognizing that behind the former drug addict, with her soft girlish features, was a woman brutalized by life. For not only was Roxanne streetwise, her hunger for financial freedom overran all else.

Forgetting her specialty, it was upon their first meeting that she'd shown him a sadistic trick to catch him wholly off-guard. For five minutes into their session and with unexpected swiftness, she had enmeshed him in a sort of metal contraption to which she then shackled his hands and feet, while rotating him half upside down and flailing him with a cane. In part this was what she imagined her client wanted, 'the Brits are into real pain' as she'd been told. But more alarmingly and sensing that his arousal seemed to pose a problem, she'd placed a halter around his neck daring to exact the 'art' of autoeroticism.

Although the practice of near-asphyxiation performed on its own can have tragic consequences Roxanne's expertise ensured that he'd been okay. But it was way beyond anything he'd expected. So when eventually she'd released him from her contraption he felt not so much sated with pleasure as enraged by his loss of control. Not only had another woman got the better of him once more, he felt humiliated at having been trapped so easily. Yet having paid for services rendered, and with Roxanne unaware of his smouldering sense of shame she'd given him her calling card.

Thus through the arrangement to go climbing with his friend Mark Tipperary in the Lake District, his visit via Leeds had a particular goal in mind.

Upon pitching his small two-man tent in a remote corner of a campsite near Ambleside, he could come and go unobserved. This made his drive to Leeds straightforward.

For this second visit, he'd phoned Roxanne on her mobile

to suggest that they go out for a meal together, offering her the going rate for a whole night's entertainment. Seeing this, as a welcome diversion from what all too often was a wearisome routine, she'd accepted readily enough.

If Christopher (and here he had decided to use his real name) had contracted her services on a basis that included an expensive dinner, with a bit of S & M thrown in at the end, then that was fine by her.

Meeting in the foyer of an up-market restaurant called 'The Lantern,' it was little more than a mile from where Roxanne worked, although in a more reputable part of the city. Compared to his casual attire, she was dressed in a black sequin skirt with a fuchsia pink silk jacket over a white lace cotton top. While her outfit flattered her contours, she'd taken care over her whole appearance - carefully manicured hands with their blood red nails, and hair freshly shampooed that hung in a blonde cascade around her shoulders. Brilliant rhinestone earrings with a diamanté plait necklace emphasized a face wholly at odds to the one of the Rottweiler dishing out her punishment. Giving her one of his own disarming smiles, it was the little girl once more whom he now greeted. Not often invited to an up-market restaurant, she seemed almost excited by the novelty of this unusual arrangement.

'You look lovely,' he felt sincere as he said it.

'Thank you!'

In contrast to the warm evening, her smile was cool and sophisticated.

Brushing the elbow of her arm they went in for their meal. Hors-d'oeuvres were of avocados and prawns. She kept to her fish-eating diet by eating poached salmon with salad, while his was a choice of venison in sweet and sour sauce, garnished with garlic herbs. They shared a bottle of Californian Cabernet Sauvignon, rounding the meal off with a sherbet fruit salad of passion fruit and tangerines, topped with cream. Both drank a coffee liqueur before Christopher settled the bill with cash.

Yet during their meal and despite her perfect English, their conversation had grown stiff and perfunctory; social niceties being exchanged like the cordon bleu titbits taken with the meal. With professional considerations still overriding any desire to be unduly sociable, the 'date' with her present client and who she had inadvertently discovered was a clergyman called Christopher, was after all no more than a contract.

After their meal and clear about her own agenda, Roxanne considered that it was safe enough to go for a short drive with him. He was after all – how do they say it in England? A 'gentleman of the cloth.'

With the night staying warm and a near full moon appearing and disappearing between clouds, he'd proposed that they visit a beauty spot known as Rombald's Moor. It was a short drive out of Leeds on the road towards Ilkley. With her agreeing to this with a 'why not', they drove through a landscape of bracken and gorse, leaving a casual witness to observe them as no different from any other courting couple.

They drew up at a secluded car park close to a high point known as Cow and Calf and from where a large vista of Ilkley Moor falls away to the east and west. One or two other cars were silhouetted in the moonlight, their occupants absorbed only in themselves, Taking a blanket from the LandRover, they walked a short distance into the gorse shrubbery where he asked Roxanne to lie on the ground and strip down to her undergarments while he returned to the car. Relaxed after three glasses of wine, she wasn't overly concerned as to what he had in mind.

He then returned with a fifty metre length of nine

millimetre rope, the sort that he and Mark would use on their climbing trip in a day or two's time. Affably, he suggested to Roxanne that he might tie her up, 'just for a few minutes and then I'll let you go. I promise not to touch you.' Aware that the fantasies of many of her clients were often of an almost playful whimsical kind, she saw the mass of rope as more comical than threatening.

Not for the first time had she posed for a client who seemed to derive satisfaction by just seeing her tied up half-naked. With a half smile, she reflected on her previous life as a computer programmer in Utrecht. There she couldn't earn in a week what she earned in a night with the likes of Christopher. What with the free meal and now 'these silly little games of tying people up', her new profession was - wasn't there an English expression for it – 'money for old rope'? But even as she smiled to herself and with his back to the moon she couldn't see the terrifying transformation.

For a while he did what he said - trussing and untrussing her as she lay on her stomach, his movements gentle almost like a caress. The rope was absurdly long as he then tied her with her legs drawn up and arms bound together in a flexible trussing knot. Known as the French Prusik, the knot is distinctive in that it can be moved by hand under tension. So although bound effectively enough by her feet and hands with the rope going around her neck, her hands could still move unrestrained.

Familiar with the essential knots used for climbing, his proficiency felt almost calming and reassuring than anything to suggest menace. He then produced a second section of white rope, not coarse at all in texture and no more than four metres in length. With this he tied two simple bowline knots around Roxanne's ankles, joining the two ends around her throat by the use of a double fisherman's knot, which tightens the greater the body weight used against it.

But as he worked the ropes, so the knots grew more lethal. Producing a further section of narrower cord he tied this around her neck while securing it to her legs, and arms using a standard figure-of-eight belay. As with a lariat that tightens under tension but which can be loosened with a free hand, so with the climber's belay when looped around a rock.

With each of the separate knots now working against each other, and with every movement of her limbs restricting her further Roxanne suddenly found herself choking. Flexing her legs or moving her arms would only shorten the new cord, all the time increasing the pressure upon her windpipe. So quickly had it happened that in wild panic, she understood she was self-strangulating for his pleasure.

With her head to one side, all she could gasp was: 'Christopher, please *undo* me, this has gone *far enough!*'

But with horror she could see his *new* face now reflected in the moonlight even as he spoke his intentions: 'This is the end of the line for you, my beautiful little bitch,' he rasped in her ear. 'I want you to die slowly and painfully. There's no one here to help you and I want you to be my victim so that I can claim you forever. Besides, I'm only doing what you tried doing to me. So don't ever think you can haunt me from the grave, for it is I who will haunt you, claiming you as my bond-slave just whenever I choose.'

The insane predator had come out of the shadows, his mad rantings proof of his deadly intent. But she managed to gasp, '*Christopher, please don't do this!* You can have me just as you want in real life. I promise to tell nobody who you are and yes, I shall be your slave forever. But *please LET ME GO!*'

Her intentions to yell were no more than a choked whisper.

With eye sockets bulging he could see in the moonlight

her normally pallid complexion starting to turn puce and then purple. Even as the cold sweat began to ruin her mascara, he gloated over her disfigurement and of the shapely limbs and torso beginning to writhe helplessly.

*'Please, help me. Don't let me die, don't do this to me!'*

With her Adam's apple engorged even as it gasped, her speech became a gurgle - small bubbles of spume forming around her mouth, leaving her tongue to flicker like a serpent.

'No way, you're on your own!' Wilkes responded. He loved the *way* she was dying - almost in total silence. Even as the perspiration poured around her straining temples, one bereft glance at the man whom she'd taken to be no more than a harmless perve told her, too late of course, that he was in a league of evil way beyond anything she'd experienced before.

*'Jesus, deliver me from this devil,'* she heard herself gasping, only to have him tug on the belay at her neck and where even as she lost consciousness, so the aura of darkness around him grew absolute. She knew she would die, as did he at the moment in the restaurant when he'd let slip his real name and profession.

Yet wishing to prolong the process, he loosened the belay as though to revive her, only for someone in the near distance to open and shut a car door. Whether she responded to this sound by uttering a few strangulated groans, she panicked him into wrenching at her neck thereby breaking it. Instantly the body went limp.

Despite having all but perfected the crime - of having a naked woman suffer and die under his total command, a sense of having been cheated once more lingered briefly. His pleasure had been interrupted not by the fact of her death, of course, but by failing to prolong the process in its final phase. But he'd killed her, done what in the restaurant he'd set out to do. So in that sense the operation had been a success.

It being a night for lovers whose ears and eyes were only for each other, the opening and shutting of a car door had been no more than a distraction. Murmured sweet nothings and the unhitching of clothing in other parts of that remote car park would have cut out all extraneous sound. So his confidence returned as he hoisted the body still caged within its mesh of ropes into the back of his vehicle and where covering her with an assortment of rugs and a car blanket, he'd driven off.

Driving in the same relaxed way as when he'd transported the body of Stacey, he planned to dump the prostitute at precisely the same location where he had disposed of the choirgirl.

By returning to the Grizedale Forest and to the same drystone wall overlooking Coniston Water may have lacked subtlety, but it was straightforward. Besides, the route to the forest was easily accessible, using a simple detour from Leeds back to his Ambleside campsite. Furthermore, as a place of concealment it had proved good enough to keep Stacey hidden for over a year and where, but for a freak event to reveal her whereabouts, she might have stayed indefinitely. So with no obvious connection between the two murdered women, the site seemed sensible enough.

As he drew near to the lay-by shortly after midnight, the earlier moonlight had become obscured by thick cloud, turning the night into near pitch-darkness. Just as last time, there was a VW campervan, only this time its occupants appeared to be fast asleep. To avoid drawing attention, he cut the engine, doused the lights and rolled into the lay-by at its far end. He was about thirty meters from the other vehicle, coming to a halt a short distance from where he'd disposed of Stacey. No signs of life stirred within the other vehicle and the road remained quiet.

Not yet cold, Roxanne's semi-naked body remained limp and flexible. Some few miles back he had freed it from its murderous trusses. For one thing he'd need the climbing rope for assisting Mark and himself over the weekend. As he stood by the wall he held the corpse fleetingly. Then, as before, he tossed it into the thick undergrowth below. He recalled how the undergrowth had proliferated some thirty feet below the whole section of lay-by, and upon hearing a faint rustling before the body came to rest, he peered over the wall. Using a powerful torch it seemed that like Stacey before, Roxanne had vanished out of sight - the effect of this producing the same wash of relief, as he'd felt before. For it was as though with the fall into the near-vertical slope below all ties between the killer and his victim were now severed.

'Easy as saying knife,' he thought to himself. In the euphoria of the moment he decided, too casually as it turned out, to pack the remainder of her belongings into a black bin liner before stashing them into some nearby undergrowth. Peering over the wall once more and checking that all was quiet in the campervan beyond, he returned to his Discovery to glide away in near silence. The only other item of Roxanne's that he had retained was her mobile phone. This he crushed under the front driving wheel of his vehicle some miles further on, before hurling the debris into some bushes.

By 2 a.m. he'd returned to his tent in a far corner of the campsite near Ambleside, the stealth of his arrival being muffled by a strengthening wind. Having a sleeping bag of expensive down and a high quality storm-proof tent, his sleep was remarkably untroubled despite a thunderstorm erupting later that night. Waking at around 7 a.m. and with the day clearing, he decided to do some strenuous hiking before his meeting with Mark later that afternoon.

# Chapter 30

As pre-arranged he met his friend at Ambleside station.

Mark Tipperary was a small wiry man, whose ferrety good looks just the right side of fifty, were retained through regular work-outs at his local gym. With no weight on him, he'd been a competent athlete in his youth and where time and opportunity allowed had sought the challenges of the rock face in later life.

Although different physically, he and Christopher were not unlike in temperament. Both tended to be loners who'd established something of a friendship at the theological college where they'd first met. By the end of his studies, Mark realized that the ordained life was not for him, choosing instead the hazardous career of becoming a playwright. Both as a writer and producer his most notable successes had been achieved more recently where, as a devotee of Samuel Beckett, he'd come to shape the style of his plays on his Irish mentor. As for having given up on his vocation to enter the Church there were no regrets.

During the course of their dinner at the hotel and reminiscing about old times, Mark suddenly came out with the most infelicitous suggestion: 'You know Christopher, I'd love to do a play about this twisted priest who, despite his perversion, manages to con the authorities and generally do pretty well for himself. What do you think? I mean, God knows, we saw enough weird and wonderful goings on at college, did we not?'

With that aplomb for which he was gifted when in a tight spot, Christopher replied, 'I'd leave that one alone, if I were you, Mark. You've got to get over your own hurts and hang-ups about the church. It's not that bad, or at least it's no different from any other large institution.'

Saying no more Mark kicked himself for his indiscretion. After all there'd been huge media coverage over the disappearance of a choirgirl from Christopher's last parish, and while Mark didn't suspect his friend for a moment, perhaps it had been a memory of that situation that sparked off the idea in his mind. A villainous priest would make excellent copy for some new drama.

They then drew up plans for their climb next day. Although it stood to be overcast, Saturday's forecast was for dry easterly winds. Just so long as the wind stayed constant and the rain held off conditions looked ideal for climbing purposes.

Mark's recent lack of practice on the rock face was more than compensated for by his enthusiasm and fitness and they'd planned what, in mountaineering terms, were some strenuous rock scrambles which included the Langdale Pikes of Jake's Rake and Harrison Stickle. Both being private men, they could think their separate thoughts whilst assisting each other where necessary

For the seasoned climber, Jake's Rake provided a steady exhilarating climb, offering no nasty surprises despite a series of short, polished walls towards the top that can be prove tricky in wet weather. But by lunchtime both climbers having made the ascent without difficulty they sat at the top admiring the panorama of lakes and dales, a view enhanced by a canopy of heavy cloud pierced by occasional shafts of sunlight.

Congratulating each other on their good physical shape, they relaxed in a nest of rocks out of the wind where they ate the picnic provided for them by the hotel. Mark, who loved the solitude of the wild open places, had on this occasion brought with him the somewhat incongruous accessory of his iPod radio. The idea had been to listen to some classical music while climbing.

With both of them now relaxing out of the wind, and with Mark still tuned into Classic FM, the one o'clock pips went. Only vaguely did he hear the same old headlines – some recent political scandal, another bomb scare and so forth. It was the news-flash that followed which drew him instantly out of his doze: 'The body of a second woman has been discovered near a lay-by yesterday morning in the Lake District, at the identical spot to that where the body of missing teenager Stacey Witcombe was discovered eight weeks ago. The murdered woman has been identified as a Leeds prostitute. Police, who are declining to release her name or to say whether the two crimes might be connected, are appealing for witnesses.'

'*Christ!*' thought Mark. 'Christopher's not going to like hearing this.' Fearing that he might have overheard already, he was relieved to see that his companion had turned away from him and, curled up foetus-like, seemed to be taking a quick nap. Although such news was likely to be common knowledge by nightfall, there was no way Mark wanted to alert his friend to it right then.

'Another body in the same place,' mused Mark, 'and here I am with Christopher in the locality where just a few weeks ago the *first* body was found.'

No details had been given as to when the body had been dumped, so maybe his friend's presence in the Lake District was pure coincidence. But the news was disquieting to Mark, and one to beg the question: Just who is this loner like myself, I wonder? I've had no problems with him as a climbing companion but maybe there is a side to him I know nothing about and . . .

He then upbraided himself: For God's sake Mark! It's your vivid imagination working overtime once more. Stop it! Yet even as the music resumed on his I-Pod with the soothing sounds of a Mozart piano sonata, Mark felt distinctly unsettled.

The afternoon stayed dry as they made their descent by way of Harrison Stickle, proceeding down the stepped skyline of its eastern ridge sweeping down to Stickle Tarn below. Although the views were stunning, Mark had now lost all appetite for any further climbing. When they got back to the hotel, he decided on making an excuse to return to London the next day.

Adjourning for a shower and cleanup they met up for a pre-dinner drink in the bar. Mark joined Christopher who, already seated, was having a large G & T. Knowing his friend to be an abstemious drinker, Christopher looked sweaty and agitated; the two empty glasses on the table beside him suggesting that he'd already had a couple. His hands were unsteady too, as he was vacantly peering into his drink

It was then that Mark made his excuse, by way of a lie: 'Christopher, old chap, I'm really sorry but I shall have to leave first thing in the morning. I've just contacted the theatre and they tell me that our lead player has gone down with some virus or other, and that we'll have to do a crash course with our understudy in time for Monday evening. I'm truly sorry but I'm going to have to leave first thing tomorrow.'

Despite saying something about it being okay, it was as though Christopher had scarcely heard him before muttering something about maybe he'd not stay himself. It was then that a repeat of the headlines did the talking that neither could own up to: 'and here are the headlines once more. The body of a missing prostitute, discovered yesterday near a lay-by at Coniston Water was found at the exact location where the remains of murdered schoolgirl Stacey Witcombe were found earlier this year. Police are appealing for any witnesses to come forward.'

No hiding now. Mark looked at Christopher who, after hesitating, returned his gaze.

'I've just heard it,' said Christopher. 'God, the Stacey Witcombe murder seems to follow me around. And now this other woman! Who was she, a Leeds prostitute or something, they said? Mark, I feel terrible. I don't seem to be free to get on with my life. My wife's left me; I've lost my job. Some people seem to persist in the belief that I'm somehow responsible for Stacey's murder. And now a second body's been found at the same lay-by where they found Stacey. What shall I do?'

Having agreed on their menu orders, they adjourned through to the dining room. Despite the peculiar coincidences Mark felt reassured by his friend's tone. It had to be patently absurd that this quiet dedicated clergyman could in any way be implicated:

'Like I've said all along, Christopher, you know that you've got nothing to reproach yourself with. You may still feel guilty that you didn't take Stacey back home that night, but that's all you can criticize yourself for. People will tittle-tattle till the cows come home. God knows the theatre world's one big gossip shop. You should hear them go on about me. Am I gay, straight, or just not interested? Folk always want to tie people like you and me down, to label us, just because maybe we're a bit different and don't keep in with the crowd.

'All you have to do, Christopher is stand your ground,' Mark advised. '*Prove* them wrong. Wait till the guy or guys who've done these murders get caught and they're banged up and convicted, and anyone who's had it in for you won't be able to do too much to make it up to you!'

'I hope you're right,' responded Christopher, appearing to cheer up a bit. Pulling Mark's reassurances around himself like a duvet, they chose to speak about general topics around climbing for a while. This gave Christopher the opportunity to tell his friend of his recent adventure in the Alps; and of how he'd saved his two fellow climbers as well as himself by slamming his ice axe into the snow using a couple of 'deadmen'. 'It was a close run thing, Christopher told him.

'Well, you deserve a medal for that!' said Mark admiringly. 'There are too many preventable deaths on the mountains these days. Scores are dying needlessly, either because climbers don't weigh up the conditions properly, or because they don't know the rudiments of safe climbing or what to do in an emergency.'

Yet despite this recent act of heroism, Christopher's mood went back to being morose. Maybe it was the G & T's talking, or the white wine that they'd drunk with their veal schnitzels, which brought him back to the topic of murder. 'But what would *you* do Mark in my situation?' he asked. 'I mean another death in the Lake District, in the same lay-by and with you knowing that I was up here both times near to the bodies' whereabouts? Even you must feel suspicious?'

'*For God's sake, Christopher,*' replied Mark. '*Stop tormenting yourself!* Who knows the second murderer, if there is a second one, could be out to play some trick like he's enjoying a sick joke. Killers often find that they have imitators trying to steal their notoriety. Anyway you'll know as well as anyone that there's no substitute for innocence. Even if the police want to question you again, you'll have your alibis making them realize soon enough that you're telling the truth.'

Then, as though talking to himself, Mark said quietly, 'I wonder how long the second woman had been dead before they found her.'

That was the question now tormenting Christopher. How in God's name had they found the body so quickly? Presuming that Roxanne's corpse would rot and lie hidden indefinitely just as Stacey's had done, what had gone wrong?

Although the husband and wife occupants sleeping in their VW motor home at the lay by had driven off that morning, oblivious of their previous night's visitor, the discovery had been made by another motorist a short time later. Having stopped off at the same lay by around 8 a.m. so as to stretch his legs and relieve himself, it was he who saw her.

Enjoying the freshness of the morning air after the night's storm, he stopped to reflect on the peaceful outline of Coniston Water beyond the trees. It was one of his favourite stopping places. Only as he lifted his foot onto the dry-stone wall to do up a shoelace did he catch sight of something red. He looked more carefully. Mannequin-like and white while pointing up from the undergrowth were the unmistakable contours of a woman's arm. It had been the vivid red nail varnish on the lifted hand that caught his attention. He could also make out a silver bracelet that had slipped down towards her elbow. With that sickening awareness of being the first to witness the scene of what appeared to be an obvious murder, the motorist had mobiled the police immediately.

The body had fallen in such a way that rigor mortis had forced the woman's arm to extend vertically up through the ferns. Had Wilkes kept her secure in her mesh of ropes, the body would never have had the freedom of movement to disclose its whereabouts. As it was the limb had risen from the undergrowth, as though pointing to the very spot from where she had been flung.

This time around the police were at a distinct advantage. The forensic department had so much more to work on with a newly discovered body rather than with a skeleton. Dental records were of secondary importance, since the identity of the victim was quickly established through the bundle of clothes and other items discovered in the black bin liner near by.

Among Roxanne's personal effects was a vivid fuchsia silk jacket and, in a small shoulder purse, a number of invoice stubs, along with a Leeds library ticket. With the evidence being so fresh, Roxanne's working colleagues related that she had told them that her last client was a man 'with a posh accent, who drove a big flash motor with the word "Discovery" written on the side and what looked like it was green in colour, at least under the street lights.'

With Mark having boarded the train back to the city, Christopher also decided on an immediate return to London, it being not so much a case of fleeing the scene of his crime as seeking the illusion of security that London offered. Had the police wished to question him, of course, they could have done so in a trice wherever he was.

But nothing seemed to be amiss as he let himself back into his flat. There was no-one hiding behind the door to make an instant arrest. Everything looked orderly, a small pile of post having been put neatly in place by the cleaning lady who came once a week on a Friday. One letter in particular caught his eye, which having arrived in Saturday's post was lying separately on the mat. Carrying the pompous insignia of Fordham's diocesan crest he tore it open immediately. The letter contained a personal message from his Lordship - Bishop Letharge:

'*My dear Christopher,*

*How are you dear boy? I do hope that you have had some much needed respite from your earlier troubles, whilst enjoying the benefits of living in London, what with all the night-life! (Just my little joke, you understand.)*

*Please contact me as soon as possible next week, since I have what is an interesting (and I hope not to be refused) proposal to put to you, regarding the resumption of your duties here within the diocese.*

*Yours, Simon F'ham+'*

The reader felt caught between the *numbness* and apprehension felt on his drive south, and the rush of *elation* that now washed over him! For suddenly it felt as though the fugitive had been purged and exonerated, like nothing bad had ever taken place. All the bad stuff belonged to some nightmare, where at the very moment when he might have cut and run, fearing that the police might have shackled him even he opened his front door, the calm and serenity that he yearned for had now come flooding back. Without so much as a whiff of suspicion in his direction, here was the good bishop making him an offer that he could not, nor should not refuse.

In his euphoria it was as though Stacey and now Roxanne were but impostors in some recurrent nightmare, trying to turn the unreal into something real. All the publicity, all the hoo-ha, even the recent troubles with his former wife and family, these too represented no more than the torments of a soul on the painful path to – was it, *holiness?* He'd heard an expression for it somewhere. Was it the long dark night of the soul, or some such? Inner demons whose torments were entirely without foundation - groundless in other words!

Blessed with his insights how fortunate then that Bishop Letharge seemed able to discern Christopher's torment, recognizing him for who he was - the saint in waiting, making his own dark pilgrimage towards sanctification. For didn't all the saints endure similar ordeals, wracked with feelings of guilt where none were necessary? Now as he luxuriated in his aromatic-soaked bath, Christopher could offer silent thanks.

That night he slept almost with the innocence of a child. After all, a man who looked careworn and exhausted might be someone to suggest guilt, if not someone out of control. So, if he reflected upon his nightmare at all or of any involvement in past events, it was only to say to himself: 'All right, Roxanne's been discovered. But she can name no names. There may have been witnesses at the restaurant that we went to. Perhaps someone might describe a distinctive-looking car, or have got a vague impression of me at the beauty spot where she died. But I've only been twice to the red light district of Leeds. It's not as though I'm a regular visitor. Having been and gone, I need never return.' He then added: 'I don't even remember seeing her.'

There was the further consolation, as he understood it, that the police wouldn't trouble themselves unduly over a missing street-girl, at least just so long as there wasn't a spate of them disappearing.

Between the delusion of his being innocent and the reality of what his memory might choose to serve up, he might also tell himself:

I know that I was up in the Lake District over the weekend, but I was booked in at the camping site in Ambleside during the time when the Leeds girl got dumped in Grizedale. Besides I was only walking and climbing at the time, with Mark vouching for me at the weekend. He'd also say how much I felt tormented over any lingering suspicions held against me over Stacey.

His vote of self-confidence returned as he smirked, and said out loud: 'So keep your head down Canon Wilkes and stay cool!'

Perfecting the art of staying cool was what he'd done to

good effect on earlier occasions. He'd already disposed of his mountain rope, which had done double duty both as a murder weapon, and in keeping himself and Mark safely hitched together. Having stuffed it into a bin-liner, along with other sections of cord he'd thrown the whole lot into a commercial skip at a service station on the M1, while taking further precautions on that Monday evening to have his car thoroughly valeted.

Thus did the honorary canon of Fordham diocese readjust his mask. He was no more than the conscientious cleric given leave of absence, following a bout of nervous exhaustion.

He had also heard how some of the worthy folk at All Saints were grieving his absence. *When might you be coming back? We really do feel for you at this difficult time. We miss your inspired leadership* provided the gist of several sympathetic letters forwarded to him by the diocesan office. Well thank goodness that Fordham's bishop was a wise man whose unswerving confidence in Christopher, ensured that he'd be back at work in the diocese before too long.

Having phoned through to the bishop's office on the Monday morning, Christopher was invited to travel up by train to meet with his Lordship that afternoon.

'Come in, come in, dear boy!' said the bishop with the affected little bow he reserved for those whom he chose to favour. 'It's good of you to come up at such short notice. Be sure to let me have your expenses before you go back.'

'Thank you, my lord, it was no trouble, really,' replied Christopher being ushered once more into the library study, with its heady ambience of Regency good taste.

'My, my, you *are* looking well, Christopher! You look as though you've got entirely over your past problems, and can't wait to get right back into harness once more.'

The bishop seemed not to observe the small abrasions about his upper cheek and temple, the fading stigmata inflicted by Philippa from some weeks back.

'Well yes, sir, my wife seems to want a minimum of fuss over our agreement to part amicably, and so there are no clouds ahead as far as I can see. I'm very much looking forward to working for you once more.'

'Good, good!' The bishop smiled paternally over his half-moon glasses while tapping a benign temple with his fingers. He especially liked it when people spoke of working *for* him. As before the prelate and his subject's highly polished black brogues seemed to wink their approval of each other.

'Would you care for a glass of port, Christopher? I feel we may well have something to celebrate.'

He accepted the cut-glass goblet, once more amply filled with what was another of the bishop's smooth vintages.

'I wonder how you would feel about preparing yourself for major responsibility within the diocese. How would you feel about that?'

Flushed with anticipation, Christopher's response was once more self-deprecating: 'I would love to do something that offered me a further challenge, my lord. But of course that's a matter of doing whatever *you* feel is best.'

'Excellent! I have been in discussions with Bishop's Council over this. It seems that Cathedral Chapter and I are agreed that given the sudden retirement of our Provost through ill health, as I'm sure you are aware, we would like to offer you the position. That is, of course, if you felt able!'

'Oh my lord, I'm not sure I'm worthy of such a high responsibility,' replied Christopher, genuinely incredulous to be offered such a post. Unction disguised as humility did its own little pirouette on the carpet, which was how the bishop liked it. But before any chink of uncertainty might threaten this proposal, the canon was swift to reply, 'I'm

## A Candle For Lucifer

honoured beyond words, my lord. Thank you, I accept!'

*'Excellent!'* said his lordship. Despite pretending to work collaboratively with his colleagues, Letharge was pure and simply an autocrat who got his way over everything. Fixing appointments as readily as he now did with Canon Wilkes had become his sole prerogative. 'That's settled then,' said the bishop. 'As there's a busy programme at the cathedral for this coming year, especially on the fund-raising front, I will need the appointment filling as soon as possible. So may I suggest an Advent commissioning service, if that doesn't sound too soon?'

Being only a few months away, Advent was in fact extremely 'soon'. *Provost indeed*! Christopher could hardly repress his glee! Who would have ever thought it? As the bishop went out to ask his housekeeper to bring in some tea, the thought, my lord, I am not worthy, slipped silently from his lips in a slime of banality.

But of course in the eyes of *this* earthly lord, Christopher was eminently worthy. Indeed Canon Wilkes was a far better choice for the bishop who, if the truth be known, had contributed in no small measure to the outgoing provost's early retirement through ill-health.

Owing to a major rift between himself and the bishop to argue that women priests should be made more welcome in Fordham diocese, the retiring provost's health had gone from bad to worse. For as the ailing provost held to his principles over this matter, so Letharge's resistance had intensified. The scandal was of course obvious, given that Letharge had before his consecration, promised to welcome all clergy regardless of their gender.

The departing provost represented that small army of casualties in the Church of England who, for a variety of reasons, can find themselves left by the wayside. Within such a group of worthy clerics who brook no servility to those in high office, not uncommonly theirs is the fate of suffering ostracism if not dismissal.

## Chapter 31

With Roxanne's body formally identified by two of the girls known to her, and with the pathologist wishing to secure most of his August Bank holiday weekend intact, the autopsy had been completed late that Friday evening.

From the rigor mortis still in place, it was deduced that the body was at the outside no more than thirty-six hours old, considerably less judging from the minimal larvae activity of a few blue-bottle eggs, freshly hatched.

A significant detail in her death was based on the partly digested contents in her stomach. She'd eaten a dinner that included avocados, prawns, salmon, red wine and passion fruit marinated, so to speak, with coffee liqueur. Here the evidence was that having been wined and dined she'd died a short time later, probably less than twenty-four hours prior to being examined; a finding verified using the vitreous humour test. By calibrating the hourly amount of potassium found in the fluid of her eyes, it was established that the woman had died between 10 p.m. and midnight of the previous night.

Identifying the cause of death was straightforward. Red blobs around Roxanne's ankles and wrists with welts around her neck and waist, along with the dried bloodstained froth around her nostrils and mouth, pointed to strangulation. An elaborate criss-cross of ligature marks indicated a weird and elaborate ritual of bondage, the bite marks on her tongue suggesting that her death had been prolonged. Despite the victim contributing towards her own death through self-asphyxiation, it was shown that her assailant had completed the process by breaking the girl's neck, the small hyoid bone having been fractured.

Pressure marks around the body indicated that the hands, almost certainly those of a well-built man, had been sheathed in what appeared to be kid-leather gloves, no fingerprints being evident. Then by plunging the lab into darkness so as to use a LumaLite, fibres and a variety of stains were lit up like fireflies. The victim's nails also revealed what under analysis turned out to be fine shreds of a nine millimetre climbing rope. Other fibres found in her teeth were of a softer white nylon texture, this rope bearing no comparison to the other.

With neither fingerprints nor semen stains being evident, some flecks of spittle not belonging to the victim were illuminated around the side of her face and left ear, as though someone had spat at her.

The police had everything and nothing to go on. The identified body provided almost pure forensic data as to the time and nature of death, as well as having been found at the near-exact location where the body of Stacey Witcombe had been left. They also knew that Roxanne had eaten a gourmet meal probably in a restaurant, and one likely to be in the vicinity of where she worked. But having been off-duty over that Thursday night, Roxanne's exact whereabouts were unclear, the last clear sighting of her having been earlier that afternoon where she'd been seen shopping in Leeds.

However after further inquiries in the red light area, it was reported that she had been asked for earlier on that

Thursday night. The man had spoken with a posh accent and been driving an off-roader with the word 'Discovery' written on the side. Subsequent inquiries produced a response from one of the diners who had left the Lantern Restaurant in Leeds, just when Christopher and Roxanne arrived. The diner described seeing a tall, older fellow white-skinned getting out of a LandRover Discovery with a pretty blonde, who 'Yes that's her all right' fitted the sad photo of Roxanne lying on a mortuary slab. He was also certain about the make of car. The waiter too, although having not taken much interest in the couple at the time, had given them a similar description, saying that the man was much older than the girl who spoke with a slight European accent and who, yes, did look like the person in the photograph.

What taxed the police was whether the second death was a copycat murder of the first, or was the killer one and the same person? Both victims were young females with blonde hair who had had their necks broken, although the concealment of Stacey appeared to have been more thorough than that of Roxanne. A small section of new tyre tread left in some curb mud close to the point from where Roxanne had been thrown was that of a 205 R15 Pirelli tyre, the type and size being typical to that used by LandRovers.

But beyond that nothing much hung together.

If the detectives who had originally interviewed the Revd Canon Wilkes hadn't much cared for his attitude, he'd held up well under questioning. Furthermore, domestic problems at home perhaps explained his reportedly strange behaviour towards Stacey's sister, a woman called Philippa, whom he had apparently been helping but who'd lodged a somewhat garbled complaint about him a month or two back.

Desperate for a lead, the police had recruited the services of a criminal profiler. Despite some glaring miscarriages of justice, offender profiling still remained popular with certain Forces, the services of a particular forensic psychologist called Dr Bob Tideswell having been especially in demand. What sort of picture might be compiled to describe the murderer of Stacey and/or Roxanne?

Tideswell's mantra was well known: 'It is perfectly possible to get inside the *mind* of a suspect, even when hard evidence is in short supply.' To make up his mental 'artist's impression' he chose to give free rein less to painstaking logic, and more to what he considered to be inspired guess-work. To do otherwise would be to disregard what was considered to be his best asset. 'One must rely on one's sixth sense' was how he put it. 'Psychic hunches are what I call them.'

But his methodology wasn't so much one of cause and effect, as one that preferred to work in reverse; seeking to profile the 'someone' who had killed Roxanne, and then to work backwards. From there Tideswell could call upon anyone whom the police suspected even in a general way, using if necessary a 'plant', so as to get inside the head of his primary suspect.

In asking, 'What *sort* of a man killed Roxanne?' he presumed that it was someone who knew her and lived in the area. The gourmet meal taken so shortly before she died suggested either someone who knew the victim, or someone perhaps who liked to impress the ladies. When a prostitute got killed, of course, the killer might well be a loner with weird sexual fantasies and poor social skills. He could be religious in a way that the infamous Yorkshire Ripper, Peter Sutcliffe, claimed to be during his killing spree of prostitutes in the nineteen eighties. There he was the respectably married truck driver who, during his spare time, claimed to be driven by heavenly voices telling him to clean up the streets.

Although the murderer could be a loner or drifter, the profile of one living a seemingly normal life was never to be discounted. Then there'd been the case of that Midlands electrician and handyman Michael Sams who fluctuated between extremes. Having killed a prostitute he went home nightly to his wife, all normal-like, as well as indulging in his other passion – of going into his attic to play with his model railway. He did the same after kidnapping a female estate agent keeping her imprisoned in his Newark workshop. There you had another one, hiding behind the disguise of the seemingly devoted spouse and even if Sams wasn't religious as such, he was certainly upright and hard working. The roll call of apparently normal individuals doing dastardly deeds on the side was legion.

So with his so-called 'psychic hunches' and not a little natural hubris, Tideswell felt confident that he could nail the Lakeside killer or killers.

'Come on old son,' said the Detective Inspector who picked him up. 'We've got some serious questions to ask.'

*''Ere, what's going off?'* asked the youth, who was quite enjoying helping to assemble a recreation area on some waste land in central Birmingham. The play area had been made available for families living in the high-rise tenement buildings nearby. Putting tools like hammers and screwdrivers to their proper use, instead of using them to wreck car doors and disable their alarms had felt strangely rewarding. Doing community service by making reparation to society wasn't always so bad.

With his Italian father's skin colouring and the blue eyes of his Irish mother he was a pleasant enough looking lad. Furthermore his slim physique made him look taller than he was. Having recently changed his long dark hair and pigtail for a low-cut Mohican, he invariably wore Nike trainers along with black Wranglers and a T-shirt. Nor was he unduly flash - a small intricate tattoo at the back of his neck depicting a mermaid draped around an anchor, a copper band on his right wrist, along with a single ear-stud in his right ear, being the extent of his adornment.

His rehabilitation from nicking cars was rudely interrupted.

'We've got some questions to put to you down at the station,' repeated the arresting officer as they bundled him into the patrol car. Nor did the questions wait for the station, for no sooner had they pulled away and viewing Merv in the vanity mirror of his sun visor the non-driving officer asked, 'What we're wanting to know Mervin is what else you did on that Thursday evening. You remember? The night when you were done for kerb-crawling up in Leeds.'

'Why are you asking?'

No response and then cryptically, 'We thought *you* might like to tell us that, Merv.'

'I dunno what you're talking about.'

Down at the station, the same officers escorted him to an interview room. Times and details of those present were addressed to a tape-recorder, before further questions were put.

'Do you have a steady girlfriend then, Merv?'

'What's it to you if I do or don't?'

'*Do* you, or *don't* you?'

'No, I don't. It's easier in my line of work not to. Anyway what's it to you?"

'Remind us again what you do, son.'

'*What the fuck's going off?* You know what I do. What do you think I'm working my bollocks off doing community service for?'

'*Language,* Merv! We're talking about what you might do *apart* from that.'

'Give me a break. What you on about?'
'We found all that stuff in your bed-sit.'
'What you mean? The readies in the freezer?'
'No, we're not on about that! We're on about the pieces of rope and black-magic stuff you got, along with the porno mags about bondage and rope tricks.'

The car thief looked incredulous. If the thought crossed his mind to say nothing until he'd got a solicitor, the line of enquiry proved too provocative.

'Come on, Merv, we know you did it.'
*'Did what, for Christ's sake?'*
'Killed the girl!'
The youth's jaw dropped.

'Good faking,' implied the glance of the DI looking at his colleague. 'We're talking about Roxanne, if your memory's so bloody short Merv. The hooker who got murdered in Chapeltown up in Leeds a fortnight ago, the one you saw earlier that week.'

'Never met her!'

'Well now, that's funny because some of her friends said that it was you who picked her up. Shouldn't have nicked that nice big LandRover, sonny. Made yourself stick out like a sore thumb!'

'I *was* up there in Leeds in the red-light district,' he replied. 'What's the big deal? That's all over and done with. The car was nicked and I was looking for a pick-up. The magistrate took care of the rest.'

'Well that's not how we heard it, Merv! The deal is that you took the girl out in your Discovery, gave her a meal and since she wasn't seen thereafter we'll ask you again: *When did you do it?*'

'I haven't a clue.' This was a foolish answer from Merv who, at the start of the session should have insisted on having his solicitor. To say that he hadn't a clue might suggest that he'd actually *been* with the girl, the night she died.

Both of his interrogators chose to read a 'catch-me-if-you-can' connotation in his last response.

'Well I can give you *a clue,* if you like Merv,' said the burly inspector who'd done just about all the questioning whether in the car or now. 'Roxanne is stitched up from head to toe, *very dead* and very autopsied lying on a slab in Leeds mortuary. Let me just jog your memory a bit.' The same photograph of the dead Roxanne was then presented to him.

It took him an age to reply, before asking: 'You saying I know her, or something?'

'Very much so, son! Are you a handy man with ropes then?'

'What are you *on about*?' Despite beginning to get seriously pissed off, the anxiety registered in his voice.

By remaining deaf to his genuine alarm, the two detectives pressed their case: 'Just that we picked up some rope in the vehicle you stole, that's all.'

'What's that got to do with it?' He recalled seeing some towing rope in the LandRover on the night of the theft.

'Because Roxanne got killed, trussed up like a cat's-cradle, and because you strangled her.'

*'That's fucking lies!'*

'Getting upset now, are we? I bet you wish that it *was* lies, Merv.'

The questions went on for some time, 'Where did you go out for a meal?' 'What did you do to her?' 'Why didn't you get rid of the rope, Merv?' when suddenly he was told. 'OK. You can go now. You'd better get back to your community service and make out you're being a good lad! You wouldn't want to upset your probation officer now, would you?'

They didn't even show him the courtesy of running him back to his place of work in the patrol car. Quite apart from them having 'shit for brains,' he cursed the Old Bill for their callousness.

Trudging the two miles back to his community project to resume work, he did so with a heavy heart. He knew that they'd not finished with him yet. More to the point Dr Tideswell's 'hunches' concerning the youth were just getting into overdrive.

'I want a pretty undercover woman PC,' ordered the profiler. 'She's got to know and chat up Costello, to see just where he's coming from. I want her to entice him, wipe his arse, make love to him if need be . . . do anything he bloody well pleases, just so long as she gets him to say that he did it, that he *killed* Roxanne.'

For all his qualifications, Dr Tideswell had a crude turn of phrase and was generally known to be hard-wired for his flashes of temper.

Barbara Meredith had only recently joined the force. Near enough a rookie, her nice looks and open expression had already caught the eye of her superiors, marking her out as a good honey trap to work in the vice squad. Despite the standing joke among the women WPCs of enjoying equal job opportunities to their *male* counterparts but with the latter being more 'equal' than others, she still wished to achieve what she could.

So with the profiler's requirements being a priority, WPC Meredith complied with the instruction for her to cozy up to young Costello by doing whatever it took to win his confidence. Originating from Birmingham as he did and with her Brummie accent she was to discover where he drank, and then by using the ploy of being a bit of a lonely heart to chat him up accordingly.

Young Costello caught the profiler's attention not just on

account of his being the driver of a LandRover Discovery, the likely car in which Roxanne had been abducted and from which a coil of rope had been recovered. It was also clear that the car thief was into some weird religious beliefs.

After raiding his scruffy bed-sit not far from Birmingham city center, the police had found a block of over two thousand quid stashed solid into the freezer department of his fridge. More serious, however, was the discovery amongst a pile of girlie magazines of a group of books about serial killers. These, plus what appeared to be the paraphernalia of a witch, heightened their suspicions.

Although his belongings were harmless enough, being but a random assortment of items vaguely associated to the occult, it was their very randomness that suggested more sinister associations. What the police took to be a voodoo object was but a mortar with its improvised pestle, used presumably for grinding drugs or incense. A Bible along with some joss sticks and a pack of Tarot cards scattered on the floor raised questions, as did a paperback copy of the I-Ching. Finding an assortment of dowel sticks, and as used in the interpretation of that oracle, only made Costello seem weirder.

Pages torn from the Bible intrigued the searchers further. Printed on Indian paper, the missing pages had been used only for the smoking of hash. But the spliff-head, if that was what he was, had even been selective in his destruction of the Bible, removing only those pages that made no sense to him. But for those ransacking his flat, a torn Bible and joss sticks scattered on the floor alongside books on serial killers and copies of *Men Only* taken together provided grounds for serious suspicion.

No allowance was made for the flat's contents reflecting the mind of a confused car thief trying to make sense of life, rather than to someone hell bent on murder.

'Hey up,' said Barbara breezily to the barman, 'Can I have a dry martini, please?' She made a point of sitting alongside the sad looking guy on the stool next to her.

For a few moments she sat sipping her drink in silence, allowing Merv to register her presence, as he usually did when a pretty, apparently available, girl came on his radar.

'Hi, how you doing?' he asked.

'So so,' she replied with a casual smile. 'But doesn't life get you down?' she spoke like someone wishing to take him into her confidence. 'My dad's been taken poorly and I'm going to have to give up my job, or at least only do it part-time to look after him.'

'Don't tell me,' he said taking a gulp from his pint glass. 'There's no one out there doing us any favours, or that's how it seems. Very often you can't do right for doing wrong. My mum, not that I can remember much that she said, told me always to look on the bright side, 'cos if you don't no-one else will for you!'

'Yep, guess that's true enough,' replied Barbara, every word of their conversation ringing clear through to the investigating team.

Seeing no reason to disguise her first name, they fell into easy conversation helped by the mutual familiarity of their Birmingham accents, and where companionably she offered to pay for a round of drinks.

He was frank over his disclosures about being a car thief and of doing some community service to make amends, 'working just around the corner as it happens, it ain't so bad,' he told her, before adding:

'I dunno. Sometimes I'd really like to do things with my life. Working with kids or summat. What I'm doing is pretty dumb. But the readies aren't so dumb, so I can't give up. Where else could you get an easy couple of grand for a day's work, nicking a motor and ringing the number plates?'

'Is that what you get?' She was good at using her eyes to express amazement.

'Depends on the motor and the market,' he replied. 'Nicking to order is the best way. The boys want a BM Coupe 525i in metallic blue or a white Lexus and you get 'em in mint condition, then you're into good money. Especially the Lexuses and Jags 'cos they're getting to be dogs to break into, what with all their microchips. But there's still ways and means. Way back I used only to nick stereos and alloys but that was pin money. Specialist motors is the one to get into.'

She drew him on for a bit about car thieving, which he did readily enough:

'Of course I've got my principles,' he told her. 'I'd never do a carjacking and I like to sell motors that ain't been tampered with body-wise. I can't be doing with those merchants who 'cut and shut' two motors and bring them together.'

'What's cut and shut?'

'You get a good front end off a write-off and a good back end off another write-off and weld 'em up. All the ringers are at it. Friggin death traps! I had a mate who bought it in one of them racing Honda Civic Rs, when the car split in two on a corner.'

'So you try to nick high-class motors and avoid the low-class ringers?' she asked.

'Yep, the story of my life!'

'Is that *all* you do?' she peered into her drink as she asked.

'Well, I'm thinking of getting into caravans. There's good money in them and they're a damn sight easier to get into. Parking 'em up's the problem' he sniggered.

She had to admire his candour: 'that's not what I meant. Do you do anything *else?*' This time she drained her glass.

'What else were you thinking of?' His expression told her

he wasn't sure where the question was leading. Half reading the innuendo, she laughed and touching him on the arm said: 'What I meant was, do you do any other sort of *crime?*'

'Nah, 'taint worth it,' he was beginning to slur his speech. 'Sides, I'd like to get my shit tog . . . . excuse me, to get me act together so as to get out of crime altogether' and picking up her glass asked if she wanted another?

'Don't mind if I do.'

Barbara didn't dislike the youth, and after some further chat they agreed to meet in the pub the following evening.

He knew that he'd be there, as did she.

They met up on a couple more occasions, before he plucked up courage to invite her back to his bed-sit.

'Sorry the place is a tip.'

'Don't worry.' They were in his living room and she was peering at his modest possessions, with its books and magazines. 'Have you ever done anything worse than theft, Merv? I see you've got some interesting books here.' She turned to look at him, bringing a mix of flirtation and mischief into her expression. 'I mean have you ever hurt anyone?'

'Not really,' the same puzzled expression creased his features.

'I mean,' she said, 'I hope you wouldn't think any worse of me if I told you I'd find it a turn-on, knowing if you'd ever hurt somebody really *badly*.'

He then told her how the police had tried to frame him for the murder of a Leeds prostitute, just because he was in a LandRover Discovery, which the police said had been the last car she was seen in.

'God, that sounds spooky.' And with a thrilled expression she asked, 'Well, *did you?* Go on tell me that you did it! It wouldn't make any difference to me if you had. In some ways I'd respect you more.'

Drawing closer and hoping to move in for the kill, so to speak, Barbara suggested, 'We can be lovers if you tell me that you hurt the girl, *any* girl.'

He didn't respond.

Catching sight of the pornographic material in his room, she tried another tack, making out that she enjoyed bondage and the like.

She got up to flick open the page of some mildly suggestive bondage scene, asking as she did so, 'Have you ever done that sort of thing to anybody?'

'Nope! *Have you?*'

The question caught her off guard momentarily.

'Uh, no, but I'm interested in why you read that stuff? You must *want* to do it if you read about it!'

'Just because you read a book on motor sport doesn't make you a racing driver,' he replied deftly. 'Come to think of it, reading a thriller about murder doesn't make you a murderer.'

She had no answer to that or to the allusion of a racing driver where in her case she was getting nowhere fast.

Meeting with Dr Tideswell sometime later, he told her not to be discouraged: 'Barbara, if at first you don't succeed, try turning up the heat a bit more.' She could write Costello a letter, making a definite offer of sex, if he admitted to having done something really violent. She could lead him on by inventing something like having had a previous boyfriend who'd been on a murder charge, and that she'd had the *best* sex with him ever. Tideswell went so far as to propose that she could punish Merv, by threatening to end the relationship if he didn't confess.

Yet despite telling the profiler, 'but he denies ever having seen the girl, let alone of hurting her,' Tideswell persisted:

'Listen, the likes of Costello will lie through their back teeth. They'll do *anything* to appear innocent, gullible even, not to mention working on their charm. But it's then that you need to watch out. It's just as well I can get three officers to you in half a minute if he tries anything on. Believe me, Barbara, the guy isn't what he appears to be!'

His forcefulness left her neither questioning his logic nor of the dubious tactics proposed with which to entrap her target. After all, Tideswell was said to be an acclaimed master in his field and she'd got her career to consider.

In a letter to Merv, Barbara enclosed more than a hint of some hard-core fantasies. The pornographic desires from her to him were far more audacious, far more *warped* than anything he'd ever said or suggested to her. So when they next met, and where his only concern was not to *lose* her he played along: 'Listen Barbara, I'm not into kinky sex. But I'm game to go along if that's what *you* want.'

This proved too much for Constable Meredith who without further ado got up saying not unkindly, 'It's OK, Merv. I'm through with you. No hard feelings!'

With the message received loud and clear by the three eavesdroppers in the van outside, the profiler flung his headphones to one side, cursing volubly. Yet undeterred, the police still arrested Costello and succeeded in getting him held on remand. A few months after Roxanne's death, he remained banged up with the police remaining persistent, and against all reason, that they had nailed their man.

It would take more than a further murder before obliging them to change their minds.

# Chapter 32

'Can you *believe* it?'

'I can believe anything that Letharge chooses to do,' replied Angela. 'He's mad, bad and a total law unto himself.'

It was early September and the press release had just announced the appointment of Canon Wilkes to the post of Provost.

'Christopher Wilkes is a psychopath. Pure and simple,' said Ben. 'There's not only Stacey; there's Frances and their broken family for whom he has no feelings whatsoever. There's the attack on Philippa who almost certainly saved her life by defending herself as she did. Following all that, there was that prostitute found only a month ago at the identical spot where Stacey got dumped.'

'It beggars belief!' said Angela. 'We'd better phone Frances, if she doesn't know already.'

She dialed through.

Ben and Angela were adjusting to their new life outside the Church. Alongside his salary cheques from the Church, good for almost a year, he had been appointed as a paid director of the charity for the homeless. This meant that along with Angela finding some freelance research work in astrology they were coping financially. They had also been provided with a larger flat, not ideal but an improvement certainly for the forthcoming baby.

'Hallo, Frances, it's me. Have you heard the latest?' asked Angela over the phone.

'No.'

'Well brace yourself,' said Angela. 'You're not going to believe this, but Canon Wilko is back in business in the diocese. And guess what, they want to make him *Provost!*'

'*PROVOST*'? Gasped Frances.

'It's *unreal* isn't it?'

'Who told you?'

'It's in this evening's *Post*. It's only a short piece. Let me read you what it says: "*Former vicar of All Saints, Ketborough, Canon Christopher Wilkes has been given the post of Provost (sometimes known as the dean) at Fordham Minster, the appointment being made effective in late November.*

"*Following the unresolved murder of All Saints' choirgirl Stacey Witcombe fifteen months ago and his divorce in June which led to his resignation, Canon Wilkes has, according to his bishop, had a difficult term of office in his former parish where he had been vicar for just over three years. However the Bishop of Fordham, Rt Revd Simon Letharge, has expressed complete confidence in his new appointee, saying that he will be ideal for the job, more especially on account of his excellent pastoral and administrative skills.*

"*Canon Wilkes and father of two, who was not available for comment, was said through the diocesan office to be delighted with his new appointment.*"'

With neither of them then speaking, Angela asked: 'Are you still there?'

'I think I'm going to throw up' was all that Frances could say before adding, 'I'll get back to you.'

Hearing the clatter of the receiver at the other end, Angela said 'God, I hope I've done the right thing.'

'Well you've hardly done the *wrong* thing,' said Ben.

'Better to let her know first than for her to hear about it second hand.'

By coincidence, Ben had just been reading an article in the national press, headed, *'what's the difference between a politician and a psychopath? Answer: None.'*

'Hey, listen to this,' he said. *'"Politicians and stockbrokers share many of the same characteristics as criminal psychopaths. The only difference is that career high-flyers usually stay within the law. Some could be said to be successful psychopaths," writes a Glasgow psychologist.'*

The article then offered a nineteen-point checklist highlighting the psychopathic personality, a type that although it works on the destruction of others, didn't necessarily include murder.

'Wilkes and Letharge fit the profile to a tee,' said Ben. 'Just for good measure, I'm prepared to wager that Wilkes can add that of a double-killer to his psycho's C.V.'

'I think we'd better go and spend some time with Frances,' said Angela.

'Right away!' agreed Ben, fishing under some paperwork for his car keys.

Few clergy, it seemed, apart from the isolated Ben Carter, former area dean of Ketborough, felt physically nauseated as such by the promotion of the new provost. Any rumblings of discontent came not so much from those deploring the appointment, as from those who felt slighted at having been passed over.

It was at the plain-speaking end of society where the anger boiled over, nowhere more so than in Ketbroough's Magpie put, and where Granville Zbierski was holding forth: 'Dat man getting promotion, 'tis bloddy wicked. Who the fock does he think he is? We ain't heard the last of him, dat's for sure. Damn, bogger, fock!'

People often laughed when Z lost it, but not this time. For although his language had gone into red mist territory, it was clear that the pub's petition with its thousands of signatures in support of the deposed Ben Carter had made not a jot of difference. Worse still, who was to say that with all their hard work they hadn't actually goaded the bishop into making his decision to promote Wilkes?

'Aye, it's beyond an outrage all right,' said landlord Nick Cocheron.

The two other Nicks were present, with Lech observing, 'I'll tell you what, I reckon if old Di Hagan were still about, he'd have run that Wilkes fellow to ground by now. He may not have said a deal but Di was nobody's fool. They said when he was in the force you could stake your life on him. He could never be doing with those fancy forensic types, forever getting up their own backsides with their sniffer dogs and computers, and all that bloody genetic fingerprinting crap.'

'Yeah, but hang on,' chimed in Nick Crooks who from an earlier conviction had just cause for respecting the science of DNA. 'It's not that forensic science hasn't made advances so much as the police aren't allowed to rely on their intuition anymore. Everything, but *everything*, has to be done by the book.'

'That's what they say,' said the landlord. 'Di was one of those guys who had endless patience and who used his detective's nose. Fair enough, you've got to prove your case. But if you don't act on hunches, you'll end up snowed under with computer print-outs and nothing else.'

'Yeah but don't forget they banged up some geyser for the murder of that Roxanne lass,' said Lech, 'and doing so on the say-so of some psychologist bloke who reckoned to have got him all weighed up, or summat.'

'There you go,' said Cocheron. 'They're all over the place.

They've got all that forensic kit to nick someone with only for some bloody psychologist to take over. Do you remember that Colin Stagg bloke who got done for that lass who got murdered in broad daylight on Wimbledon Common? They put him away for God knows how long, until it was proved that his conviction was a total set-up. Talk about perverting the course of justice!'

'It wasn't Stagg who was perverted,' added Crooks, 'but the ones who set him up. When it went to Appeal, the papers were still banging on about Stagg getting off on a technicality. But he'd done nothing *wrong*, hadn't even seen the woman, what was her name – Rachel something? He was just on the Common at the same time as she'd been there so they stitched him up. It's the profilers who want bloody locking up. Friggin' menace to society, them and their like!'

'I'll tell thee what,' said Zbierski. 'If Hagan were still about, he'd have put the shits up Wilkes, if nought else. And I'll tell thee summat else. I'm prepared to put money on it, that it was *'im* that murdered that hooker lass, Roxanne. I saw him the night that he called in at Stacey's sister's flat not so long after he'd left here and it got put about that she shot him with a stapler or summat, else he'd have gone in and done her like her sister. Wilkes is a *forkin madman!*'

The Magpie went quiet. This was a completely new revelation to them as Philippa had deliberately tried to say as little as possible about the assault. Each wondered where in God's name Zbierski got his facts from, although from past experience they'd grown to appreciate that Z made it his business to know things that they didn't.

Following up on Z's hunch that Wilkes might have killed Roxanne, another customer called Jason reminded them, 'That Leeds prostitute was found in the self-same spot as where Stacey was found. They say that Wilkes was into climbing and would often go up to the Lake District. So I reckon there's got to be a connection.'

'Why don't they just fucking well pull their finger out and arrest the creep on grounds of suspicion, if nothing else?' asked Lech.

'One thing's for certain, we haven't heard the last of the Venerable or whatever he's now supposed to be called, Wilkes' said Crooks. 'He's bad news, end of story and he'll stop at nothing. Just give it time.'

'It'll be like he's second-in-command to the bishop soon,' said Lech. 'Provosts or deans or whatever they're called, He's bloody well in charge of that cathedral place. They'll be less likely to lock him up more than ever now, leaving them to bang up somebody else, *anybody,* just so as to put the public's mind at rest. What they do is arrest some harmless sod, like they've done – someone who can't answer back. It's the usual way like a black spot on the road, where it takes three deaths in the same place before they give it serious attention.'

'So what are you saying?' asked Jason. 'Two down and one to go before they pull out all the stops? One thing's for sure, they're usually less fussed when it's a hooker who gets done.'

'Makes you bloddy, bloddy, bloddy sick,' Zbierski didn't do depression so much as rage.

Notwithstanding the shit-stirring label from his past the Pole was continuing to win begrudging respect among Ketborites. Vocal enough with local government departments to get things done, he'd got speed ramps installed to stop the boy racers near the school crossing. Almost single-handedly he'd got the council to abandon their fortnightly proposal to empty people's wheely bins, and revert back to the norm of a weekly collection. Now the failure of his petition to get any real justice for Ben Carter, fuelled by the Wilkes's promotion to Provost had turned Z incandescent: 'If I had my way, I'd bloddy well castrate that bogger and stick one of 'dem bugging devices on his cock to know every time he took a piss. What's more I'd do the same with 'dat bastard bishop.'

Although the kangaroo court of the pub's clientele might have formed a lynch mob there and then, they were far closer to knowing who was the prime suspect than those various police forces faffing about with their spread sheets on the whims of a forensic profiler.

'Enema lady!' – 'Miss Whiplash - punishment guaranteed!' – 'Dominatrix Bitch - see who's boss!' – 'Monica - spank and be spanked!' – 'Jessica, ex-nurse - this will only hurt a little!' – 'Teacher gives naughty boys some hard lessons.'

In the alien world where Katy, alias Stiletto, now worked, most thoughts concerning her father, let alone any knowledge that he'd been made up to Provost of Fordham diocese, meant virtually nothing. Of course, had she known about his latest promotion she would, drugs or no drugs, have thrown up. She *suspected,* him for who or what he was, where any promotion would simply have confirmed her suspicions that the church's charm and corruption offensive worked hand in glove.

Glaring hypocrisy nauseated her! It had been this awareness of her father from years back that had brought out the headstrong rebel in two schools where, in other circumstances, she might have excelled. And although her rebellion had taken a life-threatening nosedive into God's knows where, it was like his faked respectability deserved nothing better than her own dereliction.

'And what line of work is your daughter in, Canon? Well as it happens she's a prossy fucked up on drugs!' Katy had shared this joke with Monica.

Yet despite a drug scene that still embraced crack, crank and ecstasy, somewhere she clung onto the hope that she'd pull through. A bit like the white-water canoeing she'd done at school where, while submerged, she'd learned how with a quick jerk of her body she could bring her kayak right side up so, by a shift in attitude perhaps, might there be hidden forces to bring her back from the depths?

But as yet she had no willpower to change. For from her late teens a certain perversity had taken her into the big-time league of failure. Instead of the gorgeous daughter applauded off the school rostrum for her athletic achievements, and with the prospect of going onto a good university, Katy wasn't just your average failure. She was a car-wreck. For it seemed that early on in her life she'd been repelled by any notion of the 'good girl' image; detesting any thought of embarking on a conformist marriage with her two-point-something nuclear family.

At least, thank God, she wasn't the apple of some suitor's eye; the mannequin of some control freak demanding that she meet his every need. Having grown to appreciate that many of her preconceptions about prostitution were misconceived, she felt neither pride nor, just as importantly, chronic disgust at who she was and what she'd become. For even as addict, whore, tart, dropout, she was still Kate!

Of course, there was so much about her profession that was desperate, degrading and dangerous. The rising prevalence in child prostitution worldwide was especially vile, as were the brutal inadequate pimps who subjected many of those children to terror. She too had had to contend with the parasite pimps, and where only through willpower did she avoid those more putrid dens, from where other girls were obliged to operate. There was the furtiveness of it all, the jungle mentality by which the weakest went to the wall. But on top of all that there was to her mind the sheer farce and hypocrisy of prostitution being kept illegal.

With no wish to glamorize her trade – it was sordid and

absurd in so many ways – a fair number of them, as far as Katy could see, retained their dignity as well as their sense of humour. Many were of course damaged with poor self-esteem, some damaged irreparably, it being a profession where kinkiness might easily get to be nurtured as a way of life. But not a few of the women were selling their bodies maybe to look after children, even to get them a better education. Others were on the game to support their men folk who were on drugs or in prison, or both. In her twilight world she caught glimpses of dignity and heroism, all but absent in the so-called normal world.

Some were on the game without their husbands having the slightest idea. There was Antonia, wife of an Italian financier. He was away from their London home throughout the week, and with their children both at public school she'd become a high-class hooker working from a private penthouse doing what she did, as she once told Katy, 'just to get the hell away from my phony existence.' Besides she knew her husband was bisexual, 'always having it away one way or the other.'

Seeing no reason to conceal from the others that she was a vicar's daughter, she came to befriend the daughter of a suffragan bishop, also on the game, and another one whose uncle was an archdeacon! 'We should line them up in their robes' joked Katy, 'get them to wear a placard around their necks 'Hey guess what my daughter's a whore!' Having come across these two pros purely by chance, how many others might there be with church connections? All three girls admitted that, 'There's no way that my family knows what I'm up to. They'd never guess in a million years and would kill me if they knew!' 'As of course all good Christians should' laughed the archdeacon's niece.

They had some rip-roaring laughs as well. Jenny the archdeacons' niece was full of bawdy humour like: 'did you hear the one about the vicar having a wank, and getting spotted by the window cleaner? Well going down to pay him, the vicar asked 'how much?' 'A hundred quid,' said the cleaner giving him a knowing wink. Meekly the vicar paid up, only for his wife to ask later how much did the window cleaning cost. 'A hundred pounds.' 'Good Lord,' replied his missus all-innocent like. 'He must have seen you coming!'

There were times when laughter felt crucial, although at the time Katy had no idea that she was becoming her own therapist. She'd been *crazy* of course, crazy beyond words, to allow her to get blitzed on drugs. Nor could she blame outright Pete her loathsome dealer acquaintance. And yet, he'd been no more than a catalyst in her demise. She could have said *'No',* but opted instead to fall for his fake charms and flash motor. He was a slime-ball all right but she'd allowed herself to slither into his slime. 'Only by divine intervention,' she said more than once, 'that I never got pregnant by him.'

As a result of her addiction to an assortment of lethal substances, maybe she'd done irreparable harm to her body. But she was still *Katy,* bombed out and decadent of course. Yet more crucially, as she understood it, she was not the smiling clone of her parents, not the exemplary starlet of some phony Christian household where she could do no wrong. And it was from some deep intuition about having been true to herself, that she felt if not a sense of pride then one of occasional peace.

But two terrible engagements awaited her, the less terrible being her release from cocaine.

# Chapter 33

'Nobody I know of my age ever drinks and drives,' he said. 'When you're stoned you don't need to. You can relax at home, and there's a lot more harmful things than spending a happy weekend trip with a few roll-ups.'

Kes was a 22-year-old post-graduate student who worked part-time as a lighting technician in one of the theatres around Cambridge Circus. It was a wet evening in early December and they were in a large sweaty pub full of rowdy youths, just off the Tottenham Court Road. Younger than him by two years, Katy had met him a couple of times previously, the one evening off from work that she now allowed herself.

'I mean, my father is such a *hypocrite!*' he declared. 'He used to go on and on about my taking acid and yet would happily get tanked up and then drive off in the car, pissed as a newt. My mother wasn't much better, always making out that I was destroying myself while turning a blind eye to what my old man got up to.'

Kes gulped on his lager. 'I admit that getting on to crack was the worst mistake of my life, but I reckon it was my parents who got up my nose even more than the drug, so to speak. The facts speak for themselves. More middle-aged men get done for drinking and driving than anyone of our age. I can still hear my old man bragging, actually saying things like, 'I know what I can take' and 'I'm a better driver when I've had a few.' Like those TV ads with their slobbering wrecks paralyzed in road smashes seemed to make no impression on him.'

Sipping on her vodka and pineapple Katy was intrigued. She heard an echo loud and clear of what she most despised in her own parents, especially her father. 'My father has always acted so f...ing holy,' she said.

'That's the problem with some parents. They're so busy finding fault with their kids that they're totally blind to their own.'

She went on. 'I know I can't blame them for my own slide from pot into coke and all the rest. But I've always felt a 'sod it' attitude towards them that's got something to do with my habit. Like it's a case of *wanting* to shock them, to jolt them out of their smug self-satisfaction!'

'Has it worked?' he asked.

'Well no way in terms of my father. My mother maybe.'

'So when do we take responsibility for ourselves?' asked Kes. 'Hurting ourselves just to try and get a rise out of stupid parents achieves nothing in the long run . . . except *our own hurt* of course.'

It may have been a reprobate who had pushed Katy over the cliff – that Pete McCoy was a low-life all right. But somewhere she was responsible for her own actions. What intrigued her about this guy Kes was that he'd apparently faced up to the hypocritical influences that brought on his drug abuse, but who through sheer will-power had kicked free of cocaine. And if he indulged at all now, it was with the almost angelic pastime of smoking the old Afghan variety of dope!

She was playing with the stem of her glass.

'I mean take that lot over there,' said Kes, pointing with his drink at a group of young girls. In fact he knew some of them on account of having gone out with one of the girls six months earlier. 'There's Lilith who I was seeing last year,' he said. He nodded towards a slight girl, no more than eighteen with dyed auburn hair, matching acrylic nails and dressed almost entirely in black, and who through hooded eyes was her only acknowledgement of him. 'She's got her sister there, Nesrin and one or two of her friends all down from Newcastle. There's Lottie, who can't be older than sixteen, and I know for a fact that Nesrin and her friend are only fifteen As for that other kid she hardly looks like she's a teenager. I mean OK, they're all runaways and smack heads, but Christ Almighty, where's it all going for them and many more like them?'

Even Katy had to wonder. There they were, under-age kids acting cool with their 'sea breezers' and swigging another foul concoction in their pint sleevers, which she recalled as 'Thunderbirds' - lagers and blackcurrant juice. Sights such as these in London were common enough for the group to be known as 'pick 'n' mix kids.' These girls, all of whom were child prostitutes or rookies in-waiting, were downing their 'T's, while swallowing an assortment of amphetamines which from their colour looked like 'Double Dove' E tablets.

The other customers simply pretended that they weren't there. At least no one was saying anything, least of all the landlord or any of those behind the bar even as the girls were taking some furtive drags on something illegal.

Kes wasn't just a specialist in his subject of electrical engineering; he was wise to the everyday workings of London's nightlife. Not only had he graduated away from LSD trips and cocaine, he had distanced himself from the hypocrisy of his peers, as well as from those gullible juniors slewed out at the table opposite them.

'They just need to exercise their gray matter and get some self-respect,' he glanced once more at the girls, pity mingling with disdain. Suddenly he added, '*Shit!* I sound like my father moralizing, but you get my drift? What do you think?' he asked Katy out of the blue.

'What do you mean, what do I *think?*'

The question caught her unawares, because she who'd been in London for the past two years had pretty much chosen to stop thinking. Becoming a zombified victim to mindless prostitution, and to the mind-rotting effects induced by free-basing cocaine along with other substances hardly made allowances for *thinking*.

Kes didn't answer.

'*What do I think?* Christ, I don't know, now that you ask me. People should be allowed to do their own thing, that's what I think.'

'What, like murder?'

'Maybe.'

'You can't be serious.'

'Well, I bet there have been times when you could murder. It sounds like you could have murdered your old man. I know I could have killed my bastard father.'

Kes, whose father was an architect, had established that Kate was the daughter of a clergyman.

'Yeah, but there's all the difference in the world between *thinking* it and *doing* it! On another tack,' said Kes, 'do you think we can blame our parents for who we are?'

'Well, look at those kids,' said Katy. 'I mean they've got to be the victims of parents who don't give a toss. So, yes, of course our parents are to blame.'

'I heard it said once,' said Kes, 'that there are no damaged kids, only damaged parents.'

'I don't disagree with that,' replied Katy, not quite sure where the conversation was leading. She needed to pass the moral buck for her actions onto someone else, and it had always been her father who was the obvious choice. Cocaine fed on people who didn't like to think, or who were too bitter to do so.

Nor did she like the question that followed: 'Yeah, but when *do* we become responsible?'

Although she found herself on the defensive, she had to admit that her newfound companion was at least different. He'd not set out to make her feel guilty, so much as to ask at what point should we take responsibility for ourselves. Nor did he act all superior, and besides if the guy really had got shot of a class 'A' drug, he deserved a hearing.

'No junkie is accountable for their actions,' she said. 'Once you're hooked, it's out of your control.'

'I disagree!' he said, leaving her in questioning suspense, as he went to get them a refill.

The interlude made her want to run.

'God, I could just leave!' thought Katy. But she held herself in check. In the back of her mind she rued not just the futility of her life, but of all the money lost. She calculated the amount she could have saved if she'd never done drugs, while considering the amount she might actually save if she could *kick* the habit from thereon. It was nothing to spend upwards of £400 a day, and she reckoned that a sum of around six figures had already slipped through her fingers, hammering home the truth that as a hooker she was every bit as hooked as her punters.

Hating the truth both of the simple arithmetic and the logic that went with it, it felt as though she held a sign in front of her, 'Screw to get a screw.' For a second or two she could see just how mad everything was.

Nodding her thanks for another vodka and pineapple she

*A Candle For Lucifer*

asked, 'OK. So what *did* you do to get off crack?' Despite herself, she was genuinely intrigued.

'It's so bloody simple,' said Kes. 'That's what makes it so *bloody difficult*. There's really only one rule, and that is to *want* to get off the shit more than anything else in the world!'

Sipping on his lager, he paused to check her reaction.

'There's this independently funded drug centre in Brixton that I started going to. Since I'd been on crack for two years, nearer three, I knew it was make-or-break time. With 'H,' they say that you can carry on for twelve years before you lose your mental stability. Crack's different. You can go absent without leave in your head much sooner.'

Even as he spoke, there was a part of Kate's brain telling her not to give a fuck at what she was now hearing. Life wasn't great but she was getting by. Anyway just who is this creep? Part of her wanted to know.

Kes went on, 'Crack destroys the personality, obliterates any feeling for one's family and destroys any social conscience. Most serious drugs do that. I mean just look at those kids now,' he said glancing in the direction of the group of girls getting bombed out of their minds, eyes rolling and whose slumped postures and skimpy skirts were giving the voyeurs present a free viewing.

'What I'm saying is who gives a *friggin* damn? Society's losing its conscience without even having to go on crack. It's like so many folk are growing brain-dead without ever so much as touching any illegal substances.'

It was then that something stirred inside Katy like an action replay of words spoken from the mists of time. 'Try to guard your conscience Katy, whatever else happens in your life'! It was one of those few sayings her mother had come out with when she was having a bad time at school; a splice of audio tape whose wisdom she'd long got shot of as a hooker. But now with those under-age girls sprawling about and being mentally raped by some of the bystanders, that sentence and Kes's observations were spot-on. Most people had lost their conscience.

'So, you haven't said how you kicked the habit?' she asked.

'Acupuncture,' he said simply, draining his glass. 'And of course will-power.'

'*Acupuncture?*'

'Yep. They reckon if you can fight the first forty-eight hours of withdrawal, then you've got a good chance of coming off. Acupuncture reduces withdrawal symptoms by sixty percent. I reckon there's no way I could have hacked it *without* acupuncture. You'll never guess where they stick the needles,' he said smiling at her and waiting for her to show curiosity. She looked at him.

'In your tabs!' said Kes. 'Lots of little needles in your ears, because the Chinese reckon that there are five points in your ears that correspond to the nervous system, and that allow you to calm down.' He paused: '*Needles for needles,* you could say the only needle exchange worth having!'

He could see how the young woman with her residual good looks, despite the goose-pimply discoloured flesh, was close to make-or-break time. Perhaps she knew it too and perhaps, unbeknown to her, the prayers of her mother and friends might just be breaking through at this eleventh hour.

She was staring hard into her drink, rotating the bowl of her glass like it was a lens for her thoughts.

Their silent thoughts were interrupted by a couple of pros who'd come strutting across from the bar to try and sort out the under-age girls now lying slumped, wringing in sweat and indecent.

'*Gawd, what a mess!* 'Ere *you* in the black, *WAKE UP!*' One of the women slapped Lilith's face, bringing her round with a start.

Three or more of the girls were showing clear signs of overheating, a dangerous side effect from taking Ecstasy.

'What do you and your under-age pals think you're playing at? Haven't you got homes to go to!' The question was not a question, of course, because many of the older pros had grown alarmed by the growing tide of street children who either had no homes, or who'd fled them out of terror. Flight from one abuse into the arms of others ready and waiting to abuse them, Lilith and her small coterie had already been seen on the Charing Cross Road, selling themselves and sleeping rough.

A third pro came up and asked the doped girls what were their names. They were reluctant to tell.

'Hey, listen up! I've phoned one of them Shelter agencies to come and sort you lot out. They promised to be here in around half an hour. So sit up on your bums and don't move until they arrive, do you hear?'

The girls were rubbing their eyes while shuffling to sit up straight. The other two women stood there for a few moments before moving off, the one who'd made the phone call saying that she'd wait with the girls until help arrived.

Lilith tried to yell her protestations but her voice was hoarse. 'Why don't you just fuck off and leave us alone? We're not doing nuttin,' she croaked.

'Don't slag me off darling,' said their new minder. 'What you need is a bath and some warm shelter.'

As they were passing the bar, one of the two departing women let rip loudly at the head barman. 'Why in Christ's name do you let them drink? You can see they're under-age!'

'Hey, come on, give us a break,' the barman replied. 'Their money's as good as anyone else's, and at least they're off the streets in here.'

'Looks like they're on drugs as well,' was the parting riposte. 'The Bill ain't gonna take kindly if they catch under-age kids in here drunk, as well as stoned.'

That at least roused the other to go across and check out the kids for himself. But he chose to do nothing more.

Commendably on this occasion members from the Shelter agency arrived quickly, managing to persuade the group to go with them. Supported by their helpers and each other they staggered from the pub.

Katy felt respect for the well-built woman who said that she'd stay with the girls. Knowing her to be employed in the same area of prostitution as herself, she'd seen her around from time to time.

It took her a while to recall that she went by the name of Paratroop Sade.

# Chapter 34

Kes had her phone number. Nor did Katy refuse him when he said he'd like to see her another time when she was free.

On-duty, life resumed with the same monotony that she'd created for herself over the past year. Clients to pay the bills, clients to feed her habit; yes, clients even to fill the space of her own loneliness. Retaining her name of 'Stiletto' seemed to attract enough custom that in her variety of masked disguises kept her in business.

Still disfigured with her facial skin condition, Katy knew that the red cat suit covering her from head to toe served a vital dual purpose – that of an erotic accessory, as well as ensuring her with some job security.

Her best relationships were with the women themselves. She'd known Carla for almost the whole time that she'd been in London. Carla was a wag, a philosophical business type several years older than Katy, and a good dispenser of advice.

Nor were philosophical discussions uncommon when between appointments they'd meet in the brothel's small, improvised tearoom.

Being on the game was for Carla a 'bloody good way to earn a living, babe, just so long as you don't mess up.' By messing up, she could have meant drugs, since Carla was drug-free and comparatively wealthy. But recognizing that Katy was struggling to survive courtesy of her habit, she had counseled, 'Steer clear of the fellows, precious, or of having any *personal* life. Sure as eggs are eggs a boyfriend will mess you up, either living off your earnings or trying to get you to give up. Fellows hate not having the sort of money we get, as well as getting all sniffy and self-righteous about what we do. If you're going to have a fellow, get yourself a toy-boy and square up every time!'

She had also cautioned about pimps. 'Sometimes they can be useful but usually they're worse than a liability. Most of them are bullies and like to keep you on a ball and chain. No self-respecting girl needs a pimp. I've never had a man lay a hand on me, except when he's paying for it,' she sniggered. 'And don't whatever you do get *pregnant!*' This advice given with the urgency of what had once happened to her.

'God knows how I'd have coped if I hadn't miscarried,' she said. 'Kids completely throw you. It's just the same on the other side of the tracks. A professional woman gets pregnant, decides to have the child and forever more she's torn between her ambitions at work and her loyalties as a mother. She'll either cock up on her work, or hate the kid. What's more, if you decide to have an abortion, pros are no different from any other woman. You'll get plagued by guilt just like the rest of them.'

Then there was Debra, an ex-nurse in her early forties who, as an Angel of Love, administered anything from blanket-baths with massage to 'golden showers' and enemas. Katy found in Debra the residue of her own humour, for without seeing the disgusting hilarity of what she did and what Katy sometimes had to do, both women would have checked in at the funny-farm long ago.

Debra would tell Katy endless stories, such as one about

the client who liked to dress up as a ticket inspector on an imaginary bus.

'He'd bring all his gear in a hold-all,' she cackled. 'He got everything, black leather shoes, suit, peak cap, even the little badge with his number on it, saying "London Transport!" I had to produce my ticket from the last time we'd met, but then he'd insist that my ticket had expired and what did I intend doing about it?'

The farcical charade ended with her in her nurse's uniform unzipping his flies and giving him a hand-job, a 'blow-job', if the ticket contrived to get lost altogether! But what really creased Debra up was that her client had managed to obtain a real electronic ticket machine, 'must have nicked it from somewhere,' and would after services rendered always present her with a so-called valid ticket, until the next time.

'Everything then went back into his hold-all,' she curled up hysterically, 'and off he'd go, never anything but deadly serious with a routine always the same. I never did find out what he did in real life.'

'Probably a frustrated bus driver,' observed Kate, and they'd crack up laughing some more.

Then there was a cool Icelandic beauty, Imogen. She spoke excellent English and treated soliciting with measured detachment.

'Here it is cheap to live. At least cheap compared to my crazy land built on snow, shit and out of control banks. Maybe when I make enough money I marry a nice rich Englishman but I don't know, maybe never!' In her own more lucid moments Katy liked to engage Imogen in her philosophies. The Icelander admired Kant and Ibsen, along with the poems of Walt Whitman. Here was another pro, Katy discovered, whose intellect defied all the stereotypes.

Imogen was a walking encyclopaedia of quotations.

'Dare to make your life *extraordinary*,' she whispered in Katy's ear on one occasion, when Katy felt exhausted and nauseated at the prospect of keeping another punter happy.

'Carpe diem' – that's Latin for *Seize the day!*'

*'Ha, bloody ha!'* was all that Kate could respond on that occasion. But she still liked the diversion that such proverbs gave her.

The Icelander also came out with some great quotes on religion. '"The more I see of Christianity, the more it seems to me clear that the devil is really in charge!" – Lawrence Durrell – he was the travel writer.' She mentioned that one after Katy had found herself servicing a recently ordained Catholic priest. She couldn't believe it at first and although the cleric hadn't given her his name, he'd gone so far as to show a photograph of himself in his new robes and framed in some church porch.

'Such a waste of his manhood,' she told Imogen. 'He was really nice looking.'

Or when Katy had tied up a young fragile-looking man who later claimed to be a Catholic seminary student even as she was poking him all over with the stiletto of her shoe, Imogen duly came out with, '"Christianity has brutalized men and kept them ignorant" – Joachim Kahl.'

The consensus among the girls was that it was the Catholic clergy who were more ready to disclose their profession than those of other denominations.

On that occasion a Belgian girl called Chantelle had joined the group to talk about Dan Brown's bestseller, *The Da Vinci Code*.

'Stupid in one way, totally far-fetched!' Chantelle's English was near perfect. 'However, what was good about the book was that it spooked the Catholic Church! Got it really rattled about the Holy Grail which in the novel turns out not to be the cup at the Last Supper, but the person of

*A Candle For Lucifer*

Mary Magdalene!'

'I thought that Mary Mags was a pro like us,' observed Katy.

'So she was according to the Bible version,' said Imogen. 'But *Da Vinci* makes out that she came from royalty and was married to Jesus, and that the Grail stood for the goddess, who as Mary gave Jesus one or more children.'

'*God!* No wonder it spooked the Church!' said Katy.

'The book makes out how the Church needed to turn Mary into a whore so as to slag her off, and keep the Church an all-male outfit,' said Chantelle before adding: 'Mind you, I like the idea of Jesus shacking up with the likes of us!'

Despite her wit, Chantelle struck Katy as covering up a lot of hurts, more especially religious ones.

As for Imogen she struck Katy as being the sort of soul who could walk into prostitution and walk away from it, untroubled by many of the guilt trips that seem to perturb the British in particular. For being clinical about prostitution, she couldn't for the life of her understand why it wasn't legalized. 'You Brits make me laugh,' she said on more than one occasion, which was as much a reference to the girls as to their clients. Imogen was certainly cool.

Paratroop Sade was another – the pro who'd come to the rescue of those kids in the pub that night. Although neither Kate nor Sade worked in the same immediate locality, both being into S & M they'd met up occasionally with Sade, ever maternal, feeling obliged to give the younger girl some basic ground rules:

'Try to check out your punter first thing. They're usually OK. From my experience many who are into bondage and sado-masochism are less wacky than some of the other creeps who claim to be straight. But you can never be sure. It's the quiet ones you need to keep an eye on.'

When she put on her army fatigues, Paratroop Sade

dressed as though going into battle. But being a professional soldier, so to speak, she'd lived to tell the tale:

'For your own good, Kate, learn some martial arts. Just a few basic moves should do you. I once had a real-life marine who half-choked me to death. And then not long ago, I had some lunatic try to kill me - a right smooth-talking bastard, at least when he chose to say anything. You'll always get the bad apples who might want to top you.' She paused. 'And here's another thing. Don't ever recommend a client to see another hooker, unless you're absolutely sure. That's not because you're jealous, it's because you might endanger the other girl. I made that mistake with that smooth motherfucker I was just telling you about. I told him about that girl Roxanne in Leeds who got murdered last year. He told me his name was Nigel and the police reckon that they got some creep called Merv something, so I pray to God they got the same bastard.'

Kate remembered the reflective way that Sadie had said, 'Christ, I could never forgive myself if I thought I'd set that girl up!'

The other friend Kate began to see more of was the post-graduate Kes. It was a plutonic friendship, practical and always out of hours when she wasn't trading, but one where in a funny sort of way the theatre technician reminded her of her long-lost brother, Dom. Kes too seemed a bit bookish, but whose serious manner felt strangely comforting. Given that he'd kicked his drug habit, and wanted to help her was also remarkable.

With Carla having met Kes, and described him as an 'all right sort of bloke' Katy felt further reassured.

It was as though Kes stood for something; held out some sort of lifeline in regard to her addiction. She knew she could be a bitch at times when it came to being in denial, and she respected the fact that he'd not given up on her. It was as though his own cure offered a beacon of hope, pointing her back to a place of sanity - a living, walking example in fact that there *could* be hope beyond the dope. Still in thrall to the drug, she needed that hope; more so given her recent weight loss and what seemed like a series of asthma attacks.

Her weight had dropped off her, causing even the slightest exertion to turn her breathless. Although she could get the junk at around fifty pounds a gram, and a lot cheaper than up north, it continued to cripple her financially. For the craving seemed to intensify the weaker she became.

After a particularly bad coughing fit when she'd had to stop work once more, she phoned Kes to say that she wanted to attend the Brixton clinic so as to be given acupuncture. Cruelly he reminded her that she had got to want it, 'more than your life,' before either she could be helped, or for that matter before the clinic would be willing to receive her.

'Christ, man, I feel like I'm dying. *Let's do it!*'

'Only a handful of users *really* want to detoxify,' she was told by the woman psychotherapist. 'Can I hear it said three times that that is your wish.'

'*Yes, yes, yes!*' responded the emaciated girl with the chicken-flecked skin and running eyes, adding '*Damn you to hell!*' for good measure.

When they were drugged up, people like Katy could act quite civil and hold some sort of conversation. It was when the craving started that they'd eff and blind. Kes flinched at how some who sought a cure would arrive, just as he had done over a year ago, screaming and kicking while cursing the very souls who might bestow deliverance.

'I'm going to tell you what it will be like,' the therapist told her, 'not because I wish to alarm you but because I want you to be less alarmed when the treatment gets underway.

To prepare you that the hell of withdrawal is precisely that – *Hell!* But people like Kes have gone through it before you and others will do so after you. Your withdrawal may be more difficult Kate, given that we're responding to a cocktail of different drugs.'

She then outlined the various stages of withdrawal, telling her that the first forty-eight hours were critical but that to get completely cleansed of the drug's effects, detoxification would take a full six days. Acupuncture would continue to be given after that for a further period.

Already desperate for a fix, *any* fix, Katy had started to simper.

It was then explained to her that Kes and another assistant would stay with her at all times and where with one taking a few hours off, the other would remain at her side. The therapist's final remark was meant to give Katy some reassurance. 'The acupuncture does not cure you of itself. You will continue to crave drugs for a week or more but it will help to lessen the pain.'

'Let's go for it!' urged Kes. 'I'm with you all the way. Never forget that!'

The ordeal began around twelve hours later. Body spasms began in the form of violent yawning and equally violent shivering. The room was equipped with a mattress, blankets and numerous towels, next to which was an adjoining bathroom and toilet where she would be washed as often as was practicable. To keep her head from twisting and disturbing the acupuncture needles, she was restrained in a form of neck-brace.

Mucus and saliva began to drip, pour even, from her mouth and nose. Her eyes ran tears. The T-shirt removed from her by Kes was used as another towel with which to mop her saturated hair. A clean T-shirt was put on her and she was swathed in blankets. These in turn became saturated.

He tried to get her to drink, to replenish her dehydrated body and restore a semblance of vitality to her face, now assuming the colour and texture of a broiled chicken. Going 'cold turkey' said it all, and his heart went out to the shrunken and shivering soul, whose sleep was further hampered on account of the little needles stuck in her left ear.

Exhausted by the trauma of watching the young woman, for whom his feelings now went deeper than mere sympathy, he asked the psychotherapist, 'is there anything we can give her apart from the needles?'

'Kes, as you well know,' the other responded kindly but with finality, 'there's nothing. If she'd been on heroin, we could have given her methadone to ease the pain. But even that has to be withdrawn to bring them through fully and cleanly.'

'Yeah, I know,' he sighed, 'and methadone does absolutely nothing for the coke victim.'

'Believe it or not by just *being* here, you'll do more to bring her through than anything else. That said, you look pretty much wiped out! Take a couple of sleeping pills and crash out for a few hours. Don't worry we'll get you up before too long. As I said before, you're our secret weapon because it's you who's given Katy the *will* to go through with this.'

One of the most distressing aspects of her withdrawal followed during his absence, where she became doubly incontinent while dry vomiting in great heaving spasms. Clothes, bedding and her writhing body became an indistinguishable mess with the attendant nurse unable to do more than mop her face. Between these episodes of expelling the foul toxins from her system, Katy fell into the sleep of one whose spirit appeared to hang between life and death.

When Kes later returned he found her thrashing and

screaming on the floor. Upon eyeing him she became obscenely coquettish opening her legs and masturbating violently. With orgasmic spasms engulfing her, her emaciated belly seemed to writhe as though a nest of tumours had come alive under her skin. Yet nothing could be done, other than to let her flail in her subterranean world of rage and twisted passion.

It was after two hours that Kate went into a yet deeper sleep, comatose if not dead.

In the last critical stages of her detoxification, she slept as one of the dead. Wrung dry of her body fluids, her sleeping was regular but shallow, leaving Kes to hover close while gently stroking her face and hair. He held her hand as well while whispering gentle words of encouragement, which even if not consciously heard he hoped would strengthen the will-power of his ravaged friend. Later on members of staff managed to lower her inert form into a warm bath for further bathing.

It took a little over four days to bring her out of the thrashing, vomiting, writhing episodes and through a further twenty-four-hour period of sleep before her first intake of porridge and liquid nourishment. More sleep for two twelve-hour periods was followed by demands for cocaine, but which were supplanted with further nutritional food, mostly in liquid form. It was here that the acupuncture was said to play its first restorative role in reducing the craving.

The needles in her ears were, according to Chinese medicine, located to correspond with different parts of her nervous system, and by the end of the second week Katy's lungs and kidneys were all but functioning properly, clear of their poisons.

'Acupuncture isn't a cure as such,' she'd been told, 'rather a tool for easing the trauma of withdrawal.' The needles held no magic healing properties in themselves. The addict had to *want*, to *yearn,* to recover. The craving for narcotics of any description could she was told linger for at least two to three months. This craving had to be equally matched by a desperation to get free.

Yet even after two weeks the improvement in her appearance was so marked that Kes was able to say, 'Kate, you look like a new person.'

And having reached a plateau of peace and sanity that she'd not known for well over a year, she smiled back, 'It's amazing, I do feel *clean*.'

'There ain't nothing to compare,' said Kes triumphantly, remembering all too vividly his own deliverance.

'The longer you stay for treatment,' he went on, 'the greater your chances of success.'

'I'll stay for as long as it takes!'

In her weakness, the strength of her smile said it all.

## Chapter 35

The new provost now found himself with two properties.

For along with his London flat, Fordham now endowed him with a superb five bedroom property, pre-Georgian and converted from what had been part of an old Prebend, a residence once occupied by some of the Minster's monastic forbears. And it had been with some gentle coaxing from Bishop Letharge that the now *Very* Reverend Christopher Wilkes had gone so far as to instruct a buyer to purchase some 'suitable' furniture. And by 'suitable' this came in the form of six panel-back chairs, a large refectory table, a court cupboard, a highly ornate carved oak coffer whose patina shone like glass, plus some further period furniture for the bedroom. Although the antiques had already met with his Lordship's approval, they were not overly ornate or pretentious.

For part of him sought to live as though sympathetic to the house's ancient and austere occupants, yet without succumbing to their privations. More it was a case of the Venerable Wilkes now re-inventing himself – the sad ex-divorce aspiring to a new life of celibacy and holiness.

On looking for the services of a housekeeper, he'd given a passing thought to contacting his sister Caroline, whom he'd not seen for over thirty years. Caroline had gone to Switzerland as a ski instructor in Caux, which at that time had been the headquarters of that Moral Rearmament Movement, the organization so much loved by their parents. Having married and divorced another member of the MRA she'd written to him to express her intent of returning to England. But with all the embarrassment, not to say injustice, of his having inherited the entirety of their parents' fortune, Christopher felt it was best to leave things as they were, which meant to go on ignoring her.

Preferring that his only blood relative be relegated to history, he found a daytime housekeeper, an elderly seamstress from the Minster who would come in during the week to clean the house, as well as prepare his midday snack and evening meal.

His commissioning service as provost had taken place on the eve before Advent Sunday. Nor did it take long to install himself in his new role. He befriended the Cathedral parishioners speedily enough, although less so with the 'Chapter' or inner circle of his fellow canons, who saw to the overall running of the Minster. For it was by asking some searching questions of them over the disbursement of certain funds, that the provost stood to expose a financial scandal.

The scandal arose over an assortment of sacred vessels and reliquaries provided by various churches in and around the diocese, which had been loaned to the cathedral for safekeeping. Permission had been obtained for these glorious objects to go on an extended tour of the United States, doing so under the watchful eye of the canons. But the cost of this tour had turned out to be way over budget, putting a severe strain on the Minster's funds. Not only was public opinion scandalized that an expensive holiday had been taken on the cheap, the cathedral coffers had been depleted by almost £100,000.

Although the exhibition appeared to have been a case of bad management rather than one of outright fraud, the venerable Wilkes sought to bring the holidaying canons to book. For his part Bishop Letharge was delighted. The issue had needed to be addressed, and while no prosecutions were brought it cut the offending canons down to size. This served only to enhance the bishop's authority along with that of his provost.

Not only did Christopher demonstrate himself to be a frugal overseer of the cathedral's accounts, he liked to express his pastoral side.

He was especially well disposed towards junior members of the choir and the girl acolytes. Although in deference to the bishop's directive that it was to be a largely all-male choir, the organist and choirmaster had won the concession that girls were, at least, to enjoy the privilege of being acolytes. Like liturgical assistants the acolytes would proceed the choir up the aisle, hold lit candles during the reading of the gospel at the Eucharist and be on hand for the presentation and ablution of the communion vessels. They were always busy, more so now that Christmas was upon them, in other ways.

Of the four acolytes, there was Marianne who, on account of the other three girls being decidedly plain, stood out all the more so for being so pretty. She'd first assisted him some week's back, and now once more she was there to help for the early evening Eucharist – the occasion being Christmas Eve. The service was for those parents who, having younger children to cater for, were expected to be wide-awake first thing on Christmas Day.

It had been back in All Saints that he'd noticed how girls like Stacey enhanced their prettiness when dressed in their robes. For an evening service the effect could be further heightened in the soft glow of candlelight. And now with the candles lit and in her red cassock, white surplice and frilly collar, he found himself captivated once more. The effect of Marianne's long hair hanging in brushed and shimmering gold was divine. So for Christmas mass, whether by chance or design, he noticed too how she seemed to hover that much closer than seemed necessary.

Early on in the service she had given him a soft sensual smile, more so when she presented him with the communion wafers, followed by the dispensing of the wine from the flagon into the two gleaming chalices. Indeed, in the intimacy of the cathedral's sanctuary, it was as though whenever he looked in her direction, she rewarded him with the same sweet smile.

Memories of that last service stayed with him in particular - of how having poured out the wine and water there was the little shimmy on the cup's surface when her fingers inadvertently touched his. Then as he brought the cup to her mouth and spoke the words 'the blood of Christ,' she'd parted her lips, more for him, he supposed, than for imbibing the sacrament.

During that Christmas holiday, the girl acolyte became very much a focus for the provost's thoughts, and where for those who might have remembered, the resemblance between Marianne and Stacey was undeniable.

'I really have a problem believing in a God who is supposed to be a God of love, when this sort of thing happens,' said Tom, one of the senior tenor choristers in the choir, aged nineteen.

The acolyte Marianne McIver fancied Tom, as he continued:

'I mean what sort of God allows things like that to happen? Surely if he loves everybody, then he can give a bit of advance warning or something.'

The animated discussion, taking place in the provost's living room concerned a recent earthquake in Japan, which had taken a heavy toll of lives. Every so often he'd make his house available to allow some of the cathedral's choristers and acolytes to discuss God, and air their views. When asked to arbitrate in some of the more heated discussions, the provost had learned to respond to this sort of question as though by rote. Without actually believing anything of what he said he could always answer deftly, as he did now: 'Well, Tom, if God revealed every accident before it happened, then we would have no free will. It is free will that allows us to respond to Him of our own free choice.'

For a man so unsure of his beliefs, his memory bank of pre-set answers held up well. The plausibility attached to some of his answers even lent him an air of wisdom if not of sanctity. Some of course were not persuaded.

'I don't see what free will has to do with it,' said Josie. Josie was another of the girl acolytes, who'd grown to resent how the provost clearly favoured Marianne to the rest of them.

'Well, free will, Josie, means that we can respond to God if we so choose, but He isn't forcing us to respond.' This further autocue from Christopher's repertoire of responses only left his questioner more confused.

The scorned acolyte scowled.

An older chorister called Justin then remarked, 'I reckon the human race has got to take the blame. I mean it's all very well to blame God but many disasters probably happen because of the sort of things we do.'

'For example?' queried the provost.

'Well, for example, when there's an earthquake like we've just heard about. It's got to have something to do with the fact that we keep dragging oil and other minerals out of the ground. It's obvious that we're upsetting the earth's crust.'

'But earthquakes happened long before we did all the digging and excavating that we're doing now,' piped in Janine, a thoughtful girl of around sixteen who had shown an interest in becoming an acolyte.

'Yes, but we all know global warming is a *fact*! Look at the floods in Bangladesh! They're directly caused by the deforestation in upper India. Not only does the soil get eroded, but cutting down the forest adds to the greenhouse effect which melts the ice-caps and raises the sea-level.' This was Marianne's contribution.

From earthquakes and natural disasters to the terrorist atrocities around the world, the questions and responses did the rounds, 'Was God to blame?' and 'What happens to us after we die?' and 'What happens to people like the husband and wife who killed four of their children?'

Questions concerning good and evil tended to cause the provost some loss of composure. It was then that he left others do the talking, even though those present were weren't afraid to be forthright with their solutions. Over the matter of murdering parents, answers given by Tom and the others included, 'I reckon they should bring back the death penalty!' or, 'Let them die *nice and slow!*' or, 'A life for a life! No-one who kills children or someone weaker than themselves *deserves* to live!'

'No one who kills another *person* should be allowed to live!' Josie was out to be provocative; her resentment towards Christopher making her more so.

On one occasion Bishop Letharge was brought in to speak about women in the church. 'Should women be ordained?' was parried with evasive disclaimers from his lordship about 'a tendency to create strife and division' and 'much as I am personally in favour of women priests, I have to think about the long-term future of the diocese.' Suspecting that his sexual orientation was anything but straight, one of the more mischievous boys asked, 'Bishop,' (they got away with addressing him less formally) 'do you think that gay priests should be allowed to live openly together?'

'I have to say,' he responded with a candour that surprised even Christopher, 'that personally I can't see anything wrong with homosexuals living together. Some people claim that the Bible forbids it. But for that matter the Bible forbids the eating of some kinds of meat, and we take no notice of that today.'

Comparisons between homosexuality and the consumption of meat were lost on some of his young audience, two or three being avowed vegetarians. For them something didn't add up with the bishop's line of thought.

Tammy, a normally quite reticent teenager, then piped up: 'Men don't want women priests, because somewhere it says in the Bible that women are impure because they menstruate! That's one of the reasons.'

A collective laugh couldn't conceal the bishop's embarrassment. After all his biblical rationale for homosexual love hardly squared up to his clear prejudice against women becoming priests, on account of Tammy's observation.

It was following one of their discussions at the end of January as the group were enjoying hot drinks while munching on chocolate biscuits, that Marianne overheard Tom and his other male friends jesting about Tom's new girlfriend. 'Come on, tell us who is she, Tom!' Tammy demanded to know.

'No-one that you know,' he replied.

This disclosure had a disastrous effect on Marianne who still fancied her chances of dating Tom. After all she was pretty enough! Indeed such had been her interest in Tom that two of his friends in the group interested in her hadn't had a look-in.

'*Damn!*' she had said under her breath, leaving her feeling devastated for the rest of the evening.

Upon observing her darkening mood and, with the rest of the group dispersing, Christopher asked if she'd like to tell him what was on her mind.

Despite her good looks, Marianne McIver was a sensitive soul and one liable to get suddenly overwrought. On a previous occasion she'd told him how her mother and stepfather never bothered with her, and of how her mother was unhappy since her stepfather appeared to have little time for either of them. It was then that the provost noticed not so much the young woman as the little-girl-lost, who'd come to regard the Minster Cathedral as her new home with him as her father substitute.

On this particular night, Christopher seemed *so* sympathetic and understanding that she quite broke down. 'I'd always hoped that Tom would take me out,' she confided. 'But tonight it was clear that he's not given me a second thought. If he had done, then he wouldn't have stated loud and clear that he was going out with someone else. He's a kind person and I know that he wouldn't go out of his way to hurt me. It's obvious that he hasn't even thought about me.'

He ushered her to his Chesterfield sofa where she started to cry gently, while he sat next to her with his arm around her shoulder. Pulling her towards him so that she could cry more freely, he stroked her hair.

'Well now, Marianne, can I tell you a little secret? That's if you want to hear it.' Tear-stained blue eyes looked trustingly up at him.

'You think you've been let down. *You're not alone!* We've all been let down one way or another. *I've* been let down.'

She sat up straight now, transferring the concern that up

until then she had reserved only for herself. Nor did she object as he started to stroke her hand.

'The truth is that I've been terribly let down. My wife left me, which I'm sure you know about. But also my daughter Katy got up to no good some years ago and she ran away from home. I wanted to do everything I could for her, but I think she became upset with her mother and without any discussion just upped and ran off.'

He was watching for her reaction.

'And then can you believe what was more awful than anything that happened before? 'She turned to drugs and I've not seen or heard of her since.'

'That must be terrible!' whispered Marianne, her own worries forgotten. 'Have you got any other children?'

'I have a son but I'm afraid his mother has influenced him to have nothing to do with me. Sometimes when I'm on my own I feel like a broken man. You see, I may look confident and in control on the outside but sometimes, when I'm here at home, I too can get pretty lonely.'

Sensing that he might be getting her out of her depth, he went on quickly: 'But I shouldn't have started talking about me, when you've got all your worries.' Seeking to restore further balance to their conversation, he inquired: 'Is everything all right at home, Marianne?'

Here he pushed precisely the right emotional button to rekindle the mutual confidence between them.

'*No,*' she said, tears again welling up. '*It isn't!*' There came a short pause. 'My stepfather, apart from growing more remote by the day, seems to be withdrawing from my mother as well. We don't live like a family at all, more like three separate people. My stepfather seems completely wrapped up in his other interests, business and what's that secret society thing, the . . .?'

'Freemasons,' volunteered Christopher.

'That's it. I'm sure my mother resents him doing so much away from her, and because of how she feels she seems to resent me.'

'Would it be any good if I had a word with him?'

'No, *please don't!*' Her voice rose in alarm. 'He's the sort of man who in a fit of anger might even say that I don't belong at home anymore. He'd really resent it if he thought I'd spoken to you about him. After all, I'm of age and he could choose to have nothing more to do with me.'

'I promise not to say a word.'

Her half smile of appreciation encouraged him on.

'I know one thing. If my daughter had turned out the way you have, I'd be so very *proud* of her. It sounds to me as though you could do with a father and I could do with a daughter!'

Seeing that she liked that, he pulled her towards him again so that she nuzzled against his chest as he stroked her hair once more. He felt her nod in appreciation.

'What do you say, Marianne, if we share a little secret that I'll be your pretend daddy and you my little girl?'

Taking her stillness for acquiescence, he asked, 'How say you?'

'I'd like that,' she replied quietly.

'That's settled, then. I'll tell you what I would like.'

'What?' she whispered. Despite the intimacy she felt a little nervous as to what Christopher might have in mind.

'A *photograph* of yourself! Is such a thing possible? Perhaps a nice informal one of you on the beach, or something like that? Would you do that for me, sweetheart?'

Visibly relieved that the request was so undemanding, she replied: 'Of course, I can get one. I've got several when we went to Tenerife in the summer.'

'Could you let me have it then and, of course, you mustn't let your parents know about it.'

She had no intention of telling them.

'I must get you home,' he said taking her to his LandRover and where, with the familiarity of a father-substitute, he patted her on the behind.

It was only a short distance to her parents' home where he dropped her off five minutes later.

A few days later she presented him with a photograph of herself. Looking divine and tantalizing in her swimsuit, she was on the beach playing volleyball.

## Chapter 36

'Oh, *my God, my God, my God! What have they done? Tell me it's not true!*'

For a man usually implacable and self-possessed or, if he showed any emotion at all did so with small hand gestures or a raised eyebrow, Bishop Letharge was inconsolable. Devastated by his loss, he was flailing about even as he sobbed.

'Look at this sofa table and those Regency chairs. *Wrecked! Ruined beyond recognition!* Then there's my desk and the clock and the gilt gesso mirror *totally ruined. Oh my God, my God, my God, what am I to do?*'

Reaching a crescendo his lordship's cries to the Almighty were heartfelt, his movements akin to those of an earthquake victim foraging for signs of life in the rubble. For since he coveted his antiques more than life itself, the destruction of his treasures was as though he had indeed lost his entire family, leaving him to walk as one of the living dead!

With his Lordship having been away on a conference and not returning until later that afternoon, Mrs. Deekes the housekeeper had been uncharacteristically careless. Having slipped across to the local supermarket to get a bite of lunch she had on that occasion just pulled the door to behind her without locking up. In his absence and with both secretaries off sick with some stomach bug, she'd chosen to be a mite less careful than usual.

Upon her return, no more than twenty minutes later, she was appalled to discover the front door ajar with the downstairs hall wrecked! So shocking was the scene that she hardly dared to cross the threshold. What if the intruder was still in the house? So not until the police arrived was the damage fully assessed. Gouges had been made in the central pedestal table. Pictures in their gilt frames had been slashed and ripped. The Georgian grandfather clock had been tipped over with its glass shattered.

Nor did it end there. The intruders, armed with what appeared to have been chisels, hammers and paint stripper, had systematically gone about smashing, gouging, ripping and slurping acid over rare wood and soft furnishings alike.

The two Regency armchairs in the bishop's study boasting their original silk had been ripped and hacked at, while the Georgian desk tipped over on its side had paint stripper still running in rivulets, not only ruining two or three hundred years of patinated timber but burning holes in the Wilton carpet. Papers were strewn everywhere and although a painting had been torn from the wall to reveal a small hidden safe, it appeared that little or nothing had actually been stolen.

As the police were methodically itemizing the damage and with Mrs. Deekes still trembling at the likely repercussions of her negligence, it was then that his lordship had reappeared to offer his heart-rending cries of despair. Everything that he loved in his Palace had, like his life, been wrecked; the downstairs hall, his library and study all turned into a killing field.

'Who can possibly have done this?' he croaked.

Viewing the carnage all about him, it was as though an unknown hand had administered some coup de grace. They – it had to have been more than a single individual, surely - had desecrated all that he held dear. Not only had the raid been brazen having taken place in broad daylight, it was clearly personal in its fury - the police estimating that it could have lasted no more than fifteen minutes.

'Seems like a person or persons were very angry with you sir' was the unhelpful observation made by one of the two detectives present. 'It's amazing how much damage can get done when someone loses control. Have you any idea who might have done this?'

'None whatsoever' was all that he could mumble back.

It was then upon learning that Mrs. Deekes had left the house without locking the front door or activating the alarm, that his lordship spun round insanely to physically chase her off the premises bellowing at least ten times, *'OUT, OUT, OUT. . . !'* In his overweight and unfit condition, the outburst had left him panting and gasping for breath.

'Sounds like the bishop's barking!' smirked one officer to his companion, both of them finding it difficult to suppress their own laughter.

With his housekeeper appearing to have vanished the scene and still choking with rage, Letharge returned to what had been his study with the two officers preparing to take down his statement.

Somewhere far off he heard a question to which he could only whisper the answer. 'Yes, of course I have household contents insurance for around half a million pounds cover.' And then as though speaking to himself: 'But how can you replace a collection of antiques not only passed down through one's family, but one which I have lovingly and painstakingly acquired over four decades?' For a man who'd lost everything, he could only sob 'you can't just . . . go out . . . and buy another set of Hepplewhite hoop-back chairs, or an eighteenth century bureau in mulberry wood. What can you do with a Regency rosewood chaiselongue, when its innards have been ripped up like an old sheet and paint-stripper poured all over it? It's not like you can you just go out and buy another one around the corner.' Even as he spoke he nearly tripped over the shattered remains of his pier glass mirror in its original gilt frame.

Yet what made sense to the bishop sounded incoherent to the two officers. To their way of thinking most of the bishop's old furniture looked like so much tat anyway – certainly nothing that couldn't easily be replaced at Ikea or wherever.

'At least no-one has been physically hurt in the attack, sir,' ventured one, this producing not so much as a murmur of acknowledgement from the victim.

There was less damage upstairs, it appearing that that the intruder or intruders had made a hasty getaway through an upstairs window. But for anyone bearing a grudge against Letharge the ground floor devastation was quite sufficient. For when in the morning of that day in February he'd been his peacock self, strutting at a bishops' conference he was later that afternoon a broken man. Nor did his problems end there. With the wrecked antiques removed the following morning and only good as 'breakers', as they're known in the trade, his lordship also discovered that he was seriously under-insured.

A day or two later as he wandered through his empty palace with only rudimentary furniture in place, he knew that things could never be the same. Even Mrs. Deekes failed to put in an appearance.

*'Christ, I can't believe it!'* shouted Ben to Angela when he first

read the news in the local paper:
BISHOP'S PALACE WRECKED BY VANDALS!
'Talk about God saying, "Vengeance is mine, I will repay!" What does it mean? Who did it? It sounds like revenge, although these days it could just be vandals or junkies high on something. But I have to say that they couldn't have done it to a *nastier* chap!' quipped Ben. 'The bishop's a bastard and I'm not just saying that on account of his treatment of me. It strikes me that whoever did what they did, *knew* full well what they were doing as well as the person they were doing it to.'

Angela too found it difficult not to suppress her own sense of glee. 'I mean, it's a terrible thing to happen,' she giggled nervously. 'I hate anything of value going up in smoke or being wantonly wrecked. Remember that fire at Windsor Castle? But it does make you wonder how Letharge will cope from hereon, since he had more time for his treasures than ever he had for his clergy. It could finish him off, and thank God if it does!' She then added with an unholy guffaw, 'you don't suppose it was a gang of enraged women priests, do you?'

Ben laughed. 'I wonder how the provost feels about it,' he mused. 'He won't be best pleased, especially as I'm told he's tarted up his own little bistro with some period antiques. *Ha*! I think it's great. *THANK YOU, LORD!*' he shouted.

Two days after the break-in, an ad clerum emailed from the diocesan office announced that the bishop was suffering from ill health and shock, the message being but a preliminary one to that announcing his forthcoming retirement.

More or less around the time of the emails, the media announced: *Palace suspect arrested.* Although succinct the report spoke volumes: *A homeless youth in his mid twenties and said to be under the influence of drugs, has been picked up by the police. He had in his possession a canvas bag in which were found an assortment of chisels, screwdrivers, rubber gloves and several cans of nearly depleted paint-stripper. Initial tests have shown the youth to be connected with the crime and who, by his own admission, has confessed to carrying out the attack on his own.*

'There you go,' said Ben. 'Some speed merchant high as a kite doing the Lord's work without knowing it!'

Although the youth's name remained undisclosed publicly, he was known through the hostel where Ben and Angela worked. In fact the lad had once told Ben how he'd been a one-time chorister at another large church in the same diocese where Letharge had previously worked, and of how some ten years back there'd been some scandal about paedophilia. On the pretext of taking drugs the same lad who had then left the choir chose to say nothing more; this after having been given a sizeable sum of money.

With the young man's name having been divulged to the bishop to ask whether he wished to press charges, Letharge replied with uncharacteristic charity: 'What's the point if he's a drug addict. I wouldn't get a penny farthing from him,' adding after a pause, 'what the youth needs is some proper treatment.'

Bishop Letharge knew full well that the pressing of charges was ill advised.

Ben guessed it as well.

Yet if his lordship had shown any signs of recovery, knowledge of the youth's name was surely a factor contributing to Letharge's fatal heart attack a week later.

'Wonderful, congratulations!' Frances' eyes sparkled almost as much as those of the weary mother. The maternity ward seemed to radiate joy.

Despite being nearly two weeks late, daughter Emma had been born without complications in mid February.

Overcome with joy, Ben kept laughing and spluttering into his handkerchief.

Philippa then arrived with her daughter Rosamund, both presenting Angela with shawls, hats and cardigans, extra presents to the ones already given by Frances a few moments before.

'We've not had *triplets!*' said Angela, smiling her thanks.

As news of the birth spread, the presents began to pile into a small mountain. Gifts were especially plentiful from the parishioners of St Hilda's whose sense of guilt at Ben's enforced departure and their helplessness at not knowing what to do, served to create an affection that couldn't do too much for them. Few now cared that so suited a couple remained unmarried.

'Emma . . . any other names?' asked Frances.

'Emma Marie!'

'Do you know what they mean?' asked Philippa.

'According to one of our books Emma means "Healer of the Universe," said Angela.

'Might as well give her a challenge,' chipped in Ben and they all laughed.

Being a curious toddler, Rosamund too was fascinated by the baby.

'Isn't she lovely!' said Frances, stroking a tiny finger. 'And look at the size of her.'

'Nearly nine pounds! Like her dad from Day One!' chuckled Angela.

'Less of that,' said Ben ever conscious of being a good fifteen kilos overweight. And then adding, 'but she's got my ears all right!'

'She'd better give them back then!' said Angela laughing.

'She's fabulous! Are you going to have her christened?' ventured Frances.

'That poses a bit of a dilemma,' mused Ben.

'Doesn't much matter, not for now,' said Angela. 'HE knows that we are so grateful, and that we want the very best for her!'

'Absolutely,' agreed Frances.

Here was real joy! Any passing pleasure shown over the vendetta wrought against Bishop Letharge, and of his sudden demise, was as nothing compared to that now overflowing in the maternity ward.

Yet as she got up to leave, Frances couldn't disguise her own heaviness of heart. Following the more clinical circumstances by which she had given birth to Dominic and Katy through artificial insemination, she'd never known her former husband stoop over her and their children to demonstrate the undisguised joy as shown by Ben. Ben's wrapt attention gazing as he did upon his own Madonna and child, affected Frances deeply, and where even as she left the hospital rejoicing for the couple and their lovechild, the bitter contrast to her own wasted years hurt like hell.

Despite the furrowed brow and drawn complexion with its sleepless eyes, she was still an attractive woman. Without disguising the strands of graying hair at her temples, her figure kept trim while her dress-style remained simple but effective. For all the years of being unloved by Christopher fine weave cardigans, pleated skirts, or twin-sets and practical shoes, with a sensible amount of make-up to compensate for the ravages of the last year kept her looking more than presentable.

But if she rued the lost years for herself, she did so more for her children. Katy was in a place of near death, it seemed, while Dom was simply hurting even as he tried not to show it; forsaken by his father, crying for his mother and grieving for a sister who seemed lost forever.

Outside in the hospital grounds it was surprisingly mild, even offering a whiff of spring in the air. With the burden of her sorrows catching up with her she decided to sit down and reflect on a garden seat. 'Oh God, what about Katy?' she whispered audibly. 'What about me?'

With her divorce documents all but finalized and uncontested by Christopher, she was more than self-sufficient financially. Money wasn't the problem, for with a shrewdly re-invested inheritance and from which she'd withdrawn only tiny sums down the years, she too, like her ex-husband, was wealthy in her own right. So thank God she didn't need to ask him for anything!

But with her ex so recently promoted to provost and living in the near vicinity, she felt as distraught for herself as she did for her broken family. Much as she'd enjoyed doing up the bungalow, she needed to flee Ketborough if not the whole stinking set-up of Fordham diocese. Or as Dom kept telling her, 'Mum, you've got *to get a life!'*

When on other occasions she'd felt down, she could usually rally herself by humming a favourite hymn like Great is Thy faithfulness, or All My hope on Thee is founded. But not now, perhaps never again! Hymns like those could never compensate for the absence of human touch.

More it was a flood of nostalgic songs about love and romance, heard and memorized from the kitchen radio in the vicarage that now washed over her. She loved the swinging oldies by such as Ella Fitzgerald and Louis Armstrong; the instrumentals like Acker Bilk's 'Stranger on the Shore,' the lilting lyrics of Barbra Streisand, the impossible passion of Shirley Bassey, even the rasping sensuality of Eartha Kitt. Now as she sat in the bright sunshine, the haunting words of Nat King Cole's 'I don't want to be hurt anymore!' made her feel sick for what *might have been.* As a woman, it went far deeper than mere hurt. She felt crushed and despoiled.

'God, *why had it come to this?'* The thought screamed at her.

For in the prime of her life she'd given herself to a man who in her infatuation she'd once loved; looked up to as some knight in full armour. Yet so soon into their marriage his armour was there only for self-protection, not for any purposes of valour and passion. Now as provost he may have still walked and talked tall, but Christopher Wilkes' air of authority was that of a man of stone, no more alive than those statues, prostrate in prayer, lying around his cathedral.

From this man of stone, she'd snatched at the coat tails of another still grieving the loss of his own wife. Almost for sure she'd asked too much of Di whose early death was as much from a broken heart as from poor health. It was as though her life, along with any faith she once had had floated away like flotsam. With hopes and dreams dashed and human love all but absent, how could she feel any love for God? Some words from a Graham Greene novel came to her, 'Death was far more certain than God and with death, there would be no longer the daily possibility of love dying.'

Only then was she jarred out of her thoughts by the piercing song of a wren - the tiny creature hopping above her in the pre-budding branches of a cherry tree. So loud was its call that it seemed to be screeching against her dark introspection:

'Hey, you down there! Get with it! There's work to be done, decisions to be made. You have a son and a daughter out there needing to be loved back to sanity and wholeness.'

Like some heavenly rebuke she was jolted out of her self-pity, and where with the echo of Ben and Angela's laughter returning to her along with the freshness of an early spring day, Frances snapped out of her mood.

Half an hour after returning to the bungalow, she was delighted to hear Philippa on the phone to ask if she could come over for an hour.

The bounding barks of Snap preceded Philippa as they came up the garden path a short time later. Following the raging attack on her by Wilkes, Philippa had laid more urgent claim upon Di Hagan's collie, and where already snap had grown highly protective of her and Rosamund.

'Come in! I'm so glad that you've called, sweetheart,' said Frances.

They went straight into the kitchen with tea being a priority.

'Yes, I left Ros with her gran for an hour or so to see how you are. We all noticed at the hospital that you weren't quite yourself.'

Snap bore Frances no ill will at having been handed on to Philippa, hers being a typically effusive greeting before she went in search of her old sparring partner. Both women laughed as Sleuth and Snap renewed their acquaintance in the hall.

'Sleuth, ever the one to put on airs and graces,' said Frances.

'With Snap ever out to ingratiate herself,' replied Philippa.

'Well, it would bring a smile to dear old Di,' said Frances.

They were silent for a moment.

Sitting on stools in the kitchen, they waited for the kettle to boil.

'I really just called to check if you were okay,' said Philippa.

'I really appreciate it,' replied Frances. 'The truth is, I'm absolutely thrilled for Ben and Angela. They deserve the very best and the baby's a treasure. But . . .' her voice tailed off.

'Everything's got to you in another way,' said Philippa filling in the gap.

'*Yes!*' Frances' eyes filled up.

Snap remained pre-occupied sniffing around the corners of her old haunts.

'I suppose it's as though seeing Ben and Angela so blissfully happy has brought back everything in my own life that's been so empty,' said Frances. 'I mean if you're going to get married, one needs to do so with love in one's heart. It feels like there's *so little* love anywhere! Ben and Ange are such an amazing pair and now with their baby. It's like while they've lost everything, they know all about being happy. Obviously they're both completely responsible and yet in another way wonderfully *irresponsible*. Do you follow what I'm saying? Part of them just doesn't care about what's happened to them, or to their lowly status! Its because I love them to bits that in another way their love hurts me like hell.'

'Yes,' said Philippa. 'I know what you're saying all right. My marriage came to nothing and I suppose I've lost all interest in men because, for me, most strike me as either lecherous or treacherous, or both. I suppose if I stopped to think about it I should be depressed too. As it is I'm throwing myself into my work. But truth to tell I'd give *anything* to be as much in love as those two.'

After a pause, Philippa asked, 'By the way did I tell you mum's going to help me in the business? At least that's the idea; provided we can get the lease on the small vacant shop we've seen at the top of the High Street. That way she says she can help look after Rosamund and do some book-keeping which gives me more time doing the actual upholstery.'

'That's great news,' responded Frances. 'Which all goes to show that you've got your life ahead of you or most of it anyway. I seem to have squandered mine. I see myself winding up as a rich and embittered old divorcee whose children will end up God knows where. If I'm lucky I might still be able to hold on to Dom, but the way things are going I might even lose him.'

# A Candle For Lucifer

'Oh, *come on!*' said Philippa, with her light-up-a-room smile. 'We've got to have hope, you and me. Without hope we're all sunk! Forgive me for saying it, Frances, but stop feeling sorry for yourself! I'm telling you that because I've had to keep telling myself the same! You know that Dom loves you. I think he's a *great* fellow. What's more, it wouldn't surprise me if Katy doesn't sort her life out. So *don't despair!* Come on, show me how much you've done in the house!'

Frances made a point of lightening up.

Carrying their mugs of tea from the kitchen, they entered the living room. This one, bereft of furniture, had had the ceiling emulsioned, with two-thirds of the wallpapering complete. The transformation was already impressive.

'Well, look at this,' said Philippa marveling at the change. 'I only came in here once when Di was here. Wasn't there dowdy brown paint and smoke-stained wallpaper?' Frances nodded.

'It's unrecognizable!'

'You should have seen it when I first got started. I bungled an entire wall, mismatching the small flowers by getting them all upside down.' She laughed despite herself.

'Well, what do they say, "If at first you don't succeed . . ." Have you done any more?'

'Yes, I've given the sitting room a bit of a makeover at the front. What do you think?'

This room too had been completely painted and redecorated with a lined wall covering and everything back in place. Velvet curtains in russet gold matched a new three-piece suite. Sleuth, who had retired to languish on the settee, got up to greet Philippa.

'*Fantastic!* Everything has changed. New carpet, new furniture! Did you put up the curtains and pelmet?'

Frances nodded. 'With a little help from Dom,' Her grin

couldn't disguise her sense of pride.

'*Terrific!* You could become one of those makeover house-doctors in your own right. You've got an eye for it. I'm glad to see you've kept that old roll-top desk which, no disrespect to Di, was about the only piece of furniture I took to!'

'As it happened he left clear instructions, *not* to get rid of the desk,' said Frances. She went on, 'As for all his other stuff I took the bull by the horns and got Dominic to help me shift just about everything else either to the auction, or the dump. I'm bracing myself to do the bathroom next. Although it's a sort of therapy I'm sure to get out of my depth at some stage, and will have to call in the experts. Still, I've changed the ballcock in the toilet and again with Dom's help managed to put up a towel-rail and a replacement mirror.'

Sitting down in the revamped sitting room and with Sleuth drifting onto Philippa's lap Frances then explained 'Although I've enjoyed doing the decorating, I don't feel at home here. I mean I'm no longer cut out for Ketborough or of course for All Saints, more so with *him* just up the road as provost. I've got to get away.'

'I can understand that.'

'You know, some of the parishioners there still seem to treat *me* as the one who's at fault. Rumours persist, I'm told, that *I'm the one* to have let Christopher down, even suggesting that Di was instrumental in my divorce in some way. And now of course I'm not just his estranged wife, I'm the estranged wife of the new *provost!*'

'It's unbelievable that he's still got so much influence,' said Philippa. After the battle with the staple gun, she was ninety percent sure that he had to be her sister's killer. Had the morphing from his charm into an obscenity, as witnessed by both Frances and Philippa been what Stacey had seen too?

'God how I wish that the whole desperate saga

surrounding Stacey and that other woman Roxanne could be cleared up once and for all,' said Frances. 'I mean, they've apparently charged someone with killing the prostitute, although there are suggestions that he's been held on the flimsiest of evidence.'

'I know mum and dad, all of us, of course,' she faltered, 'will *never* rest easy until the real killer has been convicted once and for all and put away,' said Philippa. Any reference to her sister always produced tears.

A long grief-stricken silence followed.

'What troubles me in particular,' said Frances, 'is the fact that Di had some important detail implicating Christopher, or so he made out, and I simply can't lay my hands on it.'

'Do you know what the evidence was?' asked Philippa, still tearful.

Having never told Philippa about the photograph of Stacey found in the vicar's cassock, Frances was loath to do so now.

'Without such evidence as Di said he had, it still wouldn't have been enough,' conceded Frances. 'As it was he said that until and unless Stacey was discovered, what he had was of no use. What I do feel convinced about,' she continued, 'is that he, my ex-husband, will strike again and yet I feel so powerless even as I say it. I mean there he is, as large as life up in the cathedral still wowing the women, no doubt, as well as getting brownie points in other ways. Apparently he's sorted out some scandal over the cathedral's finances, leaving the bishop to state openly how Christopher has his full support.'

'Well, at least Bishop Letharge's been stopped in his tracks. The bust-up of his antiques was incredible,' said Philippa.

'The latest is that Bishop Letherge has had a serious heart-attack,' replied Frances, before adding 'Most people seem to be quietly applauding.'

'I can understand that' replied Philippa quietly. 'By the way, did I ever tell you that Christopher was paying for my rent at the flat up until the end of last year?'

'No, you didn't,' replied Frances. 'But given that Christopher has a gift for being generous to vulnerable women, it comes as no surprise. No doubt it was that which made you feel more beholden to him?'

'Precisely so! I felt beholden to him from thereon.'

*'Damn him to hell,'* said Frances. 'Think about it, Philippa! He didn't care then and he doesn't care now that his *own* daughter is a drug addict, and prostituting herself down in London.'

'I feel ashamed,' said Philippa.

'Don't be!' snapped Frances. 'And I'm not mad at *you,* Philippa. I'm just mad at what he's got away with for so long and how I've been so gullible. Added to which so few other people still seem able to see it.'

It was then that the phone rang with Ben on the line. 'I've just got back from the hospital,' he said. 'You'll never guess what's happened. I've just heard it on the local news . . .' after a short pause, Ben said, 'Bishop Letharge died this morning of a massive heart attack!'

In a steady voice so that both of them could hear, Philippa said, 'what do they say? "Don't get mad, get even"!'

Ben's voice responded down the phone, 'Maybe at long last someone bigger than us is doing the even-ing up.'

## Chapter 37

With his Lordship's death, the Very Revd Christopher Wilkes became both freer yet more isolated and vulnerable. For despite what had been Bishop Letharge's full support for his new provost, a bishop was free to remove a provost at will. Like a chess-piece he had only to cross the bishop in some way to be out-maneuvered. So in that sense while protecting him Letharge also had him between finger and thumb. Letharge's successor might well turn out to be not so kindly disposed.

So now after the pomp and splendour of a full Requiem Mass, conducted by the Archbishop of York, his lordship had been laid to his damnation. At least that was how certain women in the diocese saw the matter. For Christopher the first fortuitous consequence of Letharge's passing was to secure him his long overdue post-Christmas break. Having appeased the bishop by not taking his holiday earlier and with it being well into February, he chose to visit his London mews.

Letharge's sudden death caused Christopher also to reflect, albeit fleetingly, on his beliefs – or lack of them. Having no thoughts concerning the afterlife, he could hardly envisage his lordship now transposed onto some heavenly throne in lieu of the one, from which death had so swiftly unseated him. And much as he liked the pomp and circumstance of cathedral life, the provost still hankered for the wild open spaces where he could be on his own.

God of course, whether or not He existed, could always be conjured up in the antics of cathedral life. Lots of pageantry and ceremonials along with beautiful choral music always made one feel good inside. And he knew he could hold his own with the other canons. For although to outward appearance each looked devout, often back-stage fierce rivalries were known to erupt in the life of most cathedrals, with Fordham being no exception. This applied especially when it came to the clergy and their dress sense. A hugely expensive chasuble, for example, was commonly an item of attire coveted by one and all. As and when the occasion arose they each loved to preen themselves like so many embroidered peacocks. Again the way they chose to read or intone the various religious offices was another route for showing off. The rounding off of vowels or how certain syllables were sung, as though one's life depended on them, weren't just obsessive they reeked of the cantor praising himself. *'The Lord be with you'* and don't I sound just wonderful was how it sometimes struck Christopher. God had nothing to do with it.

Appearances were a vital part of turning cathedral life into something that it wasn't. Sharing in the life of an institution where ostentation and self-congratulations were the first deities, Christopher knew he was no different from the rest. So if he had a saving grace among all the other charades, he at least never lost his appetite for the great outdoors. And was he not being religious in some way when he felt drawn less to his cathedral and more towards the lakes and mountains?

What too of the ancient superstitions of Africa; the glimpses into voodooism that he'd secretly been shown during his childhood? If anything, a belief in fate and the magic rites of pagan Kenya seemed far more attractive than the dead brutalizing Christianity bequeathed to him by his parents. After all what of Christianity's own superstitions, none more poignant than the one of genuflecting before the lifeless effigy of Christ hanging from a cross? So it was the thought of the mountains, the existential power of Nature that had become his religion. Surely there had been no greater *religious experience* than when he'd dared to climb Mount Kenya in the teeth of a storm, defying the mountain's ancient Kikuyu god Ngai?

He was also perceptive enough to see how charm, his included, was but a front for genuine piety. For how did ecclesiastical 'charm' differ so greatly from what he believed to be his own charmed life – the sense that someone or something had always sought to protect him? He also knew there was something very powerful about his own charm. Like the mesmerizing Venus flytrap with its death-dealing fronds as he remembered it in Kenya so he seemed able to cast a spell over young and impressionable girls like Stacey and now, it appeared, Marianne!

Some nameless force seemed to be with him. Perhaps Ngai and his grotesque dwarf Gumbi had, from the upper reaches of Mount Kenya, been more enchanted than enraged by his fearless trespass. If he had any religion that had to be it – deriving comfort that maybe the old mountain god had pledged to protect him for life.

As for any western perception that speaks of the devil taking care of his own, he was more impervious to that possibility.

Back in London, perhaps it was the dare of entrapment that drew him back to the City's red-light area. He knew that he'd run the gauntlet with, was it, Paratroop Sade? Having thrown him out, she might well have warned some of the girls about 'an evil, smooth-speaking bastard being on the loose and going by the name of Nigel.' But London remained vast and anonymous and, like as not, she'd have forgotten. She had after all given no warning to Roxanne.

Having visited a theatre off Leicester Square and taken a fortifying double scotch at the Carnival Club on Old Compton Road, he went up Frith Street off the Charing Cross Road. He took out the little calling card on which he'd written down the address where he now was. He rang the intercom. 'Can I speak to Stiletto? I've made an appointment' he asked.

'Stiletto's busy right now. Do you want to leave a message?'

'Can I come in and wait, or do I have to make another appointment?'

The female voice marveled at how often these smooth 'pervs' spoke as though they were visiting their Harley Street specialist. *'Can I make an appointment?'* she mimicked their tone to herself. *'It's a matter of some urgency.'*

Mind you, what some of the classier hookers charged these days wasn't so far off the rates of a top consultant or lawyer, or so she guessed – £300 an hour being not untypical.

'We can book you in now darling, just so long as you've got ready cash?'

'Yes.'

'Come upstairs,' the female voice welded itself to the buzzer releasing its catch. Climbing some clinically clean steps painted green, he went through a fireproof door beyond which sat a Madam at her desk.

'Been here before, love?' she didn't so much look at him as look him over. She was, as he'd come to assume, typical of the female management in that profession - peroxide blonde with crimson lips, ample-bosomed with plunging cleavage. She wore heavy gold hoop earrings while smoking from a gold cigarette holder.

'No, but I booked in as Mr. X.'

'That's what I've got you down as. If you don't mind waiting, Mr. X. She'll be a good fifteen minutes yet.'

'I'll wait,' he said. 'And I've got some things to put on.'

'You can go into that cubicle over there and change. For all I care you can stay there if you don't want anyone seeing you except Stiletto.'

Her attempt at good manners was barely disguised contempt.

'Another jerk needing to cover up' was what she wanted to say.

Remaining fully clothed for the time being, he didn't have much to put on, just a black leather facemask and some patent leather gloves.

When after a few minutes he was told to go through, all that he could see was that she was clad head to toe in a red lycra cat suit, her slim physique giving the slippery effect of feline agility. The facemask was connected to the whole outfit by a zip at the neck. Her stock in trade, so to speak, a pair of bright red stiletto shoes, were conspicuous, even though she wasn't wearing them. The shoes were uncomfortable despite being kept on view amongst an assortment of implements and other paraphernalia, all placed on a shelf at eye-level.

As he stood half-naked before her, she sought to visualize him fully dressed and with his face exposed. It was a sort of photo-fit precaution, which she and the other girls developed by instinct, just in case of a problem. She could see that his head and features were well proportioned. The flecks of graying hair around his chest told her that as an older man he had an exceptionally good physique, although his strong hirsute arms with their hands sheathed in patent leather gloves appeared almost talon-like.

With the two masks confronting each other, it was he who willed her to look away, the gleam in his eyes telling her that he disliked scrutiny.

Time provided any foreplay in their erotic dance to be explored in a leisurely way. They had an hour, longer if necessary. It was necessary, as well as financially expedient, to conserve the client's orgasm to the last few minutes. So let the game begin. Knowing what he wanted, she teased him by throwing a net over his semi-naked torso. He pretended to be caught in its meshes. She stroked a whip across his haunches, and he sprang out of the trap to let it be known that she would have to do better than that, if she was to control him.

He in turn threw the net over her and pinioned her down on the floor. He then released her. Already she had a foretaste of his agility and strength.

Falling motionless to the floor, he then let her truss him with handcuffs and a chain. These devices were essentially benign, designed not to immobilize but to create an illusion of immobility; more 'fun' objects with a view to keep the sadism in check. Her whips too were more ornamental, designed to tickle rather than to draw blood. For all the macho illusions of what Stiletto claimed to be about, she'd retreated more to the tame end of S & M and intended it so. Invariably she could satisfy her customers at the lower gradations of her art and felt uncomfortable if, as sometimes happened, a client demanded from her or upon her a more punishing routine.

She could tell at the outset that this client would be no pushover. He was tall and for a man of his age seemed possessed of an inordinate strength. Nor did the mask properly conceal what was a cruel mouth and smouldering eyes that remained unrelenting with their insistence, '*Don't look at me!*'

He snapped off the 'pretend' cuffs and chain with a disdain, almost a snarl, as he demanded '*Give me some real action!*'

Even when coarsened by anger, there was a silky tone to his voice that reminded her of her father. Although the honeyed tones may have oozed vitriol, this new weirdo couldn't disguise the imprimatur of a well-educated past.

'Why were so many punters ex-public school, ex-university?' She'd asked the question many times.

'Because, darling, a privileged education often *makes* people kinky,' she could hear Imogen speaking.

Consciously she had to remain professional; suppress the growing dislike that she felt for this stranger off the streets. A stranger maybe but one who, because his type was oft replicated, was not entirely a stranger. Although an unknown quantity maybe, his voice still gave him an archetypal identity.

She drew reassurance that her panic button, hidden from view, was but a couple of paces away.

But suddenly, with the reflexes of a snake, he had seized the elongated chain from the handcuffs, wrapping it around her, at the same time grabbing a section of rope that, like her footwear, Stiletto used more for visual effect than for actual bondage. The rope, which lay in a coil, was of a thick coarse variety, the sort fishermen might use at the quayside. Although it was almost impractical for him to truss her up with, his gloved hands were strong and he made sure that the rough hemp cut painfully into her upper body. He then threw the net over her.

Sudden panic began to set in, but where to cry out would have been futile. Each den was deliberately soundproofed. Punters preferred the freedom to cry out in pain, even if the pain exacted was far below that of any literal torture chamber. Unbeknown to her he had brought with him a small section of nylon cord, the thin sort as used for a washing line. As she lay half entangled and enmeshed, he had leapt up to grab the cord that he had secreted from his trousers pocket. With lightning movements he set to work, where the more she struggled the more he enmeshed her in a spider's web of bowlines and reef knots.

Beyond any masquerade paid for with money, she began to curse him now in real fear and alarm. He liked the girl's youthful strength and when they struggled, he liked it *even more* when he knew she wasn't faking. That was the *best* part, the telltale signals of ensuing fear, the little gasps of panic and anger, the involuntary writhing and the creeping realization that it was *he* who was now in control.

Panic rightly used can be the stimulus for calling upon hidden reserves of strength. Seeking to regain her composure, Stiletto tried to stay cool in devising a plan against this smoothie, now turned monster. If she could untie the ropes, she could use some of the basic martial arts Paratroop Sade told her she'd be wise to acquire. But it was becoming critical to untangle the ropes that threatened to choke the life from her. Despite the panic button being close, it lay remained tantalizingly just out of reach.

Suddenly and unaccountably he then let her go. The speed with which he parted the knots and gave her back her freedom was part of the controlling ritual he'd acted out in his earlier fantasies. He was only *playing* with her, arousing in some primal instincts. Feigning breathlessness, he undid the ropes apologizing that she was exciting him overmuch and that he was getting too carried away.

'Maybe so,' panted Stiletto, 'but you were well out of order! Is that clear?'

Her panic subsided into relief.

He nodded and apologized once more.

The contest, if that was what it was, had left them both breathless. They were on their knees facing each other. She was a 'game' one and he found himself liking her, excited by the prospect of getting her madder still.

Although it wasn't for her to like him, she needed to take control of her own inner feelings, not to succumb to the raw hidden energy that now stirred. She saw that he had nearly half his time left. Maxine the proprietor liked the girls to complete their allotted time, only sympathizing when an appointment had to be aborted due to serious complications. A bit of 'rough and tumble' was only to be expected.

Stiletto was also motivated to see the hour through to its conclusion. Her life had undergone a sea change where thanks to her friend Kes and to the acupuncture clinic, she had kicked her coke habit into oblivion. It was a fantastic achievement, which only for those who have 'done' class 'A' drugs could begin to appreciate. Two months had elapsed since her treatment and during that time not only had she managed to make some serious savings, but her looks and strength were returning along with her sanity. Having grown increasingly fond of Kes, she'd begun to contemplate coming off the game for good.

Thinking about him made her feel better. Funny how you can get lost in your thoughts while trying to service a customer, even a head-case like this one, she laughed to herself.

As they re-composed themselves and thinking how the physical contours of the girl in the catsuit resembled those of Marianne, he tried making some conversation. 'You've got an interesting outfit here,' he remarked. 'Are you a climber with all these ropes and other tackle?'

She shook her head.

'In your line of work you must need to keep pretty fit to

deal with the likes of me,' he tried to wisecrack. He was curious to see her face.

The only benefit of smalltalk was that it frittered away a few extra minutes.

'Do you live in London?' she asked

'When I'm not elsewhere,' he replied, evasively.

'Have you visited many of the girls?'

'One or two.'

It was the end of the conversation. He alone wanted to ask the questions, having no more desire to be quizzed than looked at.

But it was enough to make her think, 'God, he sounds just like my *father.*'

The association rekindled something; an urge to return to the fight they had temporarily suspended.

She adopted a ploy, inviting him to roll onto what resembled a canvas groundsheet. Nor did he demur when she secured the end of the sheet tightly across his body with the Velcro lashings that were concealed on the other side. The groundsheet thus secured became like a straitjacket, pinning him in from his shoulders down to his knees. Of course given time he could have wriggled out of it but she was moving fast, something inside her now *wanting* to hurt him.

She slipped off her trainers and put on the red stilettos, advancing towards him with a deliberation designed to heighten fear as well as excitement. Despite the canvas affording him some protection, she stepped onto his groin and stomach using her full body-weight while rocking back on her heel, and grinning as she did so. She did this twice knowing that that pinioned on the floor he remained helpless. For some reason she was beginning to feel real hatred for this particular punter, and where in wanting to walk over the masked face he cried out in real fear.

The facemask would offer only partial protection, and how could the urbane provost ever look at his parishioners again? With a gaping hole in his cheek, a whore's stigmata, he'd be marked for life? But such was her fury at that moment that he feared not just the scarring of his face but of a stiletto entering his eye. Of course he could move his head and if need be he could bite at the pencil-thin heel, pinioning it with his powerful teeth. By thrusting his body sideways he might even shake her off him, thereby freeing himself.

But as he was contemplating this, it was her turn to suddenly mellow. In the same way that he had appeared to relent from the rope trick earlier, she straddled his body telling him that if he'd be a good boy, then she would release him. Visibly shaken but not waiting for his answer, Stiletto also shaken by her own erupting violence tore away the bindings. Never having experienced such a surge of her own feelings like that before, her rage now abated like cooled magnesium.

But if remorse came too readily to her, it was his cue to spring back onto the offensive while straddling her body with the same ferocity that triggered her earlier terror. She was on the floor and once more just out of reach from the panic button.

*Oh God, not again!* What can I do this time? Her mind raced.

His hands were around her throat, the zipped throat through which the sweat of her exertions and present panic were starting to pour like blood.

'You've pushed your luck too far this time little *bitch*! I want to see you suffer now. First, let's take a look at your face.'

Unable to reply, she felt herself blacking out.

She was aware of the zip being torn away at her throat and

of the wrenching hands over the mask. Now with the mask removed she could feel the talons around her neck. This was the bit he was waiting for. With skill he could play with her, even toy with her death just like the Venus flytrap with its encircling fronds.

And then suddenly, inexplicably, everything went very still. Five minutes ahead of time, the assailant slipped away from Stiletto's den. Slowly she returned to full consciousness.

Maxine and two other punters saw him leave. Despite looking ghostly white as well as sweating profusely she'd not been quick enough to apprehend him, other than to shout, 'Ere, what's going off?' A few seconds later and she'd rushed to Stiletto's den only to be answered with groans.

'Christ, what's he done to you darling?' she said scooping up the limp and sweat-drenched body of the girl.

'I couldn't reach the button,' gasped the other. 'Twice I needed to and both times it was out of reach.'

'What happened?' It was a question they asked of each other.

'Well, I was just going to call you to say that your next client is waiting and this is what I find, you here lying almost dead, or so it appears, and that fucking smooth-talking bastard running off half-dressed and looking like Dracula.'

'I thought I was a gonna!' said the girl. 'I really thought the second time round he was going to finish me off.'

'God, I've suddenly had a thought,' said Maxine bringing her hand up to her mouth. 'Did you get a look at his eyes?'

'Can't say he gave me much opportunity,' gasped Stiletto. 'He sure as hell didn't like me looking at him.'

'Well, I remember Sade, from across the river, telling us to watch out for this evil motherfucker called Nigel.' What's more she said, 'Look out for his eyes. They're a different shade of brown.'

*'Sweet Mother of Christ!'* was all that Stiletto could say, before fainting.

# Chapter 38

It was the nearest that he'd come to all out panic.

Engaging with his daughter in a West End brothel stirred a host of inner accusations, even as he fled back to his Cathedral the following day. On the drive back to Fordham it was worse that the voice sounded familiar: 'Try getting out of that one, provost!' 'And you thought you'd never be found out! I've never doubted that you would.'

Surely that wasn't how Katy had thought about her father all along?

*'You can run but you can't hide!'* Was that the same voice, or just the unfortunate title of a film that flashed up in his consciousness? These hateful torments reminded him of people like Mr. Zbierski, that wretched little Pole who'd made similar innuendos.

Frantically he grasped at what his own logic told him: 'Well even if I had seen her, so what? It's a free country! Anyway, best to get back to the cathedral, where I belong so as to help the diocese at this difficult time.'

Ever-conscientious let denial, if it *was* denial, be restored within the solace of his priestly robes and the cloistered arches of Fordham. What had happened would cease to have happened once he returned to work, making it no worse than other bits of the nightmare that still sought to pervade his existence.

Yet his double life was becoming increasingly difficult to sustain. The truth seemed to arrive with the same ferocity as one of his nightmare dreams, leaving him bewildered knowing which was which. He was aware of his daughter going to London and that she had a drug problem, and that when tearing away at the girl's mask it was near undeniable. Almost for sure, it had been the face of his daughter!

'But what if it hadn't been her? Or more to the point, what if *she* hadn't seen him?' he wondered. And if she hadn't, then *no* it had neither been her nor him! So it had to be a nightmare.

If Katy had shown her a photograph of her father, he mused, then the Madam on reception might have identified him, But then callously, he consoled himself, 'No way has she got any picture of me. Besides if *she's* on the game, she's no more willing to give herself away than I am to expose her.'

Even then for all his twisted logic, there was a part of Wilkes that hated any idea of the father and his daughter having been incestuous.

As a past master for turning reality into fantasy and fantasy into reality, it became harder to thwart the march of chaos and confusion going on the rampage. Stacey may have agreed to him killing her, but what of that fantasy which guilt had lain at his door over the murder of some obscure prostitute called Roxanne? Clearly the police didn't see it that way, otherwise why arrest and detain another man? He'd read somewhere about an individual called Merv Costello, languishing for his sixth month in prison.

Yet if his encounter with Katy had been no more than a dream, it was still a goddamn powerful dream if so. He'd never abused either of his children and had always been a good father, even if an indifferent one. To have met his daughter not face to face but mask to mask in, of all places, *a brothel!* Even as he denied it, the tearing away of her blindfold felt more real than anything his tortured imagination could have dreamed up!

For someone whose sleep was increasingly fitful, sustaining the pretence became less easy by the day. Such sleep as he had was full of sharp edges, a ragged contortion of different images. The face of Stacey might interchange with that of her sister Philippa. Or the extended arm and painted fingers of the whore Roxanne rising from the undergrowth, became the accusing arm of Katy dressed in her red cat suit.

Nightmares can be so cruel.

Even when seeking respite from these tortured images by calling upon distant memories of the savannahs and mountains of Kenya, these too could be gatecrashed. An apparition of the violent prostitute Paratroop Sade might appear, with the Pole Zbierski standing at her shoulder. Various police officers they too turned up in unlikely places, as did the deceased Nicholas Hagan. Mr. Hagan may have been of a gentler disposition than the rest of them, yet by not saying much that too was a worry, more so as he'd become such a close friend of his ex-wife's. And now that his former churchwarden had died could he disturb him in some way even more?

As for the other man in prison, how was he in all of this? Had this fellow Costello really killed Roxanne? It seemed confusing to think so. If not might he escape from prison with some foul purpose in mind? Several times he awoke in a drenching sweat as he thought of the wreckage done to the bishop's palace, and of Letharge's ensuing death. Did the prelate's fate foretell some evil omen upon himself? What of his *own* possessions, the antiques that he'd bought on his lordship's say-so? Would *he* die if a similar thing happened to him?

Panic had started to run amok.

The twist was that Wilkes had returned to an atmosphere of sheer calm and tranquility, living in the Cathedral's 'Close' in the company of other God-fearing men. He wasn't some desperado on the run. There were no bounty hunters wanting to take him dead or alive. Rather he remained free to go where he chose, mixing only with people who chose to ingratiate themselves.

It was only his inner self that was running flat out!

All the more thanks then to the trust, shown him by the likes of acolyte Marianne that he felt able to carry on at all. By early March, along with her visits to the youth group held in the provost's house, she'd chosen to see him on other occasions. Recently her stepfather had been inconsolable over the death of two Masonic brothers killed in a car crash, leaving Marianne to regard her home situation as going from bad to worse.

Neither provost nor acolyte could deny the emotional tie being forged between them. Yet from him to her it was rationalized as a surrogate parent/daughter love, where disowned by a drug-addicted daughter he had paternal feelings for a girl whose stepfather, appeared to have lost all interest her.

It was at a mid-week evening service of Holy Communion during Lent that the frisson reached a dangerous level. The service was a basic no frills Eucharist with no choir present and the Minster all but empty. Being the celebrant for that occasion, Christopher had Marianne to assist him once more.

Normal evening communion services typically left the nave in near-darkness with only the sanctuary brightly lit.

This enabled the worshippers to focus more easily upon proceedings at the altar. Following the usual routine and with the offerings received, the provost duly presented the communion vessels to Marianne.

Delicate fingers protruding from the sleeve of her alb transferred no more than a score of wafers to the ciborium, causing his hands to tremble slightly. With fixed concentration, she then poured the wine into the chalice in whose blood-red reflection he could see the calm image of the girl – the corn-blonde hair, and eyes which even as they looked downwards held steady with a look of love. Mercifully the chalice needed to be only half filled, preventing any spillage.

'*Oh God!*' he thought, 'the exquisite pain of being so near her, the sensuality of the libation, the image of blood and her unflinching gaze.'

With her long lustrous hair, she looked *so* like Stacey. Pliant, understanding, virginal - the altar girl in her celestial robes!

Marianne, I want to take you, drench you in the image of the wine poured out for us both!

Had he'd spoken what he'd just thought?

The calm of the Eucharistic moment seemed undisturbed.

Despite the trembling excitement from him to her, he managed to keep the goblet from staining the crisp linen of the altar, or of splashing on to the purple and gold tapestry of the altar frontal. Everything retained its air of sanctity.

Raising his hands he invited the congregation to respond: 'Thine, O Lord, is the greatness and the power and the glory and the majesty,' to which their distant echo could be heard in the darkness: 'All that is in heaven and on earth is thine. All things come of thee, O Lord. And of thine own do we give Thee.'

With her being so near, he found the language of submission and surrender almost unbearable.

Now he was embarking on the great prayer of consecration when the bread and wine took on their sacred meaning as Christ's body and blood. As he completed the prayer and as though communicating a further instruction to his acolyte, he leant across to her and whispered, 'Oh, Marianne, would you give me yourself. I'm so lonely. We're made for each other, just like a priest and sacrifice.'

*God, did I just say that?* He thought as he received from himself the consecrated elements. Yet she held her ground, so again he couldn't be sure. If he had spoken had she submitted to him at that moment?

Even had she wished it, flight from the cathedral would have been impossible. It was the highlight of the service, the foreplay between consecration and the climax of administration. Whether she froze or now offered herself he couldn't be sure, but as he went along the line of communicants, it was like they danced a freeze-frame courtship of death. He wanted her! She hovered close by. Then as the small band of communicants retreated into the darkness, she approached him once more to assist with the ablutions.

Her composure seemed to signal her compliance.

As a moment in time it had all passed fleetingly; swift enough that none in the congregation appeared distracted in any way, although for him it was another moment to savour. Forget all that nonsense about Christ being the bread and wine. It was *she* who was offering herself as his living sacrifice – she, who was asking to be devoured. Of course he'd had no intention of doing anything there in public. It was just that mentally he'd claimed her at the high point in the service, with nobody in the congregation appearing to have noticed. The fantasy of the girl with the long golden hair in her pure white alb, offering him her steady gaze, would stay with him until the time was right.

The right time was closer than either realized.

'I went to that cathedral the other night to take my mum to communion,' said Nick Crooks. 'Says she likes taking communion sometime during Lent. Wouldn't normally catch me going anywhere near the place, but mum didn't want to go on her own, so I took her. And guess *what!*'

It wasn't often that Nick Crooks had The Magpie's best story. Most ear grabbing gossip seemed to be in the sole preserve of Zbierski, so Crooks was going to milk this one, especially as it had to do with the pub's enemy number one, Canon C. Wilkes, alias the Provost.

'Jesus, you should have seen the way he looked at her,' said Nick Crooks, as he supped his pint of bitter.

He got everyone's immediate attention: 'the guy's straight out of hell and I don't care who knows it,' continued Crooks. 'I reckon Wilkes had hypnotized the lassie who was supposed to be helping him up at the altar. She looked like she was on drugs or something. Kept on looking at him like she couldn't help herself.'

'What do you reckon, Granville?' The question had come from the landlord, who by calling him Granville rather than just plain 'Z' was paying the Pole a compliment.

'I'd bloddy well lay odds-on 100-1 that he's a focking devil. You know what they call the likes of him back in my country, 'Forked tongues out of their arses.'

'It was Lucifer who got painted like that in them old Michelangelo pictures,' observed Nick Lech; so-named because of his reputation for liking nude ladies, and which had made him something of a Renaissance connoisseur as a result.

'Anyway,' went on Lech, 'if you'd laid a bet this time last

year that Wilkes was a fucking sex-freak you might have made a few bob. But not now!'

'More like the Very Reverend Christopher Lucifer,' said Cocheron. 'He can't last long. That shyster of a bishop's dead, thank Christ. And sooner or later they'll have to do something to sort out this diocese. Mind you things look like changing at All Saints.'

A further nail had indeed been hammered into the coffin of Wilkes and his authority in the diocese. A new vicar at All Saints had been appointed and it was a *woman*. What was more with her and her husband having already called in at The Magpie, she'd made a good first impression.

'Now there's a lady who deserves to be a vicar,' said Lech. 'She's got a nice accent but she wasn't standing on her airs and graces, like she was too good for this place.' He paused, 'And *nice-looking* as well!'

'You said you liked her arse,' There were times when Crooks could be really unhelpful.

Anyway they were all agreed. Revd Caroline Meggart seemed to be okay.

# Chapter 39

Despite the fine spring conditions earlier, with March going into April it had turned unseasonably cold. It was Monday in Holy Week and Marianne's visit at around seven o'clock that evening was wholly unexpected. Framed in the doorway by swirling flecks of snow, it was obvious that her call was one of desperation.

'My parents have just had an enormous row,' she was close to tears, 'and my mother's told me to get out of the house!'

'Come in, Marianne, tell me all about it,' he coaxed, opening the door wide. She looked pale and shaken. Removing her anorak, its surface glistening with a dusting of snow, he ushered her into his oak-paneled drawing room. The crackling of a log fire made the room warm and inviting, and sitting her down on his leather button-back Chesterfield, he sat alongside her.

Was *he* the father figure she longed for? She felt her hopes rising.

Choking back the tears, she faltered, 'I'm beginning to think that I don't belong anywhere, I've no family to speak of and I feel like the *orphan* I've always known myself to be. I just want to give up.'

'There, there! Hush now,' was all he felt able to say. Drawing her to him, he stroked her hair as he had done once before.

It was his tenderness that caused her to break down further and to snuggle in closer. In doing so he could feel her pink cashmere cardigan slide easily across the cream satin blouse, which she wore underneath.

But instead of being protective, her vulnerability was already exciting the predator in him. Alarmed by the suddenness of this sensation, he even considered going to make a hot drink. But it was she who held onto him as she went on: 'I just don't know what I'm going to do. I can't stay at home any longer. I'm sure my mother is jealous of me, and secretly believes that I've got something to do with their bust-up. What's more to the point is I've got nothing in common with them. They don't want me and I've got past caring for either of them. In fact, I detest them. Christopher, what shall I do?'

His senses were in turmoil. The veneer of compassion masked a steely detachment, beneath which lay the uncoiling of a twisted pleasure. If she felt bereft, so did he. It was as though the girl's dread held up some blackened mirror to reflect his cracked narcissism. The future was disintegrating before him. His family was as good as dead. Not only that something kept telling him not to kid himself – for it was *he* and no one else who had almost killed his own whore daughter. On top of all that the one man who had believed in him, Bp Letharge, was now dead.

Only half-living in the present he longed to escape into the dreams of his past. Any memory of happier times would do! Absurdly in the warm glow of his drawing room her hair captivated his senses once more, reminding him of the intoxicating aromas of the savannah. How could something so unrelated trigger off such a seductive memory of Africa?

Even as he stroked her hair absent-mindedly he could hear the laughter of his young Kenyan friends; that and the hot dry wind rustling through the grasses.

Yet Africa was both a metaphor for happiness and horror, the horror of having suffered at the hands of parents who'd abused and flayed him, and who'd nurtured within him a hatred of women. This being Holy Week he gave an involuntary start at the memory of his childhood, aspects of which had been like a crucifixion.

As she remained nestling against him, he took time to observe her shapely thighs in the well-fitting denims. Under the cashmere jumper, her breasts were well defined and firm. But even as he relished her charms, he began to hate the shapely innocence of her body into which the persona of a woman was already emerging.

The compassion was but momentary, for the girl was well on the way to losing her innocence, and if some vestige of kindness wanted to help her this was a *foreign* emotion. Was the sensation comparable to the feelings he'd had for the nun Angelique whilst on pilgrimage? Both the sister and the girl struck him as being different in some way like they understood in a way that no one else could. But he chose not to remember; the unraveling of a deeper, more inviting rage now choking all benevolence.

The man upon whose mercy she had thrown herself and to whom she'd come in her dark hour was in his darkest hour also. As she sought to consolidate her newfound security so his was disintegrating, starting to make the girl's dependence feel somehow repugnant.

Before Stacey's murder, he had loved playing the father figure, even as he had with Marianne. But the nightmare was closing in with its realities. The apparition of Katy had intensified, where she was now personally mocking the charade being shown towards the girl cosseted beside him:

'Don't even begin to pretend you can help her, *D-a-d.*' The sneering tones seemed to be just behind his right shoulder. Then, as though hissing in his ear, 'you're so twisted you could make a snake walk straight.' And then the voice said, 'What's more I know it was *you* who killed Stacey, and it was *you* who killed the girl up in Leeds.'

'*God!* Who the hell's saying these things? Is the voice giving me its *approval?* Does nothing matter anymore? Be consistent!'

Time was running out. And if he had devised any plan for making Marianne his 'once and for all perfect sacrifice' - he savoured the blasphemy of that phrase - it was being presented for priest and victim not a moment too soon. The last throw of some diabolical dice before midnight possibly?

'I mean, where can I go? Who can I run to? You seem to be the only person who understands me or who *cares* for that matter. I'm a complete misfit. I want to drop out of school and get away from everything and everyone.'

Her voice seemed to be coming from a long way off. Then with unabashed candour and looking straight at him, she added, 'I'm so glad that I've got *you!*' In saying that she stroked the front of his clerical shirt, and looked up. Like others before her, she'd been fascinated by his eyes with their different shades of brown. His eyes made him look somehow much younger that he was.

Yet vulnerability that sought to tear at long lost heartstrings now impaled itself on the razor wire of his twisted defenses. As with Stacey and his own daughter whom he had so nearly killed, the playing out of any more fatherly little games now maddened him. *He was no father!* Katy had told him as much. They'd proved this to each other many times, and never so much as in their last encounter. Still less was he the father-in-God figure to whom impressionable teenage girls persistently felt drawn.

The charmer's elixir was fermenting into the venom of the snake. Had Frances or Angela been present, they would have screamed: *'get up NOW, Marianne! For God's sake make a run for it!* You've still got a chance. Do anything but *don't stay there transfixed on the sofa!'*

Yet a moment later, enchanter and enchanted were locked into the ritual of sacrifice. Both mesmerized each other. He sensed that the forces were bringing closure to his game. Nor did the victim seem to care. Did she still trust him? Maybe his meeting with Katy and her psychic taunts had prised open some tiny crevice in his conscience. Was he *twisted,* even a devil of some sort? Maybe a legion of devils inhabited his soul, promoting him to become the very Prince of Darkness himself. With this innocent child now in his clutches he had to do justice to the same suicidal pact he'd felt for Stacey. For he too felt he'd had enough.

The same panic and rage that he felt in ripping off the mask from his daughter now seemed to well up from his spleen to his brain. Sanity even where it existed narrowed into eyes snakelike and demonic. The temptation was becoming overpowering, unstoppable, his temptress too beguiling. He would not deny himself one last opportunity for killing to perfection.

Cupping her face in his hands, he turned her towards him. He reveled in the look of hurt innocence as he held her face. Nor even then did she know that she was seconds away from death. With hands sliding down to her throat, he savoured the moment of keeping her innocence for himself, the serpent mesmerizing its prey. Bringing his thigh across hers to provide slight leverage, his fingers and thumbs met easily as they encircled the white delicate neck. He watched as her lips parted in surprise, much as they did when she'd taken the chalice.

'Don't hate me, Marianne,' he whispered. Her arms came

up and touched his sleeve but she hardly struggled. More like a tender farewell, it was a touch bearing no malice. 'It's best for both of us; best for *them* as well,' he said gently.

Sensing that she blinked her agreement, he kept his thumbs around her windpipe while lowering his fingers to the base of her neck. With but a fraction of his strength he increased the pressure, knowing that with the audible snap of her hyoid bone he had claimed her.

It was right that there'd been no violence, no unseemly struggle - the divine submission of her body going slack providing him with his demented orgasm. This time he sensed the perfect sacrifice had been fulfilled, and where with the gentlest of touches she had yielded to him. Now the only motion to signify her death came with her body slipping a short distance down the sofa, whilst a wave of blonde hair having broken free from her hair-clip fell across her face.

Part of him wished he could devour her like some giant python, swallow forever the memory that she'd ever existed.

Following the inevitable sweating and shaking fit, he remembered how quickly he'd composed himself after killing Stacey. Nor did composure entirely elude him at that moment, even as he knew his charmed life was ebbing towards its close. For it was no longer a case of *if* he were caught but *when*! It was ridiculous that he hadn't been apprehended sooner. After his deadly battle with Katy, suspicion by association already tormented his imagination. Accusing fingers from a host of witnesses had to be pointing at him. They simply had to!

For a moment he couldn't move, didn't *want* to move. Why not just sit there with the warmth of the dead girl complementing the warmth of his drawing room? Let the moment linger while watching the log embers in the fire die in the grate. He could take action later. Something seemed to be giving up on him *inside,* something he neither cared about nor wished to control anymore.

'*Enjoy the moment!*' whispered one of his demons. There was no need for further pretence, no need for the perpetuation of his silly games as charming pretender, no further masquerade of fatherly concern. The dark wheel of fate had turned full circle.

'How does it feel?' Was it another demon speaking?

He could not deny the voice. '*Good!*' he answered out loud.

Only when the front door bell rang was he brought back to the real world with his survival instincts restored in an instant. '*Christ!*' he thought. 'What shall I do?'

Going to the door and opening it he faced one of his fellow canons, mimicking an exaggerated sense of cold and stamping his feet.

'Hallo, Hugo,' said the provost. 'What can I do for you?'

The night was chilly enough not to leave him standing there, although he would have to stop him venturing any further than the hallway.

'I need to clarify a few details about our Good Friday procession,' replied the other. 'Is now a convenient moment?'

'Well, actually, I'm afraid not,' replied Christopher, 'I've just had a phone call to say that a close friend of mine up in Yorkshire has been taken seriously ill. In fact, I'm considering at this very moment whether or not to make an emergency visit.'

'I'm sorry to hear that, Christopher,' replied Hugo. 'But surely it's not advisable to go up tonight. I mean, as you can see, the weather's looking decidedly dodgy. Are you planning on driving?'

It was clear that the flurries of snow seen earlier were

increasing in the lights of the deanery courtyard.

'I don't see that I've got much choice,' replied Christopher.

'Well, can I come in just for a moment?' asked the other. The cold suggested that a visit into his living room, however brief, would be only a natural courtesy.

'Yes, yes, come in,' said Wilkes, although his agitated tone hinted clearly that Hugo's visit was ill timed. They got as far as the hall.

At that moment the phone in the hall rang leaving Christopher to respond to what clearly was a highly distressed caller at the other end. Even his visitor could hear the voice loud with anxiety, leaving him to presume that it had something to do with Wilkes' sick friend. Fortunately the gravity behind the call prompted Fr Hugo to signal a gesture that he would call another time while Christopher, looking glum, nodded his appreciation. Waving to his visitor making his exit, the provost could relax somewhat:

'Sorry, Mrs. McIver, I just had Fr Hugo at the door.'

'I feel terrible,' came the trembling voice at the other end. 'John and I had a furious row just over an hour ago and I told Marianne to clear off and she's done *just* that. What with this bad weather, I could have kicked myself five minutes later for saying such a stupid thing. You haven't by any chance seen her have you? I know she's always appreciated your kindness.'

'I'm afraid I haven't,' he replied. 'That's a worry for you. I'll certainly let you know if I hear anything – anything at all. She hasn't by any chance gone to one of her friends in the altar guild? I can't see her going far on a night like tonight.'

'I don't know. I thought I'd try you first, since she found you so helpful on another occasion when we weren't doing right by the girl.'

'I'm sure that you look after her very well normally.' The

Wilkes' charm was making its seamless return. 'Do let me know if I can be of any help, more especially when she turns up.'

'Thank you, we will!'

'Oh, by the way, please spare a thought for me' said Christopher. 'I've just heard that a friend of mine up in Yorkshire has been taken seriously ill, and I think I'll be driving up to see him … maybe even tonight.'

'I'm sorry to hear that,' responded Mrs. McIver. 'I'll remember you in my prayers. You'll need to drive carefully though. The weather's turned quite nasty. Let's hope Marianne comes to her senses and returns very shortly.'

'Yes indeed, let's hope so. Try not to worry unduly,' replied Christopher. 'Goodnight.'

No sooner had he put the phone down, than he thought, *'Christ Almighty,* they'll be sending out a search party any moment, judging from her tone of voice.'

Returning to his study the girl's body had slipped further down the sofa. Apart from her fists being clenched, she looked peaceful enough to be asleep. Where once more murder did not *look* like murder, her sublime pose helped to calm him. But Hugo's visit, followed by Mrs. McIver's phone call, plus the quick-thinking lie of needing to visit an ailing friend in Yorkshire, stirred the adrenalin that but ten minutes earlier had been so strangely subdued.

He knew that he had to hurry. Fleetingly the thought occurred to him to place her body in his Elizabethan carved coffer, a magnificent oak chest kept in his dining room and in which he might safely conceal her until morning. But no, for his alibi to hold, he had to leave that night, thereby urging him to go upstairs so as to change out of his clerical shirt, to dress more suitably and pack a bag.

It was while he was removing his shirt that he noticed how one of his green jade cufflinks had gone missing. Too late to look now, he told himself, even though he loved those subtle little ornaments to his wealth and hated it when anything that was a part of him – more especially when it was a coveted item of jewellery such as a cufflink – disappeared. Minutes later, dressed in a practical polo neck jumper with ski jerkin, thermal underwear and warm double-knit hiking trousers, he went out to his LandRover kept in the garage to the rear of the provost's manse.

Along with his London mews his vehicle was a sort of additional home in which his other self - that of the fugitive, could take flight at any time. For always fuelled up and ready with a stock of provisions, he could make his getaway at short notice. Along with such equipment as a camping stove, emergency rations, sleeping bag, ropes and a storm tent, he kept a full supply of foul-weather clothing. Incongruously he'd also left a cathedral alb lying on the rear seat.

Leaving a note for his housekeeper to explain that he'd had to make an emergency trip up north, he requested specifically that she was to dust and vacuum the drawing room thoroughly. The time was twenty to nine and he phoned another of his clergy colleagues who, whether he was in or out, invariably took messages on his answering machine after 8 p.m:

'Edward,' he addressed the voicemail, 'it's the provost here. I'm sorry but I've had to leave at short notice to go and visit a very sick friend up in Yorkshire. Father Hugo also knows and although I don't anticipate *not* returning within the next forty-eight hours, please provide cover for me if I'm not here. Although the weather doesn't look good, I feel obligated to go. Thank you so much and I trust that this doesn't inconvenience you unduly.'

Before replacing the phone, he added, 'Should you need me, you can always get me on my mobile.' He would, of course, forget to switch his mobile on.

'Now for the girl!' Mentally he already saw her as a package to be disposed of.

But before picking her up, he took some scissors to snip off a few strands of Marianne's hair before tying them into a small golden locket, which he then placed in a small mediaeval reliquary. The reliquary stood alongside an antique bracket clock on the mantelpiece in his study, the same hiding place where he kept the photograph she'd given him some time earlier. Perhaps these keepsakes represented an actual 'relic' of the martyred girl, or even a voodoo memento such as the Kenyan witch doctors practiced, in claiming both the death and soul of their victim.

Seeing that the fire in the grate was dying down to embers, he scooped up the body and taking it to the back of his LandRover placed it under a groundsheet. Outside, the moonlit sky was interspersed with clouds and flurries of snow.

He couldn't be sure why *Yorkshire* but having left messages to say that that was where he was going, he liked to keep to his word. The journey up the M1 and on to Leeds was straightforward enough. Snowploughs with their orange lights flashing were on stand-by, despite the motorway remaining clear. Notwithstanding the forecast for snow, he felt confident that the LandRover would cope on the smaller roads later on.

Leeds offered no diversions that night, causing him to drive straight through the city and taking the A660 to Otley. With the snow falling more steadily, he'd chosen to ignore his sat nav by taking the lower lying road from Ilkley up to Grassington. By then a good two inches of snow had settled on the landscape, and he knew from past experience how the more direct route via Pateley Bridge could prove treacherous.

When he reached the limestone-glaciered valley of

Wharfedale, the night sky cleared once more. In the moonlight the area looked majestic with its snow-covered slopes, and by following the narrow road to the east of the river Wharfe, he came to a remote parking spot. With visibility greatly improved, there was to his right beyond a farm gate a gentle valley sweeping upwards to an outcrop of conifers.

Wishing to conceal Marianne's body away from the road, he could see that the trees were encompassed within a broken down wall. Donning a ski-hat, kagoul and hiking boots and pulling on a pair of mittens, he lifted the body from the tailgate of his car. Being no great weight, he set about his task with vigour. Holding the body close in that way meant for the moment that the fantasy of knowing nothing of the girl's death had to stay suspended. Once she was gone she could return to his other world of phantoms.

He reached the little windbreak of trees in less than fifteen minutes. No vehicles passed the stationary LandRover below, and the location appeared to be ideal. Plenty of loose boulders lay strewn about from a section of wall that had collapsed and whose need of repair appeared neither urgent nor necessary.

With the cold accelerating rigor mortis he placed her stiffening corpse on the ground by the wall, carefully stacking a cairn of stones around and over her. He did this with apparent tenderness, like a father tucking up his daughter for a goodnight kiss. Once the first covering was complete he became more casual, as he added to the pile by throwing stones at will. Briefly he stood back to inspect the scene, checking that the stones gave no impression of having been unnaturally disturbed. It was as he began retracing his steps to the car that he felt the usual surge of relief, not even spooked as a pair of owls began to hoot close by.

By reversing back down the original track he'd taken and

with the use of a small car valet brush, he painstakingly swept each retreating footprint back to the LandRover. All being well, more snow might fall in the night and any tyre tracks left in the snow would, he trusted, pretty much typify those left by other four-by-four vehicles. It was around midnight, and confident that by daybreak the field rising up to the outcrop of rocks by the broken wall would appear undisturbed, he drove south turning west on the A65. A few miles east of the M6 he found a quiet parking spot and, wrapped up in his sleeping bag, spent the rest of the night asleep in his vehicle.

There were indeed a few further flurries of snow, as he slept better that night than he had done for weeks.

## Chapter 40

'Edward, I'm beginning to get seriously worried.' Fr Hugo had called in at his neighbour's house after conducting early morning communion.

'You mean about Christopher?' the other canon second-guessed him.

'Yes, I mean he said he'd had to go up to Yorkshire. Nor can I reach him on his mobile, and he's made no contact with us as he promised he would.'

Fr Hugo was the most levelheaded of the somewhat other worldly canons who occupied the cathedral close adjacent to the provost's house. With his slim physique topped with a shock of white hair, he bore an uncanny resemblance to a certain deceased English cardinal.

'Well, he clearly had someone very much on his mind by needing to leave so suddenly.' Edward always found it more edifying to think evil of no one.

'That's just the point,' replied Hugo. 'What worries me is that Marianne – the girl acolyte – has also been missing for over twenty-four hours.'

He refrained from elaborating on this association, in view of that other girl who'd gone missing from Wilkes' previous parish only to be discovered dead well over a year later.

But it wasn't just Hugo on that Wednesday in Holy Week left with a growing sense of panic. Others feared a connection between the disappearance of Marianne McIver and the provost. *'Pray God!'* it began to be whispered, *'that it's not so.'* But the disappearance of both Wilkes and the girl was being perceived, if nothing more, as a sickening coincidence.

The previous evening the local paper ran a short paragraph, which included a courageous admission by Mr. and Mrs. McIver.

*A seventeen-year-old schoolgirl Marianne McIver went missing last night following a row with her mother and stepfather, which both parents bitterly regret. She left the house and has not been seen since. Mr. and Mrs. McIver want their daughter to know that they love her very much, and trust that their argument can be sorted out. All they want is for her to contact them and to return home safely.*

Emotions were running high at The Magpie. Nor were niceties spared for their two return visitors, the Revd Caroline Meggart, the new vicar-elect of All Saints along with her husband Bill. Caroline's installation was due to take place a week after Easter and in visiting The Magpie for a quiet drink, she and her husband were unprepared for the conversation that ensued.

Talk of the acolyte Marianne having gone missing was started by Zbierski. 'Me, I don't like the sound of 'zis,' his voice jerked with emotion. 'There's a lassie at 'zat Minster/Cathedral place wot's disappeared. Christ God Almighty, I hope it ain't got nothing to do with Stacey.'

There was a stunned silence. Nobody needed reminding how the name of Stacey was synonymous with abduction and murder.

Nick Crooks' had nearly choked on his pint pot, as his head jerked up. *'Holy shit!'* – Zbierski's observation made him forget that there was a lady vicar present and, what was more, the successor to *him*. But the expletive did no damage, and besides he couldn't have stopped himself: 'You don't think Wilkes has got anything to do with it, do you?' With the colour draining from his face, Crooks' question came out more as an observation.

Before she could help herself, Caroline Meggart interjected, 'as it happens I understood my predecessor the provost had to go to Yorkshire on Monday night to visit a sick friend. I needed to speak to him today about my own service but apparently as yet he hasn't returned.'

Although she'd blurted this out as a statement of fact, she had, on the one occasion when she'd met Wilkes, taken an instant dislike to him. If ever a guy made her skin crawl, *he* had; her sixth sense yelling at her that something was seriously wrong with the man.

Even Z went white, as he said: 'But *she* went missing on Monday night!' It was then that he asked: 'Crooks, dinna thou say something about 'zat provost having the hots for the girl that time that thou saw her?'

'*Holy shit!*' repeated Crooks. All too vividly he remembered how Wilkes had looked at the altar girl on the night when he'd taken his mum to her service. It was only a fortnight or so ago, and where by all accounts they had to be speaking about the same girl. Nor could Z and his pals forget the way Crooks had described it, of how she'd looked at Wilkes 'like she was high on drugs or something'.

Unable to say anything more, Crooks didn't need to.

With the weather continuing cold, Marianne's prolonged absence heightened fears all round. Later on that Wednesday night before Easter, a special ten-minute showing of 'Crimewatch' was added to the evening news highlighting Marianne's disappearance. This extra news item having become common knowledge in Ketborough, Ben Carter had phoned Frances urging her to watch in.

The woman presenter produced a large head and shoulders photograph of Marianne McIver, asking: 'has anyone seen this missing schoolgirl? Marianne lives in the Midlands town of Fordham. Aged seventeen she was last seen by her parents having had an argument with them on Monday night, while then regrettably walking out. The night was cold, as it is tonight and, at first, it was assumed she'd gone to visit friends, or to meet with someone whom she trusted.'

Nobody had seen Marianne approach the provost's house and although suspicions were heightened, the police inquiry drew no immediate response.

If it was possible to bring a measure of comfort to Frances, now faced with the additional fears over Marianne's disappearance that week, the following morning's post succeeded. The letter began,

*Dearest Mum,*

*I'm not sure how to begin this letter, seeing that I have been incommunicado for so long. Anywhere here goes. I hardly dare ask how you are when I know so much of what's gone off. Probably no words are sufficient to express your true feelings, any more than are mine to express regrets. Safe to say – no doubt, we've both gone through hell. Sometime later on I'll tell you the really scary bit.*

*But let me tell you the real news from my end, KATY WILKES IS BETTER!! And when I say better, I mean CURED, unhooked, no more a junkie. Cocaine is out of my life and out of my system and I still can't believe it, even as I write!*

*You have probably guessed the direction my life went in so as to feed my habit. I'm not excusing what's happened. It was bloody terrible in so many ways. And yet, because of all that, I believe that in a strange way I am a stronger person maybe than many who've never hit the skids.*

*I know that things went completely crazy after Stacey went*

*missing. But now that you and that man whom I can no longer even think of as D-a-d have split up, I feel that I can relate to you in an entirely different way.*

*I promise that I shall come to see you in your new home very soon. What's more, I shall bring Kes. Kes is my new boyfriend and since it was he who helped me break free of drugs, I feel I owe him more than life itself.*

*Dearest Mum, I want you to know that some people may see me as the most un-Christian soul, who ever walked out on so much that others don't have! In some ways they could be right. Yet although I wouldn't describe myself as a Christian (Never have!!), I feel I've gone through some long dark night of the soul and am better for it a million fold!*

*Anyway I promise that Kes and I will see you very soon. – All my love,*

*Katy.*

*P. S. Say hello to Dom from his kid sister!*

*P.P.S. I feel sure that you would want to write or email me (if you now have one of those things!). But please be patient, I will make contact again very shortly once I've got a new address.*

Tears that had stubbornly refused to come for so long through shock, terror and dread now cascaded. Frances felt in some extraordinary way that with the healing of Katy and notwithstanding the terror at what might have happened to Marianne, there had to be an end to the nightmare soon.

Tragedy and joy vied for her attention.

With all interested parties having tuned in to the 'Crimewatch' programme, Christopher Wilkes had late that Thursday night become the sole suspect in what was widely presumed to be Marianne's abduction, if not murder.

Having been on patrol at or around the very times when the bodies of Stacey and Roxanne had been disposed of, Sgt

Dench of the Ambleside constabulary had, from the accounts given, decided that Roxanne's killer was a well-spoken, well-to-do middle-aged white male. If her vicar had killed Stacey – this being a hunch Dench had held on to, after checking out the man's Volvo registration all those months back - then the two murders could well be connected. If as seemed likely the third missing girl called Marianne had herself been murdered, then as far as Dench was concerned he had Wilkes bang to rights. Marianne after all came from very close to where Stacey lived. With two daughters in their mid to late teens, the police sergeant's emotions were on red alert. Whoever the son of a bitch was, he'd love nothing more than to run him to the ground personally.

The two police officers who had first interviewed Wilkes over Stacey and who Wilkes could only remember by their numbers 331 and 442; *they'd* seen the programme. The Magpie clientele had seen and videoed it. Most of the staff and canons at Fordham cathedral had seen it, as had Ben and Angela and Frances. Katy too had seen a photo-fit picture on the front of a newspaper that was clearly her father, as had Mark Tipperary who, no question, identified the face of his erstwhile climbing companion. And in a quiet upstairs room of a discreet Bed and Breakfast, Christopher Wilkes had seen his reflection on the screen. His landlord downstairs was aware of a man on the run, but failed to make the connection.

No longer reluctant to name him, 'Crimewatch' had described Wilkes as someone they said could' help them with their inquiries', and who was believed to have driven north from the Midlands. People were advised to be on the look-out for a well-spoken, sixty-year-old man of tall well in excess of six feet tall and graying at the temples, with the peculiar distinguishing feature of having eyes of a differing shade of brown. Descriptions were also given of his near-new LandRover. The alert applied especially to those living in Yorkshire, or in the vicinity of the Lake District, which Wilkes was known to frequent and which by common agreement, seemed to be the killer's favoured location for dumping his victims.

Although the landlord gave fleeting consideration to his new arrival upstairs, he hadn't taken much note of his appearance and chose to think no more about it. Guests, who were into climbing, as he said he was, came and went all the time. Nor was there anything disreputable about Wilkes, who having paid cash in advance made out that he'd arrived by train. He'd left his LandRover in an overnight car park nearby.

It was only with Wilkes' unarranged pre-breakfast departure that an immediate phone call was made to Ambleside police station.

With no contact having been made to Fordham diocese, the 'Crimewatch' programme had all but told the world that the provost was their main suspect on two counts of murder, and a further one of abduction; with the latter now causing the police to fear for the worst. As for that other suspect held on remand – the car-thief Merv Costello held for the murder of the Leeds' prostitute, he was growing more vocal by the day.

By leaving his lodgings early without taking breakfast, Wilkes drew added attention to himself and to his immediate whereabouts, and of all people it was Robert Dench who first spotted him just before eight o'clock that Thursday morning. Driving back towards Grasmere police station after a stint on night duty it was the LandRover's number plate that first alerted him, the registration having been chalked up on the office memory board the previous night. It left the patrolman feeling incredulous at having sighted one of Britain's most wanted fugitives driving straight past him.

'Christ!' thought Dench, 'It's *him*. It's gotta be!'

Knowing that he was tired with the weather going from clear and cold to dull and cold with a lowering mist, he had to think fast. Although the main road was passable enough having been gritted, the side roads had already proved difficult in the Ford Focus. Yet instinct made him turn around and once the rear fog lights of Wilkes' vehicle came into view, he tried to stay in sight of the vehicle while keeping his distance.

The adrenalin pumped hard. Contact made with Ambleside police station now confirmed that Wilkes was in the immediate vicinity, making Dench desperate and excited to collar the killer personally. Ever since hearing of the death of Stacey Witcombe, he knew he 'owed' it to his own teenage daughters to protect his area and, God willing, to arrest the killer should he ever venture up there again.

And now against all the odds as though by some divine fate, it was *he* who had seen the suspect and was now in pursuit. Talk about 'the Lord working in mysterious ways'! Of course, he'd had to radio through to the station to tell them that he was commandeering the police car, in order to try and make an arrest and although obliged to call for further assistance, he really did want this parson-devil for himself.

But the side roads remained treacherous, and where just before reaching Grasmere, Wilkes took a left going towards Easedale, a narrow road running parallel to the main one to the east. '*Damn him!*' yelled Dench. With the other driver ignoring the police car's flashing lights and the worsening road conditions, Wilkes was already gaining a distinct advantage.

Knowing the area well, he realized that if he followed the

road through it would return back onto the 591, allowing other police cars to intercept their quarry at the far end. But Wilkes knew that too. Although he would have preferred the higher and more rugged terrain of Mount Helvellyn to the east, the location where he now found himself could have been a lot worse. Hoping to put enough distance between himself and his floundering pursuer, Wilkes was already planning his next moves. By disposing of the LandRover and climbing the western ridge known as Steel Fell, he could camp out if need be for as long as was necessary.

Dench had difficulty staying in control. 'It's *him – no question*,' he spoke out loud. 'If he had nothing to hide, he'd have stopped long ago. Damn these bloody road conditions. This is crazy weather just before Easter, and I'm losing him.'

Recalling that it was Maundy Thursday, the sergeant reflected on the irony of pursuing a so-called gentleman of the cloth, for whom it should have been his busy time of the year – not someone taking flight through the slush and snow, trying to escape a murder charge. But with the LandRover disappearing out of sight and despite radioing for help in the hope that Wilkes might have been forced back onto the main road, Dench had to abandon the chase.

With growing satisfaction that he'd out-driven his pursuer, Wilkes managed to make a methodical and quick exit up a country track, completely unobserved.

# Chapter 41

'Bloody stupid weather,' he muttered to himself. 'Daffodils and primroses out and cold enough to freeze the nuts off a tomcat!'

Given the current cold snap, George Appleyard knew that he'd have to check out his two hundred or more ewes, many of which had already lambed. Notwithstanding his own mood, his two collies Jess and Jake were running about throwing up spangled flecks of ice, as they barked excitedly in the fresh fallen snow.

Not that the weather was bad in Wharfedale first thing on that Thursday morning, just cold. The valley was veiled in a rising mist already being burnt off by bright sunshine, but with a strong northerly wind and two or three inches of snow having fallen overnight, spring had flipped back to winter. The shepherd didn't much fancy negotiating the slippery limestone ridge leading on to the higher plateau where most of his sheep would perversely gather in all weathers. Nor was there any way he could take the quad. 'Shank's pony it is, damn it' he complained further. If necessary he would have to carry each of the lambs to the shelter, which he kept available for such contingencies.

As they careered around on the lower slopes going up to Grassington Moor, it was Jess who made a detour veering to the left. Jake was soon drawn to the spot by the excited barks of the other and with both creatures barking furiously, George felt obliged to investigate. The dogs had jumped inside a broken triangle of limestone wall where there grew a handful of tired looking conifers.

Although he could see nothing he was alerted by the same odour that had drawn his dogs to the place, and where Jess was now pawing at some rocks.

'What you got there, lass?' asked George of his companions, with both of them looking at him with their heads tilted to one side. In sensing their unease, he sought reassurance by talking to them some more. 'Calm down, calm down,' he said even as both collies started to whine and paw vigorously at the stones. 'You've probably found another dead ewe.' But even as he spoke he knew that anything dead and then *deliberately* concealed, spelt something of a different order.

Balancing himself with his stick and using his free-gloved hand, he began to remove some of the stones from the cairn whence the smell came. The dogs resumed their barking as he did so.

It was the cashmere cardigan's vivid colour that first caught his eye. Then, when he saw strands of fine blonde hair, he felt mesmerized. With a sickening awareness that he had stumbled across the corpse of a young girl, with only marginal signs of decay, he wanted to throw up and stagger away at the same time. Even as he made his discovery, he remembered hearing a news item that morning about a young girl who'd gone missing the previous night. He also recalled there being some mention of Yorkshire as well.

As he fought off nausea and dizziness and rested on his stick to steady himself, a glint of gold caught his eye. He composed himself enough to look again. There, unmistakably emerging from the side of her small left fist rested an item of jewellery whose identity was unusual, but easily recognizable. Overcoming his revulsion, he peered more closely. As though cradling some small bright creature and now balanced almost lovingly in her half-open palm rested a jade and gold cufflink.

With signals being non-existent in that place he hadn't brought his mobile, but nor did he wish to stay a moment longer. Ignoring his sheep, Appleyard ran and slid down the hill with his dogs. He had to run and stumble a further half mile to his cottage before gasping an order to his astonished wife: 'For God's sake, ring the police!'

*'Jesus wept!'* said Ben – scarcely considering how apt was his expletive in that Holy Week just before Easter.

They were sitting in numbed silence in Frances' living room, the news reports of the previous twelve hours having brought them together. Baby Emma was asleep in her pram.

'At least everyone knows now,' said Ben. 'There surely can be nobody, but *nobody,* left in any doubt as to knowing the truth about Fordham's provost.'

For several minutes they were too numb to speak. Eventually Frances tried to distract them by showing them Katy's letter. In the midst of all the other mayhem, *something* somewhere had at last happened to offset the nightmare.

Despite its pain she cherished the honesty of Katy's letter, caressed by the promise that her daughter and treasured companion Kes would call before long. In all the surrounding hell, Easter joy was, at least in Kate's situation, struggling to break through. Momentarily Ben's face lit up. *'Fantastic,* Frances! That Kes guy sounds quite something,' he said, returning the letter.

'I'm sure he is,' responded Frances quietly.

But the brief respite offered by the good news over Katy quickly gave way to the tragic disappearance of Marianne.

'Oh God, how long must it be before we are left knowing for sure?' commented Angela.

'You know I feel pretty damned ashamed that I didn't go to the police earlier,' said Frances. 'And yet, in a way, I couldn't. Do you remember me telling you about some evidence that Di Hagan said he'd got, almost immediately after Stacey's death?'

They nodded.

'Well, I never could find what Di had done with it. There's no question that he would have kept it in a safe place. He was scrupulous like that. But for the love of me I couldn't discover where it was, or what he'd done with it. Of course one clear item of evidence was the photograph of Stacey, which I'd found in his cassock. But since Di took it off me for safekeeping, I've not seen it since. And not for want of trying! I've hunted high and low, going through everything with a fine toothcomb but still nothing. Nothing at all!'

It was a form of distraction that seemed to help them. 'Well, where did Di keep his papers and valuables?' asked Ben

'He kept everything of any importance,' replied Frances - 'bills, cheque books, insurance certificates, deeds to the house, etc, all in his roll-top desk, the one item of furniture that he insisted was to remain in the bungalow and which, as you can see, I've still held on to.'

Ben got up, instantly intrigued. He was examining the interior of the desk. 'Do you mind?' he asked Frances who shook her head.

'Did you know?' he asked, 'that many desks of an earlier period had numerous concealed compartments. Some of the old Georgian bureaux would have a hidden well containing any number of cubicles and secret drawers. They seemed pretty paranoid in those days about preserving their secrets. Most of the hidden drawers went out by the time of the Victorians. But let's check it out anyway.'

A typical Edwardian roll-top, its top was already open. He pulled out a few drawers, but they were no more than drawers free of any hidden recesses lurking behind.

But then applying downward pressure with the fingers of both hands on the writing area of the desk, itself encompassed by a shallow bead surround, there came an audible click. Ben then pushed back a sliding panel to reveal a concealed drawer underneath.

'There you go!' he breathed with satisfaction. 'And look you here at *this,*' he whistled. The shallow drawer contained nothing more than a white envelope, marked, 'Incriminating evidence against one Revd Christopher Wilkes.'

Instantly the two women were on their feet, scarcely breathing as Ben opened the envelope to reveal the long-lost photograph of Stacey smiling and innocent in her swimsuit. Also there were a few penned details about the mileage of Wilkes' Volvo between when the car had been MOT'd the previous week and over the weekend of Stacey's disappearance. 'At least 400 miles unaccounted for?' had been written with a large question mark.

On a second piece of paper and written in Di's spidery hand they read: 'Got interrupted from examining in further detail the oak coffer at the back of All Saints Church, Ketborough, on the Tuesday after her disappearance.' Along with the date there then came an unanswered question: 'And where was the old sash cord and altar cover that I put in the chest, when I supervised the replacement of the window sashes?' This question clearly bothered him, as did his other observation: 'If Stacey had been placed in the coffer, which I strongly suspect, then surely fibres from her clothing or something would have been found there. My cock-up was in not checking the coffer, as I should have done, and then contaminating the evidence by putting the robes in there. Damn stupid of me. Must advise the police to <u>examine the coffer regardless.</u>'

Frances sat down too upset to speak. She could vividly recall that hot summer's day so soon after Stacey's disappearance, and of how Di had been peering inside the coffer when she'd presented him with a glass of iced tea. It must have been *she* who'd caused the 'interruption'.

With each of them feeling sick to their stomach, Angela sank to her knees and then on to all fours, while Ben being the first to recover telephoned the police. He advised them that an immediate search of the chest was imperative.

As he telephoned, all that Frances could mutter to Angela was, 'thank God I didn't ask Philippa over to join us!'

Taking Frances' hand, Angela said gently, 'Poor old Di, what with his illness and concern for you, he must have overlooked giving you this information.'

It was just coming up to midday and they tuned into the national news: 'the body of a young girl was discovered this morning in the Yorkshire Dales. Although she has not been formally identified, she was said to be wearing jeans, with a pink cashmere cardigan and cream satin blouse.'

The item ended, Ben snapped off the radio.

'*Oh, sweet Mary Mother of Jesus!*' said Angela. 'That has to be Marianne. They gave out what she was wearing last night, and I distinctly remember mention of a pink cashmere cardigan.'

A further agonized silence followed.

Seeing how agitated Ben was becoming, Angela advised: 'Look Ben, why don't *I* go to the police station. You know what you should do? Go and see the McIvers, or at least check that they are getting some attention. Quite probably the police have contacted them. Somebody like yourself needs to be with them for what looks like the inevitable.'

It was a galling duty but Ben agreed to go straightaway.

Later that day Marianne's body was formally identified in a Leeds mortuary. Dental records had no need to be checked, since facially she was easily identified from her photograph. An anorak concealed nearby under another small heap of stones contained a letter, addressed to her with some reference to plans for a 'gap year,' and a brochure about voluntary work overseas. The forensic lamp had picked up some small strands of black cotton thread in one of the girl's fingernails. Traces of saliva and sweat around her face were analyzed as having arrived there at the time of her death, not yet twenty-fours hours previously. The obvious bruising from two thumbprints was clearly visible on either side of her Adam's apple. A gold and jade cufflink would tell its own story in due course. All that was now needed was for the girl's parents to formally identify her.

Fortunately, Ben Carter who had been with the McIvers when the phone call came through insisted that he'd be the one to drive them up to Leeds. While Mr. McIver remained stone-faced and pale, Marianne's mother became inconsolable.

Maundy Thursday saw Fordham Cathedral thrown into outright confusion. The elaborate Passover supper and foot-washing ceremony planned for that evening was cancelled, while the choir was instructed not to convene for any of the Easter programme, with only the diocesan canons agreeing to conduct a silent vigil.

The panic was further compounded on account of there being neither a bishop nor a provost to offer any respite. With Letharge's death still too recent for any successor to have been announced, only a retired assistant bishop was on hand to conduct a very sombre Good Friday service, with special prayers being said for the girl and her family.

News that the Very Revd Christopher Wilkes was now the only suspect wanted in connection with Marianne's murder and other associated murders, left the diocese numb with disbelief.

'It's him! It's gotta be. *The filthy bastard!*'

Merv Costello was rooted to his small prison radio when the news of Marianne's murder came through. All the talk was of some vicar being involved and that he might be linked to two other murders including that of a Leeds prostitute. Knowing how he'd been banged up on a twisted pretext, the young car thief had grown apoplectic with rage.

The nearest that Costello could get to finding a confidante was the prison chaplain. At least *he* appeared to take seriously his protestations of innocence, when all around him other members of staff along with the inmates had chosen to convict him already. Not only that, comments from the trivial to the menacing were getting to him: 'Yeah, well there's no whore to answer for herself, is there, Costello?' Or, from a few of the inmates, 'You're just shit-scared at what's coming to you, you fucking nonce!'

In the prison code of ethics, the murder of a prostitute was only one degree better than that of child molesting. In the retribution stakes meted out on the prison landings, even the killing of your wife or girlfriend was more acceptable Having already had his food pissed in, as well as taking a glancing blow from a snooker ball stuffed inside a sock, he knew that retribution wouldn't stop at that. A further threat of sugar steeped in boiling water and flung in his face was a distinct possibility. Yet he stubbornly held out against becoming a 'vulnerable prisoner' for his own protection,

Although a VP might feel safer there was no way he was going to join the low-lifes of paedophiles and bent coppers, it being tantamount to an admission of guilt. Although sometimes it might pay to own upto non-existent guilt, since that way the system awarded you more privileges, he'd got nothing to plead guilty to. So in the twisted goings on in prison life, it felt better to take his chances and stay put! But that said he was getting seriously hacked off.

On that Good Friday, Costello took refuge in the chapel to share in an hour-long meditation of Bible readings about Christ's Passion. He sat up with a start at the bit where Pontius Pilate, having washed his hands of Jesus, said that there was nothing more he could do. But being the Passover, tradition had it that one prisoner could be exchanged for another, leaving Pilate to ask: 'And who do you want me to release in place of Jesus?' And the crowd hollered out, 'Give us Barabbas!' And the reading went on to say that Barabbas was *bad* news, a murderer and a robber.

'Christ, I'm the one who's banged up. Nicking motors ain't the same as murder. And some murdering pervert's out there large as life doing his thing with me doing *his* fucking bird,' he explained to the chaplain afterwards.

The youth was incensed. 'I've been framed by the fucking Old Bill. Some tarty bitch called Barbara tried stitching me up. *I know it!* Got me talking about what turned me on out of the ordinary - Was I into kinky sex? Even saying she'd really fancy me if I was into that sort of shit.'

When not consumed by prejudice, some prison staff can tell if there's been a miscarriage of justice. And having spoken with him before, the chaplain felt a hundred percent sure that Costello wasn't lying. This instinct was backed up when, before returning to his cell, the remand prisoner had rounded on him with a final remark:

'I don't pretend to be Christ. But I sure as hell ain't no bastard Barabbas!'

# Chapter 42

He cursed his luck as the small Ford Focus came to a halt only to slither backwards. The oppressive mist hampered his chances further. 'Typical bloody Lake District,' he moaned, knowing that to the east of the country the forecast had been for glorious sunshine.

Sgt Dench had verified all he needed to know - that the registration check done on the LandRover was in the name of Christopher Wilkes, the same registered owner of the Volvo Estate in the Grizedale forest whose number he'd checked out well over a year back. Of course back then he'd thought no more about it – 'After all, why shouldn't some vicar enjoy the delights of the Lakes, even if it had been raining cats and dogs at the time'?

No such charitable thoughts came now:

'The bastard's given me the slip!' he called back in. 'My guess is that he's tried to shake me off by making a detour, and that he'll presumably return further north on the A591. Try and get an X 5 at the other end and chuck down a stinger.' The force's two four wheel drives were the only suitable vehicles, with a stinger being the best tool for stopping a fleeing vehicle dead in its tracks.

After acknowledging his request, he was instructed to

return his panda car to Ambleside police station, sign off and provide a full report from the night before and of what he'd just seen. Technically after that he was off-duty. But *no way* was he going off-duty in his head! Nursing the panda car back onto an easier section of road he drove it back to the compound, only to ignore any form filling as to what had taken place. Sod the report along with the consequences, he told himself. Running the half a mile back to his home he was, come hell or high water, going to get a slice of this piece of action!

Praying to God that his hunch was right, his own plan was already taking shape. Dench had already guessed that Wilkes was an accomplished climber fully at home in the wide-open spaces. Forensic evidence on one if not more of the victims had specified the discovery of fibres from ropes used for climbing. Realizing that he was now on the run going nowhere, the only thing left was for Wilkes, surely, was to become as invisible as possible.

'If he tries going it alone in the mountains, then *bring it on!*' His resolve consolidated itself into those three words, as he spoke out loud. From thereon things were now personal. Ever since the dumping of choirgirl Stacey Witcombe on what was effectively his beat, the police officer and father of two teenage daughters had along with the momentum of a mid-life crisis, got himself back into full physical fitness. Above everything he was sickened by the death of the girl. But with so much of his career relegated to one to that of the sedentary form-filling, computer-literate copper, he'd needed his workouts in the mountains just to stay sane.

Might fate be giving him the opportunity for running Wilkes to ground on his own turf? It was an extraordinary outcome if so, more so as with the present low cloud no air search would be possible, and with a long bank holiday weekend's leave ahead, he was technically free to do with his time as he chose. His only oversight was not to have filled out some bloody report!

Despite a whole night shift behind him he was now fully awake, leaving his thoughts racing as he stuffed warm clothing into a backpack. Explaining to his wife that he felt morally bound to pursue the fugitive whom he took to be the Lakeside killer, she warned him: 'For God's sake darling, *be* careful!' Even as she spoke, she was making up flasks of coffee and some other suitable provisions. She knew her Bob well enough to realize that in this frame of mind, he was unstoppable. What she wasn't to know was that he'd be gone for the next thirty-six hours.

'I'm going back in the car towards Easedale Tarn. That's where I last saw him,' he told her. 'Of course he may have gone back onto the main road, in which case I'll have seen him off my patch. But if he has gone into the hills, the cloud cover is too dense for any aerial view of him.' Seeking to reassure her he then added: 'Anyway, I'll take my mobile and keep you posted.'

Theirs being a common-sense sort of marriage he was grateful for her practical level-headedness in a crisis. Even as he spoke she told herself to 'forget it', when contemplating the bank holiday weekend together that might have been.

Wisely Dench chose not to underestimate his quarry. Wilkes may have been approaching sixty but he might well be extremely fit. As a desperate man with climbing skills, he was not an adversary to trifle with. The weather also presented a challenge. Donning gear suitable for ice and snow, he knew that if the sun broke through, conditions could change markedly. But now at half past nine in the morning with the weather remaining foggy and cold, the forecast indicated more of the same.

Having seen off the fatuous flashing lights of the police car,

Wilkes couldn't deny feeling smug. Ever since their rude cross-examining of him over the disappearance of Stacey Witcombe, he felt an almost delinquent disregard for the police. Any further bouts of interrogation, with questions such as: 'Can I see your driving license, sir', or, 'might you know anything about a young girl called Marianne McIver?' were not to be contemplated. And now with news having just come over the car radio, that the body of a girl answering Marianne's description had been discovered in the Yorkshire Dales, Wilkes knew he'd crumple under such scrutiny.

'*Jesus,* they can't have found her so soon!' was all he could gasp. *'It has to be someone else!'* This seemed the only way to cope with this new eventuality, before reality kicked in: 'Anyway, I covered all my tracks!' His self-preservation sought to console him.

In two minds about chancing his arm and doubling back to take the minor road leading to Langsdale Fell, he certainly had no plans to take the main road. By turning back a mile or so on the side road, he could still reach his objective by ascending the ridge known as Steel Fell, while then cutting back in a southwesterly direction. His immediate problem now was to get rid of his vehicle, which drew attention to himself. The LandRover, too shiny by half, was what some liked to call a 'Chelsea tractor', not nearly battered enough to blend in with other farm four by fours.

Vanishing into the worsening weather was his best option.

Deliberately he drove up a rough track to a spot where he was out of sight from the road. Mud and slush almost up to the LandRover's axles meant that few others, even on foot, would be willing or able to follow, and where with a final gunning of the engine he plunged the vehicle deep into some bushes.

From the back of the LandRover he yanked out his ladder

rucksack onto which were already secured groundsheet, storm tent, sleeping bag and where in further compartments he kept a camping stove, emergency rations, and an extra pair of cross-trainers. He also donned a full set of waterproofs and sturdy trekking boots. His only regret was that his all-weather jacket was of fluorescent orange, which was fine in the event of being rescued in an emergency, but not for concealment purposes. So grabbing another item of clothing to use as camouflage he stuffed this into a side-pocket of his haversack.

Although he had no long-term plan for staying out indefinitely, he entertained the unreal notion that, by lying low, he might yet perform some Houdini-style mode of escape. Outside in the wilds, fantasy began to return once more. Was not his a *charmed* life, after all? Recalling how the bishop had given him promotion, when all seemed lost, might the charm be still working? If he couldn't vanish forever then maybe he could concoct some story to say how he'd lost his memory, and simply wandered off? Amnesia wasn't unheard of. As for the killing of any young women, whether coincidental or otherwise, he had no knowledge of them whatsoever.

Part of him still chose to think of himself as innocent. But right now, none of that mattered since he chose only to become absorbed in the wilds of nature, to be devoured by its timeless stillness and thereby reclaim his freedom. For it was a sensation that never left him, where denied the wild open spaces of nature he never lost the feeling of somehow being in his own prison.

With everything he needed, he set off at a brisk pace and, despite the deteriorating weather, headed towards the lower escarpment of Steel Fell. The dense cloud with sleet turning to snow felt comforting, in that it re-enforced his sense of being alone in the world. In places the snow was mushy and deep and despite using exposed rock where possible, he could however do nothing to conceal a steady line of footprints. Three hours into his stride and he had reached the peak of Steel Fell. On a clear day there would have been a spectacular view of Lake Thurlmere lying to the west, with Mount Helvellyn rising to the east.

Climbing in fog is easier than having to descend into it. Not that the descent from where he stood was unduly severe, it was just that by walking downwards one ran the risk of disorientation. Moving southwest in the direction of Rake Crag, the sodden peat beneath the snow along with the gradual incline reassured him that he was going in the right direction. He then circled around what he took to be Grasmere Common to his east, by which stage the enveloping fog not only hampered his progress it left him feeling exhausted. It was just after four in the afternoon.

Finding a small plateau of drier land away from the peat bog and shielded by an outcrop of rock, he decided to pitch his tent. A swollen stream bubbled with willful innocence nearby. Using his portable stove, he heated up a tin of sardines, devouring them from the tin. Washed down with a hot drink, he also ate two unbuttered stale rolls. His dessert was to chew on some dried apricot, rounded off with pieces of high glucose chocolate. On that Maundy Thursday he reflected upon how brief had been his term as provost at the Minster. But with nature now being his cathedral, so to speak, only a small part of him hankered for the role now.

Was this sad apology for a meal his 'last supper' as a free man?

It was only eight o'clock when he turned in for the night. A good night's sleep was crucial if he was to eke out his strength and keep going. Listening to the stream outside, he knew how different would be the sight of where he now lay on a bright summer's day. In the present conditions, he felt as remote as though being on Mars – *exactly* how he wanted it. But with the Bank Holiday weekend pending, backpackers in more clement conditions could venture out in droves. So would the bad weather hold?

Thankful for the temporary reprieve offered by the darkness and the fog, he'd tune into the news and weather first thing in the morning.

Glimpses of sunlight the next day told him what he most feared.

Doing so as quickly as he could, Robert Dench had returned to the road beneath Easedale Tarn, this time driving his own small four-wheel drive vehicle. Inevitably there had been some farm traffic since his pursuit of Wilkes an hour or so earlier, so he restricted his search only to a brief section of road from where he knew there were several tracks going uphill.

Hating the prospect of having to leave matters in the hands of others, if not to different forces nationwide, he only half expected to win on this one, He just hoped against hope that Wilkes might have chosen to take to the hills, thereby entering a domain in which they would both feel at home.

Painstakingly he explored each of the tracks off the Grasmere road, which led westwards towards the higher valley. Although not an expert on tyre-treads, he had a mental image of the Pirelli tyre that was standard footwear for LandRovers. Here he was further helped by the snow allowing him to identify the most recent tracks of farm vehicles left on top of the labyrinth of other tracks in the mud underneath.

His exploration was tedious and time-consuming but after almost two hours he alighted upon what he believed to be a set of Pirelli treads, disappearing up a track that funneled into what was no wider than a bridle path. He drove his own vehicle as far as he could, leaving it where the path began. Following the tracks further and going through some deep mud, he was ecstatic to discover Wilkes' LandRover about a hundred yards further on. Clearly the vehicle had been driven under maximum power, tearing a path through the undergrowth to a point where it had almost buried itself. From the vehicle a fresh set of footprints pointed in the direction of Steel Fell.

'YES!' He said, catching his breath while adding gleefully, 'and now reverend bastard I've got you on equal terms!' He made a careful examination of the herringbone footprints, so as not to confuse them with any others.

Numb with excitement, he knew that his diligence had paid off.

If anything, he'd come better prepared than Wilkes. His kit included sleeping bag, waterproofs, hiking sticks and tent. He had nourishing food, hot drinks and excellent footwear. Crucially, despite his intention only to use it sparingly, he'd brought his mobile.

The footprints offered all that he needed. In fact as he ascended towards Steel Fell, he could safely assume that the other climber had little choice but to continue onwards and up. Clearly the other man would have had a head start of at least three to four hours, and where even as he ascended towards the summit, thick cloud and sleet were making it dangerous to proceed. On a clear day he'd run up the fell, returning back via the spur known as Gibson Knot so the route was well known to him. But now, measured caution and a respect for his own lack of sleep demanded that he call a halt.

It wasn't the best place for setting up a tent but the additional fatigue of having done night duty, followed by his exertions made him pitch where he was. Fortunately the process of erecting the small dome tent was quick and straightforward. Around 2 p.m. having eaten his sandwiches, he phoned his wife to tell her that he was fine but that due to the lousy weather, he'd crash out and see how he felt later on. It was only then that he asked her to inform the police that he'd found Wilkes' car, and to tell them that he'd gone in pursuit. The delay in tipping off the police about the LandRover had been deliberate.

'For God's sake, Bob, be careful!' was all that she felt able to counsel, adding for good measure, 'Police forces the length and breadth of Britain want this Wilkes bloke. So don't go acting the hero just for its own sake.' She then added: 'Don't forget you've got your girls to consider!'

'I know, darling. Don't worry; I'll speak to you later. But if I don't', he added, 'it's only because I can't get a signal. I can hardly hear you as it is.'

Her growing anxiety unsettled him.

He wasn't sure about these mobiles. Essential in one way, but not so good when you've got an anxious wife monitoring your every move. Besides with the signal deteriorating, he chose to switch the thing off.

Upon awakening early next morning, it had been reason more than delusion that now put the fugitive's mind on red alert. With something telling him how a new day shortened the odds against his eventual capture, it also crossed his mind that it was Good Friday. He was relieved to see how the drizzle and fog still hung in the atmosphere, despite a watery sun lurking on the horizon to half suggest that conditions might improve. Earlier the local 6 a.m. news had informed him that it was he whom the police now sought, with a warning to hikers in the Lake District to be observant for a man of his description but *not* to approach him! Fortunately the weather forecast that followed advised that, in the event of, people going out hiking they should keep only to the clearly marked paths, whilst avoiding any higher climbing into the hills.

As he took an icy wash in the stream nearby, reason was asserting itself further. Were these to be his final ablutions as a free man? He could scarcely contemplate the misery of trying to wash in the confines of prison, where showers, if provided at all, were infrequent. Still worse, as he'd heard, was the vile practice of having to 'slop out'. Important then to cherish this sound of the bubbling stream, come the day when he might no longer be free. Then with two skylarks above his head, which although out of sight were breaking into full song he needed to cherish the memory.

He chose not to cook anything for breakfast, just to eat his emergency high protein rations and fill his flasks from the mountain stream. With the air staying dank and chilly, the snow lay in sullen resistance to any thaw. Good in one way, but bad in the event of any pursuer following his footprints. Unlike the snow, he felt part of his resolve beginning to melt. What was the point in pressing on up to the Langdale Pikes? Where would he go from there? He had the fleeting thought of throwing himself off some ledge. Maybe that was the simplest way.

Ending it all out in the wilds had to be preferable to any living death behind bars? And death itself was simple, no more than annihilation surely? *Oblivion!* Yet might there be torments beyond in some great 'hereafter?' Would his past victims come to challenge him in some eternal court of law? Exact revenge? If she could, he sensed how the pro Roxanne would exact vengeance at any price. So maybe death was no better than life – each presenting him with stark choices.

He liked to believe that Stacey still had feelings for him. Yet more so Marianne! For it was Marianne who clearly loved him and would welcome him home. Both had their needs. Like some fugitive child Marianne wasn't so unlike himself in his adult world, where he too felt orphaned. Loneliness was their common bond. With the mournful mist chilling everything, he now knew that he'd be discredited in the eyes of the Church, leaving him in the bleakness of his own Good Friday.

Around the same time as Wilkes woke up, Robert Dench emerged from a deep and surprisingly restful sleep. Anxiety had given way to a quiet confidence that he would reel in the escapee. For however long it took, it seemed as though God or destiny was somehow with him. Having awoken earlier at around midnight, he might have struck camp and walked on had the conditions allowed. But with the night pitch black and dangerous he was forced to stay put, allowing him to get some further sleep. Drinking his coffee still hot in the flask whilst eating more of his wife's sandwiches, he mapped out a careful strategy in his head. With the morning ahead presenting continuing mist, and with the line of footprints still visible in the snow, he chose to pace himself. Having no idea how close he was to Wilkes, he reasoned that the older and more panicky man had to tire quicker than he.

He set off at around 7 a.m, and after walking for an hour saw a break in the clouds. To see meant that he too could be seen! Pausing behind a rock, he took stock of the situation. A line of footprints was clearly visible for a good quarter of a mile or so ahead of him, and then with the mist dispersing further he spied the unmistakable silhouette of a climber. No way would he have spotted him but for the other man's bright orange outfit. There was just enough time to focus his binoculars on what he presumed was the figure of Wilkes, perhaps two miles away on a ridge known as Calf Crag, before gray cloud swept back across the valley once more to obscure his view.

Observing the gap in the cloud with growing alarm, Wilkes realized that his orange foul-weather clothing stood to light up as a beacon, in the event of conditions lifting. The chill factor still presented a problem, and so rather than remove his orange jacket he fished in his rucksack pocket to produce a full-length white priest's alb, along with its securing girdle. Having found the garment on the back seat of the LandRover and although an absurd item to wear in the mountains, it provided him with some essential camouflage.

The forecast for Easter had spoken of improved conditions and it was just a matter of how long the mist and cloud would linger. Whatever the weather, Dench now knew that he'd overhaul his target sooner rather than later.

But then about an hour later it was Dench's turn to be spotted. This time a further hole in the cloud allowed Wilkes to look back and catch a flash of light from what had to be binoculars.

*'Jesus!'* thought Wilkes. *'Is that someone coming after me already?'*

With any waning enthusiasm for flight now overtaken at the horror of imminent capture, he broke out into a near trot.

Dench tightened his grip on his binoculars. With the weather having started to break up, where in God's name had Wilkes gone? Visibility was brightening all the time only for the man in the fluorescent outfit to have vanished. Nor could he have guessed how his target had, like ectoplasm, metamorphosed into a ghostly presence moving through the snow.

For a while, the man now clad in white continued to stay invisible. Yet aware of his ebbing strength it was futile to keep stumbling on. Better to hole up somewhere and attack his pursuer unawares. Holding the higher ground offered a huge advantage. So choosing his spot, he walked further up the path only to re-trace his steps carefully, avoiding the snow where possible, so as to take up a position behind some rocks. Baiting the trap in this way by then going downwind was an old Kikuyu trick he'd learned from childhood. At that point the path was close to a near vertical drop, his ordnance survey map telling him it was a plunge of at least two hundred meters. Removing the alb and girdle along with the offending orange storm clothing, he pulled on a tracksuit top. After relieving himself, he put the alb back on while retying the girdle. He then fortified himself with some mint cake washed down with some mouthfuls of spring water. With the sugar rush reinvigorating him, he was in better shape than by running himself into the ground.

Sitting and waiting in his priestly garb, he glanced down at some primroses and violets glistening through the snow. The contrast of innocence and menace sharing the same foothold was lost on him.

The man advancing towards the crag had to be more than just some intrepid hiker - the way he was walking for one thing, stopping every so often to examine the ground. Perhaps he might even be the frustrated driver of the police car, who'd tried apprehending him near Ambleside. There was something mesmerizing about the other man's unstoppable progress, even as he halted every so often to check the footprints, not always obvious in the tufts of peat-grass and wet snow.

Yet by attacking his pursuer from behind and when he was out of breath, Wilkes believed he could still reverse this game of the hunter and the hunted. He loosened the girdle around his waist.

Methodically his pursuer drew closer, stopping but twenty yards below the rock from where with panther-like stillness, Wilkes planned his ambush. Dench was now close enough to be heard, the sound of his footsteps and steady breathing suggesting that he moved easily and well. Now he was almost adjacent to the place where he lay hidden. But it was at that point where Dench was most disadvantaged, not just with his backpack but from the exertion of his ascent – strategically far more vulnerable to the rested and unencumbered Wilkes.

In the event that he might stop and turn round, Wilkes had to move swiftly as he held his priest's girdle in one hand and a large rock in the other. Springing at the man from behind and now a few feet above him, he hit Dench across the back of his skull. The idea was that having staved in his head, it would be easy to push him over the precipice nearby.

Had he not been wearing his backpack high on his shoulders or been on the same level as his assailant, the assault could have been fatal. But the blow had been a glancing one. Partially concussed, he staggered as his attacker dragged him down onto the path, and where with both men on the ground Wilkes sought to straddle his opponent from behind, yanking the girdle around his throat as he did so.

It was the flow of warm blood, seeping down the side and back of his neck to warn him that he could quickly lose strength, thereby allowing his assailant to strangle him more easily. Dazed as he was, he made a sharp movement to roll nearer to the precipitous slope that lay on his left side. But the shift towards the sharp drop had the desired effect of dislodging Wilkes by forcing him to grab at some securing rock. Furthermore with his attacker still holding onto the rope it was the rope, which while half choking him prevented him from slipping nearer to the edge.

By bringing his hands up to the rope he could ease the constriction, and where as long as Wilkes held on they remained locked in a do or die stalemate. But with the impediment of his rucksack on his back and the precipitous drop still perilously close Dench's fate remained the more precarious.

With Wilkes then half sliding towards him it was obvious

that he wanted to shove him over the precipice. Now with the rope all but discarded, the police sergeant clung onto anything that came to hand. Suddenly with a fury-induced rush he made a lunge for Wilkes' ankle, gaining a foot or so towards safety as he did so. Then with arms and legs flailing once more he managed to scramble back onto the path, and in the split second when Wilkes was left wondering how to respond, Dench threw a flurry of punches at the other man who remained half prostrate.

The girdle with which Wilkes had tried to strangle him still hung loose around his neck and with Wilkes now winded, he made a hasty slipknot so as to tie it around the other man's wrist. But with Wilkes doing all in his power to wriggle away from the mountainous drop, it became impossible to bind both wrists.

God, he's fiendishly strong! Thought Dench.

At least by being on higher ground and having partly tethered him with the girdle, the younger man now held some advantage. But still weakened by his blood loss, the sergeant needed to secure himself on what had been the rough track that he'd been following, even as Wilkes was left smarting and breathing heavily some three feet away on the slope below. It felt tempting just to smash a rock into the man's face, so as to end it there and then. After all, Wilkes had tried using such a means to kill him.

In the next moment he wished that he'd followed his instincts, for with a sudden and totally unforeseen move, Wilkes had pulled on the rope making a grab at his left leg, once more drawing him close to the perilous edge. Only through the speed of his response and by grabbing at a clump of Wilkes' graying hair was this second attack aborted. Appreciating the other man's diabolical strength when least expected, Dench then used a rock on the side of Wilkes' temple to fully subdue him. Only then was he confident that he'd done him some serious hurt.

To stop Wilkes committing any wanton act of suicide, he then half-dragged him onto the ledge beside him. He did so by brutally yanking on the girdle on Wilkes' wrist. Nor would he take any further chances, ensuring that he had another hefty stone close to hand just in case.

It was only after recovering his breath and taking a long drink of water that Dench could attend to his own wounds. Fortunately with the blood already congealing he could tell that his head wound wasn't serious, although he admonished himself for not having worn a helmet. There were some further nasty abrasions to his hands and left wrist, and it was only as he was bandaging himself that he noticed how his captive was dressed in the garment of a priest. Not that his captor would have known, furthermore, but the hooded section of the alb now crimson with the priest's blood would have matched the chasuble Wilkes would have otherwise worn on that Good Friday.

Only after sorting himself out did he dig out some handcuffs, snapping them onto Wilkes' wrists behind his back. Although he remained inert on the path the arrested man had begun to groan.

Knowing that Wilkes had been wearing a backpack, Dench retrieved this from behind the rock where he'd been attacked, and found the orange foul-weather mountain kit and a long length of climbing rope. Only by making a belay around some rock, and securing the other end through his handcuffed arms did Dench know that Wilkes was secure at last. Secure also from taking some last leap off the cliff.

Then taking out his mobile which, despite the earlier struggle, remained mercifully operative and blessed with a clear signal, he put through a call to Ambleside police station and with rising jubilation phoned his wife, with the simple message, *'I've got him, I've got him, I've got him!* Quick, come and get me!'

The police were quickly back to him on the phone to reconfirm a fix on his location. Visibility had improved but they still needed some landmarks. Dench shouted directions. 'Fly out beyond Gibson Knot on the route to the Langdale Pike and look out for some orange fluorescent storm gear that I've laid out on the rock above!' He was assured that the police helicopter was on its way.

As he sat on the ledge, Wilkes regained consciousness and started to groan. Lying there, he looked both absurd and chilling. Clad in his disheveled alb now torn and bloody, and beneath which protruded his ribbed socks and hiking boots, his thick graying hair had clotted with blood. The anti-Christ faced with his own crucifixion. 'They tell me they had a name for you, even when you weren't a prime suspect.' Dench's lowered voice was filled with loathing: 'When you weren't dumping bodies near Coniston, and now this lassie up in Yorkshire, they spoke about you being Lucifer's assassin.' He felt sick reflecting on how Wilkes might just as easily have killed one or both of his own daughters.

'I can see why they call you Lucifer. They had their suspicions, but no proof.'

Wilkes made no response other than to groan. As an off-duty policeman, he was close to losing his professionalism, harbouring a strong wish to cut the securing rope. The fact that Wilkes was a priest repelled him further. Why not just slide him over the precipice and have done with him? He thought. Just say the guy threw himself off before I could stop him! Wilkes was a sadistic freak whom the younger man despised and feared all in one. *'Why can't I just push him off, for God's sake?'* This time he asked the question out loud.

Only the sound of the chopper's rotors saved both of them.

Following their swift and effective rescue from the

mountain, the winch-man shouted above the roar of the engine's rotor, 'They call him *Lucifer*, you know,' and then added, 'Christ, what's the son of a bitch got on?'

'It's a priest's robe,' Dench shouted back. 'He put it on for camouflage.'

'I thought the devil was supposed to dress in black,' yelled back the other.

Robert Dench spent a night being checked out at the local hospital. As it turned out his injuries were no worse than a few lacerations and a sprained wrist, enough to merit some stitches and a bandage. After a long sleep he woke up sore but exhilarated.

He recognized how over the past months, his obsessive fitness routine had in part been driven by the loathing he felt for whoever had dumped two women's bodies in the Lake District.

Another part of him felt relieved that he'd not followed through with his wish to kill Wilkes. As a policeman he had to stay professional at all times, but he'd never been more sorely tested than up there on the mountain. The tethering rope protected him as much from himself, as did the police helicopter arriving so promptly. Motivated by what he supposed could only have been a dream to catch the killer, the dream had *actually* materialized. Now with things having worked out in the way that they had, his whole body left him feeling sublimely relaxed.

Although the media were quick to pick up on him as a conquering hero, when he returned for duty on Easter Tuesday, the superintendent gave him what appeared to be a bleak look: 'Come into my office Sgt Dench,' he said beckoning him to a chair. 'I don't know what got into you or who you think you are. Technically you were off-duty, and on leave when you took the law into your own hands. Furthermore, you declined to fill in a report from your initial sighting, and in choosing to pursue the fugitive single handed, you endangered yourself instead of ensuring that you'd got proper back-up at all times – indeed from the moment you set off. Furthermore, you were remiss in giving us very late notice as to where the suspect's vehicle had been found.'

Knowing his boss to be one of the old school Dench couldn't be quite sure where his chief was going with this apparent reprimand. Surely if anyone kept banging on about using one's initiative, it had always been the super?

'But what I will say is this,' and here the other man's craggy face broke into a broad grin. 'Well done, son! I've not seen a piece of policing like that, since I was a lad on the beat. You're a credit and an inspiration to all of us Bob, and I'll see to it personally that the Chief Constable gives you a full citation. Oh, and take a week's leave on full pay!'

# Chapter 43

Both his homes were simultaneously raided that Saturday, Easter Eve. In the Manse the police homed in on his sitting room with its leather Chesterfield which, once exposed to their forensic torch, glowed in particular with small red fibres from Marianne's cashmere cardigan. Wilkes' housekeeper having had a virus on the Maundy Thursday hadn't come into work. Nor was she obliged to work over Easter weekend, thus leaving everything undisturbed from that Wednesday night. In his bedroom, they found the provost's clothes hastily stashed across a chair and on his dressing table there rested a single jade and gold cufflink; an identical match to the one found in the girl's hand.

More fibres came to light on the downstairs carpet that included some shreds of blue denim and strands of hair, even some eyelashes that all later proved to be those of Marianne. All drawers and documents were examined in his desk, every object scrutinized including those on the mantelpiece, one of which – an ancient reliquary – presented detectives with a photograph of the girl in her swimwear. The locket of blonde hair also found there provided an identical match to that from the scalp of a corpse lying on a path-lab's slab up in Leeds.

Information from Christopher Wilkes' computer in his Chelsea apartment revealed a further wealth of information. An address book of email addresses and discs showed that the provost was luring himself into a furtive web of sex rings; rings that included brutal acts of bondage done to young blonde females. Well over a hundred such pictures that Wilkes had downloaded and supposedly eradicated had been re-ghosted in the forensic department. With his sexual dysfunction and proclivity for preying on young vulnerable girls, all the evidence retrieved from his computer was proof enough that the Very Reverend Christopher Wilkes, and provost of Fordham Cathedral, was a sex freak whose perversions were declining towards outright paedophilia.

A further piece of evidence came to light. Having been advised to examine the ancient coffer at the back of All Saints, the police had painstakingly set about an examination of the chest and its contents. They'd been informed that items such as sash cord and an altar cloth had been removed, but that Di Hagan had inadvertently placed some choir robes into the chest without making any further detailed check of the coffer itself.

Being the sole contents of the coffer, the robes were examined item by item. Different fibres were removed with due diligence, and then to one side of the coffer which appeared to have been untouched by the robes were found three long strands of hair, their DNA being a perfect match to the strands of hair left on Stacey Witcombe's hairbrush.

In the week after Easter, Katy had arranged to visit her mother along with her boyfriend Kes. With Christopher Wilkes now in custody and with Kate visibly transformed it was an occasion for muted joy. Naturally they needed to steer well clear of any discussion about *him*.

Frances was delighted if not disconcerted that her

daughter was back to her old combative self.

'I mean, half the problem with drugs mum is that the soft ones aren't made legal. Cannabis is docile, even beneficial,' she reasoned. 'If fags and tobacco remain legal, then it makes a nonsense to say that smoking grass is wrong! What do you reckon, Kes?'

Having had this discussion before, Kes remained far more cautious, since he wondered whether, in his case, cannabis hadn't led him on to his taking hard drugs. Seeing him as a strong antidote to the ever-headstrong Katy, Frances found herself warming to him.

'Surely legalizing cannabis is the thin end of the wedge,' responded Frances. 'I know that the tobacco lobby is full of hypocrisy but does one hypocrisy justify another? Besides I'm told that cannabis isn't what it used to be,' she continued. 'I understand it's far more potent and dangerous than the original hippy stuff from Afghanistan. 'Cannabis-psychosis' – that's a specific medical disorder, they say and that a growing number of teenagers are at risk from suffering mental disorders.'

Although she didn't say anything, Katy was impressed. She'd never known her mother get steamed up about 'hypocrisy' before, or for that matter become so well informed. 'OK, so what about prostitution?' she had asked.

'What about it?' replied Frances, trying to sound comfortable with such an uncomfortable line of thought.

But her mother seemed genuinely 'cool' now, and gutsy enough to discuss topics hitherto unmentionable. Katy was delighted, even as she pushed her mother further: 'Well, why shouldn't they legalize it? What about all the hypocrisy *there*? At least by legalizing it, the oldest profession in the world can come out of the shadows.'

Frances knew that there might be many more discussions about drugs, prostitution or whatever in the coming months, now that her daughter had gone to hell and, 'praise the Lord', returned to tell the tale. After all, it was hard to argue against someone like Katy, who having 'been there and done that' had so much more insight into the real world, than she Frances had ever had.

What thrilled both of them was how Kate saw that her mother had started to think for herself, while Frances saw in Kate someone who'd had the courage and the loving support to emerge from the fast track to oblivion via crack cocaine.

With the arrest and subsequent imprisonment of Wilkes, the case against Merv Costello, still on remand, collapsed. What with all the forensic evidence so clearly stacked against Wilkes, everyone from the Governor to the prison staff could see that the case against him was non-existent. Even so, the prison system couldn't authorize his release:

'You'll have to wait, Costello, for a separate court to authorize your release,' the Principal Officer on his wing had told him. 'Or, of course, why don't we phone the Home Secretary for an immediate pardon?' This sarcastic response prompted the car thief to summarize the feelings of countless other inmates, in just four words, *'The whole system sucks!'* Truth to tell, the P.O. had no sympathy as he walked off.

But, of course, nothing had stopped him 'going to town' from his prison cell already. He was preparing to sue various Police Forces for wrongful arrest; for harassment; for defamation of character; the prison authorities for his victimization in prison, which could have ended in his murder. There was Dr Tideswell, the so-called criminal profiler whose case against him was based on nothing more than flawed logic, a honey-trap and the profiler's own king-size ego. 'See you in hell, Tideswell! You too, Barbara or whatever the fuck your name is!' He cursed the undercover agent with all her bitchy suggestions.

Costello would get and squeeze compensation from every quarter imaginable. The car thief had soaked himself in a study of the law during his incarceration, and intended to create maximum embarrassment for the authorities. When Costello's case did go with relative swiftness to a special court hearing, the judge ruled that Tideswell's so-called evidence should have been inadmissible in its entirety. This of itself left Costello jubilant, where the judge's findings led to the profiler being struck off the register of the British Psychological Society.

From being a zero among some of the inmates, Costello now became everyone's hero. Nor would he forget later a few of the other men, banged up for offences they swore blind they hadn't committed. He'd read somewhere that upwards of fifteen percent of those held in prison are possible victims of some sort of miscarriage of justice. *Fifteen percent!*

Four years it was said before a wrongful conviction might get overturned on appeal. *Four years!* Sometimes it was longer.

Having spent six months in prison already, Wilkes' case probably wouldn't get heard for at least another six months. But since the trial was to be at the central criminal court otherwise known as The Old Bailey, he'd been transferred to the remand section of a major London prison. At first he was sectioned in the hospital wing, but later he was deemed to be well enough to be given his own cell.

As the time for his trial drew closer, his anxiety heightened. Upon being told by his barrister that he would surely be found guilty on three counts of murder and better to enter a plea of guilty, his external calm grew fragile in the extreme. The prospect of being given three consecutive life sentences, thereby guaranteeing that he'd die in prison was intolerable. Nor, he was told, would any guilty plea on the grounds of diminished responsibility mitigate against those terms.

Having dreamt about it countless times he knew how the trial would be a one-sided farce. His QC might reason that in many respects Christopher Wilkes was a conscientious parish priest. A psychological profile might point to a damaged childhood, to a marriage that was loveless and unresolved as well as to a series of young women who, it might be argued, had been leading him on. A flimsy case might get presented that in his desire to help others, citing for example the time when he paid for the rent on Philippa's flat, people liked to take advantage of him. But as he pictured himself in the dock in his suit and clerical collar, still clinging to those outward trappings of self-respect, he knew that the Court gallery would be packed with voyeurs all agog, and but awaiting one outcome: *Guilty!*

It might be worse still, having to hear the prosecution wade into some diatribe over his dysfunctional personality, both as a priest and as a human being: Of his sadistic chauvinistic father; of his non-existent sex-life. Whatever! In his nightmares he saw images of the police smirking, the terrible Pole Zbierski, rubbing his hands in glee. And where might he hide if such true spirits of kindness such as Ben and Angela appeared in court? Then at the end after the foreman of the jury gave its inevitable verdict, there would be the judge's grisly summing up, before passing sentence.

Now on remand Wilkes' delusional tendencies yielded more and more to the cold realities about him. With the trial standing to be no more than a formality, his conviction would see him deposited within maximum-security conditions, only to die there. 'Let him rot in hell'! Wasn't that what people said about serial killers? Furthermore, as a bent priest he'd be treated as the lowest of the low; scum forced to endure a life of isolation, as well as one under constant threat.

'Shank the bastard, and you'll get some free Charlie!' The invitation to knife him for a line of coke had been already overheard for his benefit.

So if he had a semblance of a life now on remand, after sentencing he'd have *no* life. No death row as such, but there'd be no question about it. He was already a dead man walking.

Whilst in gaol he'd attended the chapel services regularly, seeking what solace he could from attending chapel. There was something comforting in just hearing the familiar words from the prayer book. Nor had the chaplain been unfriendly towards him. After all, in his public persona Wilkes liked to retain an air of pained innocence and, notwithstanding the coarse denim uniform, he could still revert to type by retaining his provost's air of importance. Then again, as a remand prisoner, he remained technically '*not* guilty,' and where having not yet been formally de-frocked he was still a man of the cloth. At least the chaplain trusted the prisoner sufficiently to bear in mind that Wilkes might become one of his servers at communion.

After one of the evening services, he'd spent a few moments in the chaplain's office referring to some spiritual problem that he'd like to discuss sometime. They were neither of them seated, and when the phone rang causing the chaplain to temporarily turn away, Wilkes had in a trice removed the other man's cassock girdle, which hung along with his other robes nearby. In mere seconds, he had stuffed the cord down his shirtfront. Failing to spot this lightning theft, the chaplain then arranged an appointment for them to meet at a later date.

Even for an instant it's all too easy for members of prison

staff to be negligent, this piece of negligence by the chaplain (*never* turn your back on an inmate) was further repeated when Wilkes returned to his wing. He was not shaken down as ought to have been standard practice, more so for serious criminals such as himself. But often there were just too few staff on duty to run through all the procedures. Besides they did regular cell searches, so with prisoners coming and going there was, as often as not, nothing to shake down. At least that was how the screws liked to argue it between themselves.

Being early autumn and with his trial drawing closer, he was in no doubt that he wanted to take the easy route, the *only* route. Having concealed a hand-written will, along with some other papers in the back of his radio, the preliminaries were straightforward enough. Weirdly, he'd also written a letter to someone he referred as his 'angel.'

Now with the girdle smuggled inside his cell, it seemed that his charmed life was given one last chance to take its final bow. At any time his cell could be searched and the theft discovered, making him realize with cool finality that *tonight* had to be the night. What's more, having been careless about his girdle, the chaplain would naturally report its loss soon enough.

His was one of the older cells, making it easy to secure a belay. Even without the hinged window and the priest's cord, death by hanging still remained the commonest and most successful means of prison suicide. But given these further advantages Wilkes knew he would not fail, *must not* fail!

Sleep eluded him entirely. At around 2 a.m. he got up from his bunk, retrieving the girdle from under his mattress. Noiselessly, he stood on his chair while readjusting the belay around the open frame and then making a noose. Given his height and the shallow drop, the soft nylon rope offered an ideal length. Not only that and despite his profuse bout of sweating, the girdle's familiar texture brought him a measure of comfort even as he rechecked the knots.

As he prepared himself, a vision returned to him of the mediaeval hatchet man he'd dreamt about in childhood. Had he disposed of others in some previous life, possibly? He'd certainly disposed of them in *this* life. Was the imminence of his self-execution no more than the revolving of fate's wheel turning full circle?

He sought to compose himself. 'Now my Stacey and my Marianne and even you, Roxanne . . . I'm coming to join you.'

Suddenly he felt as though drunk, recalling the euphoria he'd felt on Mount Kenya, or of how he felt that night in the vicarage kitchen when he'd wanted to assault and kill his wife. In an odd way, it didn't feel as though death was but moments away. If anything he felt elated, *taken over!*

He tiptoed on the chair to shorten the belay further. As he did so, beyond the grubby bottle-glass of his cell window, he had a clear view of the night sky through the open vent. The heavens were exquisite with a myriad stars, brilliant and pure, as he remembered them in the night heavens of Africa. He then secured the noose about his neck. From the futile squalor of his present confinement, it was as though the freedom of an infinite universe beckoned to him - - welcoming even. A further Kenyan flashback brought into focus a million lights, of how a multitude of flamingos and egrets might sometimes rise into the heavens. *God*, what was going on?

More recently the audible memory of the bubbling stream outside his tent came back to him, as did the call of those two skylarks.

Then out of nowhere he was reminded of a Sunday

school chorus, one that he would have sung when his father was still a missionary in Mombassa. It was as though he could hear a score of little voices chiming in: 'Jesus loves the little children, all the children of the world, black and yellow, red and white, all are precious in His sight. Jesus loves the little children of the world.'

*What unspeakable crap!* Thought Wilkes, incredulous to be tormented at such a moment by a children's chorus. Even as he dismissed the song, he saw the beautiful black face of Okutu – 'little snake.' Then there appeared the glowing faces of his other childhood friends, Namdi and Samja - they too were singing, as though urging him on: 'Hi, Chrees. Come and join us Chrees.'

Had his childhood friends passed to another shore, victims perhaps of the dreaded Mau Mau? He could hear their bubbling laughter – or was it *mocking?* Maybe he was mocking himself. As the rope jarred and he heard the chair land silently on its pillow to avoid any noise, he was transported back into childhood to sing another chorus, the words of which went. 'Jesus bids us shine with a clear light, like a little candle burning in the night . . .'

He'd forgotten how the chorus ended, because as his body twitched on its lifeless coil, so his spirit was already easing beyond the bars into the cool night. There then came a cacophony of crazy sounds, the booming notes of Widor's Toccata as played by Jonathan Sharpe on the night of Stacey's death, the hideous screeching of tree hyraxes from the mountain, interspersed with the jarring tones of Zbierski.

Nor could he be sure where he was going, but one thing he knew was that he was out of the cell racing in a direction he knew not whither. Who would be there to meet him? Might the old mountain god Ngai be there still to rescue him in some way? Or could it be the three young women whom he had killed? Worse still, could his demented missionary father emerge from the depth of Hades to escort him to the place of the damned? He knew not.

But maybe someone, somewhere back on Earth – so often perceived as the planet 'twixt heaven and hell – might someone yet be praying for the safe repose of his soul?

'*Fuck* him,' snarled Nick Crooks, 'He's cheated justice.'

'Aye, he has and all,' responded Nick the landlord. The clientele at The Magpie were incandescent.

'Still, he's admitted his own guilt, I suppose,' said Mrs. Myers. 'I think I'm happier knowing that he's dead and buried rather than locked up indefinitely. Even behind locked doors, the man scared me silly, I don't mind admitting.'

They felt vexed, traumatized and unsure of themselves. It was then that the newly appointed vicar of All Saints, Caroline Meggart, who'd endeared herself by visiting The Magpie from time to time, suggested that it might be helpful if they had a special service remembering all the hurts of people like Stacey's family, along with all the pain and frustration that those at the pub had had to face.

'Come to All Saints!' she had invited warmly. 'You've had important links with this church for several years now, and maybe by holding a simple service we can do something to heal all the wounds.'

She was as good as her word. In fact she went one better because she opted to hold the service in the pub instead. 'After all, The Magpie is only another type of church when you think about it,' she smiled.

And so prayers were said right there in The Magpie for old Jack Bishop, previous vicar and one of the pub's regulars; prayers in grateful and loving memory for Di Hagan; prayers said for the soul of young Stacey and for the two other young women murdered. Prayers were offered for the victims' families, as well as for Mrs. Frances Wilkes, the former wife of the infamous and now deceased provost. Prayers were said that All Saints would become a happy and a safe church, along with prayers said for the Magpie and for all its very special customers.

More prayers were asked for the suitable appointment of a new bishop. Caroline even felt it was right to give thanks for the very special efforts shown by Granville Zbierski, and for all the others who'd tried so hard to get justice for Ben and Angela.

Z was visibly touched that the new vicar actually took him seriously enough to *pray* for him. Deep down he'd always had a downer on himself, and the last thing he ever imagined was that a vicar – and a female one at that – might pray for him and be grateful for what he had done.

In fact the Pole really was changing out of all recognition from his old self. What's more, and here his drinking cronies did their utmost not to rib him, he'd begun to shave regularly and to wear a hairpiece!

'You want to take care, Granville,' said Crooks. 'She might ask you to be churchwarden next,' eyeing the lady vicar as he said it.

'No reason why, given time, he shouldn't be,' responded Caroline. People loved the way she smiled when she spoke, like nothing much seemed to disconcert her.

*'Now you've got to be joking!'* said Crooks.

'No, why should I be?' replied Caroline again good-humouredly.

At which point, a wave of genuine mirth rose up. The Magpie hadn't heard laughter like that for a long time.

## Chapter 44

He had kept the letter to his 'angel' well hidden before his death, it then being released to her a few days later. It began:
*Dear Angela,*

*I have written this letter on the anticipated eve of my death. Part of me doesn't know what to write or how to write. I can't put into words what I am trying to say, because I seem unable to tell what is right or wrong.*

*But one thing I feel is that you are nearer to heaven than many other people I know. Ever since our pilgrimage to Israel I had this dream of you when I knew you as sister Angelique. It was like you were some Madonna who was able to cradle in her arms the very young and the very old, the very happy and the deeply troubled.*

*All I remember from that dream was that I felt like some small child being held by you, and that I felt very reassured - very SAFE!! I had not remembered that dream until this night, perhaps because now I'm in a very dark place.*

*I beg of you <u>not</u> to hate me if I think of you in that dream as an angel. All I would ask is that when I'm gone, please light a candle for me and pray for me as I journey into the unknown.*

*– Regards, Christopher Wilkes*

'Well, get a load of this!' said Angela as she passed the letter across to Ben.

'*Holy shit!*' replied Ben. He saw that the letter had been re-directed to Angela via All Saints vicarage.

'Part of me longs to think that he is beyond all hope,' said Angela, 'and that he could never say anything to *endear* himself to me! I'm too involved with Frances and the rest to consider that I could have ever had dispassionate views about him, let alone *compassionate* ones.'

'I don't want to think of him as anything other than the devil's disciple,' replied Ben. 'I haven't got a good word to say for him, except now that he's topped himself.' He could feel his bile rising: 'I mean he's destroyed three young women, two of whom were just kids. They all had their lives ahead of them and he just snuffed them out. I can never forgive him for that! What's more he's wrecked his own family life.'

But the letter to his 'angel' rocked them to the soles of their feet. From thereon, their discussions would often revert to the subject of good and evil and what was meant by *forgiveness*. When *can* one, or when *ought* one to forgive?

He'd just been reading some commemorative article on the Peace deal in Northern Ireland, where there'd been a lot of idle talk about forgiveness and needing to move on, and he felt enraged: 'I mean, for Christ's sake, here we have evil men – terrorists pure and simple – who have been set free when they should be banged up with the key thrown away for good! Not just that, given enough time and they get invited to Downing Street to get tea and sticky buns.' He paused, 'and then they get given governmental duties. I mean, just *what* is going on here?'

They'd had this conversation before, leaving Angela to ask, 'Where is the justice for people who've had their loved ones killed, then maybe having to bump into their husband's murderer or their son's murderer walking towards them down the street? Politicians are forever doing deals with former high-jackers, and other merchants of death. Didn't the same thing happen in Rwanda, one side being asked to forgive the other for their families' murders? Yet surely most terrorists, even more so-called suicide bombers, must be brainwashed out of their skulls, as much as they are criminal?'

'All sin is sleep?' responded Ben. 'Gurdjieff said that. People only do wrong because they can't see the outcome of their actions clearly. But when people do out and out *evil* they're surely not just *asleep*. They are in effect *dead* people with no consciences!'

'So there's all the difference between sin and evil,' Angela replied. 'In fact, I'm none too taken with the word "sin," at least as it's traditionally understood. After all, how many people have got *too much* of a conscience about so-called sin – only to end up in need of therapy? Somewhere in the Bible it speaks of it as "an evil conscience." That's a good term for it, and one totally at odds to those people who have *no* conscience! So there's sin and sin!"

'So when does a murderer, a terrorist, pay his due?' asked Ben rhetorically. 'I mean there was a part of you and me that wanted to see Letharge and Wilkes dead, did we not? Should we feel guilty about that?'

They left that question suspended.

'But at another level entirely, what, for example, about that merchant of death, said to have been even worse than Hitler – Pol Pot, who spent long hours justifying to others why he believed it was right to murder *babies*, for God's sake! Nor did Pol Pot ever get brought to justice, apparently dying a peaceful death in a ripe old age. What about *him?*' Was Pol Pot simply *misguided?* More to the point was he even *HUMAN?*'

'So what about Wilkes?' asked Angela. 'I mean in one sense wasn't *he* in his own hell, even when he imagined he wasn't? From what I learned of them, his parents were pretty nasty, misguided people. And so what, if he inherited pots of money and status? Without friends and without any appreciation of who he was, maybe he was among the damned already.'

'So are you suggesting that by topping himself, he's somehow atoned for his past?' asked Ben.

'Well, if you mean do I think he's gone to hell for eternity? I can't buy into that idea,' replied Angela. 'Eternal damnation strikes me as a pretty senseless belief. Personally I believe he has another chance, many more chances perhaps, to find his true self and somehow make reparation. The Buddhist belief in karma teaches, as does Christianity, that "We reap what we sow," but that we are all on the road to nirvana or paradise. Surely Heaven is as much about finding peace for ourselves, irrespective of whether or not we're "judged" by *Someone* up there!'

'So you suppose that Christopher Wilkes will reincarnate?' asked Ben.

'My personal view is that he has to!' she answered. 'We shouldn't forget that reincarnation was upheld as a belief by the *early church,* for heaven's sake, for nearly five hundred years! It only got discredited, can you believe, by a small majority at their Council of Constantinople in AD 553. So what had been acceptable in the early church became heresy in the later one. Makes you wonder who really gets to call the shots as to what's orthodox and what isn't! So easy for Christians today to forget that the likes of Origen, Augustine, Jerome, even St Francis of Assisi, all seemed to believe in reincarnation, without so much as batting an eyelid.'

'Maybe that's where the idea of original sin comes in,' said Ben, 'that we're working off karma from a previous life.'

'Except original sin's another term I can't abide,' said

Angela. 'The Church screwed it up by giving it too many connotations with lust!'

*'And just what's wrong with lust?'* They fell about laughing as each of them spoke aloud what the other was thinking.

During that coming year, life returned to a semblance of normality for the people of Ketborough - far more slowly, of course, for those immediately involved in the drama of Christopher Wilkes.

Extraordinarily, Wilkes had left a will made out in three equal parts to his ex-wife, son and daughter. By means of a Trust, they stood to inherit almost two million pounds between them, as well as the equity from his flat in Chelsea and a number of valuable antiques. At first none of them wanted anything to do with 'his sodding blood money,' as Katy put it.

But reason prevailed, which in her case allowed her to invest the money into pioneering projects for improving the status and living conditions of prostitutes. Naturally she made a point of looking up some of her old friends, particularly Mandy who had as good as saved her life. In checking out Jenny, she was devastated to learn that the archdeaon's niece was HIV positive, even though she'd not lost her sense of humour, quipping: 'And how is your niece, archdeacon?' 'Well apart from a few spots and becoming somewhat anorexic, she's fine thankyou.'

Sometime later she and Kes became engaged. Dominic by an extraordinary feat of keeping his mind in focus went on to get a first in biology. The legacy from his father enabled him to explore cheap methods of providing drinking water for those living in the developing world, especially in Rwanda and the Sudan.

Frances chose to pass on the legacy of the bungalow given to her by Di Hagan to Philippa and her toddler Rosamund.

This enabled Frances to move away from Ketborough, but not so far that she wasn't in regular contact with Ben and Angela.

Later on, Philippa prepared to pass on Di's bungalow to her own needy parents. With its awkward staircase, they deserved better than their poorly maintained council house. 'My upholstery business is going great guns, she told them. 'Soon I'll get my own place.' Added to which she'd got engaged to a self-employed joiner – this amour being readily endorsed by Snap, who showed no misgivings about Philippa's husband-to-be. With the onset of old age Sleuth remained ever inscrutable!

After her institution as vicar of All Saints, Caroline Meggart was to pioneer a movement to get a female diocesan bishop installed. Although women were still debarred from becoming bishops, a small group had grown insistent that Fordham diocese had to adopt some of the radical initiatives it had been first set up to do. Despite no legislation even being in the offing for women to become bishops, a woman archdeacon by the name of Natalie Summers was being groomed for the task, even if for the present she stood only to get the job of being Wilkes' successor.

'*Boy*, wouldn't Bp Letharge spin in his grave now?' chortled Ben.

'Wilkes as well' laughed Angela.

Even more remarkable and but a short time after formalizing his relationship to Angela by marriage, Ben Carter was invited to return to the Church that had so rudely ejected him. Female initiatives behind the scenes had even engineered that in the absence of any formal appointment having been made for Fordham's diocesan bishop Ben be given the job of suffragan bishop.

He was so 'gob-smacked' that for a while he couldn't decide.

# A Candle For Lucifer

'After all, the Church has still got an awful long way to go if it's going to become remotely Christian,' he looked truly morose.

'Yes, but that's what you're here for!' said Angela, chiding him and laughing at the same time, 'After all, you've got a real gem like Caroline now at All Saints and rumour has it there's a new woman bishop-in-waiting who is clearly pretty switched on and fearless. Go on, I dare you. Go for it you lecherous old sod.'

Daughter Emma, who was now just over a year old copied her mother, 'Go on . . . Go for it . . .' she started, ending up mumbling the rest, despite getting the last syllable word perfect.

They fell about laughing at the child's first fumbling fall from grace. With mother and daughter telling him what he had to do, he knew he was outnumbered.

'Okay, if that's the case then the deal's got to be this,' he said. '*You* my little angel will have to be the bishop's secretary. I just couldn't be doing with one of those typical mincing females fawning around me, doing me abeyance every five minutes.'

'Is that such a good idea?' asked Angela. 'I mean, I could be tempted to lead all your flock into perdition and heresy, getting the clergy all steamed about about their natal horoscopes and reincarnation! Then what would you do?"

'Dare you!' retorted Ben.

'Dare you to dare me!' returned Angela, adding after a mischievous pause, *'My lord!'*

*'Don't ever call me that!'* roared Ben throwing a cushion at her and deliberately missing.

Emma liked that bit as well.

'Whatever you say,' said Angela getting up as though making to close the door. But then adding once more as she closed the door behind her, *'my lord!'*

Chortling, she ran to the safety of the bathroom.

Just over a year after Wilkes' death, things had changed markedly. One was that Ben had been consecrated as the area bishop for nearly six months. In fact until a diocesan bishop had been appointed and consecrated, he remained in sole charge. It was an extraordinary turnaround! Lots of ordinary folk in the diocese were overjoyed.

The other event to now wholly absorb them was the imminent arrival of their second child. No scans had been made to determine its sex, making Emma equally impatient for her little brother or sister to arrive.

If it was a boy they were in two minds about what to call him. Regardless of its associations with Wilkes, Christopher was a name that they both loved as well as being one of Angela's favourite saints, being the patron saint of travelers.

It was only two days after having been safely delivered of a boy, and still in the maternity ward that the babe's father commented:

'Look love, he's smiling.

'No darling' replied Angela. 'Babies can't smile until they're a fortnight old. It's just wind.'

But then she noticed something:

'Hey, love, take a look at this.'

With her thumb and forefinger Angela gently prised open the folds of flesh around his eyes.

*'You're not saying. . . ?'* Ben's expression was aghast.

'I'm not saying anything,' Angela replied softly.

'But it can't be. It's simply not possible!' His expression conveyed shock, even horror. To be doubly sure he needed to check for himself. But looking once more, there was no denying it. For there set in the chubby little face, their baby had brown eyes, but . . . of a slightly different shade to each other.

'Could just be sheer coincidence, darling,' she tried to console him. And half checking herself it was as though she spoke her next thought: 'But then on the other hand . . .'

Once more she became absorbed by the infant, so fragile, and cradled in one arm.

After a long pause, she then looked across at Emma seated at a table nearby with some other children. Absorbed they were all busy talking like they'd known each other forever, even as her daughter was manipulating pieces of coloured wood into a puzzle. Angela then looked up searching the eyes of her precious husband. Nothing in the whole world would bring her to hurt him.

Bringing her free arm up to Ben's head and drawing his ear down to her lips, she reminded him of the proverb upon which they both shaped their lives, and with which they were in entire agreement, *'Love conquers all!'* she whispered.

Shaking his head, he marveled at her faith. Nor somehow, could he stop himself from smiling.

As he did so, so it seemed did baby Christopher once more.

# *Epilogue*

Most people are religious, even when they think they are not! For is not religion's sole purpose there to help us make sense of our lives?

Love and a loving Creator 'God' provide the essence of all religions. Given the late Erich Fromm's psychological definition of love as being 'the only sane and satisfactory answer to the problem of human existence' the equation becomes simple: If we seek love, we seek the source of life and meaning – God. Thus are we religious!

If love is seen as being fundamental to our survival and well being, it is to that true religion as exemplified in the life of Christ that we are drawn. For this reason many people who never go to church may justifiably speak of themselves as being Christian. For it is *Churchinaity* not Christianity that is the problem! With its timeless elitism and power struggles, churchianity distorts God's love by making it conditional at best, and despicable at worst. For churchianity wears hypocrisy like a second skin, providing countless opportunities for dark forces to masquerade as light.

*A Candle for Lucifer* represents my endeavour to expose the depths to which this masquerade can descend. The book is based on a priest known to the author whilst at theological college. N was given a life sentence for a series of assaults on young girls, and who unable to face life in prison ended up taking his life.